Best Wishes,

D. P. *(signature)*

THE GHOST DANCERS

THE GHOST

SHADOW MOUNTAIN PRESS

DANCERS

A NOVEL BY G. P. SCHULTZ

THE GHOST DANCERS
© 1996 BY G. P. SCHULTZ

Manufactured in the United States of America.

First edition

Shadow Mountain Press
P.O. Box 7083
Shawnee Mission, Kansas 66207

ISBN: 0-9626324-2-2
Library of Congress Catalog Number: 96-71640

DEDICATION

To Vicki Ann, Lionel Dean, and Jake.

ACKNOWLEDGMENTS

I would like to thank the following individuals and organizations for their assistance in the research and production of the Ghost Dancers.

Lionel Ritchey for his reminiscences of Kansas City.

Bette Lilley for her help with sequences at the Art Institute.

Audrey Ottinger for sharing her notes on life in the 1930s.

Marine veteran Bob Gray for his first hand account of the battle for Guadalcanal.

The Jackson County Historical Society — Photo of Union Station.

The Kansas City Missouri Library

Andrea Warren and Anne Thomas — Editors

Synopsis by Andrea Warren

Some of the information in the novel was taken from the records of the *Kansas City Star* and the *Kansas City Times*

AUTHOR'S NOTE

Although the novel follows the exact movements of the 25th Infantry Division during World War II, the battle scenes are fictitious.

Some of the sequences in Hawaii and at Schofield Barracks were taken from the author's own experience with the 25th Infantry Division in the late 1950s.

1

From her perch in the big oak tree she could look out over the city. Below the Main Street Hill there was a flurry of activity as trains pulled in and out of Union Station. People scurried around the huge limestone and granite building, as a steady procession of cars and cabs moved them on their way. Katie wondered what it would be like to take a trip on a train. Beyond the station, the sun setting over the West Bottoms cast a glow on the tall buildings that made up the core of the city. A street car crested the bluff and headed down the hill that ran away to Old Town and the Missouri River.

The oak tree was her special place to think and be alone.

She could hear the clink of dishes as her mother cleaned the kitchen, and the steady cadence of her grandpa's snoring came from the swing on the front porch. Katie Callahan had just celebrated her twelfth birthday, and her mother had informed her it was time to stop climbing trees and to start acting like a proper young lady. She wondered why she had the bad luck to be born a girl. Boys had all the fun, while girls were supposed to be pretty and proper.

Her musings were interrupted by voices at the foot of the tree. Her fourteen-year-old brother, Shorty, and some of his friends were huddled conspiratorially below her. Silently she began climbing down through the branches so she could hear their conversation. Shorty was usually up to no good, and he attracted boys of the same ilk. Mother said he needed the strong hand of discipline that had been taken away when Pop died. Grandpa didn't have the inclination or the strength to take on Shorty.

"Federal agents are bringing Frank Nash through Union Station in the morning," Shorty said excitedly.

"Frank Nash the gangster?" Corky asked.

"No, Frank Nash the movie star," Shorty said sarcastically. Properly chastised, Corky looked down at the ground.

"How do you know?" Franky asked. Franky Rossi had black hair, a prominent nose set on a narrow face, and dark-brown eyes.

"McClusky's uncle is a cop. He heard him talking about it. Ain't that right, McClusky?"

"It's the straight scoop," McClusky said. Andy McClusky was a tall, red-haired Irish boy. It seemed to Katie that he grew a foot taller every time she saw him.

"We meet at seven in the morning, under the clock at Union Station," Shorty said excitedly. "We're gonna see us a big-time gangster."

Corky jumped back in fright as Katie dropped out of the tree. "I'm going with you," she said.

"You're going nowhere, Squirt," Shorty countered.

"I'll tell Mother you're smoking," she said defiantly.

"You tell anything and I'll hang you by your pigtails," he threatened as he threw down his cigarette and tried to wave away the smoke hanging above his head.

"Last night I heard you tell Mother you were going to stay out of trouble," she said. "You're only supposed to be at Union Station when you're working."

Shorty stared at her menacingly, and then started pacing back and forth, trying to figure out what to do with this irritant that had fallen from the sky.

"Who's she?" A voice asked from behind her.

She turned around. A boy had emerged from behind the tree. His face was tanned by the sun. He had light-brown hair, and he stared at Katie with friendly light-blue eyes.

Katie was mesmerized. He was the best looking boy she had ever seen.

"She's Shorty's sister," Franky said in disgust. "You ain't gonna let her go, are you, Shorty?"

Katie knew she should introduce herself, but as the boy stepped forward, she could feel the heat in her cheeks, and she became flustered.

"Hi, I'm Joe Wilson," he said.

She wanted to appear grown up and sophisticated, but she just stood there, speechless.

"What's the matter, Squirt? Cat got your tongue?" Shorty taunted her. "Her name's Katie, and she's a pain in the butt."

Katie controlled the urge to stick her tongue out and kick Shorty in the shins. With her shoulders held back and her head erect, she turned toward the house. "I'll see you boys in the morning," she said.

Their moans of protest followed her into the house. She didn't care anything about seeing the gangster, Frank Nash. She had only wanted to start a fight with Shorty. But that was before she met Joe Wilson. Maybe being a girl wasn't such a bad thing after all.

The next morning Katie was awake when the milk truck pulled up. She heard the clink of bottles as the milkman walked onto the porch. She climbed out of bed and put on yellow shorts and a lime-green top. Last night she had combed the pig-tails out of her auburn hair. She glanced cautiously at the mirror, and then pinned a green ribbon in her hair that matched the green of her eyes.

Outside she climbed on her bike. It was going to be a beautiful day. The air was already warming with the rising sun. She was glad summer was almost here, although last summer had been one of the hottest on record, with the temperature hovering near 100 degrees for six weeks. The family had slept outside on cots for most of July and August. Grandpa would wait until sunset and then hose down the cots and the bedding. It would be almost dry by the time they crawled into bed. Of course Pop had to be kept out of the night air because of his cough. Katie remembered lying on her cot, watching the stars, and listening to his coughing spells coming from the house. She always said a prayer that he would get better.

That summer it seemed as though she and Shorty were always being scolded about tuberculosis. "Don't hug your father — don't kiss your father — don't breathe the air near your father. Remember to boil everything your father touches, and for heaven's sake, be quiet." It was almost like having no father at all. And then Pop had gone to the sanatorium and she would have given anything to once again hear the coughing and the scolding. Pop died in January and the thought of him never coming home was almost more than she could bear. The house was so cold and quiet, and the winter seemed to last forever.

With the arrival of spring came Miss Monroe, the cleaning lady. The spring cleaning was an annual event, but this year it seemed to take on a special urgency. Katie had helped her mother and Miss Monroe clean for days on end: beating rugs, washing the windows inside and out with ammonia, varnishing and waxing the floors, and forever wiping oil dust off the furniture from the coal furnace. They boiled water in large tubs and poured it in the washing machine to wash all the cottons and the work clothes. There were so many cottons hanging on the lines out back that Katie began to wonder if the washer would wear out before she and Miss Monroe did. But the work had been a blessing and it had helped to keep her mind off Pop.

She rode a block west across 26th Street, and started coasting down the Main Street Hill. It was Saturday and the traffic was light. She turned onto 24th Street and pedaled into the horseshoe-shaped driveway in front of Union Station. The building was gigantic and always made her feel small. Pop had told her the design was based on the Roman public baths that were constructed by the emperor Caracalla, and that it was the third largest station in the country, with two hundred trains passing through every day. Pop had been the assistant station master and he knew everything there was to know about Union Station.

Over by the railway express building, a group of transients gathered on the sidewalk. They were men and boys from all over the nation who were on the move looking for work. Katie was used to seeing them lined up outside the soup kitchen on Main Street, or selling apples on downtown street corners. Sometimes they came by the house to inquire about odd jobs, or to ask for something to eat. Her mother always gave them food, and her grandfather kept a shoe repair kit from Woolworth's on the back porch. The transients would use the shoe repair kit to put on rubber half soles.

Katie leaned her bike against a lamp post and walked into the station. The grand lobby reminded of her of a palace.

It had marble floors and three giant chandeliers that weighed three thousand pounds each. They were suspended by cables from a ceiling almost a hundred feet high, and bathed in sunlight from three 90-foot-high arched windows carved in the south wall of the station. The dispatcher's voice announcing arrivals and departures echoed through the cavernous building. Katie could feel the floor shake as the huge engines chugged in and out of the station. She walked past the bronze semi-circular ticket window, and headed for the giant clock guarding the entry way to the north waiting room. It was seven o'clock, and she had arrived on time. The boys were in the entry way, engrossed in a heated discussion. With the exception of Joe Wilson, they ignored her as she walked up to them.

"Hello," Joe said.

She blushed and nodded at him.

"How are we going to know if they're bringing Frank Nash through the east or west wing?" Corky wondered.

The station was designed so that passengers arriving in train sheds below would be channeled through the concourses to the ticket windows, rather than through the north waiting room.

"That's what we're trying to figure out," Shorty said irritably. "We'll split up and take sides," he said.

"There's too many people," McClusky said. "They could pass right by and we wouldn't see them."

"And how will we meet up?" Franky asked. "Frank Nash could be outta here before we can signal the other side."

Shorty started pacing back and forth trying to think of a solution.

"Why don't you just wait here?" Katie said. "You can see all of the main lobby from under the clock."

Shorty stopped pacing and narrowed his eyes at her. The boys realized it was the perfect answer and looked sheepishly at each other.

"Now you idiots see why I let her come," Shorty said. He put his finger to his temple. "The Callahans have brains."

"Look! Over there!" Katie pointed excitedly. A man in handcuffs was being escorted by seven law enforcement officers, all carrying shotguns and rifles. They quickly formed a fan formation and headed to the east front exit of the station.

Outside the station, a new 1933 black chevrolet pulled up next to the lamp post Katie's bike was leaning against. Inside the car, Vern Miller, Adam Rishetti, and Pretty Boy Floyd checked their weapons and got out. Their mission was to free Frank Nash.

Back in the station, Shorty led his gang to the exit. "Frank Nash don't look so tough to me," he said in disappointment.

The officers moved Nash quickly across the street to a waiting car, as Shorty and his gang followed at a distance. Two of the officers leaned their shotguns against the fender of the car. One of them put his hand up and motioned for the kids to stay back while Frank Nash was placed in the front passenger side of the car. Suddenly, with no warning, two men with tommy-guns stepped from behind a waiting car.

"Put'em up! Up! Up!" they demanded roughly, motioning for the officers to raise their hands. Before the surprised officers could obey, a shot was fired and a barrage of bullets tore into the car and the officers.

"Get down!" Shorty yelled. He knocked Katie to the ground and threw himself over her. The other boys scattered all over the parking lot. The roar of guns was deafening, and then hail of bullets ended. Katie heard the roar of a motor and squealing tires. A police officer ran out of the station and fired three shots at the bandits' car as it sped away.

"Are you all right, Squirt?" Shorty helped Katie to her feet. People were screaming and running across the parking lot into Union Station. Shorty held her close to him. He could feel her heart pounding violently against his chest.

"Let's get out of here," he said.

"My bike's over there," she pointed to the lamp post adjacent to the bloody scene.

"I'll get it later," Shorty said.

"I can't go home without my bike," Katie insisted.

Scores of men were running to the car, all of them in a panic.

"Let's go get her bike," Joe Wilson said.

Katie looked at him, hopeful.

Shorty was not one to back away from danger. "Okay," he said.

They edged their way through the gathering to the lamp post. Two officers lay on the pavement, riddled with bullets, and they appeared to be dead. Another officer was wounded. Inside the car three officers were slumped in the back seat. Frank Nash was in the front seat with his head thrown back. They could tell he was dead.

"You kids get away from there!" a policeman yelled. Joe grabbed Katie's bike off the lamp post and they retreated across the parking lot.

"Are they all dead?" Katie asked.

"I think they're just wounded, Squirt," Shorty lied.

She put her arms around his neck and held him tight. "I'm glad you're okay." Katie loved her brother. They teased and fought, but they were close in things that mattered. "You know I won't tell mother we were here."

"I know you won't, Squirt." He was proud of her because she hadn't whimpered or whined. She was a tough kid, even if she was a girl.

Joe gave her the bike.

She nodded her thanks, thinking how brave he was, and then turned back to her brother. Shorty was still mesmerized by the scene. Years later Katie could recall his look of awe and excitement, and she knew it was the defining moment when she began her fight to keep him from falling into a life of crime.

That evening Katie peered over her grandfather's shoulder and read the headline of the *Kansas City Star*: "FIVE SLAIN AT STATION: Gangsters Slaughter Government Agent, Two City Detectives, Oklahoma Police Chief and Convicted Bank Robber Early Today."

Katie had guessed that Shorty lied to protect her. She still felt queasy when she thought about the bloody scene in front of Union Station, and she felt sorry for the men who were killed.

The screen door slammed. Shorty walked into the room.

He looked at the headline and raised his eyes questioningly at Katie. She shook her head, letting him know they were in the clear.

"What are you reading, Grandpa?" he asked

"There was a massacre at Union Station."

"No kidding?"

"They were taking Frank Nash to the federal penitentiary in Leavenworth, and someone tried to free him. I bet Johnny Lazia and that bunch of hoodlums in the north end were involved."

Shorty walked back to the kitchen. Katie followed. "Mom home yet?" he asked.

"No." They were both worried someone had seen them at the station and had told their mother.

Joe Wilson was back on Katie's mind. He wasn't part of Shorty's gang so she wondered about the connection.

"How did you meet Joe?" she asked Shorty.

"At the ball field. He's one heck of a pitcher, so we let him on the team."

"Does he live close by?"

"Yeah. Over on Union Hill. He and his family just moved into the neighborhood. Why all the questions, Squirt?"

"Just wondered."

They heard the screen door slam. Shorty rolled his eyes hopefully at Katie.

"Did you hear about all the excitement, Father?" they heard their mother ask. "There were some people killed at Union Station."

"It's in the paper, Ann," Grandpa replied.

Katie and Shorty walked cautiously into the living room.

"Hello, Katie. . .Egan." She and Aunt Martha were the only ones who could get away with calling Shorty by his given name.

Katie walked over and gave her mother a kiss on the cheek and got a hug and kiss in return. Shorty never hugged or kissed anyone.

"Now you understand why I don't want you hanging around Union Station when you're not working, Egan," she said.

Shorty nodded his head.

"How was work?" Grandpa asked.

"Hard to get anything done with people running up and down the stairs all day talking about the killings," she said, kicking off her shoes. She worked for Tom Pendergast as a secretary at Democratic headquarters at 19th and Main. Boss Tom ran the city from his second-floor office. All day long a steady stream of cronies, politicians, and working men and women sought favors from the huge political boss who controlled the fortunes of the city.

A knock sounded at the screen door and Katie went to answer. McClusky and Corky were standing on the porch. Katie opened the door for them. She saw Franky on the porch swing. He never tried to come in the house. Some of the boys were comfortable inside, and some were not. She looked around for Joe Wilson, and her heart sank when she didn't see him.

McClusky went to confer with Shorty.

"Are you in the clear?" Corky asked Katie.

She looked at his freckled face and light curly brown hair. He was skinny and smaller than the other boys, and seemed the least likely person to be hanging out with Shorty. Perhaps it was his talent for drawing. He could pick up a charcoal pencil and sketch anything. Shorty would bet a stranger a nickel that Corky could draw an exact likeness of any movie actress, and Shorty would always win. Shorty had Corky's actresses pinned all over his bedroom walls.

"Yes," she answered. It felt good to be in on the secret, to be part of the gang.

"Where's Joe Wilson?" she asked.

"He had a date," Corky replied.

"Oh." She felt a knot of jealousy forming in her stomach.

"Not falling for Joe, are you, Katie?"

She blushed.

"Joe has all the girls chasing after him. Even the older girls." Corky said enviously. He secretly wished that Katie would notice him because he thought she was terrific.

"I just wondered," Katie said defensively. How could she have expected Joe Wilson to notice her? It was silly to have even hoped for such a thing. Her mother was right. It was time to stop climbing trees and start acting like a proper young lady. She felt childish and awkward, and she knew it was going to take forever to grow up.

2

When he was still in grade school, Shorty had been a good enough player to become the number one catcher on the neighborhood baseball team. He was much younger and smaller than the other boys, so they called him Shorty. He didn't mind, any name was better than Egan. He loved everything about catching. From his crouched position behind home plate he was in control, calling for pitches, positioning infielders and outfielders, and most of all, protecting home plate. He guarded it with a vengeance, and a run scored against his team was a personal insult. With his stocky stature and reputation as a fighter, he was an intimidating force. When he had on a catcher's mask, chest protector, shin guards and spikes, he was formidable. Opposing runners dreaded a confrontation at home-plate. It was not enough to tag them out. Shorty loved to hit people. He would rise out of the dirt and make them eat the ball. Even when a runner scored unopposed, he was allowed only a tip of home plate. If the runner tried to take more, his reward was a sharp elbow in the ribs and an invitation to meet after the game.

Shorty conferred with Joe Wilson at the pitcher's mound. It was a hot 4th of July day and they were playing their arch rivals from the west side. On a previous play the right fielder had sprained his ankle and they looked to the bench for help. The bench was empty. Joe looked to the grandstand and spotted his little brother, Scooter. He motioned for him to come out onto the field. Scooter ran out to the pitcher's mound. A white scottish terrier followed close behind. Scooter had to crane his neck to see Joe from under the bill of his Saint Louis Cardinals baseball cap.

"Scooter, take right field," Joe ordered.

"What!" Shorty yelled. "He can't play right field."

Joe reached down, grabbed some dirt, and started rubbing it into the ball. "He's a player," Joe said.

"He's a midget," Shorty argued. "How old are you, Scooter?"

"Eight," Scooter answered.

"Eight! He's eight years old?" Shorty was incredulous.

Joe and Scooter stood on the pitcher's mound as Shorty stalked back and forth, cursing to himself, until the umpire walked out to the pitcher's mound.

"Are you guys going to play ball, or are you going to forfeit?"

"Okay, Okay," Shorty said.

"And get that mutt off the field," the umpire ordered.

"He's not a mutt," Scooter challenged. "His name's Whitey."

The umpire shook his head, and Whitey followed Scooter to right field.

"Don't throw anything on the outside of the plate," Shorty ordered. The next batter was right handed and Shorty didn't want him going to right field. Shorty took his position behind home plate. He looked to right field, and all he could see was grass and a Cardinals baseball cap. He shook his head and prayed for a strikeout. It was the top of the ninth, with one man out and a runner on first. They were one run ahead. Two more outs and they would win the game. He called for an inside fast ball and got a called strike. Two pitches were balls, and then Joe threw another strike. He called for another inside fast ball. It was too far inside. The count was 3 and 2. The batter would be waiting for a pitch on the outside corner, so Shorty called for an inside curve. The ball came spinning in toward the outside corner. The batter swung and hit a fly ball to right. The runner on first was off with the crack of the bat. Shorty sank to his knees in defeat. He watched as the white ball tumbled out of the clear blue sky toward a Cardinals baseball cap circling down below. Whitey was yapping and jumping in the air. All of a sudden a glove came up, and Scooter caught the ball. He ran as fast as he could for a few steps and then threw the ball to the first baseman, doubling up the runner.

Joe walked to home plate. Shorty was still down in the dirt muttering to himself. "He caught the ball. The midget caught the ball."

"What's the matter, Shorty?" Joe said. "I told you the kid was a player."

Everyone was cheering and slapping Scooter on the back.

Shorty took off his catcher's equipment. He was still muttering and shaking his head when Scooter walked up to him. "Can I be on the team?" he asked.

"No," Shorty said. "You're not old enough."

Scooter walked dejectedly away.

Shorty remembered what it was like to be told he was too young and too small.

"Hey Scooter," he said. "How would you like to be the equipment manager? You can practice with the team."

Scooter looked around at Shorty. A smile creased his face, and he nodded his head.

"That was a great catch," Shorty said. Scooter ran happily away.

McClusky threw his first baseman's mitt into the bag. Franky and Corky came out of the stands.

"Lets change into our swimsuits and hit the lake," Shorty said. He was their leader and they never questioned his orders. At first their friendship had been one of necessity. Shorty, Andy, and Corky were the only three Irish kids in a German/Polish neighborhood, so they stuck together. Their neighborhood, perched on a bluff above Union Station, was called Dutch or German Hill because of all the German immigrants who had settled there.

Franky lived below Dutch Hill in a tenement house filled with Italian immigrants. He was a shark at marbles and was always sneaking into the neighborhood to play the German and Polish kids. The older German boys would let him get his marble bag full of brightly colored agates and then they would take it away from him. Shorty, Andy, and Corky were walking by a vacant lot one day when they saw the German boys beating on Franky. Since Franky was outnumbered, they had jumped into the fray. Shorty had a reputation in the neighborhood for fearlessness. He was a bulldog and he would never back down. He didn't win every fight, but he exacted so much damage from an opponent that the German and Polish boys left him alone. The fight had lasted only a few minutes before the German kids ran off. Franky had some cuts on his face and a black eye and Shorty took him home and patched him up.

From that time on, hardly a day passed that Franky wasn't sitting on the Callahan front porch waiting for Shorty. He became an inseparable part of the Irish gang. The four boys took some verbal razzing. The other kids called them the three potato heads and the dago, but that only helped solidify their loyalty to each other. After a while the name calling stopped, and they were accepted in the neighborhood.

The boys started walking toward the boathouse. The day was hot with no hint of a breeze. Around the lake all the picnic tables were full of people celebrating the holiday. Many would spend the night in the park. Shorty and the boys were offered food at every table. They ate hot dogs and watermelon and drank ice-cold lemonade.

After lunch they dove into the cool waters of the lake. Corky swam up next to Shorty. "Have you seen her yet?" he asked.

"Don't worry. She will be here."

But Corky was worried. At the age of 18, he was the only one left in the gang who was still a virgin. Shorty had fixed him up with Shirley Polansky. At 19, she was the youngest of the four Polansky sisters. Shorty said they all liked to do "it" but Shirley liked "it" best of all.

Corky dreamed of doing "it" all the time. With dreams about to be realized, he was losing his nerve. He wasn't quite sure what to do. If he asked Shorty or one of the guys, they would tease him unmercifully.

"Maybe this isn't such a good idea," he said.

"Don't worry, Corky," Franky said, reading his mind. "She will put it in for you." All the boys laughed, and Corky ducked underwater to escape embarrassment.

"Are we going to stay for the fireworks tonight?" McClusky asked.

"No way," Shorty answered. "Jimmy Dorsey's at the Pla-Mor. Girls will be there from all over the city."

"Can you get us in?"

"Is my name Shorty Callahan?"

At 18, Shorty was already a man about town. He had quit his job at Union Station, and during the summer he and Franky ran numbers for a bookie joint on Twelfth Street. It was easy money, and he was meeting people who could steer him to more lucrative pursuits.

"There she is!" Franky pointed.

A girl in a red swimsuit walked out of the boathouse and spread her beach towel on the pier. She was tall and heavy set. Her breasts were her most striking feature.

"Look at those tits," McClusky marveled.

"Okay, Corky, make your move," Shorty ordered.

"Listen, Shorty . . ."

"Do it, Corky! Just go over there and ask her to swim. Once she's in the water, start feeling her up."

"How can we do it in the water?" Corky wondered.

"You don't," McClusky said. "A fish might bite off your worm."

Franky dove under the water and playfully bit Corky on the leg.

"Ouch!" Corky yelled.

Shirley Polansky looked over at them and then turned away.

"When you get her good and hot, take her over into the woods behind the boathouse," Shorty said.

Corky knew there was no going back. They would tease him forever. With his heart pounding he swam over to the pier and started treading water while he worked up his courage.

"Hi, Shirley," he finally said. "Would you like to come in for a swim?"

She looked at him from over her sunglasses, and he blushed. She smiled, took off the sunglasses and slithered into the water. Her breasts looked like balloons as they floated toward him.

"Hi. Are you Shorty's friend?"

"Yes. My name's Corky Oliver."

"Nice to meet you, Corky."

"Same here," he said, treading water. "Want to swim out a ways?"

"Why don't we go under the pier where we can talk?" Shirley suggested.

"Okay." He followed her under the pier.

They sat in the shallow water. She moved her leg against his.

"Do you think I'm pretty?" she asked.

"You're beautiful." Corky felt the softness of her leg and smelled traces of her perfume. Water dripped off her hair and fell in glistening pellets down the mysterious cleavage between her breasts. She reached under the water and grabbed the inside of his thigh.

He thought his dick was going to burst. He had to hold on. If he came in his swimsuit, Shirley would tell and the kidding would never stop. He leaned over and kissed her on the cheek.

"That was nice," she said. "I was doing this as a favor to Shorty, but I really like you." She put his hand on her breast, and he squeezed very gently.

She kissed him and he squeezed harder. Her lips tasted warm and sweet. He felt her tongue in his mouth, and then her hand was around his swollen member. He pulled her swimsuit down. Her breasts jumped out at him, and got delightfully in the way of his every move. She scooted back out of the water, slipped out of her swimsuit, and lay back on the sand. He marveled at the black bush between her legs and the thin line of hair that traced to her navel.

"Hurry, Corky," she whispered in his ear. He pulled his swimsuit down. Franky was wrong. She didn't have to put it in for him. He plunged into the black bush, found his way, and suddenly everything was warm and wonderful. He buried his face between her breasts and pounded the bush in a steady rhythm. Shirley was starting to moan. He didn't want it to end, so he held back, listening to her moans of pleasure. She started moving faster and faster until he was no longer in control. He felt her body tense. "Don't stop. . .Don't stop," she moaned. . .and he let go.

They lay together in the sand, contentedly listening to the water lap against the pier. After a while she leaned over and kissed him on the cheek. He heard the rustle of a bathing suit and the parting of water as she slipped into the lake. He smelled a last trace of perfume, and like a mermaid in a fairy tale, she was gone. When he looked around three faces were smiling at him from out in the water.

"I think he made her come," McClusky said in wonder.

"Nah," Shorty said. "She faked it to make him feel good."

Although Shorty wondered why she had never faked it for him.

"What's your secret, lover-boy?" Franky teased him.

Corky blushed. He pulled his bathing suit up and rolled into the water. There was a new-found look of respect on the faces of his friends and a feeling of confidence beating in his chest. "Come on. I'll race you guys across the lake," he said.

Katie leaned against the door of Shorty's bedroom as she watched him adjust his bow tie in the mirror. He was moving his body and his feet to the music playing on the radio.

"Come on, Shorty," she pleaded. "I just have to see Jimmy Dorsey, or I'll die."

Shorty laughed. He turned away from the mirror and danced across the room to get his shoes.

"Please, Shorty. I'll keep out of your way, I promise."

The brass section lit up the radio, and Shorty started playing his imaginary trumpet.

"I'll do anything you ask for a whole month," Katie begged. "Clean your room, iron your clothes, be your slave."

Shorty raised his eyebrows teasingly as he jitterbugged back to the mirror.

She bit her lip to keep from smiling. Shorty could really dance.

"You have to be 18 to get in, Squirt," Shorty said, moving his shoulders back and forth to the music. "That leaves you two years short."

"I look older," she said. "And quit calling me Squirt."

He bowed graciously, mocking her. "Yes, Miss Katherine, whatever you say."

She followed him to the bathroom, trying a different tack. "I'm in a spot, Shorty. I bet two of my friends a dime that you could get us in the dance. I told them you could do anything."

"Flattery, flattery," Shorty said teasingly. "It will get you a lot of places, Squirt, but not in to see the Jimmy Dorsey orchestra."

"Okay," she pouted. "Grandpa's at the lodge hall, and Mother is going to Aunt Martha's. I'll just stay here by myself on the 4th of July."

"Someone has to be with the cat," Shorty said, as he grabbed his coat and danced his way out the door. When he realized she wasn't behind him, he turned around. She was still leaning against the bedroom door, looking dejectedly down at the floor.

Shorty frowned and let out a deep sigh. He couldn't stand to see her unhappy. "If you're not at the Pla-Mor by eight o'clock sharp, Shorty Callahan won't know you," he said.

She ran into the hall and hugged him around the neck. "Thank you, Shorty."

"Go on and get yourself dressed," he said, embarrassed.

Katie and her two friends were blocks away when they heard music from the Pla-Mor drifting out into the warm summer evening. They quickened their pace up Main Street. Earlier in the evening they had put on layers of lipstick and makeup in a vain attempt to appear older. Katie wanted to hear the Jimmy Dorsey band, but her main motivation was to see Joe Wilson. She had slyly asked Shorty if Joe would be at the dance. She had seen him frequently over the years: at ball games, church, and picnics, and when he came by the house to see Shorty. She was always polite, but at a loss for words around him. No one knew she had a crush on him, not even her girlfriends.

Franky Rossi was talking to a couple of girls in front of the Pla-Mor. He excused himself and motioned for Katie and her friends to follow him into the alley. They walked around to the back of the building and stopped at an open window. "Make a fist and put your arm in the window," Franky said.

"Why?" Katie asked.

Franky sighed irritably. "Just do it," he ordered.

Katie was first to go. She reluctantly put her arm in. Someone grabbed her closed fist and pressed something on the top of her hand. She withdrew her arm and looked at the purple lettering.

"What's this?" she asked.

"It's your ticket into the Pla-Mor."

"How did Shorty get the stamp?"

"What do you care?"

"I just wondered."

"Shorty has a couple of good-looking girls occupy the doorman while he takes it," Franky explained.

"That's dishonest," Katie said.

"Nooo!" Franky mocked her. "Maybe you girls should go to church and pray for him." He started walking out of the alley. The brass section of the Dorsey band blared out the window and blew away any of Katie's moral considerations. She and the girls followed quickly behind. At the entrance to the alley, Franky put up his hand for them to stop. "Wait a few minutes until I get inside," he ordered. He didn't want to be seen with any fresh-faced, under-age bobbysoxers.

Katie and her girlfriends waited impatiently for a few moments and then walked to the door of the Pla-Mor. The doorman gave them a curious stare. Like brides with new diamonds they put their hands out for examination, and the doorman waved them through. They waited until they were out of the doorman's sight and then whooped and laughed with delight at their good fortune. Katie surveyed the huge ballroom, which could accommodate over 500 couples. The wood dance floor was laid over 7,000 hair felt spring cushions that would give a quarter-inch. Everyone said the floor was like dancing on a cloud. The girls found a corner where they could watch the dancers. With swishing skirts and popping gum, they tapped their saddle shoes to the beat of the music. Katie spotted Corky back against the wall. He had his sketch pad and charcoal pencil and was busy sketching the scene in front of him. He spotted Katie and the girls and walked over.

"Hello, Katie."

"Hi, Corky. Do you know Marie and Judy?"

"Sure."

"What are you drawing?" Katie asked.

"Just some sketches of the dancers." He turned to Judy. "Would you like to dance?"

"Yes," Judy replied.

Corky put his pad and pencil on a table and moved with Judy out onto the dance floor.

Katie was surprised. Corky was usually shy and reserved, but tonight he seemed confident and somehow more grown up.

The dance floor started jumping as the band played "In The Mood."

"Come on Katie," Marie said, taking her hand, "let's dance." The two girls started jitterbugging to the music. The night was hot and sultry and all the windows around the dance floor were open. The Dorsey band members had already shed their sport coats. In the middle of the floor some dancers were putting on an exhibition. They were called "shiners" because of their acrobatic dance moves. Katie's eyes roved around the ballroom searching for Joe Wilson. The music ended, and out of breath, she and Marie retreated back to their corner of the ballroom.

"Corky!" Shorty yelled, as he worked his way toward them through

the crowd. Franky and McClusky followed close behind. "I've been looking all over for you," he said exasperated. "Quick. Draw me a picture of
Betty Grable."

Corky retrieved his pad and pencil and started sketching.

Marie and Judy bashfully eyed Shorty. He was stocky, with wavy
brown hair, brown eyes, and a puggish, flat nose that had been broken in
a fist fight. He wore a white sport coat, black pants, and a black bow tie.
Judy and Marie thought he was a dream.

"Are you ladies enjoying the dance?" he asked.

"Oh yes. Thank you for getting us in," Marie said.

"My pleasure," Shorty bowed graciously, then snapped his fingers at
Corky. "C'mon, c'mon, I don't have all night."

Corky quickly finished his sketch, tore it off the pad, and handed it to
Shorty. Shorty eyed the sketch. "Yeah," he said. And without so much as
a thank you, he and his two companions melted into the crowd.

Katie turned to Corky."Why do you let him order you around like
that?"

Corky shrugged. "He doesn't mean anything by it. That's just the way
he is."

"Well I think it's rude. He's lucky to have you for a friend."

"Actually it's the other way around."

Katie looked at him questioningly.

"With Shorty for a friend, I don't have to worry about being hassled
by anyone. That's a big help when you're an artist in this neighborhood."

"Protection," Katie said.

"I guess you could say that."

"You use his brawn and he uses your talent as an artist."

"That's just a small part of it. You should see him with my Grandma.
Her eyes light up when Shorty comes by the house. She doesn't get out
much and she sure loves it when Shorty stops by." Corky lived in an old
rundown house on the east side of the neighborhood. His parents were
dead, and his grandfather had been killed in a railroad accident. His
grandmother barely got by on a small pension from the railroad.

"Shorty has a way with words, all right," Katie said. "People are
either afraid of him, or fooled by his bluster."

"That's because they don't know him," Corky said. "And they don't
see him for the good person that he is."

Katie thought how lucky Shorty was to have Corky for a friend.

"What is he going to do with the picture of Betty Grable?" Judy
asked.

"Ice breaker," Corky answered.

"Ice breaker?"

"I'll show you." Corky walked away from them, and then, imitating Shorty's cocky stride, he walked up to Judy. "Excuse me, Miss. I thought you might like to see a sketch of a girl who looks just like you." He handed the sketch to Judy.

"Why that's Betty Grable," Judy said, playing along.

Corky grabbed the drawing and studied it carefully. "Well, what do you know. It *is* Betty Grable."

The girls laughed with delight.

"Does it work?" Katie asked.

"Almost every time. Shorty has a way with the girls."

Katie looked across the dance floor. She saw Joe Wilson and her heart skipped a beat. He was dancing with a beautiful, black-haired girl. She looked older and sophisticated. Katie wondered if she was a college girl. She felt a pang of jealousy as she watched them glide across the floor. The girl made her feel immature and totally inadequate.

"Who's the girl with Joe Wilson?" she asked nonchalantly.

"Nancy Davidson," Corky answered. "She's a debutante. Lives out on Ward Parkway." He wanted to dance with Katie, but he could tell that she was gone on Joe.

Katie kept her eyes on Nancy, wondering what it would be like to be all grown up and in Joe Wilson's arms. The song ended and she continued to stare. Joe looked across the room and their eyes met. Katie watched as he excused himself and started walking toward her. She shifted her feet nervously, but her gaze never faltered. She could feel her heart beating, and the palms of her hands were wet and clammy.

Joe stopped in front of her. "Hello, Katie."

"Hello, Joe."

"Are you having a good time?" he asked.

"Yes. How about you?"

He nodded.

"Is that your girlfriend?" Katie asked. It was more of a challenge than a question.

"No. Why do you ask?"

Katie blushed. "I just wondered."

Joe couldn't believe how grown up she looked. Her auburn hair fell to the top of her shoulders and was parted by a green barrette that matched the green of her eyes. She had a thin nose set between slightly hollow cheekbones, and her dimpled chin jutted from a jaw that seemed set in determination. He had been fascinated with her from the day she had first jumped out of the tree and informed Shorty that she was going with them to see Frank Nash at Union Station. Until this moment she had always seemed so young and out of reach.

The band started playing, and the vocalist began singing. Corky and Marie headed for the dance floor.

"Would you like to dance?" Joe asked.

"No," Katie answered. She saw Judy's mouth dropped open in astonishment.

"Why not?" Joe asked.

"You have someone to dance with."

"You act like you're mad at me."

"Maybe I am."

"Why?"

"You figure it out," Katie said, wondering why she was acting this way. They stood for a few moments with their eyes locked, and then Joe retreated back across the dance floor. He kept looking back at her with a puzzled expression on his face.

"Why did you do that?" Judy asked.

"I don't know," Katie said miserably, as she watched Joe go back to the arms of his debutante. The night that had shown such promise had lost its luster, and she wished she were anywhere but here. "I'm going home," she said.

She sat on the porch swing, gently pushing it back and forth with her bare feet. Out on the horizon the sky burst with color as fireworks lit up the night. An occasional pop pop of firecrackers interrupted her solitude. Inside the house the living room fan hummed diligently against the hot, humid night air. Her mother and her grandfather were still out enjoying the celebration. Shorty would probably be out all night. She still couldn't believe what had happened at the Pla-Mor. What right had she to be jealous of Joe Wilson? He would probably never speak to her again. She pictured herself in his arms, dancing across the floor of the Pla-Mor. In frustration, she took a deep breath, leaned her head back, and looked up at the stars flashing brilliantly in the night sky. A car stopped in front of the house. She heard a car door close, and footsteps. It was probably Shorty, stopping by the house for something. She was too lost in thought too care.

Joe walked up on the porch. The house was dark. He was debating on whether to knock on the door when he heard the swing creaking back and forth. Then he saw her sitting in the moonlight with her head leaning back on the swing. He took a seat on the porch rail and sat for awhile, quietly watching her.

When Katie raised up, she saw him, and caught her breath.

"I think you owe me an explanation," he said.

She was too stunned too speak. And besides, her heart was in her throat.

He moved off the rail and sat beside her on the swing.

Her mouth felt dry and full of cotton.

"What were you mad about?" he asked.

"Why do you care?"

"Do you always answer a question with a question?"

Katie was silent for a moment. "I guess I owe you an apology."

"No. You just owe me an explanation. Why wouldn't you dance with me?"

She turned and looked at him. "I was hoping you had figured it out."

"Maybe I have," he said. They sat quietly for a few moments watching the fireworks burst on the horizon.

"Do you remember the day we first met? You jumped out of the oak tree." Joe pointed to the giant oak in the front yard. "And right into Shorty's plans to see Frank Nash at Union Station."

"I didn't think you would remember."

"I remember all of our meetings. They just didn't add up until tonight."

She turned and looked at him. "Why tonight?"

"I guess I finally realized I'd just been hanging around waiting for you to grow up."

"I wanted to dance with you," Katie said.

"You did? Then. . ."

"I was jealous of Nancy Davidson," she blurted out. She expected him to laugh. Instead he slipped his hand in hers.

"I've been thinking about this for a long time," Katie said, looking at him. "Please don't do this unless you mean it."

"Katie Callahan, I believe you owe me a dance."

She went inside, turned on the radio, and dialed through the stations until she found some music.

He led her off the porch and into the yard. "I want our first dance to be under the stars," he said. At last she was in his arms, and they began dancing to the music. She was lost in the moment and hardly noticed the dew on her bare feet. The stars glistened above them, and on the horizon puffs of color from fireworks lit up the night sky. These things only happened in dreams and in the movies, she thought. The song ended. Their eyes locked, and then his lips were moving invitingly toward hers. She closed her eyes and he kissed her. His lips were warm and wonderful, and everything she had dreamed her first kiss would be. She pulled away and stepped back. "What about Nancy Davidson?" She asked.

"Who?" Joe answered.

Katie smiled contentedly and rested her head on his shoulder.

3

The next morning Katie sat at the kitchen table dreamily staring at her cereal. Her mother sat across from her reading the paper. "Was Joe Wilson waiting for Egan last night?" her mother asked suspiciously. "No. He came by to see me."

"Joe is quite a bit older than you."

"Only two years," Katie said.

"What's he going to do now that school is out?"

"He's going to college."

"Where?"

"Either Kansas City College or Rockhurst."

"What does he want to be?"

"A writer."

"What kind of writer?"

"He wants to write novels."

"Oh?" Her mother's voice had a hint of disapproval.

"What's the matter with being a writer?" Katie challenged.

Her mother put down the paper and straightened her hair net. "Your grandmother had a term for writers, artists, actors, musicians, or anyone of that ilk. She called them ghost dancers."

"How come?"

"Because most of them don't live in the real world. They work odd jobs and barely get by while waiting for the big break that hardly ever comes. Like ghosts, dancing around the fringes of society. She advised me to keep my distance."

"Why?"

"Because they don't mind starving for the sake of their art, and she didn't want me starving with them."

Katie eyed her mother suspiciously. "Why did the subject ever come up?"

Ann Callahan blushed. "Before I met your father, I dated a musician."

"What happened?" Katie was curious. "Did Grandmother try to make you stop seeing him?"

"No. She let the romance run its course. He went on the road with a band, and we lost touch."

Katie knew that she and Joe would never lose touch.

Ann Callahan sipped her coffee. "Your grandmother always said that it's just as easy to fall for someone with a profession."

"Love is a lot more important than any profession."

"So you think you're in love?"

It was Katie's turn to blush.

"I think you should only be dating boys your own age," her mother said.

Katie began eating her cereal. There was no way to explain that all of her girlhood dreams had come true, and that she would never date anyone but Joe Wilson.

Joe sat at his desk organizing his notes. He was always jotting down things that happened during the day or writing character studies of the people he met. His notes were resource material for the historical novel he hoped to write. He had decided to set it in the neighborhoods on the bluffs above Union Station. He lived with his family on Union Hill in an old Victorian home that had a spectacular view of the city. From his second-floor bedroom window he could look out over the gravestones and monuments of Union Cemetery where the city's pioneers were buried and see a visual history of the city. He had a bird's-eye view of the green concourse and stone monuments of the Liberty Memorial. The national memorial was dedicated to those who had lost their lives in service of their country in World War 1. And off to the northeast in the Dutch Hill neighborhood where Katie lived, he could see Our Lady of Sorrows Church perched majestically on a bluff overlooking the city. The church was the protectorate and spiritual symbol for generations of immigrants who had settled the Dutch Hill and Union Hill neighborhoods. To the north in the center of his view was Union Station, the gateway to a city that provided plenty of grist for a novel, from powerful political bosses and notorious gangsters, to the country's best jazz and blues bands, and a wide open reputation for gambling and good times that had continued unabated since the days of the wild west.

Everyone but Katie was fodder for his novel. He wanted to keep her all to himself. At first he had dismissed his feelings for her because she was Shorty's kid sister, and then at the dance he had taken one look at her and fallen in love. He knew it was love because it was like nothing he had ever felt before. She was feminine and practical with an edge of toughness carried over from her tomboy days that made her self assured, yet there was also a girlish sort of vulnerability that she let surface once you got to know her. He knew that she was the person that he wanted to spend the rest of his life with.

"Hi, Joe." Scooter stuck his head into the room.

"Hey, Scooter. Come on in. Where have you been?"

"Playing with the guys down on Signboard Hill. What are you doing?"

"Trying to get something down on paper."

"Do you want to pass some ball after dinner?"

"Sure." Scooter was constantly after him to play baseball. Scooter loved the game and spent most of his time at the ball field. His given name was Michael but Joe had dubbed him Scooter because of the way he darted after ground balls. He was only 8 years old, but he had the potential to be one of the best baseball players in the neighborhood.

"What are you writing about?"

"Some things that happened today."

"What things?"

"Descriptions of the neighborhood and notes about some of the interesting people I've met."

"I don't like to write," Scooter stated matter-of-factly.

"You might when you're older."

"Maybe," Scooter said, unconvinced. "When is Katie coming over?"

"Tomorrow after church. Do you like her?"

"Yes. She's really neat."

"I think so too."

Joe watched as Scooter scanned the room. He could tell there was something on his mind.

"When do you go to college?" Scooter asked.

"Next month."

"Oh."

"I"m going to be living at home, so nothing will change. We can still talk after school and play ball in the evenings."

"Won't you be busy with homework?"

"I'll still make time for us."

"Okay, Joe," Scooter seemed relieved. "Mom says dinner will be ready in a few minutes."

"I'll finish up and be right down."

Katie glanced over at Joe as they sang from the hymnal. She was nervous about having dinner at the Wilsons'. She wanted to make a good impression and she hoped they would like her.

Father Dugan moved to the front of the congregation. "Let us take a moment to invite God into our presence."

Katie bowed her head and whispered a silent prayer. When everyone was seated she made a visual survey of Our Lady of Sorrows Church. The stained glass windows depicted Christ in various stages of carrying the cross on the road to Calvary. The artwork was beautiful and inspirational and helped her feel the presence of God. At the front of the church a host of angels held a crown above a statue of Jesus on the cross, and a bank of candles flickered on either side of the altar. Her faith in God and the church had always given her strength in day-to-day living. Father Dugan had been a big help when Pop had died. An image of Pop came to mind. She and Shorty were kids, sitting on his lap. They would wait for him to take the large shiny railroad watch from the pocket of his vest. He would hold it out and they would listen to it tick. The watch was as steady and dependable as Pop. When a train whistle blew, he would look at the watch and recite the number of the train and whether it was on schedule. They had moved up on Dutch Hill so Pop could listen to the train whistles. And then he got sick and nothing in life seemed dependable anymore. Father Dugan and the church had helped her through those hard times. The resonating voices of the choir brought her back to reality. She took a deep breath and whispered a silent prayer for serenity to carry her through dinner at the Wilsons'.

Joe looked across the table at her and winked. She smiled at him. All of her fears had proved groundless and she was getting along famously with the Wilsons.

"Would you like some dessert, Katie?" Mrs. Wilson widened her light blue eyes, coaxing her to accept.

Katie was stuffed but she couldn't refuse. "Yes. Thank you."

Mrs. Wilson rose from the table. She had a willowy figure and the same light-brown hair as Joe.

"I'll help you clear the dishes," Mr. Wilson said. In contrast he had dark hair and hazel eyes and he was not much taller than his wife.

"Can I help?" Katie asked.

"No indeed. You are our honored guest," Mr. Wilson replied. "And we owe you a debt of gratitude. You managed to get Joe away from his writing to attend Sunday mass. That's something we haven't been able to accomplish."

"I've recently become a lot more religious," Joe said with a smile.

Over dessert, the conversation turned to politics. The Wilsons were both high school teachers. Mr. Wilson taught political science and Mrs. Wilson taught history. A requirement of the household was that everyone be current on world affairs.

"I fear what is happening in Europe," Mr. Wilson said. "The Germans are parading their nationalism again. You would think the slaughter of millions in the last war would have curbed their militaristic impulses, but they're rattling the sabers again."

"Let's not bore Katie with our concerns about the situation in Europe," Mrs. Wilson said.

"I read in the paper that a majority of Americans don't want us involved in another European war," Katie replied.

Joe had warned her about Wilson dinner table topics and during the past week she had brushed up on current affairs so she could hold her own in a conversation.

"That's true enough, Katie, but the peace-loving people of this country will have to keep enough pressure on President Roosevelt to keep him from caving in to those who would involve us in another war."

"If America hadn't become involved in the last world war Germany might have won," Joe said.

"That may be true, Joe," Mr Wilson replied. "However, we feel that negotiations could have prevented the war in the first place."

"In most disputes I would agree, but there are dictators bent on world domination and sometimes you have to take a stand."

"We had better head off this discussion," Mrs. Wilson said. "Once we get started on politics, Katie, it can go on forever. Why don't you show Katie your room, Joe?"

"Okay, Mom."

"Thank you for the dinner," Katie said. "It was delicious."

"Come on, Katie. I'll show you my room, too." Scooter took her by the hand.

Katie sat at Joe's roll-top desk. Scooter had been called away to another baseball game. "Your parents are really nice."

"Thanks."

"They seem worried that we might go to war."

"They're pacifists. They spend a lot of time working for the peace movement. My grandfather was killed in World War 1 and my mother never got over it."

"You don't agree with their views?"

"I do to a point. Where we differ is that I see the need for a strong military in case negotiations fail."

Katie eyed him thoughtfully. "There's something that's bothering you."

He looked into her hazel eyes. Her intuition about him was more proof that there was something special going on between them. "Yes. I have to find a way to tell my parents that I've signed up for R.O.T.C. in college."

"That will be difficult. If it will help, I'll be with you when you tell them."

He leaned over and kissed her. "Thanks for the offer, but I had better face this one alone." She kissed him back. "We had better not get started at this. Your parents showed a lot of trust leaving us alone in your room."

"You're right. They also know a morally strong Catholic girl when they meet one."

She kissed him again and then pulled away. "So this is where you write." She ran her hands over his antique desk. "Yes. The desk belonged to my grandparents."

"What have you been working on?"

"A character study of your brother."

"Really? Will he be in your novel?"

"I might use some of his traits and mannerisms."

Katie became reflective for a moment. "I'm worried about him."

"Why?"

"He's spending a lot of time down on 12th Street with the wrong crowd and I'm afraid he's going to get hurt."

"Shorty has always been able to take care of himself."

"I know. But he might get involved in more than he can handle."

"He's the kind of person that has to be allowed to make mistakes. He's smart, but he also thinks that he's indestructible."

"You *have* done a character study," Katie said.

"I just observe. I don't have any answers."

She squeezed his hand. "It's nice having you to talk to. Let's go back downstairs and visit with your parents."

August 1938

Shorty and Franky left a crap game in the basement of the Dixon Hotel and started walking east on 12th Street. Neon lights began flickering on as Kansas City's street of sin announced itself to the gathering darkness. The sounds of jazz and laughter filtered out of the pool halls, bars, and strip joints. Fans blew the musty smell of cheap perfume and stale tobacco out into the night. With a nod of his head Shorty acknowledged the bouncers and prostitutes stationed along the sidewalk. The street was like a carnival, each arcade a different experience for fun-loving adults. Shorty and Franky were well known along the street. They had graduated from running numbers to working for the Bonatto family, providing protection for gambling joints owned by the organization. Shorty's goal was to make some quick money so he and Franky could open their own bar and supper club in a fashionable part of town. They had to dish out a few bumps and bruises when customers welshed on their bets, but that was life in the gambling business. They never seriously hurt anyone and there was easy money to be made. The two young men were always dapperly dressed. They had on fashionable white shirts, light tropical trousers, and white shoes.

"How are we going to handle this?" Franky asked.

"Don't worry," Shorty answered. "Just leave it to me."

One of the gamblers on the street was suspected of skimming money from the crap tables, and Shorty and Franky were ordered to take care of the problem. How they handled the matter would be a test of their loyalty and determine their future status in the organization.

"We should have brought along a gun," Franky said.

"You keep forgetting that we're the good guys," Shorty replied. He turned off the street and walked into a dimly lit tavern.

"Sammy here?" he asked the doorman. The man pointed his thumb toward Sammy's office. The boys walked back. Sammy was on the phone. He motioned for them to sit in chairs that fronted his desk. Shorty shook his head. Sammy noticed the determined look on Shorty's face and hung up the phone. When he stood up to shake hands, Shorty hit him with a straight right hand. The blow broke Sammy's nose and splattered blood all over the desk. Sammy fell over his chair and landed on his back. Shorty was on top of him in an instant with his hand around Sammy's throat. He pinned him to the floor.

"We need your car keys, Sammy." Shorty rummaged through Sammy's pockets until he found the keys. Then he pulled Sammy roughly to his feet. "Let's go." He pushed Sammy toward the back door. He saw the desperate look on Sammy's face. "Don't even think about calling for help," Shorty said. "You've got no chance with the guys Bonatto will send next. "

Sammy held his nose in pain. He nodded his head. Shorty was not like the rest of them. He might have a chance with Shorty.

Outside they got into Sammy's car. Sammy moved behind the wheel and turned the ignition. "What are you going to do with me?"

"Head south on Main Street," Shorty commanded.

Sammy held a handkerchief to his nose and did as he was told. There was no use trying to deny anything. All he could hope for was a deal. "Listen, boys. I have some money put away."

"Shut up and drive," Shorty said. "Dead men don't tap their bank accounts."

"I'll be reported missing," Sammy said. "You guys were the last ones to be seen alone with me."

"You got no family, Sammy. Your doorman's on our payroll, and the pimps and whores you run with could care less if you disappear."

Sammy digested the words. He knew Shorty was right.

"Sixty thousand dollars," Sammy said matter-of-factly, putting his only trump on a desperate situation.

Shorty sucked in his breath. Sixty thousand dollars was a lot of money. He wasn't about to kill anyone for the Bonatto family. He had just wanted to scare Sammy. If he used his wits he would get a fortune in the process. He mulled over the risk, and decided to take the chance. "Where's the money?"

"Let's hear the deal," Sammy said. He now had the first card of a hand, and he was a master dealer.

"How much did you skim? And don't lie to me," Shorty threatened.

"Fifteen thousand," Sammy answered.

Shorty guessed it was closer to twenty. "We give twenty thousand back to Tony Bonatto. We keep twenty, and you leave town with twenty," he offered.

Sammy now had the full hand. He knew the boys were making no more than a hundred a week. All he had to do was raise the ante. "Thirty thousand for me, and I'll head for the coast, change my name, and never be heard from again," he bargained.

Shorty mulled it over for a moment to make Sammy sweat. The ten grand he and Franky would split represented a year's pay. "It's a deal," he said.

Sammy pulled the car over to the side of the road. Under Shorty's watchful gaze, he retrieved a briefcase from the trunk and handed it to Shorty. They continued south on Main as Shorty opened the case and stared at the bundles of greenbacks.

"The twenty dollar bills are wrapped in bundles of a thousand,"

Sammy said.

Shorty counted out thirty bundles and tossed the money in Sammy's lap. He closed the briefcase.

"Where do you want me to let you off?" Sammy asked.

"Union Station," Shorty answered.

Sammy turned west off of Main and headed for the station. Moments later he pulled to a halt in the parking lot.

"Get out," Shorty said.

"Now wait a minute," Sammy pleaded. His 1935 cream-colored Cord Phaeton was his most prized possession.

"How can we convince Tony we finished our business if we don't have the car?" Shorty asked. He read Sammy's expression and knew he had played his hand better than Sammy had expected.

Sammy breathed a sigh of defeat. "Take care of her, boys," he said sadly as he stuffed bundles of money in his pockets and got out of the car. "She's a sweet old girl."

"Buy a ticket under an assumed name," Shorty ordered. "And don't even think about coming back."

"Kansas City will ring as Waterloo in my ears," Sammy said.

Shorty had no idea what that meant. He knew Sammy read a lot of books. He watched Sammy hurry into Union Station, and then he slipped behind the steering wheel of the touring car. Franky climbed into the front seat. Shorty put his hands lovingly on the steering wheel. He and Franky smiled at each other. "We are going to get more pussy in this car than even I can imagine," Shorty said. He allowed himself a moment of revelry as he pictured them driving around town, picking up girls waiting for the streetcars. And then he remembered Tony Bonatto, and the serious business at hand.

"When we get to Tony's place, here's what I want you to say. . ."

Shorty parked the car on Delaware Street. They walked a block east to the City Market, then entered a building under the Bonatto Produce Company sign. One of the workers on the dock pointed to the stairs. They walked up to Tony's office. Tony was at his desk, finishing off a plate of rigatoni. He motioned for them to come in. Tony Bonatto was a big man. He was over six feet tall and weighed two hundred and fifty pounds. He was 35 years old, with dark black hair, large brown eyes, and a flat nose that had been broken several times during his years an an enforcer for the mob. His round head protruded from broad muscular shoulders. Behind his back everyone called him Tony "No Neck"

Bonatto. Tony wiped his mouth with a napkin. "Franky, my boy. It's good to see you." Tony got up and put his arm around Franky.

"Hello, Uncle Tony. You remember Shorty Callahan?"

"Sure. How you doing, Shorty?"

"Fine, Mr. Bonatto." Shorty knew to keep his distance and let Franky do the talking. Several years ago Franky's family had moved out of the tenement hotel and into the Italian district known as Little Italy on the north side. Italians had a family thing about business. They were always hugging and kissing, and calling each other uncle and brother. Shorty accepted the fact that he was not of the blood, and would always be an outsider.

"Did you take care of our problem, Franky?"

"Yes sir."

"Any problems?"

"No sir." Franky laid the briefcase on Tony's desk.

"What's this?" Tony asked.

"You pay us to collect the money, so we collected the money."

Tony was intrigued. He opened the case, and his eyes widened when he saw the money.

"Twenty thousand dollars," Franky said.

A smile crossed Tony's face and then he looked suspiciously at the boys. "Solly!" he yelled. "Get in here!"

A little man in a green visor walked out of a back office and stood before them. Solly Weinstein was the numbers man for the organization.

"How much do you figure Sammy skimmed from his joint on 12th Street?"

Shorty felt a trickle of sweat run down his back. Solly looked him in the eye, and then scratched the gray hair behind his right ear. "A minimum of ten thousand and a max of twenty," he said confidently.

Tony still wasn't satisfied. "How much did you boys keep for yourself?"

The two boys looked at each other guiltily for a moment. Shorty prayed that Franky would get the words right. He had coached him all the way from Union Station.

"Shorty wanted to keep fifty dollars to pay for a new outfit, but I told him you was good for it, Uncle Tony."

Shorty took the cue and stepped forward. He pointed to Sammy's blood that had spattered on his shirt and pants.

Tony took the rubber band from a bundle of twenties and gave each of them a hundred dollars. "I'm always good for it. Tony Bonatto never forgets a favor."

The boys headed for the door. Shorty stopped and turned around. "I almost forgot, Mr. Bonatto. Sammy's car is parked over on Delaware Street. Here's the keys." Shorty had already surmised that Tony did not want to be connected to the property of a murder victim, but he had to offer the car to cement his loyalty to the organization. "We'll catch the streetcar back to 12th Street," he said.

"You boys keep the car for a job well done," Tony said in his most benevolent manner.

Shorty walked over and shook his hand. "It's a pleasure to work for you, Mr. Bonatto."

"You bet it is, Callahan, so don't get too smart for your own good. If you get my meaning?"

"I understand, Mr. Bonatto."

"Good. Now get out of here. I got work to do."

The boys were exuberant as they walked out into Market Square and over to Delaware Street.

"What a day's work," Franky said. "Five grand each and a beautiful touring car. You sure know how to handle Tony No Neck."

"Tony knows we took some dough," Shorty said. "What's killing him is that he doesn't know how much. I figure we can keep giving Tony his fair share of the profits on 12th Street and still make a bunch of money. It's time we quit being errand boys and start setting up our own organization. If an ape like Tony No Neck can make this kind of dough, just think what we can do. We can make enough for two supper clubs."

"Don't get on the bad side of Tony," Franky warned. "I've seen him take guys apart with his bare hands."

"Tony is fat, lazy, and living on his reputation," Shorty said. "I'll bet you your five grand that I can whip his ass."

Franky looked over at Shorty's smiling face, and they both started to laugh. Franky wasn't about to bet his money, because he knew damn well that Shorty could do it. Franky looked at his watch. "What time are we supposed to meet McClusky?"

"Ten o'clock at the Chesterfield Club. His cousin is here from Oklahoma and he wants us to meet him. I'll change clothes and then we'll pick up Corky." With the canvas top pulled back on their touring car, and bundles of money to spend, they headed south to Corky's house.

"Wow!" Corky exclaimed as he surveyed the touring car. Where did you get this?"

"A gift from our employer," Shorty said.

"Is there a body in the trunk?"

"Get in the car and don't be a wise ass," Franky said.

Corky climbed in the back. "Umm," he said thoughtfully. "No blood on the seats."

"A wise ass and a comedian," Franky said, as they headed for the Chesterfield Club.

McClusky sat at a table with his wide-eyed cousin. It was obvious to Shorty that the thin, sallow-faced Okie was right off the farm. He had seen the forlorn, hungry look on hundreds of drifters who had left the dust bowl and migrated to the city looking for work. The Okie was eyeing the waitresses, who had nothing on but their jewelry.

"This is my cousin, Duff," McClusky said. The boys introduced themselves, shook hands, and sat down.

"Duff's been speechless since we walked in here," McClusky continued.

"What's the matter, Duff?" Shorty asked. "Don't they have naked girls in Oklahoma?"

Duff shook his head in wonder and kept staring. "I've always dreamed of being in a room with naked women, but I never thought my dreams would come true."

The boys laughed.

"What brings you to Kansas City?" Corky asked.

"Trying to find work," Duff said. "After our farm went under, my mom, dad, and two sisters headed for California. I decided it would be best for everyone if I struck out on my own. Andy's family has been good enough to put me up for a couple of weeks."

"What happened to your farm?" Corky asked.

"The dust claimed her," Duff said solemnly. "It was a sad day when we had to leave," He looked bewildered, as though he was still trying to sort out all that had happened.

Shorty ordered them a round of drinks. "What kind of work are you looking for?" he asked.

"Anything that pays. I've got my name on the list for the WPA and the CCC."

"My uncle's trying to get Duff on the city payroll, but the city's way overstaffed," McClusky said. "He had to go directly to Boss Pendergast to get me in the police academy."

"You made it," Shorty said delightedly. He punched McClusky on the shoulder. "Congratulations."

"Thanks," McClusky said. He shook hands with Corky and Franky. "I hope I can get through the training."

"You'll make one hell of a cop," Shorty said. "Now let's celebrate. The drinks are on me." He called a waitress over and whispered in her ear. Moments later she was back serving the drinks. Shorty slipped her some money and then helped her up onto the table.

Duff was mesmerized as she started moving her naked body in front of him, dancing erotically to the music. She slithered down to her knees and shook her breasts in his face. He turned red with embarrassment, but he was not about to turn away. The girl rose to her feet. She turned around, and with a seductive look at Duff, bent over and left nothing to his imagination.

"Watch this, Duff." Shorty took out a silver dollar. He held it on the table in the tips of his fingers. The dancer moved over and slithered down to the beat of the music. The boys watched in rapt fascination as she moved seductively closer to the coin. As the drums rolled, she lowered her thighs and expertly snatched up the coin with the lips of her vagina.

Duff's mouth dropped open in astonishment. The dancer slipped off the table and went to fetch another round of drinks.

"Where did she learn to do that?" Duff wondered.

"Liberal arts class in college," Corky said.

"He thinks he's Will Rogers," Franky said to general laughter.

"Where do you work, Corky?" Duff asked.

"He's an artist," Franky said. "Artists don't work. It gets in the way of their creative nature."

"Creative?" Corky asked in mock astonishment. "Where did you ever hear that word? You haven't been trying to read again?"

"You wise ass," Franky said to general laughter.

"Next week I start work at a grocery store down in the west bottoms," Corky said. "I hope to save enough money to attend the Art Institute."

"Yeah, and when you graduate you get a little piece of paper that allows you to starve to death," Franky said.

"Don't you two like each other?" Duff asked.

The boys laughed.

"They tolerate each other," McClusky said. "Corky's always trying to be everybody's conscience, and that's a heavy load when you're dealing with Shorty and Franky."

"You think I've got a heavy load," Corky said. "Wait until you swear to uphold the law with these two for friends."

"What do you guys do?" Duff asked.

"We provide security for the entertainment industry," Shorty answered.

Corky laughed, but beer got caught in his throat and he coughed it up all over the table, much to the amusement of the others.

Corky finally caught his breath. "Security for the entertainment industry," he said unbelievingly, and they all started laughing.

Duff just looked at them in bewilderment. Shorty wiped his eyes. "Sorry, Duff. It's an inside joke. How would you like to go to work for Franky and me?"

"Golly, I need work, but I don't know anything about the entertainment business." Shorty tried not to look at Corky, but he couldn't help himself, and they all howled some more.

"I'll teach you all you need to know," Shorty said when he gained control. "Can you handle yourself in a scrap?"

"Where I was raised, you learn to fight," Duff answered.

"A hundred a month to start," Shorty said. "Is that okay?"

Duff was dumfounded. It was more money than he had seen in years.

Shorty took a bundle of bills out of his pocket. He peeled off five twenties and placed them in front of Duff. "An advance on your salary. You'll need to get some new clothes and an apartment."

Duff was speechless. He looked like he was about to cry. "Okay, come clean," Corky said, saving Duff the embarrassing moment. "Where did you guys hide the body?"

The next afternoon Shorty knocked on Corky's screen door. From the shadows inside the house he could see Granny Oliver shuffling toward him on her cane. She made it to the screen door and a smile lit up her face.

"Hello, Granny."

"He's still asleep, Shorty. You boys must have made a night of it."

"We had to celebrate Andy McClusky getting on the police force."

With a smile, Granny nodded her approval. "You want me to wake him?" she asked as he walked into the house.

"Nah. I'll get him in a minute. How are you doing, Granny?"

"Fine, fine. My gums are a little sore, so I left my teeth out."

" I brought you the August issues of *Life, Look*, and the *Saturday Evening Post*." He placed the magazines on the coffee table.

Granny moved her hands lovingly over the magazines, imagining the wonders inside. "Thank you, Shorty. You're trying to spoil me."

"Now and again I have to bring my best girl a present."

Granny's eyes sparkled and she smiled coyly. "Sometimes you make me feel like a young girl again, Shorty."

It was Shorty's turn to smile. "I better get Corky out of bed before he sleeps the day away."

"Wake up, sleeping beauty." Shorty pulled the pillow out from under Corky's head.

Corky sat up, yawned and looked sleepily around. "What's up?" he asked.

"Go put on something nice," Shorty ordered. "We have an appointment with some people."

"Who?"

"Never mind, just go get dressed."

Corky came out of the house tucking in his shirt, and Shorty said good-bye to Granny. Fifteen minutes later he steered the touring car through the gates of the Art Institute. The 26-room red brick mansion loomed above them as they parked under the portico. The old Meyer mansion had been converted to use as a haven of education for artists and art students. The mansion was surrounded by eight acres of beautifully landscaped grounds that were covered with rare trees, plants and shrubs.

"What are we doing here?" Corky asked.

"Come on." Shorty got out and Corky followed him inside.

A secretary eyed them as they approached the registrar's office. "Help you?"

"Yeah. I'm Shorty Callahan. This is Corky Oliver. We're here to sign Corky up for the school year."

"What are you doing?" Corky asked in surprise. He was dead broke and couldn't possibly pay the tuition.

"You'll have to fill out these forms," she said, handing them over.

"How much?" Shorty questioned.

"Seventy five dollars a semester."

"How much if we pay the full four years? Do we get a discount?"

"Well. . .I don't know. . .it's never come up before," she hesitated.

"Let me talk to the head man," Shorty said.

"Listen, Shorty. . ."

"Don't interrupt me when I'm negotiating, Corky."

A man came out of a side office. "Hello, I'm John Morgan."

"Mr. Morgan," Shorty shook his hand. He introduced Corky. "We want to sign Corky up for the school year. I was wondering what type of discount you offered if we pay the full four years."

Mr. Morgan folded his arms across his chest and looked sternly at Shorty. He guessed the two young men were carrying out one of the pranks that were always being hatched on campus. The country was trying to work itself out of a depression, and hardly anyone had the tuition for a semester, much less the full four years. But he was a good sport, and he would play along. "You pay for four years, and you get a five percent discount," he said.

Shorty frowned at him like he was the world's biggest cheapskate. "You're using money that I could be earning interest on," he said.

Mr. Morgan winked at Corky. "Okay. Ten percent."

"Now that's more like it."

Mr. Morgan gasped as Shorty took out a bundle of twenties and started figuring. "With the discount that comes to $540 dollars. He counted out the bills on the secretary's desk.

"I'll need a written receipt," he said.

Corky and Mr. Morgan stared at the money in shock.

"When do classes start?" Shorty asked.

"September 5th," Mr. Morgan recovered his speech and held out his hand. "Mr. Oliver, let me welcome you to the Art Institute."

Corky shook it, thinking that Shorty was the best friend that anyone could have. He followed Shorty outside under the portico. "I can't tell you how much this means to me, Shorty. I never dreamed it would happen. If there"s anything. . ."

"Oh shut your yap, and quit acting like a sob sister," Shorty said. "You better graduate from this place, or you'll have me to answer to. And keep your eyes open for girls. These artistic types like to experience the finer things in life." He raised his eyebrows playfully at Corky.

Corky laughed and shook his head in wonder as he followed Shorty to the touring car.

4

W here did you get the car?" Katie asked suspiciously.

"What's it to you, Squirt?" Shorty said as he sipped soup from a pot on the stove. "I think you're getting involved with the wrong people, and you're headed for trouble."

"Do you, now?" Shorty mocked her. He patted her head.

Katie knocked his hand away. "Yes. You think you're so smart, and you're going to end up in jail."

"Will you come visit me?"

"Why can't you be serious?"

Shorty reached over and pinched her cheek. "Because you're my lee-tle baby sister," he said, making baby talk.

Katie pulled away. "You're going in the wrong direction when you should be going to college, or working a decent job."

"The wrong direction? I have a new car, a pocketful of cash, and for your information, I'm on a rocket to the stars."

"Hah! You're on an express train to Leavenworth, and you're too stupid to see it."

"Now, Squirt. Let's not resort to name calling." Shorty poured some soup out of the pan and into a bowl.

"Father Dugan asked about you."

"Ah, Father Dugan. So that's what this is about. Trying to get me back to church."

"Father Dugan cares about you. He says you have a lot of potential."

"He's right."

"Don't be so cocky. I worry about you."

" I worry about you too, Squirt."

"You do?"

"Sure. I wonder what will happen to my little sister when Joe Wilson dumps her for one of those beautiful girls who are always chasing him around." Shorty saw her look of uncertainty, and realized he had hit her in a vulnerable spot. He put his arm around her. "Hey, I'm only kidding. Joe is lucky to have you. If I see him with another girl I'll break his arms."

"There, you see." Katie had fresh ammunition. "Your solution to any problem is to hurt someone."

"It was a figure of speech."

"No. It was a good example of how your mind works."

"I'm going to miss these heart-to-heart talks," he said.

"What do you mean?"

He hesitated for a moment, trying to find an easy way to say it. "I'm moving in with Franky. We're getting an apartment downtown."

Katie knew this would happen eventually, but she still felt unprepared. Shorty had always been there for her. When Pop died, he had helped with the loneliness and the despair.

At night, when she was lonely, or afraid of an approaching storm, she would call to him across the hall and he would turn on the antique musical carrousel that Pop had given him for his birthday. The music from the carrousel always made her feel safe and secure because it meant that her brother was close by. He had hung around the house on her birthdays, and made it easy for her in the neighborhood. No one teased or bothered Shorty Callahan's sister.

"What about us?" she asked.

"Listen to you. I'm only going downtown."

"But why?"

"It's time for me to get a place of my own."

"Mom and I need you. Who will I talk to?"

"You have Joe Wilson."

"So that's it. You've been waiting around for someone to come along and take me off your hands. If you stay I'll give him up."

Shorty looked behind her back. "You have your fingers crossed."

"Okay. I won't give either of you up. Take me with you."

Shorty laughed. "I can see Franky's face when I tell him: Listen, Franky, my 16-year-old sister. . ."

Katie frowned. "I get the point. Have you told Mother?"

"No."

"What if she says you can't go?"

"Sure," he scoffed. "What can she do?"

Katie shrugged in defeat. Things would be different if Pop were alive. Shorty never mentioned Pop but Katie knew he missed him. It was like Pop's death had given Shorty a hard shell, so that he hid his feelings and struck out at the world. "You don't always have to be the tough guy, you know."

Shorty shrugged.

Their mother walked into the kitchen, interrupting Katie's sermon. "What are you two arguing about?"

Katie raised her eyes at Shorty, daring him to tell.

"I'm moving out next week."

"Oh." She was taken aback for a moment. "Do you think you're ready for that, Egan?"

"Yes. I'm a grown man."

"Eighteen is hardly a grown man," she said. Shorty had been squeezed by the two Callahan women before, so he plotted a hasty retreat. "I know how hard you've worked to keep us together, but it's time for me to go," he said to his mother. It was the first time he had ever paid her a compliment.

He saw her shoulders slump and her hands go to her eyes. Katie moved over and hugged her. "Nothing will change," she said. "I'm sure he will be showing up here every day looking for a free meal."

Ann Callahan wrapped her arms around Katie, and held her tight. "When are you moving out, Egan?"

"Next week."

She dabbed her eyes with a handkerchief. "Our last week together as a family," she said tearfully.

Shorty was prepared for this and refused to feel guilty.

"Aunt Martha invited us out to Lake Forest for the weekend."

"I've made plans to be with my friends," Shorty said.

"You can bring your friends. They can sleep on cots out on the porch."

Shorty knew she wasn't fond of his friends, so this was quite a concession. Katie's eyes pleaded with him to accept.

He decided to agree, and do Katie a favor in the process. "I'll come if Katie can invite Joe Wilson."

His mother gave him a look that let him know he had gone too far.

"What's the big deal?" he said. "The whole family will be there to chaperone."

"All right, Egan. Katie can invite whomever she wants."

He winked at Katie. The sparkle in her eyes told him that all was forgiven.

Katie looked up at the early evening stars as Joe guided the canoe across the lake. A red glow above the west hill was all that remained of the setting sun. Around the lake, bullfrogs raised a steady chorus, welcoming the dusk. A beaver raised his head, realized he was being pursued, and ducked under the water. Up ahead a flock of Canada Geese flapped their wings, preparing to take off. With a cascade of spraying water they rose into the evening sky, honking at the gathering darkness that instinctively moved them on their way. Katie watched as they circled the lake and flew across the red glow on the horizon. "How beautiful," she said in wonder.

"Like a painting," Joe agreed.

"You can use it as a scene in one of your books."

"If I ever get one started."

"We've been going together for a year and I've never read anything you've written."

"Is it important?"

"Yes. I want to know everything about you, not just what you want me to see."

"My writing is a lot like your old oak tree. A private place where I can think and be alone. You've never asked me to climb your oak tree."

"You would think I was silly."

"No I wouldn't."

Katie smiled, making a mental note not to press him about his writing. She put her hand down and made a ripple in the cool, still waters.

Joe looked around at the picturesque homes bordering the lake. "This is a nice place."

"In the old days these lands were used as hunting and camping grounds by the Kaw, Wyandotte, and Delaware Indian tribes," Katie explained. "They used the fresh-water springs that bubbled out of the ground. Legend has it that Chief Spotted Tail of the Wyandotte is buried on the point of the west hill."

"Has your family lived here long?"

"Since 1916. In the old days Uncle Ray had a hunting and fishing cabin in the upper lake. When he married Aunt Martha he built her the house up on the hill."

Across the lake a scoutmaster barked orders to a canoe full of Boy Scouts.

"The Boy Scouts own the property to the northwest," Katie said. "They use the lake for training exercises."

Joe held the paddle out of the water and let the canoe drift. In the distance, lights from the community clubhouse flickered out into the dusk. "Are you taking me to the dance tonight?" he asked.

"No. I might have to share you. Out here I get to keep you all to myself."

"Likely story. You probably have a boyfriend you don't want me to meet."

"You've found me out," Katie said. "Paddle the canoe closer to the clubhouse so we can listen to the music." The call of an owl carried out of the hills. It was answered by an owl in the upper lake. The moon's reflection lit their way across the water. "This is perfect," Katie said, as Joe put down the oar. She slipped back and snuggled up to him. He put his arms around her and they let the canoe drift as they listened to music flowing from the clubhouse.

"Do you love me, Joe?"

"You know I do."

"You couldn't love me as much as I love you."

"How much is that?"

"So much that I don't know how to say it."

He held her chin in the palm of his hand and kissed her gently on the lips. "Do you swear by the ghost of Chief Spotted Tail of the Wyandotte?"

Katie laughed. "Yes. I swear by the ghost of Chief Spotted Tail that I will always love you."

The romantic moment was interrupted as a car screeched to a halt. The occupants noisily piled out onto the lakefront. In the light of the gas lanterns Katie could see that the girls were draped all over the boys and that everyone carried beer bottles.

"Oh, no," Katie said. "It's Shorty." She could see that he had been drinking, and she guessed that he had brought some less-than-proper ladies out to the lake. "Quick. Row us to the bank. If Aunt Martha sees those girls she will just die."

"Why?" Joe asked as he paddled to the shore.

"Aunt Martha is the last of the Victorian ladies. We'll never hear the end of it if she's connected in any way with improper behavior."

Corky spotted her coming toward them in a fury. He stepped forward and tried to ward her off. "I tried to talk him out of it, Katie, but you know how well he listens."

Katie walked around Corky and grabbed Shorty by the arm. She pulled him over to the side. "How could you bring those girls out here?" she hissed.

"You obviously have not looked at those girls," he answered. "They are the finest the Chesterfield Club has to offer."

"You know what I mean. Aunt Martha will be furious."

"Not if you don't tell her." One of the girls walked over. "Come on, Shorty," she pouted. "You said we could go swimming."

Franky and McClusky stood a few yards away, not wanting to risk

Katie's wrath.

"Where are your swim suits?" Katie asked suspiciously.

"In the car," Shorty lied.

Katie started to go look.

"Tell you what, Squirt." Shorty put his arm around her. "Me and Corky will go up to the house and see Aunt Martha. She thinks he is going to be the next Norman Rockwell."

"Terrific," Corky said. "Use my sterling reputation with Aunt Martha to get what you want."

"Don't be difficult," Shorty said as he pushed Corky toward the house. "Just go in and start some artsy talk with her and everything will be fine."

"What about the girls?" Katie asked sternly, as she stood there with her hands on her hips.

"I will explain everything to Aunt Martha, and even ask Uncle Ray to come and chaperone our evening swim."

Katie eyed him suspiciously as she followed him up the hill. She knew her brother, and this was too easy.

When they arrived at the house, Katie led them inside. The house was one of her favorite things about coming to the lake. It had solid oak floors, high ceilings, and spacious rooms that were filled with antique furniture and family heirlooms. It was a great home to explore and Aunt Martha could recite a fascinating story about each heirloom. Uncle Ray had been in the construction business and he was always remodeling rooms or adding on. He had kept his hunting and fishing cabin in the upper lake to accommodate unexpected guests that always seemed to show up on holidays. She led Shorty out to the porch where her mother, grandfather, Aunt Martha, and Uncle Ray were chatting.

"Hello, Egan," his aunt Martha greeted him with a kiss on the cheek. She was in her seventies and always wore long flowing dresses with a brooch at the neck. "You brought Corky with you," she said delightedly. "I had your painting of the lake framed and hung in the living room. Did you see it?"

"Yes, Ma'am. It's kind of you to hang it in such a prominent place."

"Well not at all. My friends are all envious."

"It's good of you to say so."

"Hello, Uncle Ray."

"Hello, Shorty. How are things in the city?"

"Good, Uncle Ray."

"I brought some friends out, Aunt Martha. I was wondering if it would be all right if we went for an evening swim?" Aunt Martha's eyes went up suspiciously.

"Just some boys and girls from the neighborhood," he reassured her. "I came up to ask Uncle Ray if he would chaperone."

"How thoughtful of you Egan. I don't see the harm if you keep the noise down."

"Thank you, Aunt Martha."

"Now, Shorty. . ." Uncle Ray started to protest when he saw Shorty's eyebrows go up, signaling a promising evening. He rose to his feet. "Don't mind helping out the young folks at all," he said.

Shorty knew his Uncle Ray had a weakness for the ladies.

He had run into him several times on 12th Street where they had traded conspiratorial winks before going their separate ways. He also knew the telescope Uncle Ray kept in his upstairs bedroom for observing wildlife and the stars was really used to seek out beautiful young bodies on the lake front.

"Will your friends be spending the night, Egan?"

"Just Corky, Aunt Martha."

"Very well," she said, relieved.

"We had better not keep our friends waiting," Shorty said. "We don't want to be rude."

"Have a nice time," Aunt Martha said.

Katie pulled Corky aside before he went out the door.

"What's a silver dollar girl?" she asked.

Corky shrugged. "What do you mean?"

"I distinctly heard Shorty whisper something to Uncle Ray about a silver dollar girl."

Corky played dumb and hurried out the door. He chastised Shorty as they went down the hill behind Uncle Ray. "You're abusing Aunt Martha's hospitality."

"How?"

"You misled her about boys and girls from the neighborhood."

"Ha," Shorty shot back. "What about you? Thanking her for putting your painting in a prominent place. You didn't even notice the painting."

"Yeah, well. . .I didn't want to hurt her feelings."

Shorty laughed and slapped him on the back. "You did good with the artsy talk."

Back at the car, Shorty introduced his Uncle Ray. "You remember Franky Rossi and Andy McClusky."

"Of course." Uncle Ray shook hands. "And this is Peggy." Peggy was a thin red head with playful green eyes. "This is Mae." Mae was average height, with brown hair, brown eyes, and well developed breasts that pushed seductively at her blue cotton summer dress. "And say hello to Rita." Rita was the silver dollar girl. She had short black hair, black eyes, and a beautiful body that made her the favorite of customers at the Chesterfield Club.

"Is the rope swing still in the old sycamore tree, Uncle Ray?"

"Indeed it is, my boy."

"Then away we go."

Shorty parked the car on a hill over-looking the upper lake. The branches of the old sycamore tree loomed out over the water.

"McClusky, reach in the glove compartment and get that bottle of schnapps for Uncle Ray."

"Shorty, you're trying to spoil me. I'll do my guard duty on the ridge right over there," Uncle Ray said, pointing to a ridge above them. "If anyone ventures close I'll give a whistle." He cradled the schnapps in his arm and headed up to the ridge. It would give him the best vantage point to watch the girls.

"All right everyone," Shorty said. "Last one to get undressed is first on the rope swing."

The boys pretended to be nonchalant, but their pulse quickened as they glanced at breasts and bottoms popping out at them in the moonlight.

Mae lost the contest, and she was first to go. "It's too high," she said, holding gingerly to the rope and looking down into the darkness.

Shorty came up behind her and grabbed a share of the rope. "Me Tarzan. You Jane," he said. "We go in water together."

Mae laughed. Franky shoved them off the ledge, and out over the lake. Mae screamed and Shorty let out a Tarzan yell as they fell into the lake. They laughingly made their way out of the water. Shorty followed her glistening buttocks back up the stone steps to the top. "Okay, give a nice stretch and let Uncle Ray see those beautiful tits," he said. "We want to reward him for being a good sport."

Mae pulled her shoulders back in a seductive pose, letting the moonlight glisten off the water beading on her breasts.

"I don't know what it's doing for Uncle Ray," Shorty teased, but it's obvious what it's doing to Corky." Corky burned with embarrassment as everyone laughed.

"Come on, Corky," Peggy said. "Go with me off the swing."

"Be careful," Franky teased. "He might spear you with that thing on the way down."

"I'll take my chances," Peggy said.

"Whoa, Corky," Franky said. "You might have more there than you can handle."

Peggy reached over and squeezed Corky's swollen muscle. "I think he will be able to handle it just fine."

Everyone hooted and hollered as Franky pushed them out over the lake and they fell into the water.

Franky and Rita went next, and then Mae went off the swing with McClusky.

"What happened to Corky and Peggy?" Shorty asked, peering down at the lake.

"I heard some moaning and groaning out in the water," Rita said.

"Corky!" Shorty yelled. "You had better behave, or I'll tell Aunt Martha!"

A Tarzan yell came back at him from out of the darkness.

McClusky returned from the car with fresh beers for everyone. Franky and Mae were in an embrace a few yards away.

"Post time!" Shorty yelled, getting Frankie's attention.

"What's the bet?" Franky asked. He and Shorty were always making bets: the horses, pool, baseball, the weather, even the color of someone's socks. "Rita and I will stand you and Mae. We'll be the horses and the girls can be the jockeys. The couple that can go off the swing and stay together all the way to the bottom of the lake are the champs."

"You're on, Callahan. Don't let him cheat, Rita."

Rita laughed. She climbed on Shorty's back. Shorty grabbed the rope and McClusky gave them a shove out over the lake.

"Hi yo, silver dollar!" Shorty yelled. There was laughter, and then a loud splash.

Mae climbed aboard Franky and they were shoved away into the darkness. Fifteen minutes later, McClusky was still sitting alone under the rope swing, wondering who had won the contest and what had happened to everyone.

Shorty and Corky spent the next day sailing on the lake with Katie and Joe. The night before, McClusky and Franky had taken the girls back to town in the touring car.

The family was gathered around Aunt Martha's dining room table after the evening meal.

"I had a call this morning from the Watts," Aunt Martha said. "They live on the upper lake. Someone was making these terrible Tarzan calls throughout the night and keeping them awake. Do you know anything about that, Egan?"

"Indeed I do, Aunt Martha. We were all gathered around a campfire out on the point, toasting marshmallows and trying to hear Uncle Ray's stories about the old days. It was hard to concentrate with all the noise from the upper. I'm surprised at the riff-raff that's allowed in here these days."

Corky had to cover his mouth to keep from laughing.

"Security certainly isn't what it used to be," Aunt Martha agreed. "I'll speak to the Board of Directors. Did your uncle entertain you with his knowledge of the stars?"

"Yes, Ma'am. Uncle Ray said he saw some things last night that he had never seen before. Ain't that right, Uncle Ray?"

Uncle Ray coughed uncomfortably. "Indeed it is my boy. It was an experience not soon to be forgotten."

"I'm glad you were able to tear him from the radio for one evening," Aunt Martha said. "Monday through Friday he listens to 'Amos 'N Andy,' and on Sundays it's the 'Jack Benny Show.'"

"Da Kingfish do like to listen to da radio," Shorty said.

"Dat's true, Lightnin," Corky chimed in to general laughter. "He sit der fo all of da day, an most of da night."

"That reminds me," Uncle Ray said looking at his watch. "H.V Kaltenborn will be on in a few minutes. His program is on the crisis in Europe."

"I don't know what all the fuss is about," Grandpa said. "They should let Hitler have Czechoslovakia and be done with it. The Europeans are always going to be in one territorial dispute or another. They've been going at each other since before the Crusades. It's certainly none of our business."

"Chamberlain meets with Hitler in two weeks," Uncle Ray said. "My guess is he will sacrifice the Czechs to appease that little two-bit dictator. If he does, Europe will be in for it."

"Not necessarily dear," Aunt Martha said, agreeing with Grandpa. "Hitler is just trying to recover the original German homelands. Those countries certainly aren't worth going to war over."

"You can say that because it's not your country," Uncle Ray countered. "Hitler will keep pushing until someone stands up to him."

"You can't blame France and England," Ann Callahan spoke up. "Their populations were decimated in the last war."

"Well, they had better stiffen up, or these kids will have to go over there and save their bacon again," Uncle Ray pointed to the young people around the table. "What do you think, Shorty?"

"Uncle Ray is right. If someone takes a punch at you, you had better punch back. It's the law of the streets. Countries are no different."

"Well put, my boy," Uncle Ray said.

"Well, I can't imagine this country ever going to war again," Aunt Martha said. "The people are against it. That socialist in the White House won't go against public sentiment." Aunt Martha, a staunch Republican, would not even speak the name of Franklin Roosevelt, a man she felt was a betrayer of his class.

"Especially now that we're coming out of the Depression and starting to prosper," Grandpa agreed, showing support for his sister and fellow Republican.

"Hitler has given notice to the European powers that he means business." Joe spoke for the first time. He's renounced the Treaty Of Versailles, reoccupied the Rhineland, annexed Austria, and now he wants Czechoslovakia. The European powers are practicing appeasement at any price, and it will cost them in the end."

"Well said, Joe." Uncle Ray had another ally. "You seem very well informed."

"Thank you, sir. My parents are both teachers, so we have a lot of discussions about world affairs around the dinner table."

"And your parents are predicting war?"

"My parents are pacifists, so they're praying it won't happen. With the situation in Europe, and Japanese aggression in the Far East, they're not very optimistic."

"Do you think America can remain neutral?"

"I don't know, sir. It seems unlikely."

"Your radio show is on, dear," Aunt Martha said, thankful for the reprieve from the unpleasantness of world affairs. "I think I'll retire to the sewing room."

"I'm going to the study to read," Grandpa said.

Katie helped her mother with the dishes and then went out to the porch swing with Joe. Shorty and Corky had walked down to see what was happening on the lake front.

"Do you miss being with the boys?" she asked.

"No. Why would I miss it?"

"I'm not naive. I know what boys like to do."

"Is that so?"

"Yes. You might be having more fun with Shorty." Joe squeezed her hand reassuringly. "Thanks, but I would rather be with you."

"We can't be married until you're out of college. Do you think you can wait that long for. . ."

"I'll be ready when you're ready. Isn't that what love is all about?"

"I guess so. Sometimes I ache all over just thinking about us being together."

"I know," he said, squeezing her hand. She rested her head on his shoulder. Through the glass on the french doors she watched her mother move about the kitchen.

"How come your mother has never remarried?" Joe asked. "She's a fine looking woman."

"I don't know. It's hard to picture her with anyone but Pop, so I haven't thought too much about it. She's never seemed interested in anything to do with romance since Pop died."

"I bet that changes when you and Shorty leave."

"Perhaps," Katie said. It was a gentle reminder that her brother was leaving, and her world was changing. They talked for another two hours. Shorty and Corky came home and stretched out on their cots. Everyone else had gone off to bed. Katie went inside and put on her pajamas. Joe undressed and slid into his cot. She returned to the porch and lay down on her own cot next to Shorty.

"Shorty?"

"Yeah, Squirt."

"Are you glad you came out for the weekend?"

"Yeah. It's been great."

"You're a bad influence on Corky."

"Yeah. I know."

Corky chuckled. "I'm glad you can see what I'm up against, Katie." He loved her sense of humor. She would always be Joe's girl, but it was enough just to be near her.

"I loved his line about roasting marshmallows around the old campfire," Katie said. "I almost choked on my dessert." Shorty and Corky started to giggle, and Joe and Katie joined in.

"You can never put anything over on Katie," Corky said.

"She knows you better than anyone."

"Ain't it the truth," Shorty agreed.

After awhile everyone settled down. Katie watched the moon settle over the lake, and listened to the steady hum of the locusts. Joe and Corky had fallen asleep. She knew instinctively that her brother was still awake.

From the Boy Scout camp to the northwest the sound of a bugle playing taps penetrated the darkness. The notes carried crisply over hill and valley, and rolled gently across the lake.

Day is done. . .
Gone the sun. . .
From-the-lake
From-the-hill
From-the-sky
Rest in peace
Sol Jer brave
God is nigh. . ."

As the last note faded, Katie felt a wave of apprehension. It was the same feeling she used to get when storm clouds rumbled, and she would run to Pop.

"Shorty."

"Yeah."

"Do you think there will be a war?"

"I don't know."

She thought about the irony of an artist and the son of pacifists lying here beside a tough guy like Shorty. And then she realized it wasn't ironic at all.

"Shorty."

"Yeah."

"If there's a war, you have to watch out for Corky and Joe."

There was a moment of silence. "Yeah. I'll do that," he said.

She looked out at the stars and yawned, feeling very secure next to her brother.

"Good night, Shorty."

" 'Night, Squirt."

5

Shorty sat in the bar of the Dixon Hotel having a drink. He had spent the last couple of months setting up his own small organization on 12th Street that skimmed money from card and crap games. He used Duff to keep an eye on everything that happened on the street. Duff was the best investment he had ever made. The Okie was fearless and he was loyal. With his gangly appearance and "aw shucks" attitude, he was 12th Street's version of Gary Cooper. Duff always had a kind word and a coin for anyone down on their luck. The pimps and gamblers on 12th Street eyed him with wary respect, and the whores, dogs, and derelicts loved him.

Shorty looked up as Solly Weinstein slid onto the stool next to him. Solly ordered a scotch and soda from the bartender. Shorty wondered why Solly always wore the same rumpled brown suit and soiled green visor. Word on the street was that he was a millionaire.

Solly looked over at him. "Have you spent the ten thousand, kid?"

Shorty swallowed hard. He felt his pulse quicken and a dryness in his throat. How could Solly have found out about the money?

"What are are you talking about? What ten thousand?"

Solly grinned around his scotch glass. "Don't play dumb with me, kid. I been around too long."

Shorty let out a sigh of resignation. "If you knew, how come you kept quiet?"

Solly shrugged. "We Irish have to stick together."

Shorty laughed. "That's a good one. Now tell me the real reason."

Solly took out a cigar and expertly unwrapped it. "Tony Bonatto knows you're setting up your own games on the street."

Shorty shrugged. "I'm protecting Tony's interests. He gets his share."

"He doesn't want a share. He wants it all."

"So he sent you to give me the word."

Solly lit his cigar. He savored the first few puffs before replying. "Tony doesn't know I'm here." Solly scrutinized Shorty. "I'm a good judge of character, and I know you don't have the heart for this business, kid. I'm advising you to get out while you can."

"I'm doing okay."

"You won't always be able to escort a competitor out of town. What if you have to kill someone?"

"Let me worry about that."

"You could end up dead."

Shorty mulled over the finality of Solly's words. "If Tony knows about Sammy and the money, how come he hasn't come after me?"

"You don't know?"

Shorty gave him a questioning look.

"Your mother works for Boss Pendergast, and you're a catcher on one of Pendergast's baseball teams. If Tony hits you he has to answer a lot of questions from the Irish mafia. You create more complications than you're worth."

Shorty had considered the possibility that his mother's job with Pendergast might pay dividends. "So you're saying I have a free ride?"

"You do for the time being. The word is that Judge Reeves and a grand jury are going to indict Boss Pendergast on income tax evasion. I don't envy you if he goes to prison."

"I'll take my chances. The Pendergast's have been running this town for sixty years."

Solly finished his drink and got up to leave. "Don't bet on it, kid. If Pendergast takes a fall, you better pack your bags."

"Thanks for the warning, Solly."

Solly put his hand on Shorty's shoulder. "Take my advice: make some quick dough, and then get into another line of work."

As Solly walked away, Shorty breathed a sigh of relief.

With Pendergast's protection he could expand his operation and not have to worry about Tony No Neck.

Franky finished talking to a girl at the end of the bar. He walked over to Shorty. "What did Solly want?"

"He says we're making Tony nervous."

"*He's* nervous. That's a joke. What about me?"

"Relax," Shorty said. "Tony thinks we're in tight with Boss Pendergast. I want you to start raising our stake in the games."

"Maybe we should get out while we can. We don't want to push Tony too far," Franky warned.

"Let me worry about Tony." Shorty finished his drink. "Let's go. I need you to drive me out to the house. Katie has shamed me into coming for Sunday dinner. She's having Joe and Scooter over for Halloween. After you drop me off, go by and get Duff, Corky, and McClusky. Come back for me around 7.30 so I'll have an excuse to leave."

Katie placed her grandmother's fine china on the dining room table. She positioned the silverware so that it was lined up to perfection. She wanted everything just right for her first dinner party. Her mother and grandfather had gone out for the evening. She pictured how it would be when she and Joe were married: a home, children, rituals. "Do you need any help, Katie?" Joe called from the living room, interrupting her thoughts.

"No, thank you. It's almost ready."

Joe and Scooter sat on the couch reading the sports page. Joe took Scooter with him whenever he could. He didn't want him to feel left out. Katie understood and was very supportive of their relationship.

Shorty walked into the house. He saw Scooter and immediately went on the attack. "Was I right, Scooter? Huh? Huh?" he tickled Scooter in the ribs. Scooter covered up with his arms and tried to get away.

"They got lucky," Scooter said, laughing.

"Lucky?" Shorty was incredulous. "The best baseball team of all time got lucky?"

"The Cardinals are still the best."

"Sure they are. Let me see if I've got this right. The Cubs beat out the Cardinals for the pennant, and then lose four straight to the Yankees in the series. That makes the Cardinals the best team in baseball."

"Wait until next year," Scooter said.

"Not next year, or any year," Shorty countered. "Listen to these names: Gehrig, Gordon, Crosetti, DiMaggio, Dickey, Henrich. They've won the world championship three years in a row, and they'll do it again."

"How about, Mize, Medwick, Owen, and Slaughter," Scooter countered. "The Cardinals will be back."

"Dinner's ready," Katie announced, breaking up the friendly argument.

"This looks great, Katie," Joe said, as everyone sat down.

"Thank you." Katie said, surveying the roast beef, baked potatoes, green beans, and salad.

"I didn't know you could cook, Squirt?"

"I'm learning."

"How you doing in college, Joe?" Shorty asked.

"Okay. I can't wait until Katie is with me next year."

"You're going to college?" Shorty asked in surprise.

"Yes. I've talked it over with Mother, and she thinks we can swing it financially."

"I thought you wanted to marry Joe and be a housewife."

"I do. I also want to be a teacher and help with the finances."

Joe smiled. "Your mother has her convinced that she will starve if she marries a writer."

"It's the Irish in her," Shorty said. "She will have all your dough in a piggy bank under the bed."

"It never hurts to be frugal," Katie replied. "However, money isn't that important to me. I want to be able to make a living, and I love being around children. A teaching career will allow me to do both."

"I think she's being influenced by my parents," Joe said. "They think the world of Katie."

"There's not much money in teaching," Shorty said.

"There's more to life than money," Katie countered, with a tone of disapproval that Shorty knew was aimed at his lifestyle.

"You're not going to preach, are you?"

"Not until we're alone."

"How are you and Franky getting along in your new place?" Joe asked, heading off the argument.

"Not too bad," Shorty answered half-heartedly.

"You've discovered that you need a cook and a maid," Katie guessed.

"Do we ever. We invited Duff to move in with us, but he took one look at the place and turned us down."

"He's the boy from Oklahoma?" Katie asked.

"Yeah. He's coming by tonight with the gang. I'll introduce you."

After the meal, Joe went in to help Katie with the dishes. Scooter went into the living room and turned on the radio. Shorty lit a cigarette, and started reading the paper. He was deep into the sports page when Scooter called him into the living room. "This radio program is really good, Shorty."

"What is it?'

"Mercury Theatre. Orson Wells is doing a program called 'War of the Worlds.'" Shorty moved closer to the radio and heard the announcer say something about a space craft landing in Grover's Mill, New Jersey. Shorty was intrigued. He settled in with Scooter to listen to the program.

A half-hour later there was a knock at the door. "Nuts," Shorty said irritably at the interruption. He went to the door and saw Mr. Pavlich, the next door neighbor, in a high state of agitation. "Have you heard the news on the radio?" he asked excitedly.

"What news?" Shorty asked, thinking about the war in Europe.

"A meteor has landed in New Jersey. We're being invaded by Martians!" his voice shook with terror.

Shorty shook his head at the man's stupidity.

"Come out here," Mr. Pavlich motioned, seeing the doubt on Shorty's face.

The street was full of people. They were all looking up at the stars and talking excitedly. Radios were turned on full blast up and down the street. Mr. Pavlich walked down into the yard to talk to another neighbor.

"Scooter!" Shorty called excitedly. "Get out here."

Scooter didn't want to leave the radio, so he poked his head out the door. "What's up?"

"Look out here. They think it's for real."

"What?"

"'War Of The Worlds.'"

Scooter walked out onto the porch and saw all the people pointing at the sky.

"I'm packing the family in the car and heading out to the country," Mr. Pavlich called from the yard. "I'd advise you to do the same."

"It's just a radio pro. . ." Scooter tried to say before Shorty's hand went over his mouth.

"Thanks, Mr. Pavlich," Shorty said. "We'll be right behind you." Mr. Pavlich ran across the yard to his car.

"Are you sure this is really a scam, Scooter?"

"Sure. They said so before the show started."

Shorty clenched his fists and his face was a picture of ecstasy.

"Uh, oh," Scooter said. "What are you thinking?"

Shorty put his arm around Scooter's shoulder and led him inside. "You're only dealt a hand like this once in a lifetime, Scooter. Are you with me?"

Scooter grinned.

"Go in the kitchen and get Joe and Katie. Act like something terrible has happened." Shorty knew they would be smooching, and would not have heard a word. He turned the lights low in the living room for added affect.

Scooter opened the kitchen door. "Joe! Katie! Come quick," he shouted fearfully. They hurried into the living room. Shorty had his ear to the radio, a grim look on his face.

"What is it?" Katie asked.

"Shhh," Shorty said, his eyes wide, and a look of terror on his face.

They gathered around the radio, listening intently, as the announcer described the alien creatures.

"What's happening?" Joe asked, concerned.

"They interrupted all programming with a news bulletin a few minutes ago," Shorty said. "A spacecraft of some kind landed in Grover's Mill, New Jersey."

"It's a joke," Joe said.

"If you think it's a joke, go look outside," Shorty said.

Katie and Joe went outside and started talking to the neighbors. They watched as Mr. Pavlich and another neighbor hurriedly packed the kids into the family car. The entire block seemed to be in a panic. They ran quickly back inside and fell on their knees in front of the radio.

"What will we do?" Scooter asked in fright.

"Just stay calm," Shorty said.

The announcer continued in an excited voice and confirmed that the aliens were an invading army from the planet Mars. Shorty watched as Katie gasped, her hand going to her heart. "What should we do?" she asked. Joe put his arm around her and held her tight.

"Maybe we should get out of the city," Scooter said, worriedly. "What about Mom and Dad, Joe?"

They all jumped in fright as footsteps hit the porch, and Franky, Corky, Duff, and McClusky burst through the door.

"What's going on?" Franky asked. "The street's full of people talking about an invasion from Mars."

Shorty held up his hand. "Listen."

The announcer described the terror that was taking place in New York City and said he would stay on the air until the end.

Shorty paced the floor, deep in thought. "We have to figure out what to do. Where's Mom and Grandpa?"

"They went out to a restaurant."

"Whatever it is, nothing can stop it," Scooter said nervously, pacing back and forth next to Shorty. "They've beaten the army, the air force. We've got to get out of here."

"You're right, Scooter. Katie, you, Joe and Corky start packing some food. The rest of you go upstairs and get all the sheets and blankets from the beds. Take everything. We may be out in the country for days or even weeks."

"What for?" Franky asked. "It's all happening on the East Coast."

"How long do you think it would take a spacecraft to get here?"

Shorty asked. He snapped his fingers. "Like that. Now move, move, move," he shouted. "We don't have much time."

Scooter and Shorty could barely control themselves as they listened to footbeats pound up the stairs.

"What will we put the food in?" Katie yelled frantically from the kitchen.

"Use pillow cases," Shorty replied. He could hear the upstairs bedrooms being torn apart, as sheets and blankets were ripped from the beds. In the kitchen Katie and Joe were frantically slamming cabinet doors. He and Scooter managed to hold it together until everyone arrived back in the living room. McClusky, Duff, and Franky were draped in sheets, and blankets, and Katie, Corky and Joe had pillow cases of food balanced on their shoulders. Shorty was going to make them pack the car, but they looked so ridiculous that he burst out laughing. He and Scooter laughed so hard that they fell on their backs in the middle of the living room floor, kicked their feet in the air, and howled.

Katie and the other boys stared at them for a moment, not realizing what was going on.

Shorty caught his breath. "Listen to these two words very carefully," he said. "Happy Halloween." Katie and Joe looked at each other sheepishly, realizing they'd been had. "How could we have been so gullible?" Joe said, shaking his head.

"You dirty. . ." Franky started to say.

"Ah, Ah," Shorty interrupted. "I would strongly suggest that unless you people are dressed for Halloween, you take off those sheets and blankets, and get my mother's house back in order. I mean. . .do you really think she's dumb enough to believe that you tore up her house and looted her cupboards because you were running from Martians?" He and Scooter howled with laughter on the living room floor, as Katie and the boys burned with embarrassment.

"If it's the last thing we do," Corky said, "we'll get you two for this." The threat made Shorty and Scooter howl even louder.

6

MAY 1939

At the Art Institute, Shorty sat with Corky under a maple tree. A slight breeze rustled the leaves, reflecting sunlight off the lawn. They were surrounded by shrubs and sweet smelling flowers. A chorus of robins, cardinals, and blue jays chattered around the grounds searching for food.

Two girls walked past and smiled at the boys. They smiled back.

"Ah, springtime," Shorty said. "When a young man's fancy turns to girls."

Corky smiled wryly. "What does springtime have to do with it? Girls are open season where you're concerned."

Shorty ignored the good-natured jab. "Sometimes it's enough just to sit back and admire God's handiwork," he said.

"Did you say admire, or abuse? And you had better leave God out of this."

"I mean, let's face it. There's a reason girls were designed to stick out in all the right places."

"Easy access," Corky surmised.

"College is doing wonders for you."

"I don't need college to know that I'm sitting next to a pervert."

"Speaking of girls. This is your second year of school, and you have yet to fix me up with one of these artistic types."

"Maybe they'll dedicate a plaque to me. The man who kept Shorty Callahan from soiling the women of the art world."

"Fine friend you are."

"Actually there is a girl. . ."

"I knew it," Shorty said. "You've been holding out on me."

"Not exactly. If you meet this girl, you'll fall in love, and that will be the end of Shorty Callahan."

"Fat chance. Falling in love is for sob sisters. I only fall in love for a night or two."

"You'll fall in love with Emma. Everyone does."

"That will be the day." Shorty said.

"Okay. But don't say I didn't warn you. Come on, I'll introduce you. She should be over at the sculpt shack." They stood up and started walking across campus.

"Sculpt shack?" Shorty questioned.

"The former owners had two greenhouses. We use one for sculpting and the other for painting," Corky explained. "Emma is a sculptress."

"Sounds like she may be good with her hands."

"I'm amazed at how you can reduce everything to sex."

"Twelfth Street," Shorty said, smiling. "I'm a product of my environment. If this girl is so special, how come you're not dating her?"

"Because we're good friends."

"Not your type, huh?"

"She could be. It's just that her friendship became more important to me than romance."

"In other words you kept her from me until you knew nothing would develop."

Corky smiled. "I guess I did."

Shorty slapped him on the back. "It's good to know my dough is not being wasted on your education. I'd have done the same thing."

"But don't think I'm doing you any favors," Corky said. "I'd be surprised if you get to first base."

"Just give me my turn at the plate, and watch me hit a home run," Shorty said, as they entered the sculpt shack.

A class was in session. Shorty and Corky slipped into seats in back of the room.

In front of the class, an instructor walked around a nude model as he pointed out various sculpting techniques. He had long fingernails that whirled around the woman's stomach, breasts, and neck.

Shorty raised his eyebrows suggestively at Corky.

Corky put his fingers to his lips, telling him to be quiet.

Shorty listened as the instructor droned on. He kept his eyes on the model. A few minutes later, the instructor dismissed the class.

It was then that he saw her. She was surrounded by a group of students; all of them chattering away as they moved toward the back of the room. She had long black hair that fell past her shoulders. As she moved closer, he saw that her eyes were brown. Like a queen being escorted by her subjects, she moved regally ahead, politely listening to the comments and observations of those obviously trying to impress her. She wore a long-sleeved, tattered man's shirt, worn jeans, and penny loafers. As the group passed by, she glanced at him, and he felt butterflies churn in his stomach.

Corky tried to penetrate her escort. "Emma, there's someone I want you to meet."

"We're going over to Teddy's Tea Room," she said above the din of her entourage. "Come and join us," she yelled as she was swept out the door.

Shorty stared after her, mesmerized.

"Uh, oh," Corky said, looking at him. "Lovestruck, and you haven't even met her."

"Well, I'm about to," Shorty said, as he and Corky followed the students out the door. She was beautiful and there was a presence about her that set her apart. Something mysterious that in a single glance said: "I'm Emma, follow me if you dare." He knew he had to be careful. If he fawned over her, he would become one more member of her entourage. He realized his heart was pounding and he felt a trickle of sweat run down his back. He loosened his tie and reminded himself not to act impressed. "That has to be the worst-dressed group of people I've ever seen."

"Sculptors," Corky said, shaking his head. "They're weird. They live for self expression. Free love and all that kind of stuff."

"Emma?"

"I don't know about Emma. I can tell you that she has her own way of looking at things."

Feeling very much the outsiders, they followed the rag-tag group of sculptors across campus.

The Tea Room was located in the basement of the main building and run by a retired artist named Teddy. He was not only the owner, but the father figure and confidant of many of the students. In his role as benefactor, he had inadvertently become rich, trading food for original paintings from students who later became famous in the art world.

Emma and the sculptors were sitting around a table in the corner. Shorty and Corky walked over. "Emma, this is Shorty Callahan." Shorty took her hand. It was warm to the touch and made his pulse quicken.

"Hello, Emma."

"Hello," she said, pulling her hand away. She scrutinized him. "Why the name Shorty?"

"It's a long story," he said.

She turned back to her fellow sculptors without giving him a second glance. He and Corky took seats on the fringes of her entourage. Her reaction had hurt his feelings. She was the girl of his dreams, and she was ignoring him. He listened to about twenty minutes of conversation about three-dimensional representations and abstract forms and other artsy crap that he had absolutely no interest in, and then suddenly she was speaking to him.

"What do you do, Mr. Callahan?"

"I'm in the security business."

"Oh, really? Corky must have been mistaken when he said you were a gangster." Her eyes were full of amusement.

Corky turned red with embarrassment, and her entourage laughed.

"What did you think about the presentation in the sculpt shack?" she asked mischievously.

Shorty stared back at her. So that was how it was going to be. Use Shorty Callahan and his ignorance of the art world for the amusement of her friends. He was expected to say something half-way intellectual so they could have a big laugh at his expense.

"The class was so inspiring that I was on the edge of my seat," he said. "I kept waiting for the instructor to slice her tits with his finger-nails."

There was dead silence at the table as Emma and Shorty stared at each other.

"I believe Emma was referring to the artistic aspects of the presentation," one of the sculptors said.

"Were there artistic aspects?" Shorty asked. "I guess I was too busy looking at the models tits and ass to notice."

"Listen, wise guy. Who do you think you are?" One of the sculptors rose out of his chair.

"Yeah," another one said.

"Why don't you rejects from the fashion world step out on the lawn and find out," Shorty threatened. "You can give me some tips on my wardrobe."

Emma put her hand up and whispered something to her friends and they obediently sat back down.

Corky stood up. "Come on Shorty, let's go." Corky gave Emma a "Why did you do this?" look. She glanced at him and then turned away. He and Shorty left Teddy's Tea Room.

"I owe you an apology," Corky said when they were outside.

"Nah. I owe you one. I'm sorry I lost my temper."

"I don't know why Emma acted that way."

"I do. She wanted to get a reaction out of me, and like an idiot, I fell for it."

"Why would she do that?"

"Why do women do what they do?" Shorty asked, exasperated. "If I passed her little test, maybe I would get to follow her around and kiss her feet."

Corky smiled wryly. "Come on. Admit you were impressed."

"No way. I've seen her type before. She comes from money, and she thinks the world revolves around her pretty little head."

"You're right about the money. Her father's a banker, and the family lives in Mission Hills."

"I knew it."

"But that's all you're right about. There was some sort of falling out when Emma decided to become an artist. Her father had her life all laid out for her: Vassar and marriage to a blue blood. She rebelled and came to the Art Institute."

"Hah," Shorty said sarcastically. "How can you rebel when you're fed from a silver spoon? It's a ten-minute drive to her mansion in Mission Hills."

"Emma has a small apartment over there." Corky pointed to an apartment building across the street. "She works summers and weekends as a tour guide at the Nelson Art Gallery to pay her tuition and her room and board."

"Oh," Shorty said. "Well, I better get going. By the way, how's Granny Oliver?"

"She hasn't been feeling too good lately."

"I'll stop by with flowers and some of her favorite magazines."

"She would like that, Shorty."

"Congratulations on finishing another year of school." Shorty said as he got into his car. "I'll see you later."

He started the car and headed out the gate. He had managed to remain calm around Corky, when all he could think about were Emma's laughing brown eyes. "Emma." he whispered her name. He could still see the expression of amusement on her face, and he could feel the butterflies churning in his stomach. It was obvious she was used to men following her around like lap dogs. She had even had her way with him. He had shoved her mind games back at her, but she had made him lose his temper. The problem was that now there was no way to contact her without joining the pack. He sighed. Why did love always have to be so complicated? Maybe one of the girls at the Chesterfield Club could help him forget about her.

Solly Weinstein sat in his cubbyhole of an office. He listened as Tony Bonatto talked to four of his henchmen in the outer office.

"Boss Pendergast entered Leavenworth Prison today," Tony said.

"You want us to hit Callahan?" one of the henchmen asked.

"No. Pendergast's organization is still intact. We'll wait awhile so it won't appear that we're making a power move against the Irish on 12th Street."

"How long?"

"Six months," Tony said, as he puffed on a Cuban cigar. "Give me Callahan for a Christmas present."

Shorty and his gang sat in the Cord Phaeton outside the Nelson Art Gallery. Two weeks had gone by since his encounter with Emma. He had tried everything to get her out of his mind, but nothing had worked. He had to see her again, even at the risk of becoming a lap dog.

"I know why we're here," Corky said. "To see if art will soothe the savage beast."

"Shut up, wise ass," Franky said.

"Tell me, Franky. Who was Michelangelo?"

"Old guy. Used to paint houses in my neighborhood," Franky replied.

The other boys howled with laughter.

"All right, knock it off," Shorty said. "Does everyone have their pieces of paper?"

Duff, McClusky, and Franky held them up. Corky had written down questions about some of the paintings Emma would show on her tour. Questions that were difficult if not impossible to answer.

"Who's going to read Franky's for him?" Corky asked.

"Up yours, you little twerp," Franky said.

"Corky, get lost. We don't want Emma to see you."

"That's the first intelligent thing you've said today," Corky muttered as he got out of the car.

"Okay, let's go." The boys followed Shorty into the gallery. They were dressed dapperly in white suits and panama hats.

Shorty looked around. The building was huge and reminded him of Union Station.

"She has the next tour," Shorty said. "I'll linger behind and listen in the hallways."

Emma appeared. She looked beautiful as she always did, but she also looked professional. She was dressed in a blue blazer and a gray skirt, nothing like the tattered clothes of their last meeting.

Shorty hid behind a column and heard her welcoming remarks. Her voice made his heart race. She led the group down the hallway and they entered a room. The first painting was a Van Gogh. Shorty listened as she described the artistic aspects of the work.

McClusky held his hand up and Emma pointed to him.

"Do you think Van Gogh's use of swirling brush strokes was a result of his madness?"

"I don't know. . ." she stammered. "Perhaps they were."

"I heard his sister was an artist," Franky said. "Is that true?"

"I'm not sure," Emma said. She knew Van Gogh's brother was an art dealer, but had heard nothing of a sister. She moved on to the next painting, a Gauguin. She was into her spiel when Duff raised his hand. She pointed to him.

"Gauguin left his wife and five kids. What became of them?"

Emma fidgeted with her hair as the tour group waited for her answer. "I have no idea," she finally said.

McClusky raised his hand. "Why do you think Gauguin abandoned the objective view of impressionism for strong contours and psychological content?"

Duff and Franky looked at him wide-eyed. McClusky shrugged his shoulders and pointed to the paper. Emma rubbed her forehead. She could feel perspiration forming under her blazer. "Perhaps he needed a change of style." she said.

"Why?" Franky asked.

"Sometimes a change can spark creativity," Emma explained.

"Why?" Duff asked.

Shorty was in the hallway enjoying her discomfort.

"Let's move on to the next painting," Emma suggested.

"I guess she didn't know the answer," Franky said, very loudly.

"You would think these tour guides would be trained," McClusky said, as Emma gave him a dirty look.

Shorty let his gang harass her through a few more paintings, and then he called them off. They were sitting on the steps when Emma came out of the building. Shorty waited off to the side.

Emma glanced at them and tried to hurry past.

"Sometimes art can be very intimidating," Shorty said.

His gang started laughing, and Emma turned around.

"It happened to me once," Shorty said. "A group of sculptors tried to have a good time at my expense."

Emma smiled wryly and bit down on her lip.

"Very uncomfortable feeling, as I remember," he continued.

"All right, Callahan. I owe you an apology."

"I accept." He introduced Duff, Franky, and McClusky.

She nodded. "You went to a lot of trouble to get even, Callahan."

"Getting even wasn't my motive."

"Oh?"

"Have lunch with me and we'll talk."

"Can't. I have an appointment. It was nice meeting all of you." She started walking across the lawn to the Art Institute.

"Take the car," Shorty said to his gang. "I'll take the streetcar." He took off after Emma.

"You're mad at me," he said when he caught up with her.

"Actually, I'm flattered that you would take the time to stage that little drama. Why did you, Callahan?"

"I wanted to see you again."

"Why?"

She was teasing him with her eyes. "You're not falling in love are you, Callahan?"

"I've never been in love. What's it like?"

"Can't eat. Can't sleep. Can't get her off your mind."

Careful, Shorty, he reminded himself. Don't let her know you care. The image of the lap dogs came to mind.

"Must not be love. I'm eating and sleeping just fine."

She gave him a knowing look as they crossed the street to her apartment building.

"Where do you live?"

"Second floor."

"Can I come up?"

"I told you. I have an appointment."

"Boyfriend?"

"None of your business."

"I'd like to meet him."

She eyed him thoughtfully for a moment. "Okay. Come on."

He followed her up the stairs to her studio apartment.

The furnishings were sparse. Sheets covered a couch and two chairs, and the walls were bare. Two sculpting tables held works in progress. They fronted a patio that looked out over the Art Institute. Emma went to a sheet covered object over in the corner. She pulled off the sheet. It was the statue of a man.

A knock sounded at the door and Emma went to answer. "Hello,

Julio. This is Shorty Callahan." They shook hands. Julio was six feet tall, with black hair, and the physique of a Greek god.

"Let's get started," Emma said.

Julio started taking his clothes off while Emma molded the statue. When he was completely naked she studied him and started to work.

"Don't you usually have a chaperone for this type of thing?" Shorty asked.

"It wouldn't do, Callahan. How could I squeeze his weenie with a chaperone in the room?" She challenged Shorty with her eyes.

"Don't try to be funny." he shot back.

"Why would I try to be funny? Sometimes I have to sculpt an erection. How do you think I get them erect?" Shorty turned red. She had made him jealous, and she knew it.

"Isn't that why you came up here, Callahan? To have your weenie squeezed?"

A look of amusement crossed Julio's face.

"I can have my weenie squeezed in a lot of places," Shorty said.

"Then why are you here?"

"I'm beginning to wonder."

"Are we getting mad, Callahan?" Her eyes never left Shorty, as she walked over and squeezed Julio's penis. "One of the benefits of artistic expression," she said. Shorty was seething.

"It's no wonder the lap dogs are always following you around."

"That's right. I'm a bitch in heat."

"Why are you doing this?"

"Doing what?" She walked back to the statue and went to work.

"I just want us to be friends," Shorty said.

"We both know what you want."

"I don't need this." Shorty turned to leave. "I made the first move, the next one is up to you." He went out the door and slammed it behind him.

Julio raised his eyes at Emma. "Nice ass," he said. "If it doesn't work out, can I have his telephone number?"

Emma ignored Julio as she angrily kneaded the statue with her fingers. Something had clicked when she had met Shorty. She was determined not to let love complicate her life. An artist needed total freedom and she did not want to get bogged down in a relationship. She would have to stay busy and try to forget about him.

7

Katie walked hand in hand with Joe across campus. They had just finished enrolling for the coming school year.

"Oh, Joe," she said excitedly. "I can't tell you how many times I've pictured us together like this. College is going to be so much fun."

He laughed. "It's great having you here." She glanced over at him as they walked along.

"What?" he asked, reading her expression.

"There are some beautiful girls on campus. It's lucky I'm here to protect my interest."

"Don't trust me, huh?"

"Resolve can weaken in the Garden of Eden."

"My love for you conquers all temptation."

Katie tugged on his arm and stopped him under the shade of a walnut tree. She put her arms around his neck and gave him a long, lingering kiss.

"Wow!" he said, catching his breath. "This is the education I've always dreamed of."

"We may need a chaperone to keep us apart."

"Who wants to be apart?" he asked, nibbling on her lips.

A member of the faculty walked past, and cleared his throat disapprovingly.

"Uh, oh," Joe said. "You've only been on campus for a day, and we're already in trouble."

"I should know better than to date the campus lecher," katie teased. She pulled away from him and started running toward the parking lot. He caught up with her and jumped in the car. "I can't believe your mother invited me out to the lake for Labor Day weekend."

"You've managed to impress her this past year. She no longer disapproves."

"Why the change?"

"I think she finally realized that you're not trying to seduce her only daughter."

"Oh yeah?" Joe raised his eyebrows seductively.

"Well, at least until after we're married."

"So let's get married."

"It's tempting, but we would end up with ten kids and ruin our chance at an education."

"You're too practical," he said, starting the car.

"And don't you forget it. I'm a product of my Grandmother Callahan. She always said that abstinence breeds character."

Joe raised his eyes to the heavens. "Thank you so much, Grandmother Callahan."

Katie laughed. "Let's go pick up Corky and Scooter and head for the lake."

"You'll watch out for Scooter around the water," Mrs. Wilson said, concerned.

Joe kissed his mother on the cheek. "Scooter's a great swimmer, Mom."

"We'll watch him anyway," Katie said, reassuring her.

Scooter bounded down the steps carrying a towel that held his swim suit and toilet articles. "All ready to go," he said excitedly.

"What are you and Mr. Wilson going to do this weekend?" Katie asked.

"I think we'll just relax a bit, and get ready for the school year."

Mr. Wilson walked into the room. "So, we're off to the lake are we?" He put his arm around Katie's shoulder. "You need a weekend of rest and relaxation before starting the school year."

"Come on, let's go," Scooter said impatiently.

Mr. Wilson looked at Katie and Joe. "I said rest and relaxation and you have to keep up with this guy." He ruffled Scooter's hair with his hand.

"We can handle him," Katie said. "If he gives us any trouble we'll turn him over to Aunt Martha. She knows how to handle 10-year-olds."

Whitey started barking and jumping on Scooter.

"He goes crazy whenever he thinks Scooter is going to leave," Mrs. Wilson said.

"Let's take him with us," Katie offered.

"Could we?" Scooter asked hopefully.

"Sure. Why not. We're staying in Uncle Ray's fishing and hunting cabin in the upper lake. He's going to chaperone and he loves dogs."

"Well, off with you then." Mr Wilson gave Katie a hug and put his hand gently on Joe's shoulder. Scooter kissed his mother, and he followed Katie and Joe out the door.

Corky was waiting at the entrance to the Art Institute. He greeted them and tossed his bag in the car. "My date will be here in a minute. Before she arrives, I need to ask all of you a favor. If Shorty's name comes up in conversation, please refer to him as Egan."

They looked at him questioningly.

"Trust me," he said.

Emma walked up to the car. "Katie and Joe, I want you to meet Emma Stephens," Corky introduced them.

"Hi Emma," Katie said.

"And this is Scooter," Corky said, as he and Emma climbed into the back seat.

"Can I sit next to you?" Emma asked.

"Sure." Scooter said, staring at Emma. She was beautiful and she smelled great.

"You forgot to introduce this guy," Emma patted Whitey on the head.

"His name is Whitey."

"Hi, Whitey." Emma rubbed Whitey's ears, and he barked his approval.

Joe headed the car for the lake.

"How's your mother and grandfather, Katie?" Corky asked.

"They're fine."

"And your brother, Egan?"

"I'm worried about him. He came to dinner last Sunday and just moped around the house. I've never seen him so down."

Corky had noticed it too. Shorty had not been himself all summer. The change started when he had first met Emma. Corky knew that Shorty had fallen for her, and he was guessing that Emma felt the same. She was always inquiring about Shorty in a sly sort of way.

"I'm surprised Aunt Martha invited us out after Egan's antics last year," Corky said.

"Aunt Martha is very forgiving where Egan's concerned," Katie answered.

"Is Egan coming to the lake?" Scooter asked, getting in on the name game.

"Yes." Katie answered.

"Great. He's my pal."

"Are you a painter, Emma?" Joe asked.

"I'm studying sculpting."

"How interesting."

"Thank you for the invitation," Emma said. "I hope I won't be in the way. It's wonderful to get away for the weekend."

"We're glad to have you," Katie assured her.

At the lake the family gathered around the dinner table.

"When did Egan say he would be here, Katie?"

"He didn't say, Aunt Martha. You know how he is."

"Yes dear," Aunt Martha sighed in resignation. "We'll keep his dinner in the oven."

"Corky, how did you manage to capture this lovely creature?" Uncle Ray asked, looking at Emma.

"We're just friends," Corky said, as Emma blushed. She had swum in the lake and lain in the sun all afternoon. She felt totally relaxed as she sipped from her glass of wine. Katie's mother was so kind, and her Aunt Martha was a genteel woman. The entire family had made her feel welcome. Corky was fortunate to have such wonderful friends.

"What project are you working on, Corky?" Aunt Martha asked.

"I'm not doing much of anything Aunt Martha." Corky was like a member of the family, and it seemed perfectly natural for him to call her Aunt Martha.

"You artists are always so secretive about your work. Why is that, Emma?"

"We're superstitious — afraid we'll jinx ourselves if we discuss a work in progress."

"That makes perfect sense," Aunt Martha said.

They were well into the meal when they heard footsteps coming up the walk next to the house and Whitey barking excitedly.

"Whitey!" Shorty patted Whitey on the head, and opened the door. "Where's Scooter Wilson? Scooter you owe me. . ." he stopped in astonishment when he saw Emma sitting at the table. He felt a bead of sweat form at the back of his neck.

Emma stared at him in shock. "What are you doing here?"

"I was going to ask you the same thing."

"She's my date for the weekend," Corky said. "Emma, this is Katie's brother, Egan," he said, grinning over his deception.

Shorty took a seat at the table.

Emma stared in amazement. She could not connect this family with Shorty Callahan.

"You two know each other, Emma?" Katie asked.

"We've met."

Aunt Martha went to the kitchen and retrieved Shorty's dinner from the oven. "We've missed you this summer, Egan. How have you been?"

"Fine, Aunt Martha." He could not take his eyes off Emma.

"He's fibbing, Aunt Martha," Corky said. "Actually he's been moping around all summer."

"Oh? Why is that, Egan?"

Shorty gave Corky a dirty look.

"It all started when he met this girl at the Art Institute," Corky continued. "I think he's in love." He winked at Katie. Shorty blushed.

"Shorty, in love?" Katie questioned.

"Eat your dinner, Squirt."

"I can't picture Shorty Callahan in love," Katie teased. "She must really be something. Tell us about her, Shorty. What's she like?"

"Get off my case, Squirt."

"She's something, all right," Corky said. "Trouble is, she's independent and hard-headed like Shorty."

"Can I have a word with you in the other room?" Shorty asked threateningly.

"No, you may not," Corky replied. "I am not about to leave Aunt Martha's dinner table. This food is delicious."

"Why, thank you, Corky," Aunt Martha said. "Egan is fortunate to have you for a friend. You always seem so interested in his welfare."

Corky smiled at Shorty.

"If you like this girl so much, Egan, why don't you bring her by the house?" his mother asked.

"You're all jumping to the wrong conclusions," Shorty said. "I met this girl, but we didn't hit it off."

"How come?" Emma asked, challenging him with her eyes.

Shorty met her gaze. "She let me know very quickly that she wasn't interested."

"How did she do that?" Emma asked.

"She embarrassed me in front of her artistic, high-brow friends, and then she let me know I wasn't going to interfere with her lifestyle."

"You read a lot into a girl having a naked man in her room," Emma said.

The only sound in the room was Aunt Martha sucking in her breath. Everyone looked at each other, and then at Emma.

"I would be very surprised if it was just one," Shorty said confrontationally.

"Oh, you would, would you?" Emma challenged. "What is it you're trying to say?"

"I don't have to say anything. I know what I saw."

"Perhaps you should work at being a little less shallow, Callahan. Maybe my reluctance had an entirely different meaning. Maybe I didn't want to get romantically involved and complicate my life."

"What about Julio?"

"Did it ever dawn on you that maybe Julio likes you better than he likes me?"

"You mean Julio. . ."

"You figure it out."

Katie looked wide-eyed at Corky. "Wow!" she said. "This is going to be an interesting week-end."

Later, after everyone had finished listening to the radio and had vacated the living room, Aunt Martha took Katie's hand. "Come along, girls," she said. Emma followed them into the bedroom.

Katie knew the ritual by heart, and she knew better than to protest. Aunt Martha was childless, so she mothered Katie shamelessly. The hair brushings had started when Katie was a little girl and continued through her formative years.

The lavender lace skirt on Aunt Martha's dressing table matched the lavender lamp shades on either side of the mirror. Katie sat down on the cushioned bench and scanned the items that were familiarly etched into the foundation of her girlhood. The metal jewelry box that she loved to explore; the glass top displaying all the wonderful trinkets against a pink velvet setting. The purple, pink, and white perfume bottles made of crystal, each fragrance conjuring up images of romance in exotic places. The china powder box, and the powder puff she loved to dab on her cheeks and always used to excess because it made her feel so girlish.

"We ladies need some time to ourselves," Aunt Martha explained to Emma.

"It's her way of saying it's time to spoil me," Katie said.

Aunt Martha took the pins from Katie's hair and let it fall around her shoulders. She grabbed the pearl-handled brush and started expertly brushing through the auburn strands. For Katie, each stroke was like a soothing massage. When she was relaxed and under the spell of the brush, Aunt Martha could pry anything out of her.

"Come sit with me." Katie reached out and took Emma by the hand. Emma joined her on the bench. They looked at each other's images in the mirror.

"Are you going to torture my brother through the entire weekend, or show him some mercy?" Katie asked.

Emma smiled. "I'm still debating. What do you suggest?"

"Sometimes he can be insufferable," Katie said. "But he has a good heart, and it's obvious he cares for you."

"I almost fainted when he walked into the dining room. I still can't believe he's your brother and a member of this family. It just doesn't fit."

Aunt Martha took the pins from her mouth. "Egan is just like his great uncle, Clarence. He thinks life is one grand adventure, and he plunges along absolutely fearlessly, never taking responsibility for his actions."

"What about his lifestyle?" Emma asked.

"You mean the gangster image," Katie said. "We've had some awful fights about the direction his life is taking, but we don't want to alienate him." Katie eyed Emma in the mirror. "You would certainly be a positive influence in his life."

"I'm strongly attracted to your brother, but like him and his uncle Clarence, I shy from responsibility."

"Can't you just be friends?" Katie asked.

Emma shook her head negatively. "Passion has a way of turning friendships into commitments."

"Well, you had better do something," Aunt Martha said, as she saw Shorty's image in the mirror. "This is the sixth time Egan has walked past the bedroom door."

"Seventh," Katie said, as she and Emma laughed.

Aunt Martha put the pins back in Katie's hair and positioned herself behind Emma. She began brushing Emma's jet black hair. "You have the hair and eyes of an Indian princess."

"The coloring comes from the French heritage on my mother's side."

"Careful," Katie cautioned. "Under the seductive spell of the hair brush, you will tell Aunt Martha everything." Emma smiled. She closed her eyes and enjoyed the pampering. It had been a long time since anyone had brushed her hair.

"Do you live alone, Emma?"

"Yes, Ma'am."

"Are you from Kansas City?"

"Yes."

"And your parents go to the expense of keeping you in a place of your own?"

"I pay my own way," Emma said defensively. "My parents don't agree with my lifestyle."

"Oh," Aunt Martha tried to restrain her curiosity so she wouldn't offend her guest. "It's important for a young woman to establish her independence."

"Yes," Emma agreed.

"You should always remember to keep a channel of communication open to your parents," Aunt Martha said. "Regardless of what you may think, they will always love you."

Emma bit her lower lip. Katie was still holding her hand. It felt so good being one of the girls again.

"When's the last time you talked to your mother?" Aunt Martha asked, reading Emma's expression.

"Months."

Aunt Martha stopped brushing and held Emma's head gently in her hands. "Promise me you'll go see your mother when you get home."

Emma nodded. The family setting and everyone's kindness made her realize how much she missed her family. "I promise."

"Now, the two of you get on your way. Uncle Ray will walk you to the cabin in the upper lake."

Katie raised her eyes at Aunt Martha.

Aunt Martha sighed. "I'm getting so forgetful." She reached for one of her perfume bottles and dabbed the cool liquid on her middle finger. She lifted Katie's auburn hair and touched the soft spot behind each of Katie's ear-lobes, and then she did the same with Emma.

"The best part," Katie said, satisfied. She got up and gave her Aunt Martha a hug. "Shorty Callahan, here we come."

In the kitchen, Ann Callahan pulled a sudsy plate from the hot water, dipped it in the rinse water, and then handed it to Joe.

"Thanks for inviting me out for the weekend," he said as he wiped the plate dry.

"Well, Katie always seems so much happier when you're around."

"I hope so."

Ann submerged a pan in the water and began scrubbing. "I need to apologize to you, Joe. I had some misconceptions about you when you first became friendly with Katie. I wanted her to date someone her own age."

"I'm not only older, but a Ghost Dancer to boot," he replied.

She laughed, embarrassed. "Katie told you."

"Yeah. It scared me so bad that I locked my pen and paper away for weeks," he joked.

"I want you to know it was nothing personal. I became very protective of her after her father passed away."

"She really misses her father," Joe said. "She talks about him all the time."

"Yes. They were very close."

"I will never put my writing career ahead of Katie's welfare. I mean that."

"It sounds like you two are getting serious."

"We plan to be married after college."

"Oh. I'm not surprised."

"Then you don't mind?"

"No. It's obvious you're in love."

Joe glanced at her. "I don't mean to pry, but I was wondering how you've been getting along?"

"Well I. . ." Ann was flustered for a moment.

"I know it's hard to support a family by yourself, but you seemed to have managed very well."

She nodded. "It was difficult at first, but with time I've gotten better at it. I couldn't have managed without help from Egan and Katie."

"Hey, Joe." Katie poked her head into the kitchen. "It's time for us to head for the cabin."

Uncle Ray and Scooter were up ahead with the lantern, leading the group to the cabin in the upper lake. Whitey darted happily in and out of the lantern's light.

"After Shorty's antics last year, I'm surprised we're allowed back in the upper lake," Corky said.

"What happened?" Emma asked.

"Never mind," Shorty said defensively.

"Shorty invited some friends out to the lake and they caused quite a stir," Katie said.

"It no doubt had something to do with the opposite sex," Emma guessed.

"I know why I was invited out for the weekend," Shorty said, trying to fend them off. "To provide amusement for my friends and family."

"Poor misunderstood thing," Katie teased. "He wants to make a good impression, but his past behavior keeps getting in the way." She winked at Emma.

"That's okay, Squirt. Have a good time at my expense. I don't mind."

Katie reached out and took his hand and then took Emma's and joined them together. "All I ask is that you hold hands until we get to the cabin." She dropped back next to Corky and Joe and left them alone.

Shorty and Emma walked for awhile in silence. He was conscious of the warmth of her hand and the smell of her perfume. The moon beamed brightly down on the lake, and the stars seemed to shine with added luster.

"Maybe Corky's right," Emma finally said. "We can be friends."

Shorty squeezed her hand. "If that's what you want."

She looked over at him. "What do you want?"

"I don't know. I've never felt like this."

"Like what?"

"Can't eat, can't sleep, can't get her off my mind." Emma smiled, and squeezed his hand. "When we first met I was worried about becoming a lap dog like the rest of the guys in your entourage."

"And now?" Emma asked.

Shorty stopped walking, looked up at the moon, and howled like a bloodhound.

Emma started laughing.

"The Shorty Callahan we all know and love is back!" Katie yelled, as they walked up the steps to the cabin.

Uncle Ray flipped off his lantern and turned on the cabin lights. He had driven up earlier in the day with their belongings. "I put all the bags in the bedrooms," he said. "I hope you enjoy your stay." he turned to leave.

"Where are you going?" Katie asked.

"Home. To sleep in my own bed."

"But you're supposed to chaperone."

"Chaperones are for people who need them, Katie Callahan. You and Emma are not among them. I bid you a pleasant good night."

Katie hugged him and kissed him on the cheek. "Good night, Uncle Ray, and thank you."

Shorty and Emma sat in rocking chairs on the porch. The moon was high in the sky and the bullfrogs croaked loudly down on the lake. An occasional wild bird joined in the chorus.

Inside Scooter and Corky were playing checkers. Katie and Joe had gone for a walk.

"I finally have you all to myself," Shorty said.

"Uncle Ray said you could be trusted."

"No. He said you and Katie could be trusted. He knows me better than that."

"Shorty Callahan; the wayward son."

"You've been talking to Katie."

"She's a delight, and you have a wonderful family."

"I guess you were kind of surprised when I showed up?"

"Shocked would be a better word."

"I'm that bad, huh?"

"You're an enigma. How could someone leading your lifestyle come from such a wonderful family?"

"Aunt Martha says it's in the genes."

"Uncle Clarence," Emma said.

Shorty grinned. "You've already heard the story. I wonder what Katie and Aunt Martha would do if they didn't have me to worry about."

"You're lucky they care about you."

"How about you? Do you care about me?"

"Ah ah, Callahan. None of that. With caring comes commitment."

Shorty took her hand. "And you're not about to commit to anything, are you?"

"Not if I can help it."

"How does this no commitment thing work?" Shorty asked.

"What do you mean?"

"I mean, where do we draw the line? Is a kiss a commitment?"

"Well. . .no."

"Good," Shorty said. He stood up and pulled her into his arms. He kissed her, and her lips were as warm and soft as as he had imagined.

"Why did you do that, Callahan?"

"Because I've been thinking about it all summer."

"What else have you been thinking about?"

He kissed her again. "How much I would like for us to be friends."

"Something tells me you would like to get very friendly," she whispered.

He was enchanted by the moonlight glowing in her dark brown eyes, and by the perfume Aunt Martha had dabbed behind her ears. "If we can be friends, I'll try to control myself," he said, kissing her on the neck.

Emma pulled away from him. "Like Corky said, we can have fun without a commitment."

"You make the rules and I'll follow them," Shorty said.

"See, you're already being sarcastic."

"Why are you so afraid of a commitment?"

"Because I value my freedom and I don't trust men."

Corky opened the cabin door and walked out onto the porch. "Let's lower our voices, children. I just put Scooter to bed."

"Sorry," Emma apologized.

Corky sat down on the porch railing. "I assume you two are getting things worked out?"

"Yes, thanks to you," Emma said.

"Don't thank me yet. I feel like a man who has mixed two kegs of dynamite."

"Surely we're not that bad," Emma said.

"I just hope it works out, because I'll have to pick up the pieces."

"You're too good to us," Shorty said.

"How true." Joe and Katie came up the porch steps.

"Is everybody ready to turn in?" Katie asked.

"I'm sleeping with Emma," Shorty announced.

"Don't you just wish," Katie said sternly. "Come on, Emma." Katie took her firmly by the hand. "You're sleeping with me."

Shorty laughed. "Good night, ladies. And don't forget to lock your doors and windows."

Later, Katie and Emma lay in the big feather bed.

"Did you and Shorty work things out?"

"We're trying."

"Good."

"You and Joe seem to be a perfect match," Emma said.

"Thank you. It was love at first sight."

"Are you going to get married?"

"Yes. After college."

"That will be a while," Emma said.

"It seems like forever," Katie agreed.

Emma yawned. "I haven't felt this relaxed in a long time."

"The sun and the water," Katie said.

"And the wine and the hairbrush," Emma added.

"I'm glad you came out for the weekend."

"So am I."

"Good night, Emma."

"Good night, Katie."

Through the open window Katie could hear the wind tugging at the branches of the giant cottonwood tree. She breathed a sigh of total contentment. Life was wonderful: She had Joe, she was fulfilling her dream of going to college, and now she could enlist Emma in her battle to get Shorty straightened out. The sound of the wind mixed with the croaking of the frogs and she drifted peacefully off to sleep.

The next day Katie sat with Emma on the porch. They watched Corky sketch a drawing of the lake. In the distance they could see Shorty, Joe, and Scooter fishing on the water. Corky had been listening to Katie go on about Shorty's lifestyle and how she was afraid that he was going to end up in jail.

"There are so many other things he could do if he would just get away from that environment," she said.

Corky put down his chalk and studied his drawing. "Maybe your brother isn't the 'John Dillinger' you make him out to be."

"You're always making excuses for him," Katie countered.

"That's because I see both sides of him. The good and the bad."

"What good could possibly come from criminal activity?"

"Gambling isn't exactly criminal activity. It's not like he was a murderer or a bank robber."

"But that's where it could lead," Katie said.

"Shorty has a strong sense of right and wrong," Corky reassured her. "He won't cross the line."

"You seem awfully confident about that," Emma said. "What makes you so sure?"

"The good things he does for people."

"What good things?" Katie asked. "Name one."

"I'll name several. When Duff first came to town, he was broke and didn't have anywhere to live. Shorty gave him a job and a place to live. He also gives Duff money to take care of the hungry and homeless people on 12th Street. I've seen him give Father Dugan money for the Catholic Mission. He also takes the time to come and see my grandmother because he knows she's lonely, and he paid my tuition so I could go to the Art Institute."

"He did?" Katie asked in wonder.

"That's right. He knew he might not have the money later, so he paid the full four years." Corky paused and studied his drawing. "Don't ever let on that you know this, but Shorty started giving your mother a monthly allowance. I think it's to help pay for your education."

Katie looked at Emma. "I feel so stupid. I had no idea."

"Well, I thought you should know," Corky said. "Don't stop trying to reform him, just give him credit for the good that he does."

"I will. And thank you for confiding in me."

Later in the morning the boys finished fishing and walked back to the cabin. As they all gathered on the porch, Katie greeted her brother with a hug.

"What was that for?" he asked.

"I just felt like doing it," she said.

Shorty eyed his sister warily. "Is she going to start preaching, Corky?"

"I don't think so," Corky replied.

"Isn't that your Uncle Ray?" Emma asked, looking down the road.

They all turned to look.

Uncle Ray was walking rapidly up the road. "Something's happened," Shorty said.

A few moments later Uncle Ray made it to the porch. He sat down to catch his breath.

"What is it?" Katie asked anxiously.

Uncle Ray took out his handkerchief and wiped his face. "It just came over the radio. Germany has invaded Poland. France and England are going to declare war on Germany."

Katie felt the wave of apprehension return. Why did some distant war keep intruding on her idyllic little world, and why did it fill her with such dread?

Joe put his arms around her and held her tight.

"What do you think it means for us, Uncle Ray?" Shorty asked.

"There's a lot of isolationist sentiment in the country, so we'll be able to stay out of it for a while. But the Europeans have a way of pulling us into their squabbles. They found out in the last war that they can't defeat the 'Hun' without us."

Katie looked out on the lake. A sailboat was lazily floating with the wind. She said a silent prayer to ward off world events, and made a vow to put them out of her mind. No far-off war was going to tarnish the luster on her last weekend of the summer.

Scooter Wilson took the snap from center and dropped back to pass. His receiver went down ten yards and cut across the wide expanse of brown lawn in front of the Nelson Art Gallery. Scooter arched the ball through the falling snowflakes and over the heads of the defenders. He watched as it tumbled majestically into the arms of his receiver. "Touchdown!" he yelled happily, as he rushed to celebrate with his teammates.

It was Thanksgiving Day. The traffic on 47th Street was already beginning to back up as everyone rushed to the Country Club Plaza to watch the annual lighting ceremony that kicked off the Christmas season.

Scooter retrieved his football and waved good-bye to his friends. Night was beginning to fall and he had to hurry. Shorty was having his annual party at the Villa Serena apartment building. It was an event everyone looked forward to, when family and friends gathered in an apartment overlooking the Plaza to excitedly count down the last seconds until the switch was thrown that turned on a hundred thousand colorful bulbs that outlined the stores and shops.

Scooter jogged to the heart of the Plaza, tossing the football back and forth in each hand. As he walked across the Wornall Road Bridge to the Villa Serena, he pretended to be Washington quarterback Sammy Baugh. He dropped back for a pass to leading receiver Charley Malone. The falling snow had slickened the ball and it slipped out of his hand. The football fell over the railing and dropped twenty feet into the dry bed of Brush Creek. Scooter pretended he was recovering a fumble as he ran down the creek bank, scooped up the ball, stiff-armed an imaginary defender, and ran up the opposite bank. As he emerged from under the bridge, he heard a man's voice above him say something about Shorty Callahan. Curious, Scooter stopped to listen.

"We'll hit him when he comes out of the Villa Serena," the man said.

"We should get a bonus for this one," another man replied. "Tony No Neck has waited a long time to get rid of that ungrateful Irish asshole."

"Is the back of the Villa Serena covered?"

"Yeah. We got Chico in the parking lot. With this crowd of people it should be a cinch job."

Scooter stayed put until the voices faded into the mass of people crossing the bridge. He scrambled up the creek bank, zigzagged like a halfback through the crowd of Christmas shoppers on the sidewalk, and ran across the street to the Villa Serena.

Shorty was in a holiday mood as he poured Emma a glass of wine. The party was a welcome respite from the war news coming out of Europe and Asia. Joe, Katie, and Corky were putting the last touches on the Christmas tree. The rest of the gang and the other guests stood at windows, looking down at the mass of people gathered for the lighting ceremony. It was a tight fit in the apartment for the fifty people Shorty had invited.

"Whose apartment is this, Callahan?" Emma asked.

"I rent it from a friend of mine. He spends Thanksgiving skiing in Colorado."

"Is this where you bring your girlfriends?"

He raised his eyebrows playfully at her. "I'll spare you the details."

Emma narrowed her eyes at him.

"Ah, Ah," Shorty said. "Those are the kind of looks that lead to commitments. If you want me all to yourself, all you have to do is get down on your knees and beg."

"You're going to keep pushing this commitment business, aren't you, Callahan?"

"Not me. I like dating other girls."

"Then why do you keep showing up at my door?"

"I feel sorry for you. I thought it was obvious."

Katie walked over with Joe. "Do you two need a referee?"

"Your brother amuses me," Emma replied.

"It's her way of saying she loves me," Shorty countered.

"Why don't you call a truce in the war of romance and try to make it through the holidays," Katie suggested.

"A truce would spoil all the fun," Emma said.

"As a gift to me," Katie said. "Your truce will be my Christmas present."

"What do you think, Callahan?" Emma asked.

"Okay. No more fighting until the first of the year. Should we seal this bargain in the bedroom?" Shorty asked playfully.

"That will be the day," Emma said.

"You behave yourself," Katie scolded. "There will be plenty of time for that when you and Emma are married."

Emma's mouth dropped open in shock. "Married! Where did you ever get an idea like that?"

"You know what they say about opposites attracting."

"Yes. And I don't believe a word of it."

They were interrupted as Scooter hurried up to them.

"Shorty, I have to talk to you," he said, trying to catch his breath.

"I'll take Green Bay over Chicago and give you six points," Shorty said.

"It's not about football."

"Okay. Seven points," Shorty offered.

Scooter shook his head in exasperation. He grabbed Shorty's arm and started pulling him toward the bedroom.

"Must be man talk," Shorty said over his shoulder. Scooter led Shorty into a darkened bedroom. "Listen, Shorty. I was underneath the Wornall Bridge when I heard two men talking. They said they were going to hit you when you came out of the Villa Serena."

Shorty walked over to the window and looked out. "What did they look like?" he asked, concerned.

"I only heard voices. They talked about having the back of the Villa Serena covered."

"Go get Franky and Duff," Shorty ordered. "And keep this to yourself."

Scooter ran to the door.

"Hey, Scooter," Shorty called.

Scooter stopped and turned around.

"You're a real pal," Shorty said. "I owe you one."

Scooter grinned and hurried out of the room.

Franky and Duff walked into the room, drinks in hand.

They were enjoying themselves as they waited for the plaza lights to come on.

"What's up?" Franky asked.

Shorty motioned them over to the window. "We've got company. Look under the street light at the end of the bridge."

Franky and Duff peered out the window, looking down on the sidewalk below. The snow was falling harder; the large white flakes starting to cover the ground.

"It's Sal and Nicki D," Franky said. "What are they doing?"

"Waiting for me," Shorty answered.

"Are you sure?"

"Scooter heard them talking."

"I told you we should have quit while we were ahead," Franky scolded. "What are we going to do now? Those guys are professional killers."

"Go look out a window and see who's covering the back door," Shorty ordered. He paced the room, pondering his predicament. Sal Marconi was Tony Bonatto's enforcer. He was always dressed immaculately in the latest fashionable suit, starched shirt and tie. Sal was a perfectionist. He felt a smudge on his attire was a much greater sin than assault or murder.

Nicki Dalporto was Sal's henchman, an ex-fighter who had taken too many punches to the head. A lot of punch drunks ended their careers with a pleasant disposition, but Nicki D. had gone the other way. He had a sadistic streak and he loved to hurt people.

Franky and Duff hurried back into the room.

"It's the Spic," Franky said.

Chico The Spic Morales was a short, wiry Puerto Rican who used a knife to make up for his lack of stature. He was a professional carver and he loved his work.

"If Tony sent these guys, he's not messing around," Franky said. "What are we going to do?"

"We've got the advantage, so we're going on the offense," Shorty replied.

"Right," Franky said derisively. "They have guns and knives. What are we going to do, fight them with snowballs?"

"That's not a bad idea," Shorty replied. "Now listen up. . ." Shorty slipped away from the party, and headed for the back door of the Villa Serena. He started whistling "Jingle Bells" as he pushed open the back door and walked out into the falling snow. Chico was 30 yards away. He saw Shorty and his hand went into his coat pocket. Shorty walked briskly ahead. Twenty yards from Chico he stopped, bent over, and started making a snowball. The snow was wet and perfect for rounding into a ball. Shorty made two snowballs and put one in his coat pocket.

"Chico!" he yelled in recognition. "Merry Christmas to you!" Shorty moved ahead ten yards. He drew back his arm and hit Chico in the chest with a snowball. Shorty could see the look of indecision on Chico's face. Chico kept his eyes riveted on Shorty as Shorty reached back to throw another snowball.

The diversion gave Duff and Franky time to slip up behind Chico. Duff dove for the little Puerto Rican. He wrapped his arms tightly around him and they went sprawling into the snow.

"Hold his arms!" Franky yelled. "He'll cut us to pieces if he gets loose."

Franky bent over and pried Chico's fingers from around the knife. They stood him up and searched him thoroughly.

"This guy has enough blades to be a circus performer," Franky said as he tossed four knives down a storm drain.

Chico glared at them menacingly.

"Take care of him," Shorty ordered, as he hurried away into the falling snow.

Franky and Duff took Chico over to the car and shoved him into the back seat. They sat on either side of him.

"What should we do with him?" Duff asked.

Franky opened the blade on the knife and wagged it under Chico's nose. "Chico's a big man with the girls. Ain't that right, Chico?"

Sweat started to form on Chico's forehead, and he looked at them with a sickly grin.

"I wonder how much the girls will like him when we cut off his nuts."

Chico's eyes widened. "Listen, you guys. . ."

Franky turned the blade around and punched Chico in the adams apple with the handle of the knife. Chico fell forward with a loud moan, and started gasping for breath. Franky grabbed Chico's hair and jerked his head back.

"Don't let us see you anywhere in this town again, Chico," Franky warned. "If we do, you can kiss your nuts good-bye." Franky pulled a coughing Chico out of the car and stood him up. He punched him hard in the stomach, and Chico fell to his knees, sucking for air.

"The next time you're banging one of those Spanish girls, remember to send us a word of thanks for sparing your manhood," Franky said. He kicked Chico in the balls. Chico doubled up on the ground in pain. Franky and Duff turned away and headed off in search of Shorty.

Shorty turned the corner and walked north across Ward Parkway. He could see Sal and Nicky D. up ahead. They were intently watching the front of the Villa Serena. Shorty bent over. With his left hand he scooped up a handful of mud from under the snow. He walked quickly ahead. When he was five yards away he doubled up his right hand into a fist. "Merry Christmas, Sal." In surprise, Sal and Nicky D. turned to look. Shorty hit Nicky D. in the nose with a solid right hand. Blood sprayed all over the freshly fallen snow. The force of the blow knocked Nicky D. head over heels down the bank of Brush Creek. Before Sal could recover, Shorty locked his arm, preventing Sal from going for his gun. Shorty put his face close to Sal's. "I thought this might go well with your attire," he said. He took the mud and wiped it down the front of Sal's new camel coat. Sal looked at the mud, and then at Shorty, and then back at the mud. His eyes widened in disbelief, and a look of total outrage covered his face. Shorty unlocked his arm and hit Sal hard in the stomach. Sal was in his forties and he had gone soft. The air went out of him and he sank to his knees. Shorty turned and started running west on Ward Parkway. Sal would be livid. It would cloud his judgment and give Shorty the edge he needed. Shorty ran through the falling snow into the heart of the Plaza. He tried to lose himself in the happy throng of holiday revelers waiting for the lights to go on.

Back in the apartment, Katie looked for her brother. The lighting ceremony was seconds away and she couldn't figure out where he was.

"Beats me," Joe said. "When was the last time you saw him?"

"Scooter was pulling him toward the bedroom," Emma said.

They all converged on Scooter.

"Ten, nine, eight, seven. . ." the countdown had begun. Everyone turned to look out the windows. "Three, two, one. . ." The lights came on, outlining all the buildings on the Plaza, and thousands of people cheered the beginning of the Christmas season.

"Merry Christmas, Joe."

"Merry Christmas, Katie."

Katie gave Emma a hug. "Merry Christmas, Emma."

"And to you Katie," Emma said.

"Now where could that brother of mine be?" Katie wondered, as she walked over to Scooter.

"Merry Christmas, Scooter," she said.

Scooter looked at her warily. "Merry Christmas, Katie."

"What were you talking to Shorty about in the bedroom?"

"It's personal," Scooter said defensively. He kept glancing at Katie as she circled slowly around him.

"It would take a real crisis for Shorty to miss the lighting ceremony," she said.

Scooter remained silent.

"You and Shorty have become real pals."

Scooter nodded his head.

"And you would never betray a friend."

Scooter slowly shook his head.

"Unless that friend were in trouble," Katie said. "And then if you were a true friend you would have to tell."

Scooter looked at her with uncertainty. "I promised I wouldn't."

Katie put her fingers to her chin, pretending to ponder the problem. "If I were to make a guess where Shorty is, then you wouldn't be telling, would you?"

"No." Scooter seemed relieved to find a way out of the problem.

"Is he sick?" Katie asked.

Scooter shook his head.

"He's with another girl."

"Why would he?" Scooter asked in wonder. "He has Emma."

"Thank you, Scooter," Emma said.

"He was called away on business," Katie guessed.

"Nope."

"Then he's in trouble."

Scooter nodded his head in the affirmative.

Katie decided to go for the worst possible scenario, and then work her way back.

"Someone wants to hurt him," she said.

"Some gangsters are after him," Scooter replied.

Katie grabbed him by the shoulders. "Are they here in the apartment building?"

"No. They're somewhere on the Plaza," Scooter said, pointing to the window.

"Come on," Katie said. "We have to find him."

Shorty moved quickly through the Plaza. He kept glancing over his shoulder to see if he was being followed. A clean white carpet of snow covered the ground creating a perfect setting for the thousands of holiday revelers moving in and out of the stores. He knew the Plaza well since he had once worked for the electrical company that put up the Christmas lights. He stopped on the corner next to Santa Claus, who was ringing a Salvation Army bell. Shorty reached in his pocket, grabbed a couple of five-dollar bills, and dropped them in the bucket. When he turned around, Nicky D. was staring at him from across the street. Shorty started walking ahead. Sal Marconi appeared from around the corner, blocking his way. Shorty searched for a way out of the trap. Seeing a group of Christmas carolers outside a restaurant, he joined the front row of the choir and started singing. Sal and Nicky D. closed in on him. Sal had a smug expression on his face and Nicky D. held a handkerchief to his nose.

Shorty knew that while Sal and Nicky D. were not the brightest guys in the world, they were smart enough not to shoot him in front of a group of witnesses. Surrounded by the happy faces of the carolers, Shorty thought it ironic to be singing songs of Christmas joy to a couple of goons intent on murder. "It came upon a midnight clear, that joyous song of old. . ." Shorty sang along with the choir.

A noisy gang of young men headed toward them from down the street — revelers getting an early start on the Christmas cheer. They were yelling and pushing each other back and forth on the sidewalk.

At the moment Sal stepped in front of Nicky D. to let them pass, Shorty lowered his shoulder, and, like a fullback, rammed the boy passing in front of him. The punishing block knocked the boy into his companions and they in turn fell into Sal and Nicky D. They all lost their footing on the slick sidewalk and tumbled headlong into the street.

The girl next to Shorty screamed as he took off running down the street. He darted up alleys and hurried quickly in and out of stores until he was sure he had lost Sal and Nicky D. At the Skelly service station he turned east on Ward Parkway and hurried through the falling snow. As he passed an alley, a blow hit him in the side of the face. Everything went black for a moment. When he recovered he was on his back, looking up at the gently falling snow. The side of his head felt like it was on fire. Someone had him by the collar of his coat and was dragging him into the alley. Shorty chopped the hand away. He spun around in the snow and whipped his feet at the ankles of his assailant. Nicky D. swore. His feet went out from under him and he landed on his back. Shorty was on him in an instant. He punched Nicky D. in the head as hard as he could. Shorty felt one of his knuckles pop. It was like slugging a piece of concrete. Nicky D. hit him on the chin with a straight right hand and Shorty went tumbling out of the alley and back onto the sidewalk. The blow cut his chin and he could feel warm blood running down his neck. Nicky D. let his full weight fall on top of Shorty in a body slam. Shorty felt the air go out of him and he lost consciousness for a moment. When he woke up, Nicky D. was choking him. Shorty knew he had to act quickly or he was a goner. He reached his hand back for a strand of Christmas lights glowing at the base of the building. The electricians he had worked with had taught him how to change bulbs in an instant. Nicky D. was choking him harder. He was about to pass out again. With his last breath he got the bulb unscrewed, scrapped some snow in the empty socket, and rammed it into Nicky D.'s bulbous nose. There was a flash, a scream, and the smell of burning flesh. Christmas lights went out all over the Plaza. Nicky D. fell off him and landed on the sidewalk in an unconscious heap. Shorty rubbed his throat and finally caught his breath. He left Nicky D. on the sidewalk. Someone would find him and the police would soon be swarming all over the Plaza. Shorty staggered down the sidewalk. There was a ringing in his ears and he could barely focus on objects in front of him. He turned south on Wornall Road and headed across the bridge, unaware that Sal Marconi was following close behind.

Katie and the gang had searched everywhere. They were pacing nervously back and forth in front of the Villa Serena when the Christmas lights came back on. Katie spotted Shorty staggering across the Wornall Bridge. "There he is!" she yelled. They raced through the snow toward the bridge. Sal Marconi closed the gap between himself and Shorty. He would push the gun against Shorty's back, and squeeze the trigger. The loud pop would be just another noise in the Christmas celebration. As he moved up behind Shorty some people came running at Callahan from across the bridge. He put the gun back in his pocket and faded back into the crowd.

"What happened, Shorty?" Katie asked frantically. "Are you okay?"

Shorty had his back to her, holding onto the bridge railing, his face contorted in pain.

"Get me to the car," he said to Joe and Corky.

"Oh, no you don't," Katie said. "You have some explaining to do."

"Not now," Shorty gasped.

Katie was determined, and she was mad. She grabbed him by the arm and turned him around. He winced, his body full of pain from Nicky D.'s slam. He looked at Katie. His face was battered and bruised, and blood from the cut covered his white shirt and tie.

Katie stared at him in shock.

"Come on, let's get out of here," Joe said, as police sirens started converging on the Plaza.

Corky and Joe were helping Shorty into the backseat of the car when Franky and Duff arrived. They opened the car doors and slid quickly into the front seat.

"We have to get you to a hospital," Katie said.

"We'll take care of him," Franky cautioned. "We have our own doctor."

"I'll go with you."

"No. I don't want you involved in this," Shorty said. "Joe can take you home."

Emma saw the worried look an Katie's face. "I'll go with him," she said, as she slid into the back seat next to Shorty. The doors slammed and the car sped away through the falling snow.

Shorty leaned his head back on the seat and let out a sigh.

Emma held her handkerchief against the wound on his chin. "I've waited a lifetime to do my Bonnie Parker impersonation," she said.

"Don't be funny."

Emma looked out the car window at the falling snow.

"Your lifestyle is beginning to wear on your sister. She deserves better."

"If you're going to preach, Franky can let you out on the next corner."

"This is the first time I've seen you practice your profession, Callahan. It isn't very becoming."

"So go find yourself a Mission Hills banker."

"My. Aren't we being hostile. Maybe you can work on your attitude in prison."

"Listen, Shorty," Franky interrupted. "We either have to start carrying guns or give this up and open our supper club."

"No guns." Shorty said.

"What are we going to do about Uncle Tony? He's going to send these guys after us again."

"Tony won't try anything for awhile. He'll be a nervous wreck wondering how we're going to get our revenge."

"We gotta start carrying guns," Franky said.

"No guns," Shorty said firmly.

"Tell me this isn't real, and I'm in an Edward G. Robinson movie," Emma said.

Shorty leaned his head painfully back against the seat. He was in no mood for Emma's sarcasm. "Life can be difficult when you have to leave Mission Hills and associate with the lower classes."

"I can handle the lower classes, Callahan. It's no class that causes me problems."

"Then why are you here?"

"When I get you to a doctor, I'm closing out my Bonnie Parker routine."

"Sounds like an ultimatum."

Emma looked at him. "I never took this gangster business very seriously, Callahan. I was wrong. You could have been killed tonight."

"If I wanted a sermon, I'd go to church."

Emma's eyes flashed with anger. "Katie may have to put up with this, but I certainly don't."

"So cancel my invitation to the mansion in Mission Hills," Shorty said sarcastically. "I guess I won't be meeting mom and dad after all. Franky, stop the car over there by the taxi stand."

"I should have known better than to let myself get involved with you," Emma said.

"Are we involved? I guess I missed that part."

"That's real cute, Callahan," Emma said as she angrily got out of the car. "And don't bother showing up at my door again."

"See that she gets in the cab," Shorty said to Duff.

"Have a nice life, Miss Emma. I'll look for you in the society pages," he called after her as she stalked off through the snow. He couldn't keep her with him. There was no telling what Tony Bonatto would do next. If Emma were hurt he would never forgive himself. He would hide out for a while until things calmed down, and then he would try and soothe things over. The snow was falling harder, covering the windows of the car. He thought back to when he was a kid. He, Katie, and the gang would grab sleds and gather at the top of the Main Street Hill. Through the window the street light was getting dimmer. He fought to stay focused on the light, but it slowly faded away and he passed out.

E mma paused for a moment outside the door of her father's study. When she was a little girl the room had always seemed so large and intimidating. She remembered how fast her heart used to beat when she was called downstairs for one of his lectures. They usually consisted of a list of those things he expected of her if she was to take her place in the family business and in society. The conversation invariably turned to the accomplishments of her brother, Robert, and her sister, Elise. Her father used them as prime examples of the things she could achieve if she applied herself. Robert was a graduate of Yale and a partner in the bank. Elise had graduated from Brown with an accounting degree. She was a consultant in the bank's trust department. Emma hardly knew either of them. Robert was fifteen years her senior and Elise, fourteen. By the time Emma came of age, both were married and had families of their own. The only time she saw them was when her father summoned them in to the Stevens family court to be used as role models or to sit in judgment regarding one of her transgressions.

Emma's break with her family had occurred two years ago on a hot August night. She was outside the mansion in the back seat of a roadster owned by a junior vice president of her father's bank. He was 32 and married. They were deep in the throes of physical passion when her father arrived home unexpectedly. The full moon had left nothing to his imagination. She had been banished to her room for a week and the vice president had been shipped off to a St. Louis branch of the bank. The obligatory family meeting had been convened and she was called into the study. Her brother and sister sat on either side of their father with those pious, condescending looks on their faces that always infuriated her.

"And what do you have to say for yourself, young lady?" her father demanded.

"About what?" she asked blandly.

"You know perfectly well what I mean."

She looked around. "Where's Mother?"

"She's not feeling well."

"That means she's drinking."

"We're not here to discuss your mother, so don't try changing the subject. Let's talk about the scene I happened upon the other night out in the driveway."

"Okay." Emma's tone was matter-of-fact.

"You're not ashamed?"

"Why would I be ashamed? I'm a grown woman and perfectly capable of making decisions."

"You? A grown woman?" he scoffed.

"The vice president of your bank certainly thought so."

"Don't you be impertinent with me, young lady."

Emma looked at the smug faces of the three members of the family court and for reasons she couldn't explain she no longer felt intimidated. "If it isn't tolerated, then why do you do it?"

Her father paused for the longest moment. "What do you mean?"

"Why do you have affairs with other women?"

He glared at her for a moment as the blood rushed to his face. Her brother and sister stared at her, wide-eyed. "Now you listen to me, young lady. My personal life is none of your business. I may have made a few mistakes during the life of my marriage, but. . ."

Emma spoke before she could think. "A few mistakes? Come now, Father. You're a legend at the country club."

"How could you be so disrespectful?" her older brother reproached her. "You act like a tramp and then try to cover it up by attacking Father. Your behavior is disgusting."

Emma looked blankly at this brother she did not know. "My behavior is none of your business."

"Anything that reflects on this family is our business," Elise hissed.

"Ah. The father, the son, and now the holy ghost," Emma said mockingly.

"I'll ignore that," Elise replied sharply. "How could you have been so careless? What if you had become pregnant?"

"Not likely."

"How can you be sure?"

"There's a product on the market that prevents that sort of thing. It's called a rubber."

Elise flushed. "I could understand a slip of this kind with someone your own age, but certainly not with a married man. Just what were you trying to accomplish?"

Emma was fed up with Elise and her pious attitude.

"You're probably not familiar with the experience, but it's called an orgasm."

"Now you listen to me. . . ."

"Don't let her get to you, Elise. That's what she wants," Robert said. "She's just going through a stage of adolescent rebellion."

Emma cast her gaze on Robert. "What would you know about rebellion? You couldn't get out of bed without directions from Father. And in case you haven't noticed, I'm years past adolescence."

"Then why don't you act like it?"

"Maybe you should be examining your own behavior."

"What's that supposed to mean?"

"There's a rumor going around the club about you and the wife of a certain lawyer. But I'm sure there's nothing to it." She watched with satisfaction as the anger welled up in his face.

"How did you get to be such a spoiled brat?"

"I've had great role models."

"I think I've heard quite enough," her father said wearily. "Perhaps you'll acquire a different perspective when you're away at school."

"I'm not going away to school," Emma said defiantly.

"I beg your pardon."

"You heard me."

"You'll do as I say."

"Not any more. I'm going to school at the Art Institute."

"And just how do you intend to pay the tuition?"

"I've been working as a tour guide at the Art Gallery and I'm not the least surprised that you haven't noticed."

"And how will you live?"

"I'm moving into an apartment across from the Art Institute."

There was a stunned silence in the room.

"You actually think you can support yourself by working at the gallery and doing that stuff that you do?" Robert asked scornfully.

Emma narrowed her eyes at him. "'That stuff' is called sculpting and this conversation is over." She had turned away and marched upstairs to begin packing her belongings. Her heart was pounding and her knees were weak. Could she make it on her own? For a moment she thought of racing downstairs and begging forgiveness from the family court. But she knew it would mean sacrificing her art and her independence. She continued packing.

That was two years ago, and now that she had firmly established her independence, she had an uneasy truce with her father and the rest of the family. She opened the study door and walked inside. "Hello, Father."

"Hello, Emma. I just wanted to see if there was anything else you needed before we left town."

"I'm fine."

"It's good of you to have the Christmas party. The young people would have been disappointed. It's become quite a tradition."

"I've always enjoyed it."

"Who will be your co-host?"

"I'm hosting alone."

"Oh." He seemed surprised, but she knew that he was pleased.

Her mother entered the room. "It's time to go, dear." She squeezed Emma's hand. Her father patted her on the shoulder. They never hugged or kissed her.

"We'll call you on Christmas day."

"Have fun." She watched as they gave last minute orders to the servants. Then the car pulled away. It was a scene she had witnessed many times. At first they had asked her to go on these trips, but she came to realize that she was just extra baggage — the mid-life baby her parents had never wanted and had never felt comfortable with.

The servants dispersed and she was left alone. Her footsteps echoed off the winding marble staircase that led to the second floor. She sat in her bedroom in front of the mirror and started taking the pins from her hair. As night began to fall she glanced out the window and saw a solitary light in the mansion across the way. It seemed to symbolize the loneliness she felt. She missed Shorty, Katie and the gang so much. At first Shorty had been just another way to get back at her father, so it had surprised her when she had fallen in love with him. The ultimatum she had given him about his criminal activity had backfired. He hadn't come begging for her forgiveness as she had expected and now she was alone again, the poor little rich girl. The gang would sure get a laugh out of that. They thought she was so confident and in control. If they only knew!

She still wasn't sure why she had had the affair with the bank vice president. Maybe she just wanted her father's attention. She had fallen for Shorty because he was interested in her as a person. But she was constantly fighting a paradox. She had to have a man around who wanted and needed her, yet a permanent relationship was out of the question. Her father and brother were proof that men could not be trusted.

She picked up a piece of soft clay and started kneading it with her fingers. Her sculpting had always been her antidote for loneliness. After awhile the loneliness abated and she became lost in her art.

The week before Christmas Katie and Joe were snuggled on the living room couch. Lights from the Christmas tree illuminated frost-covered windows. Outside the wind howled, blowing freshly fallen snow against the window panes. Katie moved even closer to Joe. "Listen to the wind," she said.

"I'm glad we stayed home," he replied.

Katie had wanted to see the premiere of *Gone with The Wind*, but the weather had turned bad so they put off the movie for another night.

"This is how it will be when we're married," she purred contentedly.

"No. When we're married we'll be in bed under the covers."

She kissed him, and then nibbled playfully on his lips. "Katie Wilson," she whispered. "I like the sound of it."

Joe kissed her passionately, bending her backwards on the couch. She could feel the hardness of him pressing against her pelvis. She never had to worry about him going too far. He would build to a point, and then pull away, determined to wait until they were married. For now it was enough to be in each other's arms, experimenting with just how far they could go without going all the way.

"Whew," Katie said, slipping away. "I need to catch my breath."

Joe started rubbing her shoulders. "It got hot in here all of a sudden," he agreed, kissing her neck.

"Stop that," she said, pulling away from him. "You know what it does to me."

"Do I ever."

She turned around and pushed him back on the couch, then crawled on top of him and started pecking his face with kisses. They both started laughing and fell off the couch into a heap on the floor.

The front door opened and Shorty walked into the living room. He looked down at his sister entangled on the floor. "What's this, tag team wrestling?" He brushed the snow from his coat.

Embarrassed, Katie and Joe scrambled to their feet. Katie straightened her skirt and brushed at her hair. "We weren't expecting you," she said.

"No kidding," Shorty said, with a friendly glare at Joe.

Katie flushed. She hadn't seen her brother for a couple of weeks. She kissed him on the cheek. "Your chin looks a lot better. How do you feel?"

"A little sore, but I'm okay."

Shorty had holed up for two weeks, waiting for word from the street that he was in the clear. Everyone had survived the Christmas lighting ceremony, although Nicki D. had some serious burns. The police handled it as a gang-related problem and refused to get involved.

"Are you safe?" Katie asked.

"Yeah. So quit worrying."

"Listen, Shorty. . ."

"If you're going to preach, I'm going to leave."

Katie bit her lip. She wanted to tear into him, but she knew it would only drive him away. "What brings you out on a night like this?"

"Corky called. Emma invited us to a party. I came by to see if you and Joe want to go."

"You made up with her?"

"Sort of."

"We thought we'd spend the evening here, listening to the radio."

"Then how come the radio's not on, Squirt?"

Katie blushed again.

"I think the two of you had better come with me and cool off," Shorty suggested.

"Sounds like it might be fun," Joe said, playing the peacemaker. "Where's the party?"

"Mission Hills."

"Really?" Katie said, her interest instantly piqued. "Emma invited us to her home in Mission Hills?"

"What's so strange about that?"

"I don't know. Emma has never shared that part of her life with us."

"Maybe she thought it was time we met her friends," Shorty said.

"What in the world am I going to wear?" Katie wondered aloud.

Katie, Joe, Shorty, and Corky sat in the car in the Mission Hills district, looking up the hill at the English Tudor mansion. The home sat on eight acres of terraced lawn and was surrounded by gardens covered with a blanket of snow. The home and gardens commanded the entire face of the hill.

"I'm not going in there," Katie said.

"Come on, Squirt, they're people like us. They just happen to have money." Shorty tried to bolster her confidence.

"Can you imagine living in this palace?" Corky whistled. "I can't wait to get inside."

Shorty drove around to the back of the mansion and parked the car. Through the windows they could see a variety of Christmas decorations and bright, colorful lights. The faint sound of big band Christmas music drifted out into the night. A car pulled in next to them and two women got out. They headed for the mansion. Shorty noticed their casual dress and figured they were part of the staff. "Let's go," he said. They stepped out into the freshly fallen snow and followed the women down some steps and into the servants quarters.

"Where are we going?" Katie asked suspiciously.

Shorty ignored her as he looked around.

"Do you have our invitation, Corky?" she asked, feeling very intimidated by her surroundings.

"Me? Are you kidding? An invitation to this place?"

"Why yes. Shorty said Emma called you and invited us to the. . ." Katie stopped and glared at her brother. "Oh no," she said. "You wouldn't do this to me."

"Now just relax, Squirt. It's going to be okay."

"Oh, how embarrassing." She had worn her best casual clothes, never suspecting that it was a formal party.

A butler appeared in the hallway. "Servers or kitchen?" he asked.

"Servers," Shorty said confidently.

"This way," the butler directed.

Shorty gave the thumbs up sign as he followed the butler down the corridor. "Your serving jackets are here," the butler said, stopping beside a closet. "There will be someone upstairs to instruct you on the proper procedure."

"Thank you," Shorty said, as the butler walked away.

"I think I'm going to have a heart attack," Katie said, as Shorty helped her into a white jacket.

"Just calm down, Squirt."

"But what will Emma think?"

"Tell her you're working your way through college."

"You've got a lot of nerve," Corky added.

"Ain't it the truth," Shorty agreed.

"We should leave you here by yourself," Katie threatened.

"Yeah, but you won't. You're too curious about what's going on upstairs."

Katie let out a sigh. Her brother knew her too well. She might never get another chance to explore a mansion in Mission Hills. She took a deep breath and followed Shorty up the stairs toward the sounds of music and merrymaking. They opened a door and walked into a ballroom filled with formally dressed couples and excited chatter. Katie looked up at two chandeliers sparkling like crystal above a polished oak dance floor. Christmas decorations accented stylish furnishings and a giant Christmas tree flashed majestically in a corner of the ballroom.

"Wow," Katie whispered.

Shorty spotted the upstairs butler giving orders to the staff and walked over to him. The butler stiffly nodded his head toward a table covered with glasses of champagne. Shorty took the cue. He led his companions over to the drinks and they all picked up a tray. With another wave of his head, the butler ordered them to circulate, and they obediently started weaving their way through the guests.

Shorty scanned the room, looking for Emma. He had spent a miserable three weeks away from her. He served his last drink and was headed back for another tray when he saw her standing in a corner of the room. She had on a red evening dress that was cut low and accentuated her breasts. A strand of white pearls was gathered around her neck and her black hair was spun up into a bun. She looked so beautiful that all he could do was stare and feel the rapid beating of his heart.

"Circulate!" the butler whispered in his ear.

Shorty grabbed another tray and headed for Emma. She was surrounded by four young men, each of them vying for her attention. He walked up behind her. "Would any of you like a drink?" He saw her stiffen when she heard his voice, but she kept her composure and refused to turn around. "How about you, Miss. Would you like a drink?" Shorty moved around and faced her. She had a quizzical expression on her face, trying to figure out what was going on. She narrowed her eyes at him as she took a glass of champagne. Shorty retreated across the room. He knew that her curiosity would get the best of her, and she would have to come looking for him.

Emma excused herself from her admirers and started after him. She stopped walking and scanned the room, when suddenly she was bumped from behind.

"Oh, I'm so sorry," Katie said, looking down at the champagne that had spilled from her tray. When she glanced up, she was looking at Emma.

"Emma!" she said.

"Katie! What are you doing here?"

Katie turned red with embarrassment. "Emma listen, I. . ."

"Hello, Emma," Corky said, as he hurried past with his empty tray.

"Hi, Emma," Joe said. "You better get with it, Katie. The butler's watching."

"Have you all taken part-time jobs with a catering service?" Emma asked.

"Not exactly."

"Then what?"

Katie sighed. "My brother was desperate to see you again. He tricked us into believing you had invited us to the party. When we arrived he led us downstairs and the butler assumed we were part of the catering service."

Emma stared at Katie for a moment, picturing the absurdity of it all, and then she burst out laughing.

Katie looked around. "Please don't embarrass us, Emma. I'm so sorry. this never would have happened if I'd. . ."

Emma put her arms around Katie and hugged her. "I would never do anything to embarrass you. Now take that silly jacket off." She motioned for Joe and Corky to come over and then she led them into a den off the ballroom.

"It's so good to see all of you again." she hugged Joe and then Corky. "Welcome to Oak Hall."

"We'll get Shorty and say good night," Katie said.

"You'll do nothing of the sort, Katie Callahan. You are my guests and I insist that you join the party."

"We couldn't possibly. We're not dressed."

"It doesn't matter."

"It does to me."

"All right then. If you insist." Emma pushed a button on the wall and a maid appeared.

"Yes, Miss Emma."

"Edna, this is Katie Callahan." The maid nodded.

"I want you to take Katie up to my closet and find her something to wear."

"Yes, Miss Emma."

"And also take these gentlemen to the guest closet. I'm sure they can find something appropriate to wear."

"You're going to a lot of trouble," Katie said.

"I'm kicking myself for not sending you an invitation in the first place. I just didn't know how to handle it without inviting your brother."

"Shall I send him upstairs to get dressed?" Katie asked.

"No. I think he should continue working for awhile. It will serve him right. We may never get another chance to have Shorty Callahan wait on us."

Katie smiled. "What a wonderful idea," she said, as she followed the maid up the stairs.

"You, boy! Another drink for the ladies!" Corky yelled across the room at Shorty. Shorty glowered menacingly at him.

"You can't get decent help any more," Corky said to Emma. They were all gleefully ordering Shorty after drinks and appetizers.

Katie was having a wonderful time. She had on a pale green evening dress, and she was surrounded by admiring young men. Emma took her by the hand and pulled her away from her admirers. "Look over there," Emma pointed to the dance floor where Joe had girls lined up waiting to dance with him. "That's what happens when you date the best-looking guy in the city."

"Isn't he just gorgeous?" Katie said. "Sometimes it's hard for me to believe that he's mine."

"Yes, he is gorgeous," Emma agreed. "And so are you."

Katie blushed. "How much longer are you going to punish my brother? He's been miserable without you. How many men would have gone to this much trouble to be close to the woman they love?"

"In spite of everything, you will always stick up for him, won't you, Katie?"

"The night you had the argument with Shorty, he said those nasty things to drive you away. He was afraid you might get hurt."

Emma looked at her questioningly. "How do you know?"

"Franky told me."

"I was so mad that I never considered he might be looking out for my welfare." Emma paused for a moment. "I'll tell you a secret. I was afraid your brother was never going to show up here."

Katie laughed.

"If you will excuse me, I'll go rescue him from the butler."

Shorty was serving a drink when Emma came up behind him. "Would you like to dance?"

Shorty turned around. "Sorry, Miss, but I'm not allowed to mix with the guests."

"Make an exception," Emma said, grabbing him by the arm. "I'll clear it with the butler." She led him onto the dance floor as he shed his serving jacket. The music was slow and soft, and she was in his arms.

"You look terrific," Shorty said.

"Thank you. You went to a lot of trouble, Callahan. How did you know I was giving a party?"

"I stopped by earlier and saw the guests arriving."

"How did you know I was here?"

"Your apartment's been dark for three days. I figured you were home for the holidays. I kept driving by until I saw you greeting your guests."

Shorty looked around the dance floor. "This place is really something. It makes me realize how far out of my league I've been playing."

"Want to give up the game?"

"Couldn't, even if I wanted to."

"Why not?"

"Because I'm in love with you."

Emma stopped dancing and looked into his eyes. "Maybe you have love confused with infatuation."

"I'm confused about a lot of things, but not about my feelings for you."

Emma sighed and rested her head on his shoulder. "Do you realize how uncomplicated my life was until I met you?"

"And how boring," Shorty said.

Emma laughed.

"When do I get to meet Mom and Dad?" Shorty asked.

"I would love to introduce you, but my parents are spending Christmas in the Bahamas with some of their friends."

"Likely story. They're probably hiding behind the curtains until you get rid of the riff-raff."

"I've never known you to have an inferiority complex."

"I've never been in a place like this."

"I'll introduce you to my parents when they get home."

"You've made up with them?"

"We have a truce going through the holidays."

"I guess that means we can set the wedding date."

"You're impossible," Emma said, shaking her head.

It was Shorty's turn to laugh.

It was after midnight and Katie, Joe, and Corky were back in their street clothes. Emma hugged each of them at the back door.

"We've danced the night away and I feel like Cinderella," Katie whispered in Emma's ear.

"Except you already have your prince," Emma whispered back.

"Thanks, Emma," Joe said. "It was quite an evening. I apologize for being a party to the break in."

"Don't start apologizing for my brother," Katie said. "You won't have room for anything else in your life."

"Amazing," Shorty said. "I give you a wonderful evening, and you still give me a hard time."

"Poor misunderstood baby," Katie said, pinching his cheek. "Let's get out of here and let Emma get some sleep."

"Shorty is staying here," Emma said matter-of-factly.

Katie's mouth dropped open. "Emma!"

"Don't get the wrong idea, Katie. Shorty and I have some things to talk about, and then I'll have the butler escort him to a guest room."

"You had better assign someone to guard your door," Corky said.

"Keep it up, Corky," Shorty threatened. "You're already on my hit list."

Everyone laughed.

"Are you going to be by yourself on Christmas Eve, Emma?" Katie asked.

"Yes."

"Come to the lake. We have the clubhouse on Christmas Eve. It's a family tradition."

Emma had been dreading being alone on Christmas Eve. "Thank you, Katie. I would love to come."

"Good night everyone," Emma yelled as she watched them run through the falling snow to the car.

"Well, alone at last," Shorty said.

"Follow me, Callahan." She led him up a wide, winding staircase to the second floor. They walked down a passageway past a series of bedrooms to the end of the hall. Shorty was wide-eyed as he looked at the various paintings and elaborate furnishings. Emma opened another door, and started climbing a narrow staircase that led to the next level.

"Where are we going?"

"My studio." At the top of the stairs she opened a door and flipped on a light. They were in an attic room that held numerous works of sculpture in various stages of completion.

"When I was a little girl this was my secret place," Emma explained. "A place where I could be alone and never be bothered by anyone. The room is off-limits to family and staff alike." Outside the wind whistled in the eaves of the mansion.

"It's toasty up here," Shorty said.

Emma walked over to a statue and took off the covering. "I'm glad you're comfortable, because I need you to get undressed."

"You what?"

"You heard me. I do some of my best work after midnight, and you have a body that I've always wanted to sculpt."

"Now wait a minute. . ."

"Come on, Callahan. I'm sure you've taken your clothes off in front of women before."

"That's different."

"Oh . . . so we do admit to our bad behavior."

"You're twisting everything I say. It's just that we're friends and I wouldn't feel comfortable."

"What would make you feel comfortable?"

"If you want me to model, then we get undressed together."

Emma stared at him, mulling over the challenge. "All right, Callahan. Have it your way."

Shorty watched as she unsnapped the pearls from around her neck and placed them on a table. "Unzip me," she ordered.

Shorty walked over and unzipped her dress. She kicked off her heels and slipped out of her dress. He could feel his heart pounding as he looked at her firm upturned breasts pushing against a white satin bra.

"Come on, Callahan. Stop staring and start undressing."

"Yes, Ma'am." Shorty started tearing at his clothes, keeping his eyes riveted on Emma. He watched as she unsnapped her bra and let her breasts fall free. They were firm and full, with wide nipples that seemed almost purple in the light. She slipped out of her ivory-colored underpants and stood naked before him. He turned away from her and slipped out of his shorts.

"What's the matter, Callahan? Too embarrassed to let me see?"

"It's just that . . . you know . . . you're so beautiful and I have this condition."

"A deal is a deal, Callahan."

He turned around and left nothing to her imagination.

Emma stared for a moment. "That certainly isn't the reason they call you Shorty, is it, Callahan?"

"I didn't think artists were supposed to notice such things."

"That would be hard to miss. I'll just have to work around it," she teased.

"It would be a lot more fun if you worked with it," he replied.

"Are you propositioning me, Callahan?"

"Since the day we first met."

She stood seductively before him, challenging him with her eyes. She had made no move to work on her sculpting.

He started walking slowly toward her. "It's time, isn't it, Emma?"

She remained silent, staring at him with those gorgeous brown eyes.

"I've wanted to make love to you from the moment I first laid eyes on you," he said. He pulled her to him and felt the warmth and softness of her body. They kissed and caressed each other until they could wait no more. As they were spinning to the floor, Shorty grabbed a covering from one of the statues and put it under her back. They kissed and fondled and she arched against him. "We've waited so long, Callahan." She caught her breath as he entered her gently, but firmly, and they became lost in a steady passionate rhythm. He was vaguely aware of the howling winter wind as it tugged at the eaves of the attic. A shutter was banging against the side of the mansion . . . she was so warm and beautiful, and he had been so patient. . . She moved furiously against him and he held on, not wanting it to end, clinging to the edge . . . He couldn't wait any longer. "Oh, God . . . Callahan."

They lay on the floor in each others arms, listening to the wind brush snow against the mansion. She rolled over on top of him and sat up straddling his waist, then took the pins from her hair and shook her head, letting her black hair fall around her shoulders.

"You're so beautiful," he whispered. He cupped his hands around her breasts. She kissed him and started seductively moving her hips. "I apologize, Callahan. We really rushed through that one."

"Couldn't be helped," he replied.

"This time we'll make it last."

"I may need some time to refresh the troops," he said.

"You underestimate yourself," she said, taking him in her hands and squeezing firmly until he was ready. "See what I mean?" Emma helped him find his way and they were together again. She started the rhythmic movement, her breasts moving exotically back and forth, and her black hair tumbling into his face.

"You're going to kill me," he whispered.

"If you last until dawn, Callahan, you'll know you're going to make it," she whispered back.

"Jesus," Shorty said, in awe and anticipation.

Shorty was awakened by the sun shining through an attic window. Emma was wrapped around him, snuggled under the warmth of the sculpting cover. He kissed her on the cheek and she stirred.

"Good morning," he said.

She sighed, and slowly blinked her eyes open, trying to get her bearings. Then she pushed away from him. "You're not going to get any ideas about this changing anything."

"Me?" he said derisively. Why would spending the most wonderful night of my life with the woman I want to marry change anything?"

"You know how I feel about marriage. We can still be good friends."

"Stupid me. I thought only people in love behaved this way."

"You know what I mean. I'm not about to be trapped behind a picket fence with a bunch of little Callahans."

"There are worse things."

"No, there aren't. At this point in my life, losing my freedom would be the worst."

Shorty sighed. "I don't want to spoil last night with another fight."

Emma snuggled closer to him. "I'll be your girl, Callahan. All I'm asking is that you don't tread on my independence."

"I guess that means I won't be meeting Mom and Dad after all."

"On the contrary. I'll introduce you when they get back from vacation."

Shorty felt the warmth of her breasts pushing against him and his interest turned to other things.

"What's that I feel, Callahan?" She kissed him gently on the lips.

"I believe it's something that's going to come between good friends," he replied.

She giggled as he threw off the sculpting cover and rolled on top of her. "Being good friends is not half bad," he said.

"I thought you might make the adjustment," she replied seductively.

It was a cold, crisp, Christmas Eve night. Katie and Joe paused on the front porch of the clubhouse and looked at the full moon shining brightly down on a blanket of snow and ice covering the lake.

"It's beautiful," she said.

"Beautiful, but brrrrr. . ." Joe replied, shivering. "Let's get inside where it's warm."

Katie grabbed his arm. "Not until you kiss me."

"Our lips will stick together."

"What's wrong with that?" She moved her lips invitingly toward his.

"We're putting off more steam than an engine," he whispered as her lips pressed against his.

She came up for air, and clung to him, pulling him close.

"What's the matter?" he asked.

"Everything is so perfect, Joe. I don't want any of this to end."

"It's going to be okay," he said, wrapping his arms around her and holding her tight.

She raised up and kissed him again.

They heard tapping on the huge picture window of the clubhouse and

Katie and Joe turned around. The whole gang was gathered at the window applauding. Embarrassed, Katie grabbed Joe's hand and led him inside. "Merry Christmas everyone," she said.

"Come on, Katie," Corky took her by the hand. "We're going to warm up our voices before heading out into the cold to sing Christmas carols."

McClusky was at the piano. Franky sat on the stool next to him.

"What are you going to play, Franky?" Corky asked. "Gershwin or Cole Porter?"

"I'm going to play my knuckles off your forehead, you little twerp."

"Now, now," Corky teased him back. "You know how Aunt Martha feels about violence on Christmas Eve." Everyone laughed and McClusky hit the keys and stared playing: "God rest ye merry gentlemen, let nothing you dismay . . ." and everyone joined in to sing. They were into their third song when Aunt Martha poked her head into the room. "The sleigh is here. Hurry along."

Outside they all climbed into Uncle Ray's vintage sleigh. The two horses pawed the snow as they blew steam into the cold night air.

"Bundle up!" Uncle Ray shouted.

Shorty snuggled up next to Emma, and pulled a blanket over them.

"Away we go," Uncle Ray shouted. The horses took the cue and began prancing ahead. They passed by a giant spruce tree, lit with hundreds of colorful bulbs. Christmas lights sparkled in the darkness from all of the homes on the lakefront.

"Stop here at the Wallace house." Aunt Martha ordered.

They climbed out of the sleigh, and one of the carolers ran through the snow and knocked on the Wallace's front door.

Uncle Ray reached under the seat and pulled out a box of candles. Shorty lit the first candle and passed them around until everyone held a flickering flame. The Wallace family gathered on the front porch, and the carolers began softly singing "Silent night, holy night, all is calm, all is bright." Katie looked up at the stars shining brightly down from above, and at the carolers basking in the glow of candlelight. She squeezed Joe's hand and he smiled at her. She was so happy, and everything was so perfect that she vowed to always remember this moment. She whispered a silent prayer of thanks to God for all that He had given her.

10

Shorty looked out the window of his office. The setting sun cast a red glow on the buildings overlooking 12th Street. Down the block a few stragglers from the work-a-day world were locking up their businesses and heading home, leaving downtown to the night people. He put his feet up on his desk and loosened his tie. His war with Tony Bonatto was coming to a head. Last night Tony's goons had beaten up two runners and stolen the day's gambling receipts. There had been a mysterious fire in one of the bars Shorty controlled. If he didn't do something to retaliate, things were sure to get worse. He thought about taking Katie's advice and getting out of the business. He had enough money for the supper club, but he needed more for Katie's education. It was his responsibility as the man of the family to see that she was educated. And he wanted a nest egg just in case he was lucky enough to win Emma. If he could hold on another six months he would have all the money he needed. He called Franky into the office. "We're going after Tony Bonatto."

"Terrific," Franky said derisively. "Let me guess. We're not going to use guns."

"Why use guns when we can use our brains?"

Franky looked at him questioningly.

"Is Tony still fooling around around with those two high school girls you were telling me about?"

"Every Friday night at the Muehlebach Hotel."

"Are they willing?"

"The Cincatto twins? Are they ever. I would sample some of that myself, but word might get back to Tony."

"How old are they?"

Franky shrugged. "Couldn't be more than 17."

"What makes them so willing?"

"He gives each of them a C note. Those girls will hump their brains out for a hundred a week."

"Tony could have a lot of girls. What makes the Cincatto twins so special?"

"Ooh la la." Franky shaped the female form with his hands. "Tight little asses and tits that won't quit. Word on the street is that they like to experiment with the kinky stuff. If you know what I mean."

"Spare me the details. I'm getting worked up."

"Tony likes for them to dress up like cheerleaders: saddle shoes, bobby sox, and no underwear."

"Would you quit. I'm not going to be able to stand up."

Franky laughed. "So what does this have to do with getting our revenge on Tony?"

Shorty leaned back and put his hands behind his head. "I bet Tony's wife would like to meet the Cincatto twins."

Franky's eyes widened. "You can't do that, Shorty."

"Why not?"

"Because it goes against all the rules. Families are off limits. You know perfectly well it's an Italian thing."

"Do I look Italian?"

"No, but. . ."

"Then I don't have to play by the rules."

"C'mon, Shorty. Don't do this," Franky pleaded.

"I'll pass the word on the street that you were not involved in any way," Shorty said. "That will keep you straight with the Italian community. Now I need for you to get me a detective's badge from one of the cops on our payroll, and tell that 'would be' motion picture director to get his ass up here. I have a way he can make up the back rent that he owes me."

Shorty knocked on the Bonatto family's front door. It was Friday night and Tony's goons were off duty. A young girl answered. She appeared to be about ten years old.

"Can I help you?"

"Mrs. Bonatto please."

"She's busy," the girl said.

"Tell her it's urgent."

"What's it about?"

Shorty narrowed his eyes at her. "Go get her, you little twerp."

"Mom! Mom!" the girl hurried away.

"What's all the commotion about?" A rotund, black-haired woman appeared.

"Mrs. Bonatto, I'm detective Callahan." Shorty showed her the badge.

"What's the problem, officer? Has something happened to my husband?" she asked with concern.

"We're detaining him on a small matter, Mrs. Bonatto. He says he was with you last night. Is that correct?"

"It most certainly is," she said with relief. "I don't know why you people insist on trying to blame my husband for everything that happens in this city."

"Sorry, Ma'am. Tony sent me here to bring you downtown so you can confirm his alibi."

"Oh. I didn't realize you were a friend of my husband. I'll be right with you."

Shorty stopped the car in front of the Muehlebach hotel.

"What are we doing here?" Mrs. Bonatto asked.

"I talked the captain into interrogating Tony in a comfortable room. You know how he hates to be seen at the police station."

"Oh. That was very thoughtful of you."

Shorty escorted her inside and they rode the elevator up to the second floor. "If you will wait here for just a minute I'll see if the captain's ready for you." Shorty pulled a chair up, and Mrs. Bonatto sat down. He hurried down the corridor and tapped on the door next to Tony's suite. The door opened and Saperstein, the 'would be' motion picture director, peered out.

Shorty pushed open the door and walked inside. "Talk to me, Saperstein."

Saperstein put his finger to his lips and motioned Shorty over to take a look. Shorty peered into the vent next to the camera. Tony and the girls were naked on the bed. There was a lot of moaning and groaning going on.

"You should have been here earlier," Saperstein said. "I swear to God those two girls are double jointed."

"Have you got it all on film?"

"Yeah. And thanks for the two months' free rent. I would have taken this assignment for nothing."

Shorty took another look through the vent. "Damn!" he said, disappointed. "They're putting their clothes back on."

Saperstein turned the bill of his baseball cap around and took a peek. "Nah," he said. "They're getting dressed up like cheerleaders. It's how the guy gets his nuts off."

"Unbelievable," Shorty whispered, as he watched one of the twins pick up a set of pom poms.

Saperstein put his hand over his mouth to keep from laughing. "Keep watching," he said. "You won't believe this."

Tony lifted the skirt of one of the Cincatto twins, bent her over the bed, and started doing it dog fashion. The other twin stood in front of him holding the pom poms. She started doing a cheer from Tony's high school football days.

"Go Eagles! Go Eagles! Sis Boom Bah!" She speeded up the cadence and Tony started moving faster and faster. "Go Eagles! Go Eagles! Sis Boom Bah!" She started shaking the pom poms in a frenzy.

"I don't know what you have planned, but this will be the third time he's gotten his jollies," Saperstein said. "He's either going to pass out, or have a heart attack."

Shorty went out into the hall. "I think they're ready to see you now, Mrs. Bonatto." The desk clerk at the Muehlebach had given Shorty the room key to clear a gambling debt. Shorty turned the key slowly in the lock and opened the door. Mrs. Bonatto walked into the room. "Go Eagles! Go Eagles! Sis Boom Bah!" Tony was into his final thrusts when he looked around and saw his wife. Shorty watched from the door as the Cincatto twins screamed, and Tony's dick melted like ice cream in August. With surprising agility for a large woman, Mrs. Bonatto recovered from her initial shock and ran across the room at her husband. She started yelling in Italian and pummeling him with her purse, scattering the twins like bowling balls. Shorty quietly closed the door and headed down the hall to the elevator.

The next evening, Shorty, Franky, and Duff were laughing hysterically at Saperstein's movie when the call came.

"You prick. You're a dead man," Tony's voice threatened over the telephone.

"Hello, Tony. Is this a social call?"

"Laugh it up when you're six feet under," Tony said. "When you break the rules, Callahan, you have to pay the price."

"You mean rules like statutory rape?" Shorty replied.

There was a pause on the other end of the line. "What do you mean?"

"I gave the Cincatto twins a couple of C notes to pose with their birth certificates."

"So what. You will never get them to talk."

"Don't have to. When you called we were all enjoying the movie."

"You were what?" Tony asked in disbelief.

"Watching the movie. Your buddies at the city market will get a kick out it. Especially the part where your wife is pounding your pecker with her purse. And the pom poms were really a nice touch, Tony. Now listen carefully: If you or your goons cause me any more trouble, a copy of the movie goes to the District Attorney. He would like nothing better than to put your sorry ass in Leavenworth." There was dead silence on the other end of the line. "And one more thing," Shorty said, as he held the phone out to Franky and Duff. They all started chanting: "Go Eagles! Go Eagles! Sis Boom Bah!"

Graham Stephens sat in his office on the top floor of the Stephens Bank building. From his lofty perch he had a panoramic view of the city. This past weekend Emma had brought home the latest example of her misguided lifestyle: a small-time hoodlum named Shorty Callahan. It was unbelievable that she would even associate with this type of person, much less think she might be in love with him. It was further proof of how mixed up and rebellious she had become. This Callahan character was exactly the type of person the city was trying to eliminate — a remnant of the corrupt Pendergast organization that had crippled the city's progress for half a century. Graham and his Republican friends had been instrumental in sweeping out the remains of the Pendergast organization from city hall and establishing a reform mayor dedicated to cleaning up the nest of gamblers and prostitutes contaminating the city. He picked up the phone and dialed the mayor. It was time to call in some campaign debts.

Shorty sat next to Emma in a booth at the Linwood Ice Cream Shop. It was his favorite place for a treat. He and Katie had been coming here since they were kids. Shorty looked at his watch and frowned. "I wonder where they are?"

"Coming through the door," Emma said, as she waved to Katie and Joe.

"Hello," Katie said. She leaned over and kissed her brother on the cheek, and then slid into the booth next to Joe.

"What movie did you see?" Emma asked.

"*Goodbye, Mr. Chips*," Katie replied.

"It was a tear-jerker," Joe said. "Katie went through two handkerchiefs. How about you guys?"

"I wanted to see *Wuthering Heights*, but Shorty talked me into *Stagecoach*."

"Be careful, or you will spend the rest of your life watching westerns," Katie warned.

"Let's order," Shorty suggested.

"What flavors do they have?" Emma asked.

"I'll have Eddie call them out."

"Don't you dare!" Katie threatened.

"What's the matter with you?"

"Don't play dumb with me. You know perfectly well what I mean."

Shorty ignored her. "Hey Eddie!"

Katie kicked her brother in the shins.

"Ouch! That hurt."

"I mean it, Shorty," Katie hissed.

"What's going on?" Emma asked.

"Eddie has a hair lip," Katie whispered. "Shorty thinks it's funny to make him call out the flavors."

Emma looked over at Shorty and shook her head. "You can be really disgusting."

"Okay, Okay," Shorty said. He pulled his shins out of harm's way. "Hey Eddie!" he yelled. "What flavors do you have?" Katie lashed out at Shorty's shins and missed.

"Snoclate — Snrawberry — Snuti Fruti —" Eddie started calling out the names.

"Why are you biting down on your lip, Squirt?" Shorty asked. I hope you don't think this is funny."

Katie ducked her head under the table.

"Marnshmellow — Scnerry —" Eddie continued.

Shorty peered under the table. Katie had her hand over her mouth and her shoulders were shaking uncontrollably.

"Would you mind sitting up, Squirt? You're really embarrassing me," Shorty chided her.

Katie sat up and put her hands over her face. One glance at Shorty and she would crack up. "Make him stop," she said, hating herself for laughing.

"Thanks, Eddie!" Shorty called out.

Katie took a couple of deep breaths and managed to compose herself. She looked over at Shorty.

"Okay, Squirt. What's it going to be?" Shorty asked. He leaned over and put his face close to Katie's. "Snoclate or Snrawberry?"

Katie covered her mouth to keep from laughing, but her entire body was shaking.

Shorty looked at Joe. "You have a lot of nerve bringing this girl out in public." Shorty nudged her with his shoe. "Come on, Squirt. Eddie is coming to take our order." Katie composed herself.

Eddie took their order and was back a few minutes later with the ice cream.

"Thanks, Eddie," Shorty handed him a twenty dollar bill. "Keep the change."

Eddie nodded his thanks.

"Expensive ice cream," Joe said.

Shorty shrugged. "Eddie has a wife and five kids to support."

The door of the ice cream shop banged open and two burly looking men in rumpled suits walked in. They scanned the room and then headed for Shorty's table.

Shorty glanced up. "Hello, Mulvany. What brings you to this part of town?"

"My never-ending pursuit of truth, justice, and the American way," the detective answered sarcastically. His partner chuckled. "You ready to go downtown, Callahan?"

"I'm under arrest?"

"No," Mulvany chided him. "You're master of ceremonies at the mayor's birthday party. He sent his personal car for you. Now stand up and turn around." The detective took out a pair of handcuffs.

Shorty looked for an avenue of escape. The door banged open again and two uniformed policeman stood in the doorway holding billy clubs.

"Don't even think about it, Callahan," Mulvany warned.

"What are the charges?" Katie asked.

"Mulvany let his gaze fall on Katie. "Who are you?"

"His sister, and you have no right to arrest him without telling him why."

"Take your pick, little sister: extortion, gambling, bribery — big brother has his hand in a bit of everything. Ain't that right, Callahan?" Mulvany pulled Shorty out of the booth and handcuffed him.

"What's going on, Mulvany?" Shorty asked. "I've got friends at city hall."

"If you had friends, Callahan, I wouldn't be here. Anyone with Pendergast connections is going out with the garbage."

"So what does that make you, Mulvany?"

"That's good, Callahan." Mulvany shoved him roughly toward the door. "We'll see how much of a wise-ass you are behind bars."

"Call Franky," Shorty said to his friends. "He'll know what to do."

Shorty had spent the night in jail waiting for Franky to post bail. He paced back and forth in the cell, staring at the stark grey walls. It was driving him crazy to be confined. Franky had to get him out of here. Down the hall a key clicked and a heavy steel door opened. He listened intently as footsteps came down the corridor. Andy McClusky appeared from around the corridor.

"Hello, Shorty."

"Andy. What are you doing here?" He was glad to see a friendly face.

"I thought you might need some company. I also brought you a visitor."

"Oh yeah? Who is it?"

Tony Bonatto walked around the corner. He slowly walked in front of the bars scrutinizing Shorty. "You look good, Callahan. I slept better with you behind bars."

"Don't be a smart ass, Tony. This was a dumb move on your part. Did you forget about the movie?"

"That's why I'm here, Callahan. I figured you would be blaming me."

"Who else would want me in jail?"

Tony laughed. He lit a cigar and blew the smoke into the cell. "You're not as smart as I figured, Callahan. One of the first rules of business is to never get on the bad side of big money."

"What do you mean?"

"I mean that you should learn to keep your dick out of the society pages."

Shorty looked at Tony with a puzzled expression.

"When I heard you were arrested, I did some checking. It seems that a prominent member of the banking community is not too happy that you're humping his daughter."

Shorty lunged at the bars and took a punch at Tony. A former street brawler, Tony gracefully sidestepped the blow, and laughed even harder.

"What's the matter, Callahan? Are you in love with this society broad?"

"You watch your mouth," Shorty threatened.

"You better give your dick some brains. The blue-bloods don't like the lower classes tapping their daughters."

"You get your fat ass out of here," Shorty said.

"Okay, Callahan. I just wanted to set you straight. I didn't want that movie floating around town."

McClusky took Tony by the arm and started escorting him away.

"Hey, Tony!" Shorty called after him. "You remember the day you called me about the Cincatto twins?"

"Yeah. What about it?"

"The movie went in the trash the moment I hung up the phone."

Tony stared at him. "You're a real piece of work, Callahan."

It was Shorty's turn to laugh.

After he escorted Tony through the door, McClusky walked back and stood outside the cell. "You have another visitor."

"Who is it?"

"Katie. She's been here since the sun came up."

"Don't let her in," Shorty said. "She couldn't handle seeing me cooped up like this."

"That's what I figured, so I've been stalling her. Franky and your lawyer should be here soon."

"Thanks, Andy. Tell Katie to go home. I promise I will meet her there."

"Okay, Shorty. You better have a good lawyer. The courts are really cracking down on anyone even remotely connected with Pendergast. Graham Stephens has a lot of clout with the new administration, so things don't look too good. Maybe I should talk to Emma."

"I'll handle this my own way. But thanks for helping."

"Okay. I've got to get going. I'll check back to be sure you got out on bail."

"Thanks, Andy."

Katie was waiting in the living room when he walked into the house. She hugged him. "Are you okay?"

"Fine."

"What does your attorney say?"

"We can beat the charges."

Katie studied him. "Don't lie to me, Shorty."

He sighed. "Okay, Squirt. The city has a good case against me. The lawyers seem to think it might be better if I plead guilty and throw myself on the mercy of the court. If the city is spared the expense of a trial we can work out a deal where I get a short sentence."

"How short?"

"One to two years."

Katie turned away with a look of dejection.

Shorty put his arm around her. "Hey, it's not that big a deal. I'll be out in time to see you graduate from college."

"I know how much you hate to be confined. You couldn't stand being in prison."

"I'll be okay." Shorty tried to comfort her. "If I agree to cooperate with the court, they will move my sentencing date back to the Christmas holidays when the judges are more lenient."

"What are they charging you with?"

"They're calling it extortion. In order to do business I had to collect a 'nut' for City Hall."

"What's that?"

"A percentage of the money made by anyone operating a business on 12th Street went to the boys downtown."

"Then why aren't they prosecuting everyone?"

"I turned the money in, and someone at City Hall kept a payment book listing the names of all the collectors."

"Oh." Katie looked at him with concern. "What does Emma say about all of this?"

"I haven't told her."

"What about Mother?"

"There's no point in letting her stew for the next six months. Let's wait until the sentencing date to tell her."

"When will that be?"

"The eighth of December."

"Okay. But you have to promise me that you will tell her yourself when the time comes."

"Okay. I promise."

Katie put her arms around her brother and held him tightly to her.

"Way to go, Callahan," Emma said as she kneaded the head of a statue. "Katie said you were destined for prison, and you worked very hard to fulfill her prophesy."

"I can see that you're all broken up about it. I'll run into the bathroom and get you some kleenex."

"Is that what you expected — hysteria and tears?"

"I never know what to expect where you're concerned."

"Well don't expect me to do my Bonnie Parker routine and wait for you. That just isn't my style, Callahan."

Shorty took a deep breath and fought to control his temper. "Lately we seem to be either making love or fighting."

"That should tell you something about the long-term stability of our relationship."

"Then maybe we should end it now, before you soil your reputation."

"I believe that suggestion was just made by my father."

"News travels fast."

"My father has friends at City Hall."

"Are you going to take your father's advice?"

"I haven't decided."

"You had better make up your mind. I don't have a lot of time to waste. If you want to break-up, just say so."

"Sounds simplistic, but I'm trapped by my conscience. If I walk away, I've left you in your hour of need. Stay, and I become the girlfriend of a convicted felon."

"I must have missed the love and caring part."

"You missed it when you decided to pursue your lifestyle instead of taking the advice of your friends and family."

"So where does that leave us?"

Emma paused, searching for words. "I think we should go back to being just good friends."

"You mean forget about the physical part of our relationship because I'm going to prison."

"I think it would be best."

"Talk about shallow."

"What would you have me do, take a vow of celibacy and spend two years pacing outside prison walls?"

Shorty walked over and opened the door. He turned back and faced her. "I wouldn't expect that at all, Miss Emma. It would require some loyalty on your part and also some class. Why don't we just forget that we ever met. It will make it easier on both of us." He walked out and quietly closed the door.

Emma stared after him. She would have taken it better if he had yelled at her and slammed the door. She looked at the statue and realized she had kneaded the head into oblivion.

11

Emma answered the knock at her door and pulled back in surprise. She stepped aside. "Come on in, Corky." Since her break-up with Shorty she had made a conscious effort to stay away from anyone connected with him.

"How have you been?" he asked, walking past her into the apartment.

"Fine. How about you?"

"Okay."

"Want to sit down?"

"No thanks. I just stopped by to invite you out to the lake for the 4th of July weekend."

"At Katie's urging, no doubt."

Corky nodded.

"One last stab at match-making. I thought she would have given up by now."

"You know how persistent she is."

Emma went back to her sculpting. She was wearing a black smock over her jeans, and her hair was tied up with a blue bandana.

"You don't have to keep avoiding me," Corky said. "We were friends long before you met Shorty."

She paused. "I thought it would be easier this way."

Corky walked across the room and looked out the window. "We've missed you this summer."

"And I've missed all of you."

"There's something I have to tell you, Emma."

She waited.

"Everyone in the gang knows this but you and Katie. Shorty made us promise to keep it from you."

"What are you talking about?"

"You're one of the reasons Shorty is going to prison."

Emma stopped sculpting. "What?"

"Your father put pressure on the mayor to have Shorty arrested and prosecuted."

"I don't believe it. Why would he?"

"To put an end to your relationship."

"If this is true, then why didn't Shorty tell me?"

"He didn't want to cause any more of a rift between you and your parents."

"Are you sure about this?"

"Andy McClusky has relatives working at every level of the police department. You can confirm it with him."

Emma knew it must be true. "I'll talk to my father," she said.

"It's too late for that. The prosecutors won't drop the charges. They're out to prove that the new city government is working for reform. Shorty will have to do time."

Emma reflected for a moment. "I've been a complete fool," she said softly. "Shorty tried to protect my relationship with my parents, and I didn't even care enough to offer him my support when he needed me."

"You didn't know."

She shook her head in disgust. "I was thinking of myself and how lonely I was going to be with Shorty in prison."

"You had every right to be concerned."

"I was wrong and you know it."

"It's not too late to make things right."

"I'm not so sure. We had some harsh words."

"Trust me. Come to the lake."

"You're a good friend, Corky. I sometimes wonder why you put up with me."

"Because you're one of the people I admire. It took a lot of courage for you to walk away from an easy life and pursue your career as an artist. And you've been great for Shorty. Everyone in the gang thinks that you're the best thing that ever happened to him."

"Now you're really making me feel bad."

"Then you'll come?"

"Let me pack some things and I'll be right with you."

Shorty had decided to make the most of his last summer of freedom. He was spending a lot of time at the lake: fishing, playing golf, and just lying around in the sun. He had not seen Emma for several months. He missed her fiercely and couldn't stop thinking about her. After months of feeling sorry for himself and moping around, he had invited Rita, the silver dollar girl from the Chesterfield Club, out for the 4th of July celebration.

The hot afternoon sun beat down on his back as he lay on the dock watching a sailboat drift listlessly on the water. He was getting apprehensive as his sentencing date drew near. Prison was something that happened to hardened criminals, so he had never taken Katie's warnings seriously. In perfect hindsight, he wished he had listened to her. Rita lay next to him. He could feel the softness of her foot against the back of his leg. She looked beautiful and alluring in a one-piece blue bathing suit. He knew he was the envy of every man at the lake. He nudged her with his leg. "You getting well done?"

"This sun is delicious. I'm going to bake all afternoon."

"Don't overdo it and spoil our evening. I want to be able to touch that beautiful skin."

She rubbed her bare foot over his. "Just remember that I have to be at work by ten."

"You'll be too tired to work."

She smiled. "You're probably right, but this is one of the club's biggest nights of the year."

"I can't believe you're choosing the club over the frog hunt."

"Frog hunt?"

"Every July 4th eve, me and Katie go frog hunting with Uncle Ray. We catch frogs for the July 4th frog jumping contest."

"Sounds slippery and slimy."

"It is. But we have a lot of fun."

Rita yawned. "I'm getting sleepy. The beer and the hot sun have done me in."

"Me too." He nudged closer and put his arm over her. In the distance he could hear the pop of firecrackers exploding in the hills around the lake. He listened as the thump, thump of the diving board catapulted laughing kids into the cool waters. Over by the dam a dog was barking. He drifted off to sleep.

He was awakened some time later by voices chattering away next to him. He unlinked himself from Rita and slowly opened his eyes. Katie was sitting next to Joe, and Corky sat next to . . . Oh God . . . it was Emma! She glanced at him with a look of amusement.

"Are you going to introduce me, Callahan?"

Rita stirred and yawned herself awake.

"Rita, this is Emma Stephens. And this is my sister, Katie."

"Hi, Emma, Katie," Rita said sleepily.

"Hello, Rita. That's a stunning bathing suit," Emma said.

"Thanks."

Shorty squirmed uneasily. Emma had on a two-piece black bathing suit that accentuated her black hair and brown eyes. She was a match for Rita and more.

Emma took Corky's hand. "Let's go swimming."

Shorty watched as they ran to the end of the dock and dove into the water. He spent the rest of the afternoon and early evening watching Emma swim, sail, and sunbathe on the lake. She totally ignored him, and never once glanced in his direction. Her presence had made him forget all about Rita. She was a good friend and he would not hurt her feelings, but he was glad when she finally said her good-bye and left.

Twilight had descended on the lake. Shorty tossed the frog net and burlap bags in the canoe. He carefully laid the spotlight on the seat. Katie and Joe had already shoved off and were paddling out into the lake. Emma and Corky were up at the house talking to Aunt Martha. Emma still hadn't spoken to him again or paid him a bit of attention. "Are you ready to shove off, my boy?" Uncle Ray asked.

"Let's go," Shorty said. He started to push the canoe out into the water.

"Mind if I come along?"

He turned around. Emma was standing on the beach. She had on an old tee shirt, shorts, and she was barefoot. Shorty could feel the butter-flies start to churn in his stomach.

"We would love to have you," Uncle Ray said. He helped Emma into the middle of the canoe. Shorty climbed into the bow. Uncle Ray settled into his position as oarsman and pushed them away from the beach. Night was falling and stars glittered around a crescent moon. Shorty could smell the faint scent of Emma's perfume.

The bow of the canoe split the still waters around the point as Uncle Ray headed for the first dock. He put the paddle in the water and expert-ly slowed the canoe. Shorty shone the light under the dock and it landed on the beady eyes of a giant bullfrog. "Look at him! He's huge!" Emma exclaimed.

"Don't make any sudden moves," Uncle Ray warned. Emma held the burlap bag they would use to hold the frogs. Shorty ducked his head as the canoe went under the dock. "Steady now. . . steady. . ." Uncle Ray said. Shorty kept the spotlight trained on the bullfrog. "Emma, take the light and hold it on him," he said. He switched the frog net to his right hand as Uncle Ray guided the canoe closer to the beady eyes glowing just above the surface of the water. Shorty lunged over the end of the canoe and put the net over the frog. The frog instinctively jumped and Shorty turned the net over. "Got him!" he yelled. He held the top of the net in his fist as the bullfrog fought for freedom.

"We got us a jumper!" Uncle Ray said, pleased.

"Can I put him in the bag?" Emma asked.

"You really want to?"

"Sure." She reached down into the net and grasped the cool, slimy body of the frog.

"Careful now," Shorty warned. "He's a fighter."

Shorty opened the bag and Emma dropped in the frog. He tied the top of the bag.

"Way to go, Emma," Uncle Ray said. "You sure you haven't done this before?"

Emma laughed. "Let's go catch another one," she said excitedly. Shorty beamed at her.

Later, after he had helped her catch several frogs, he put the last catch in the bag and surveyed the lake with his spotlight. "I can't understand why we haven't run into Katie and Joe. I wonder how many frogs they've caught."

Katie and Joe had their blanket spread in a grassy spot out on the island. They lay on their backs looking up at the stars. From the outer reaches of the lake they could hear an occasional yelp of delight as Shorty, Emma, and Uncle Ray caught another frog.

"We should feel guilty," Katie said.

Joe smiled contentedly. "It was an easy decision. You and moonlight will win out over Shorty and bullfrogs every time."

Katie leaned over and started making frog noises in his ear. "Gerump . . . gerump."

Joe laughed and pulled her close. "Look over there!" he pointed. A shooting star streaked across the night sky before burning away on the horizon.

"Bad luck," Katie said.

"You're superstitious?"

"Isn't everyone?"

"Not about shooting stars."

"My grandmother said that if you saw one, someone you knew was going to die."

"Do you believe it?"

"Of course."

"Should we start warning all of our friends and neighbors?" he teased her.

She rolled over on top of him. "Make fun of my superstitions, will you." She started tickling him in the ribs. He laughed and tried to cover up.

"Katie, is that you?" Shorty's voice called from close by.

"Shhhh!" Katie said. She and Joe hugged the ground as the spotlight shone on the willow trees above them. The canoe passed by the point of the small island. They watched as the light flickered away in the distance.

"Whew," Katie said, relieved. "That was a close call." Joe kissed her on the lips. "Lovers caught in a passionate embrace," he said. "Word will spread of our scandalous affair and Aunt Martha will never live it down."

"The Scandal of Lovers Island," Katie whispered. She laid her head on his chest and listened to the steady beating of his heart. "I love you, Joe."

He squeezed her affectionately. "I love you too, Katie."

"Will our lives always be so perfect?" she sighed contentedly.

"Probably not. But we'll manage as long as we have each other."

"I feel that way too."

He kissed her again.

Music from the July 4th dance drifted out of the clubhouse and carried across the lake. Joe rose to his feet and pulled her into his arms. "Something for us to remember when times aren't always so perfect," he said. He wrapped his arms around her, held her close, and started slowly dancing to the trumpet blowing softly across the water. She put her arms around his neck and swayed back and forth with the music.

"I wish this night would last forever," she said. "Let's see that it does."

She hugged him and kissed him.

Suddenly, a spotlight bathed them in light.

"I knew it!" Shorty shouted from out in the lake. "How many frogs have you caught, Squirt?"

Katie and Joe turned away from the bright light and kept on dancing. "Ignore him and maybe he will go away," Katie said.

"You're not using any of our frogs tomorrow!" Shorty yelled. "This was supposed to be a team effort and you two are goofing off!"

"The stage lights are on us," Katie said. "It must be time for our number." She and Joe began singing with the music.

"All right wise guys! You think this is funny?"

"He's been out with the frogs too long," Katie yelled. "He's gurrrumpy." She could hear Emma laughing.

Uncle Ray guided the canoe up to the island. "I have to get Aunt Martha to the dance," he said. "I'll take the frogs and you two can ride back with Katie and Joe." Emma and Shorty climbed out onto the bank, and then shoved the canoe away from the island. Shorty held the spotlight on Uncle Ray long enough for Emma to see him give her a conspiratorial wink.

Shorty turned his attention back to his sister. "Well, what do you two have to say for yourselves?" he asked, confronting them.""

Emma moved between them. "Sorry we interrupted such a romantic moment. Do you mind if we join you?"

"We'd be delighted," Joe said.

"Come on, Callahan. Let's go over here." Shorty held the light and followed her to a spot a few yards away. "Turn off the light," she ordered. "I want to dance." He flipped off the spotlight and put it down. The music from the clubhouse was soft and mellow and she was in his arms.

"Have you missed me, Callahan?"

He pulled her close. "Don't you wish."

"I could tell you were suffering when I saw you wrapped around Rita."

"You probably won't believe me, but Rita was my first date since we broke up."

"No. I don't believe you. But it's nice to hear."

"Are we going to be friends again?" he asked.

"If you'll have me."

"Why the change of heart?"

"You were right. Life was boring without you."

The song ended and he kissed her.

"That was nice, Callahan."

For the first time in months he felt light-hearted and he had something to look forward to. The band started playing another song and he and Emma continued dancing. He could hear Katie softly singing the words to the music. Above the island an occasional rocket streaked across the night sky. With the moon, the stars, and the music, it was the most romantic moment of his life.

The next day, July 4th, Shorty teamed up with Emma and Corky and entered the canoe, sailboat, and swim races. During the frog jumping contest, Shorty's huge bullfrog sat on the dock and refused to move. Emma and Katie laughed hysterically as Shorty lay face down on the dock in front of the frog, begging him to jump. When the contest was over, and it was time to release the frogs, Shorty's bullfrog made the longest jump of the day. Everyone cheered heartily as he made two huge leaps across the dock and out into the lake.

The night before, Aunt Martha and Katie had hovered around Emma like protective hens. He knew it was because they hadn't seen her for a while. When it was time to say good night, Emma had shrugged helplessly and looked at Shorty apologetically with those beautiful brown eyes, and somehow all of his disappointment had melted away. It was enough that she was here, and they were together again. Later, when Emma had slipped out of her bedroom, they had sat together on the porch holding hands. He couldn't explain it, but somehow their relationship had changed. They had talked most of the night and never managed to get around to anything else. When he had awakened this morning, there was a certain satisfaction in knowing that for the first time in his life he was good friends with a woman other than his sister.

The holiday festivities had died down and dusk was settling over the lake. Everyone sat expectantly on the front porch waiting for darkness to fall so they could view the fireworks display that would be launched from the island. Uncle Ray placed a pitcher of Aunt Martha's fresh lemonade on the table. Aunt Martha followed with a sugar bowl from her silver service. "Come on, everyone. A glass of lemonade will refresh you," she said.

Katie leaned back in a white wicker chair and listened to the tinkling of spoons and the filling of glasses. Over on the porch swing Emma and Shorty were holding hands and whispering to each other. It was so good to see them together again. Joe and Corky took time off from setting off firecrackers to have a lemonade and then they returned to the front yard and continued to scream and yell with delight and act like they were ten years old. Katie tucked her bare feet under her white cotton summer dress. Her skin felt tingly from the hot sun and the water games had sapped her energy. She was having a great time, and now she could sit back, enjoy the glow from the day, and watch the fireworks.

"Here's your lemonade, sweetheart," Aunt Martha said, handing her a glass.

"You spoil me, Aunt Martha."

"Nonsense." Aunt Martha sat down and looked her over. "You be sure and rub yourself down with some Jergens before going to bed."

"Yes, Ma'am."

"What a lovely summer dress."

"Thanks. Mother took me shopping at Harzfelds."

"I was in there the other day trying to find something to wear," Aunt Martha said. "Every dress had Joan Crawford shoulders. I can't understand why fashion designers want women to look so unfeminine."

Katie smiled. If Aunt Martha had her way, women would be walking around in lace dresses and suffering in tight corsets.

Andy McClusky greeted Joe and Corky and walked up to the porch. He still had on his uniform.

Shorty jumped off the swing and greeted him. "Andy. It's good to see you. I didn't think you could get off work."

"Hello, everyone," Andy said.

"Get him a glass of lemonade, Egan," Aunt Martha ordered.

"Thank you, Ma'am," Andy said. "But I can't stay. Can I see you inside for a minute, Shorty?"

Emma and Katie glanced nervously at each other as Shorty followed Andy into the house. Aunt Martha put her hand on Katie's arm and gave her a gentle pat. A few minutes later Andy came out onto the porch alone. He excused himself and walked out the door. Shorty failed to appear so the girls marched into the house. They found him sitting in the kitchen, staring blankly at the wall.

"What is it, Shorty?" Katie asked.

He came out of his trance and looked at them. "It's Granny Oliver. She's passed away."

"Oh, no," Katie said, thinking about the shooting star. "Corky's going to take it hard," Shorty continued. "Granny was all the family he had."

"Do you want me to talk to him, dear?" Aunt Martha asked.

"Thanks, Aunt Martha, but this is something I have to do." Shorty got up and walked slowly out of the house.

When Corky came into the house, the girls surrounded him and offered their sympathy and support. Corky went into the bedroom to get his things.

"This couldn't have happened at a worse time," Katie said. "He's lost his granny and in a few months Shorty has to go away."

"We'll all pitch in and watch out for him," Emma said.

Shorty handled all the funeral arrangements and for the next two weeks, stayed close to Corky. When Corky refused to move in with him and Franky, they moved into Granny Oliver's house with him. It turned out to be a perfect arrangement. Corky kept Shorty and Franky in line and would not tolerate their slovenly living habits. They in turn kept him occupied, and would not let him get down in the dumps about Granny Oliver.

Summer and fall passed much too quickly for Shorty. As the days rushed by, he tried to steel himself for his December appointment with the court.

Emma walked quickly past her father's secretary and into his office. She had been to the bank only once before — for "career day" when she was a junior in high school. She had known even then that she wasn't going to join the family business, but she had pretended interest to please her father. Now she did a quick survey of his office. It was bigger than her apartment, full of expensive furniture and had oak bookshelves lining the walls. Her father sat at a large round desk in the middle of the room. He had a panoramic view of Old Town and the Missouri River.

He looked up, a smile of pleasure on his face. "Well, this is a surprise."

"Hello, Father."

"I must say that I never expected to see you here. Sit down."

She took a seat beside his desk and came right to the point. "I know about the part you played in having Shorty Callahan arrested. I'm curious to know why. What has he ever done to you?"

Her father cleared his throat. "He's not the type of person you should be associating with."

She glared at him. "You mean he's going to prison because he doesn't quite measure up?"

"Emma, you know perfectly well that it's much more serious than that. Your 'friend' is involved in criminal activities."

"Don't make him out to be a gangster. He's involved in gambling."

"Am I missing something here? I thought gambling was a criminal activity."

She leveled him with a steady gaze. "I believe I've seen you exchanging money with your friends on the golf course."

"That's different. A friendly bet is not to be confused with organized gambling."

"I'm not here to debate the fine letter of the law. Shorty has never seriously harmed anyone and he has been extremely kind to me. If he has broken the law he could do some kind of community service work to pay his debt to society rather than going to prison."

"That's up to the judge."

"You can use your influence on the court."

He leaned back in his chair and scrutinized her. "We might work something out if you will agree to stop seeing him."

"No."

"Then there is nothing more to say."

Her voice became low and intense. "I thought we had set our differences aside, but it's obvious that you're still trying to control my life."

"Someone has to," he said firmly.

"What is it about my life that is so difficult for you to accept?" she shot back.

"Only that you have no future. You can't make a living in the arts. Most artists are bums!"

"Thank you, Father."

His face reddened. "I didn't mean you personally."

"Oh, I think you did. You can't see that there's more to life than a profit-and-loss statement."

"I've made a very good living for you and the rest of the family."

She stared at him. "At what cost? Have you ever tabulated the bottom line of your personal life?"

"I think you've said quite enough, Emma."

"Not quite." She stood up. "If Shorty Callahan goes to prison, you won't be seeing me again." She turned and stalked out of his office.

The Sunday before Shorty's sentencing date, he had put his affairs in order and explained the situation to his mother. She broke down in tears and lamented all of the things she must have done wrong. It had taken her awhile to recover, but she finally accepted the fact that he was going to prison. She and Katie invited all his close friends over for a quiet Sunday gathering — a last get-together before he had to go away. All the Christmas decorations were set out so they could decorate the house and tree.

"Hand me the star, Squirt," Shorty said as he balanced himself on a chair.

Emma, Corky, and Joe were placing colorful bulbs on the tree. Scooter and McClusky sat at the kitchen table stringing popcorn while Franky and Duff placed evergreen boughs over the doors and archways. Although everyone was trying to make it a joyous occasion, Shorty knew they were just putting on an act. "Scooter, go over and turn on the radio," he said. "We need some Christmas music to liven up the party."

Katie grabbed some tinsel and started draping it on the tree. She was just going through the motions. The thought of her brother in prison had taken all the joy out of the holidays. That morning at church she had sought out Father Dugan and they had prayed together for Shorty's safe return.

"How about going to church with me this evening?" She looked hopefully at her brother.

"Are you kidding? Sally Rand is at the Tower Theatre."

He read her look of exasperation.

"Hey. It was a joke."

"I'm sorry. I guess I'm a bit on edge."

Shorty came down off the ladder and gave her a hug. "You're going to be okay."

"I wasn't worried about me."

"Hey, everyone!" Quiet down!" Joe yelled through the din of conversation. "There's some kind of bulletin coming over the radio."

There was a moment of silence and some static and then a man's voice broke in excitedly. "I repeat. There has been a Japanese attack on the island of Hawaii! There has been a Japanese attack on the island of Hawaii! Information is sketchy, but it is reported the United States naval base at Pearl Harbor has been bombed and there is great loss of life. The battleships *West Virginia* and *Oklahoma* are burning. . ."

Katie's heart was in her throat. She looked around. Everyone was frozen, staring at the radio.

"Maybe it's another 'War Of The Worlds,'" Scooter said, breaking the silence.

"Not this time, Scooter," Shorty replied as everyone came out of their trances and gathered around the radio. The announcer continued to repeat the bulletin.

"What do you think, Joe?" Shorty asked.

"I think we're at war."

"You know how unreliable these news reports are," Katie said hopefully. Her eyes met Joe's and she knew her idyllic little world had come to an end. Joe put his arms around her. "You're right. We'll just have to wait until these reports are confirmed," he said, trying to comfort her.

The next day the headline in the *Kansas City Times* read: "JAPANESE BOMBERS RAID U. S. MILITARY BASES." The Japanese had struck over a wide area of the Pacific, inflicting heavy damage on

Honolulu and at the naval base at Pearl Harbor.

The entire nation waited in nervous anticipation for President Roosevelt's speech to a joint session of Congress on December 8th.

The gang met at Katie's house and gathered around the radio for the 11:30 a.m. speech. They were also going along with Shorty to his 2 p.m. court appearance.

Katie still held out hope that somehow the President would keep them out of the war. There was talk of a negotiated settlement. She bit her lip nervously and held tightly to Joe's hand as the familiar voice of President Roosevelt came clearly, calmly, and confidently over the air waves. "Yesterday, December 7, 1941 — a date that will live in infamy — the United States of America was suddenly and deliberately attacked by the naval and air forces of the empire of Japan." Katie listened as the President told of Japanese deception and the attack on American shipping on the high seas.

"Last night Japanese forces attacked Hong Kong," the President continued. "Last night Japanese forces attacked Guam. Last night Japanese forces attacked the Philippine Islands. Last night the Japanese attacked Wake Island."

Each "last night" spoken by the President was a blow at Katie's hopes for a negotiated settlement.

"With confidence in our armed forces, with the unbounding determination of our people, we will gain the inevitable triumph. So help us God. I ask that the Congress declare that since the unprovoked and dastardly attack by Japan on Sunday, December 7, 1941, a state of war has existed between the United States and the Japanese Empire."

Joe switched off the radio. No one in the room spoke.

Shorty sat next to his lawyer, waiting for the judge to appear. The courtroom seemed stark and foreboding. He was apprehensive and he kept nervously tapping his fingers on the side of his chair. He had not only let down his family, but he was going to be in prison when his country needed him most. He had an empty feeling in the pit of his stomach and he knew the time he would spend in prison would be an eternity.

He turned and made a quick survey of the courtroom. Katie and Emma both gave him looks of encouragement. Franky and Duff gave him the thumbs up sign. Corky was at the side of the room whispering something to Joe and McClusky.

"All rise!" He stood as the white-haired judge entered the courtroom. Shorty guessed that he was near seventy. The judge sat down and everyone followed his lead. He began reviewing the case and the charges against Shorty. When he was finished he leaned back, and with a reflective look on his face took off his spectacles and began cleaning the lenses. When he was finished, he placed them carefully on the rim of his nose and surveyed the courtroom. "Mr. Callahan, do I understand that you wish to enter a plea of guilty?"

Shorty stood up. "Yes, your honor."

"Ordinarily," the judge continued, "this would be an easy case to pass judgment on. However, the events of the past few days tell us clearly that we are not living in ordinary times."

Shorty felt a glimmer of hope.

"I have here several letters of recommendations on your behalf, Mr. Callahan." The judge held them up for everyone to see. "One is from Father Dugan, the priest at your church. Another is from the McClusky family whose service to the community is well known and exemplary. Another is from an accountant named Solly Weinstein; and another from a prominent member of the banking community."

Shorty guessed that Emma had put pressure on her father, and Solly was trying to help him again.

The judge leaned over the bench and scrutinized Shorty.

"There are two underlying themes in these letters, Mr. Callahan. One is that you're not the hardened criminal the prosecution is making you out to be; and the other is that you're just the kind of young man we are going to need to win this war. Would you and your counsel approach the bench, please."

Shorty moved forward with his lawyer.

The judge took off his spectacles and rubbed his eyes.

"Mr. Callahan, I have four grandsons who are going to have to fight in this war, and that played a big part in my decision. You have a reputation as a fighter, so we're going to put that talent where it can best be served. If you are in an armed services uniform by March of this year, your sentencing will be set aside. If at the end of your military service you have an honorable discharge, this entire proceeding will be stricken from your record."

The courtroom erupted in cheers.

"And don't think I won't be checking up on you, Mr. Callahan," the judge warned.

Shorty was so relieved and happy that he just stood there dumbfounded. He was not going to prison! He was going to do what he did best, and that was to fight, and fight for his country at that. He put all protocol aside and marched up to the judge and put out his hand. "Thank you, Your

Honor. I won't let you down."

The judge shook his hand. "See that you don't, Mr. Callahan. This proceeding is closed." He banged down his gavel.

The next thing Shorty knew, Katie and Emma had their arms gleefully wrapped around him, and the rest of the gang was slapping him on the back and offering their congratulations.

12

New Year's Eve, 1941/42

The Christmas season had been a blur for Katie. The war had changed everything. All of her plans for the future were put on hold as she tried desperately to get her life in order. She was doing her best to convince Joe not to drop out of college and join the service. Shorty would be joining up soon and it might be months or even years before she saw him again. How would she ever adjust to life without the two of them!

"You seem preoccupied," Joe said.

"I have every right to be," she replied irritably. "I thought we were building a life together, and you want to run off and fight some stupid war."

"I don't have a choice."

"Everyone has a choice. Your parents are pacifists. You could become a conscientious objector."

"Oh sure. And how would I ever face anyone again? Especially your brother."

"What has my brother got to do with this?"

"Everything. What should I do? Send him off to fight the war for me?"

"There will be plenty of men to fight the war."

Joe sighed in frustration. They had been going at it like this since the President's declaration of war on Japan. "This is no longer someone else's war, Katie. Our way of life is threatened. Each of us will have to contribute something if we're going to win."

"Oh, pooh. We'll win the war with or without your help. After all, it's just Germany and Japan against the rest of the world."

"You're not even being rational. Germany is invading countries all over Europe, and Japan is crushing any resistance in the Far East. It will be up to America to stop them."

Katie turned away from him. He walked over and put his arms around her. "Hey. It's New Year's Eve. Why don't we forget about the war for awhile and enjoy ourselves."

Katie knew he was right. She was making herself and everyone around her miserable. "I'm sorry. It's just that nothing is working out the way I planned."

He kissed the back of her head. "We'll just have to put our plans on hold for awhile."

"I know I'm being selfish."

"Promise me you'll snap out of it."

"Okay. I promise. Where are we meeting the gang?"

"Under the clock at Union Station."

"Then let's go celebrate," she said, putting on a brave face.

Union Station was bustling with activity. The bright red caps of the baggage handlers bobbed everywhere as they moved briskly about the station. The lobby was packed with thousands of people who had come to celebrate New Year's Eve.

Soldiers, sailors and draftees milled about the station waiting for trains, and a group of carolers were gathered around a giant Christmas tree in the Grand Lobby, singing songs of the holiday season.

Katie scanned the area under the clock for Shorty and the gang. Beneath her, she could feel the coal-fired locomotives churning, and she could hear the doormen yelling the call to trains over the din of the crowd in the north waiting room.

"Happy New Year, Squirt." Shorty walked up and put his arms around her.

"Happy New Year," Katie said, returning the hug.

"Where is everyone?"

"Fred Harvey's restaurant. We wanted to get out of the crowd, so everyone's in the bar waiting for our reservations."

"You reserved tables?"

"Don't worry. Dinner is on me."

"Won't that be expensive?"

"It's a new world, Squirt. Why save money I might not get to spend."

Katie pulled away from him. "Don't you ever say anything like that again!"

"It was just a joke."

"Well I don't think it's anything to joke about."

Shorty glanced at Joe. Joe raised his eyebrows, advising him to leave it alone.

"Happy New Year, Joe." Shorty held out his hand and Joe shook it.

"Happy New Year to you, Shorty."

"C'mon. Let's go meet the gang," Shorty said. They followed him as he weaved his way through the lobby and into the restaurant located on the east side of the station.

Katie saw Emma waving to them from a corner of the bar. Duff, Franky, McClusky, and Corky were with her. "Happy New Year." Katie and Joe greeted everyone and sat down.

"Have you ever seen such a crush of people?" Emma asked.

"It looks like the entire city has showed up to have a good time."

"And we plan to," Shorty said as he ordered drinks for everyone.

"What did you find out at the recruiting office today?" Katie asked as she settled into a chair.

"Good news," Shorty replied."The army recruiter is a friend of mine. He advised me to wait a couple of months and he can get us all assigned to the same basic training unit. Right now the Army has all the volunteers it can process, and they're shot-gunning them all over the country."

"You're all volunteering?" Katie asked.

"It's either volunteer now, or get drafted later," McClusky said. "We want to join up together."

"That's right," Shorty said. "There's a good chance we can all be assigned to the same outfit and go overseas together."

"Why the Army?" Katie asked. And then she remembered that Pop had been in the Army.

"We want to fight," Shorty answered. "The Army gives us the best chance of getting into combat."

Katie's heart sank. She started to protest, but then remembered her promise to Joe.

"You might end up in a quiet office job," Emma said, verbally stating Katie's hopes.

"Not me," Shorty said confidently. "I'm going to kill Japs."

"That's right," Franky said. "We want to pay back those dirty bas—" Franky looked at Katie and caught himself.

"Dirty rats," Corky corrected him.

"That's right," Franky said, as everyone laughed.

It was close to midnight. The gang had broken up and gone their separate ways. Franky, Duff, and McClusky had dates with the girls at the Chesterfield Club. They never brought the girls around Katie because they knew she would disapprove. Shorty sat in the bar of Union Station's Westport Room with Katie. Corky was dancing with Emma, and Joe had gone to the restroom.

"Would you do something for me, Shorty?"

"Sure. You name it."

"Talk Joe out of going into the service."

"Come on, Squirt," Shorty said, squirming in his seat. "I can't do that."

"Oh yes you can. Joe will listen to you."

"How can I ask a man not to defend his country? It's unpatriotic."

"Nonsense. Joe can do something here at home to help the war effort."

Shorty sighed. "You know this goes against everything I stand for."

"Please, Shorty. Won't you do this one thing for me?"

He shook his head in resignation. He had never been able to refuse her anything. "All right. I'll do what I can."

Joe came back to the table and sat down. They made small talk for a few minutes and then sat for a while watching the dancers.

"What are your plans, Joe?" Shorty asked.

Joe looked at him questioningly. "What do you mean?"

"You know. The war effort. What will you do?"

"I'm joining up with you guys."

"Listen, Joe. . ."

Joe turned to Katie. "It's not going to work, so you may as well give it up."

Katie narrowed her eyes at him and leaned back in her chair in frustration.

"What's going on?" Emma asked, returning to the table with Corky.

"These two are trying to convince me not to join the service," Joe replied.

"Sounds like a reasonable request," Emma said, showing her support for Katie.

"Is that how you really feel, or are you part of the grand conspiracy?"

"It's how I feel. They will call you eventually, so why not wait until you have to go?"

"What if everyone had that attitude? Who would fight the war?"

"All of these guys who can't wait to be heroes," Emma said, pointing to the servicemen swarming all over Union Station.

"I believe that's called letting someone else do the dirty work for you. Isn't that right, Shorty?"

Shorty raised his eyebrows and took another sip of beer. He wasn't about to say anything that would upset Katie.

Joe turned to Katie. He was tired of the constant fighting. They were wasting the time they had left together. "Here's the way I see it, Katie. I can either join up with Shorty and the gang, or I can join alone. There are no other options, so you decide."

Katie looked into his light blue eyes and knew she had lost. He was making his declaration in public so there would be no backing down. As had happened so many times in her life, the only person she could rely on now was her brother.

She let out a sigh and resigned herself to the inevitable. "Then I want you to go with Shorty," she said.

"C'mon everyone," Corky said. "It's almost midnight. Let's go out into the lobby where we can see the clock."

The lobby was tightly packed with merrymakers, everyone watching the clock in eager anticipation of the New Year. Katie looked around at all the faces. They were laughing and full of gaiety. Everyone seemed determined to have a good time in spite of what tomorrow might bring. Suddenly the clock struck midnight and the station erupted in cheers and merrymaking.

"Happy New Year, Katie," Joe put his arms around her and gave her a kiss.

"Happy New Year, my darling." She held onto him with all her might as the wild celebration swirled around Union Station. After a few minutes the din subsided and it became almost quiet, as if everyone had suddenly realized the implications of the new year with the country at war.

It was then that she heard it. The song began building on the west side of the station and worked its way across the throng of people holding hands in the Grand Lobby: "Should auld ac-quaint-ance be for-got and nev-er brought to mind? Should auld ac-quaint-ance be for-got, and days of auld lang zyne? For auld — lang — zyne, my dear. . ." Katie stopped singing as she started to choke up. For the first time, she realized she was-n't alone. They were all in this together, and would have to rely on each other. She felt a real kinship to her fellow man, and she vowed that from this moment on she would make the most of every moment she had left with Joe. Her Grandmother Callahan had always said that life usually worked out for the best, so she was going to count on that and stop being a burden to everyone.

Joe squeezed her hand. "Are you okay?"

"Yes. Come on everyone," she said. "We don't have any time to waste."

"Where are we going?" Shorty asked, as he started the car.

"Home," Katie replied.

"Home? I don't want to go home. It's New Years Eve."

"Take me home," Katie insisted.

Shorty was in too good a mood to argue, so he headed the car out of the station and made a right turn up the Main Street hill. He parked the car in front of the house.

"Everyone out," Katie ordered.

They piled out into the cold night air. A full moon illuminated the house.

"Over here," Katie said, as she led them over to the giant oak tree in the front yard.

"What in the world are you doing, Squirt?" Shorty wondered.

She took Joe's hand and led him under the tree to the exact spot where she had first laid eyes on him. Everyone gathered around.

Katie paused, savoring the moment as she gazed at the night sky. The stars twinkled brightly through the branches of the oak tree. And then she had eyes only for him.

"Will you marry me, Joe?"

Joe stared at her in complete surprise.

"Katie! There's a war. . ."

"Answer my question," she said matter-of-factly. "Will you marry me?"

Joe was exasperated."Katie, our plan was. . ."

"Will you marry me?" she asked firmly.

Joe was silent for a moment. His eyes locked on hers.

"Yes," he finally said. "You bet I will." She wrapped her arms around his neck and kissed him as everyone recovered from their initial shock and offered their congratulations.

"Are you sure about this, Squirt?" Shorty asked.

"I've never been more sure of anything in my life."

"When will the wedding be?" Emma asked.

"Two weeks," Katie answered.

"Where?"

"If it's okay with Joe and his parents, the wedding will be at our church. We'll have the reception at Lake of The Forest."

"Two weeks!" Aunt Martha said in shock. "How can we possibly be ready? We hardly have time to send out the invitations!"

The look of panic on Ann Callahan's face let Aunt Martha know they had better come up with a plan. "Have you ordered a dress?"

"Well. . .no. Katie just told me yesterday. I haven't had time to do anything."

"Then we will have to buy something in stock and pray we have time for alterations. I'll make an appointment with Miss Tutwieler at Harzfelds Bridal Shop." Aunt Martha rolled her eyes to the heavens. "Oh, the impulsiveness of youth," she said in exasperation.

Ann Callahan began nervously biting her lower lip.

Aunt Martha realized she had gone too far with her concerns. She took Ann by the hand. "Oh, my dear. We women always act this way about a wedding. It's part of the ritual. We're in a state of panic right up until the last minute, but we always manage to pull it off. I promise you that Katie will have a wonderful wedding."

Ann Callahan smiled. She gave her Aunt Martha a hug. "Thank you, Aunt Martha. I knew I could count on you."

The wedding day was a flurry of activity. Katie was caught in a whirlwind of church decorations, caterers, flowers, and a hundred other things to make ready. She said a silent prayer of thanks for her mother and her Aunt Martha. As the 2 p.m. wedding drew near, she left all the details to them and concentrated on her vows. She was not the least bit nervous as she stood in the back of the church holding on to her grandfather's arm. Most of her life had been devoted to this moment and she could hardly wait to begin. Her only regret was that Pop couldn't be here. She carried a small white bible that belonged to her grandmother. Her dress was made of white silk net and trimmed in chantilly lace, and she wore her mother's finger-tip veil of bridal illusion with a tiara of chantilly lace. She could feel her Aunt Martha's elastic garter made of blue ribbons and lace pressing gently against her thigh. The bridesmaids were up ahead, giving her nervous glances of encouragement. Emma was the maid of honor. She wore a gown of pale blue net and carried a large sunburst effect of pink carnations. Marie and Judy, Katie's girlhood friends, also wore pale blue dresses and carried an assortment of carnations. Aunt Martha had worked wonders with the flowers under war-time conditions. As the wedding march began, Katie held tightly to her small white bible and cradled a single white orchid on her arm. As she started down the aisle she looked at the smiling, admiring faces of her family and friends gathered in the church. At the altar, surrounded by flowers and bathed in candlelight, Father Dugan waited with bible in hand. Shorty stood beside Joe. Katie could tell that he was taking pride in his role as best man. And Scooter looked all grown up in his role as bearer of the rings. She took it all in so she would remember every detail for the rest of her life. And then she was standing next to Joe, listening to the words of Father Dugan. As she faced Joe and repeated her vows she felt a real sense of satisfaction and gratitude that her girlhood dreams had come true, and when Father Dugan pronounced them man and wife she was so happy that she beamed and then she kissed Joe tenderly on the lips.

The reception had been going on for three hours, and everyone was having a grand time. The wedding had rescued family and friends from the winter doldrums and the worry of war. Champagne was flowing, and the dance floor was packed with young couples keeping the beat of the boogie woogie.

Outside, a snowstorm was building in intensity. Through the picture window of the clubhouse Katie could see snow squalls swirling across the lake.

"We had better get out of here if we're going to make it to Arizona," Joe said.

"Okay. You can tell Shorty to bring the car around."

A few minutes later Shorty gave the signal that all was ready.

Katie rounded up everyone in the gang and led them to a spot in front of the roaring fireplace. She put her arms around Emma and they held each other for a moment.

She hugged and kissed all the boys. "Joe and I love you, and we want to thank you for everything," she said. She took Scooter aside and assured him that he was not losing Joe and that he would always be a part of their family.

Joe kissed Emma and shook hands with all the guys.

"Let's go," Shorty said. "The car is running."

At the front door of the clubhouse Katie hugged her mother and Aunt Martha. "Thank you both for everything."

"Have a wonderful time," her mother said through her tears. And then Katie was facing her brother. "How can I ever thank you enough?"

Shorty reached into his pocket and discreetly slipped her an envelope. "Some dough for your honeymoon," he said.

"I couldn't possibly. You've paid for the reception," she whispered.

"Just take it and have a good time," he said.

She put her arms around him. "I love you, Shorty."

"Yeah, yeah. Now get out of here before you get snowed in," he said.

As they ran to the car, rice and confetti mixed with the swirling snow and rained down on them. They yelled their good-byes and jumped in the car.

"Have a wonderful time, Katie! Good-bye, Joe! Drive carefully!" Joe put the car in gear and Katie rolled down the window and continued to wave as they drove away. The tin cans behind the car were partially muffled by the snow.

"I don't know how far we're going to get in this stuff," Joe said, peering through the windshield.

"Stop when you get across the bridge," Katie said softly. "We'll remove the tin cans from the back of the car."

The snow was cascading down as they both got out and removed the cans from the back bumper. They threw them in a trash bin and jumped back in the car.

"Now turn the car around," Katie said.

"What?"

"Turn the car around. We're not going to Arizona. At least for a few days."

"You're kidding. I thought we. . ."

"Would you rather be in Uncle Ray's cabin with me, or out on the highway fighting a snowstorm?"

"You're not only beautiful, but resourceful. How are we going to pull it off?"

"Uncle Ray is a co-conspirator. When the coast is clear he will wave a lantern from the clubhouse porch. Everyone will be inside out of the storm. We'll just be another pair of headlights passing in the night."

Joe leaned over and kissed her. "You're wonderful."

"Thank you. I've waited most of my life to be with you and I don't intend to wait a moment longer."

He kissed her again. Katie kept one eye on the porch.

A few minutes later the light of a lantern slowly moved back and forth at the clubhouse.

"There it is!" Katie said.

Joe pushed on the gas pedal and they drove back across the bridge and through the gate. The party was in full swing as they came abreast of the clubhouse and slipped past.

"We made it!" Katie said, letting out a sigh of relief. Joe headed the car for the upper lake.

"Who knows about this?" he asked.

"Just Uncle Ray and Aunt Martha. They will tell Mother later tonight so she won't worry about us driving in the snow. We'll park the car in the garage where Uncle Ray keeps his canoe and fishing gear."

Joe glanced over at her. "Are you nervous?"

"A bit. How about you?"

"More excited than nervous."

"Me too."

They parked the car in the garage, grabbed their suitcases, and headed up the hill through the falling snow.

"Isn't the snow beautiful, Joe?"

"Yes. It's a wonderful setting for a wedding night." They set their suitcases down on the porch and he opened the door. "Welcome home, Mrs. Wilson." She let out a yelp of delight as he picked her up and carried her into the cabin. A warm fire was burning in the fireplace.

"Uncle Ray is so thoughtful," she said. They took off their coats and scarves. "You look like a fairy princess with your hair covered in snow," he said. He pulled her to him and kissed her. "Your nose is cold."

She laughed and kissed him back.

They held each other tightly, enjoying the warmth of the fire.

"I'm trying to slow down," he whispered.

"I know. So am I."

He retrieved the suitcases and they started exploring the cabin.

"Look in here," Katie said, pointing to the cupboards. "We have a week's worth of food." They both nervously moved about the cabin, making small talk, and eventually ended up in the bedroom. He pulled her to him and held her close. "I've waited so long for this moment that I don't know how to begin."

She began taking the pins from her hair. "I'm going to get ready in by the fire." She carefully extracted the white lace negligee from her suitcase and went into the other room.

The fire was crackling as she slipped the negligee over her head and let it fall softly onto her shoulders. It made her feel feminine and special and added to the anticipation of the moment. Firelight was dancing off the walls as she entered the bedroom.

Joe stared at her in awe. "You are so beautiful," he said, reaching his hand out to her.

"So are you, my darling." She took his hand and they climbed into bed. When they were under the covers, they kissed and fondled each other until they could wait no more. "I always knew it would be wonderful, but I had no idea," she whispered. "I love you, Joe."

"I love you too, Katie."

Outside, the wind had died down and snow was falling gently on the roof of the cabin.

The band had played the final song, and departed. The last of the merrymakers said their good-byes and Uncle Ray turned off the ballroom lights. Shorty and the gang watched as he locked the front door of the clubhouse. They were having too much fun to give up the party. "I wonder if anything is open in town," Shorty said.

"You're not going to town in that condition," Uncle Ray said. In the glow of the porch lights he looked into the youthful faces surrounding him and felt a touch of sadness. This might be the last party for these young men and women in a very long time. They were going off to war and only God knew what would happen to them. He looked out on the lake. It had been frozen solid for two weeks. "You do know what this is a perfect night for, my boy."

Shorty looked at him questioningly.

"We haven't had one for ages and you use to love them," Uncle Ray said.

"A skating party!" Shorty said excitedly. "What a great idea."

"You go up to the cove and get a bonfire started," Uncle Ray commanded. "I'll take Emma up to the house and get her something warm to put on. I'm sure we have enough ice skates for everyone, but do we have enough anti-freeze?"

Shorty patted his coat pocket. "We have an ample supply, but you might want to bring some schnapps."

"Come on, Emma. There's not a moment to waste."

The gang had brushed snow off the glaze of ice. Shorty was skating back and forth in a wide arc, in and out of the light of the bonfire. He had worked up a sweat and had shed his coat.

"Hey. You're really good," Emma said.

He skated up next to her. "My ice-skating is not bad either," he teased her.

"Ha, ha. You do look awfully handsome in that tuxedo," she said seductively. She grabbed the scarf around his neck and held on as they began ice dancing across the lake.

"You're not bad yourself," he said.

"Watch out, Sonja Henie," she replied.

It was his turn to laugh.

Over on the bank of the cove, Uncle Ray was deep in his schnapps as he told stories of the old days to the boys gathered around the campfire.

"It was a beautiful wedding," Emma said.

"Yes. Why don't you marry me and we'll have a wedding of our own."

"Because that wouldn't be fair to either one of us."

"Joe and Katie didn't feel that way."

"We are not Joe and Katie."

He made a turn with his skates and came to an abrupt halt. "What's that supposed to mean?"

"Joe and Katie have had a long-term commitment."

"And we haven't? I wonder whose fault that is."

"I know. And I accept full responsibility."

He pulled her close and kissed her on the lips. "I love you, Emma. Let's get married."

She pulled away from him. "The judge was right, Callahan. It's going to take people like you to win this war. If you're spending your time pining after me, you won't make a very good soldier."

"So you're turning me down to help the war effort."

She smiled wryly. "Something like that."

"I guess that means you won't be waiting for me when I get back."

"I think it best not to make promises that circumstances might not allow us to keep. I have a feeling that it's going to be a long war."

"And when it's over and I come home, you'll probably be married to a doctor or a lawyer and settled down in Mission Hills."

"Not likely, but not impossible. Why do you think so little of my staying power?"

"Because you're a free spirit."

"And you're a dedicated family man, aren't you Callahan?"

"I could be, if I had you."

She melted for a moment and put her arms around his neck.

They held each other tightly as the snow fell gently on the frozen lake.

"Hey! You guys cut that out!" Corky yelled from the bonfire. "You're going to melt the ice!"

Shorty and Emma skated over to join everyone at the bonfire.

13

T he ten weeks after the honeymoon were the happiest of Katie's life. She and Joe had moved in with her mother. They had all agreed that it would be pointless to spend the money on a place of their own with Joe going in the service. It was a perfect solution; with Shorty gone they had the entire upstairs to themselves, although they had to share a downstairs bathroom with her mother and her grandfather. Katie thought it magical that she could sleep with Joe in the same room she had grown up in. It was such a wonderful feeling to wake up in the middle of the night and know that he was beside her. In the morning, after her mother left for work and her grandfather went to work in his "Victory Garden," she and Joe would share the bathroom. It gave them time to talk and plan the day before their first class.

They had both taken part-time jobs at the Post Office to help pay their room and board. Katie sorted mail and Joe loaded mail trucks. When the work day was finished they rushed home to help prepare dinner for the family. After the evening meal, everyone gathered around the radio to listen to the latest war news. In the Far East the Japanese Empire continued its relentless march south into Indochina and the East Indies, and in Europe Nazi Germany reigned supreme over the entire continent. Only Britain stood alone under the blitz of German bombs. In the spring of 1942 the shadow of the war loomed menacingly over the lives of all Americans.

For the sake of decorum, Katie and Joe would hang around downstairs for a few hours before retiring to the upstairs. With the daily routine, their marriage was setting a pattern. Katie felt that if the war would just go away, her life would be perfect. She said a prayer every night for a quick victory by the Allies and she refused to listen to any talk of Joe's departure, convincing herself that something would happen to end the war. Joe, Shorty, and the rest of the gang had already signed up to join the Army. The recruiter was just waiting for the right slot so he could send them all together.

Katie and Joe sat on the porch swing. The dogwood trees and flowers were in full bloom. A light rain was falling.

"Smell the flowers," Katie said, as she breathed in the evening air. "Isn't spring wonderful? We have to plant lots of flowers when we have a home of our own."

"And a couple of dogwood trees," Joe said.

"And of course I have to have my very own oak tree."

"Only if you promise not to live in it. The neighbors might talk."

"I'll try not to be an embarrassment to you."

"Here comes your brother," Joe said, as he recognized Shorty's car coming up the street.

"What's he doing here on a Saturday?" Katie wondered.

Shorty parked the car. He climbed out and ran through the falling rain onto the porch.

"What brings you back to the old homestead on a rainy Saturday morning?" Katie asked.

"Just checking on the newlyweds," he said, brushing the rain from his hair. "It looks like you're getting settled in."

"That's right," Katie confirmed. "So I hope you're not here to claim your old room."

"That's just like a woman: beg me to stay and then refuse to take me back when I leave."

"Poor baby," Katie sympathized. She got off the swing and gave him a hug. "You know you can come back any time you like."

"Thanks, but I'm afraid my roommates couldn't get along without me."

"How's Emma?" Katie asked. "We haven't seen her for a while."

"That's because you two never leave home."

Katie blushed.

"We'll all go to the show sometime soon," she said.

She looked at Shorty in concern. He seemed uncomfortable and it wasn't like him to stand around and make small talk. She sat back down next to Joe with every intention of quizzing him.

"I'd better get going," Shorty said.

"Going? You just got here." She was aware that he wouldn't look at her.

"Could I see you alone for a minute, Joe?" he asked.

Katie read her brother's expression and her heart sank. She squeezed Joe's hand. "Whatever you have to say, you can say to both of us," she said, dreading what she might hear.

Shorty hesitated, wondering how to begin. "I heard from the Army recruiter today. We have our orders."

Katie had steeled herself for this moment, but the words still left her breathless and unable to speak.

"Where are we going?" Joe asked.

"Fort Warren. It's in Cheyenne, Wyoming."

"When will we be leaving?"

"Next Saturday."

"What time?"

"We meet at Union Station at 5 p.m."

Shorty turned to leave. He paused for a moment and looked back at his sister. "I'm sorry, Squirt."

Katie recovered her tongue. "No you're not," she said hatefully. "You can hardly wait to leave and go fight your stupid war."

"Come on, Katie," Joe said. "That isn't fair."

Katie bit on her lower lip as it started to quiver. "I'm sorry, Shorty. I didn't mean that."

"I know you didn't."

Katie stood up and hugged her brother. He returned the hug. "I'd better go tell Emma," he said.

The next week was frustrating for Katie. She vowed to savor every moment with Joe, but time proved elusive, and their precious moments slipped quickly away. By mid-week she was a nervous wreck, so she sought out Father Dugan at Wednesday mass. He encouraged her to be more supportive of the war effort and the personal sacrifice Joe was making for the country, and he suggested that she concentrate on helping others and leave to God the things she could not control. Her talks with Father Dugan always made her feel better. He had even agreed to come to Union Station on Saturday evening to see the boys off.

She slept fitfully on Friday night with her arms wrapped tightly around Joe, afraid that if she let go for a moment she would wake up and he would be gone. The bedroom clock seemed to mock her as it ticked away the seconds until his departure. When the dawn broke, she propped herself up on one elbow and studied his face, recording every nuance, so she would remember it in the lonely nights ahead.

He stirred and opened his eyes. "Did you sleep at all?" he asked as he yawned himself awake.

"Like a baby," she replied.

"Liar."

He pulled her to him and held her tight. "We'll always be together, Katie."

"I know. Time and distance can never separate us."

He rolled over on top of her and kissed her on the neck. "I may have another together in mind."

She giggled and kissed him back.

"Maybe we should spend the day in bed," he suggested.

"Can't. We have to go see Scooter and your parents. We can be together some more this afternoon."

"I love you, Katie."

She closed her eyes and hugged him back, praying that she would be brave for him and not fall apart. "I love you too, my darling."

Emma slowly awakened. She uncurled herself from Shorty and looked at the clock. "Come on, sleepy head," she shook him. "Time to wake up. It's almost three o'clock."

He reached for her and she laughingly slipped away.

"You said our last afternoon together would be memorable and you were right," he said. "I can hardly move."

"You'd better get some energy, soldier. Haven't you heard there's a war on?"

Shorty looked at her reflectively. "I'm going to miss you, Emma."

"After that effort, I would certainly hope so."

"You're not going to be serious even for a moment, are you?"

"What's there to be serious about?"

"We might not see each other for a very long time."

She got up and started putting on her clothes. "Would you feel better if I wept and begged you not to go?"

"No. That would be too much out of character."

"Careful, Callahan. I sense a fight brewing."

"You will promise to write?"

"Of course."

"And you'll keep an eye on Katie?"

"Yes."

Satisfied, he crawled out of bed and started putting on his clothes. "I guess it's time for me to go win the war," he said, with an air of cockiness.

She put her arms around him. "Now there's the Shorty Callahan I'm going to miss."

Joe stood looking out the window of his boyhood home on Union Hill. The dogwood trees made a splash of color above the green of Union Cemetery. At the Liberty Memorial a line of people waited to ride the elevator to the top of memorial tower. The bell in the steeple of Our Lady Of Sorrows Church began ringing the call to Saturday mass. Joe took it all in so he would remember every detail.

Scooter burst into the room.

"Katie says it's time to go, Joe."

"Okay."

Scooter stood silently beside his brother, taking in the view. "Katie is going to miss you," he finally said.

Joe glanced over at him, knowing what he was really trying to say.

"You'll check on her for me?"

"Sure."

"You can talk to Katie while I'm gone, Scooter. She would like that a lot."

He considered. "Katie's nice, but she can't play ball."

"No, but she can be a good friend, so I hope you will give her a chance." He put his arm around Scooter. "We'll write to each other and I'll be back before you know it."

"Okay, Joe."

He glanced one last time out the window and then he and Scooter headed down the stairs.

Their mother was putting on a brave face, but Joe could tell she had been crying. "I'll be okay, Mom." He hugged her and then he shook hands with his father.

"Although we don't agree with your decision to join the service, Joe, we are proud of you for standing up for your convictions."

"Thanks Dad. I'm proud of you and Mom for standing up for yours." He took Katie's hand and headed for the door. "We'll meet you under the clock at Union Station."

Katie and Joe sat on one of the straight-back oak benches in the north waiting room of Union Station. The family members of all the boys had gathered to say their good-byes. Katie took Joe by the hand and they walked over to an empty corner of the station where they could have some privacy.

"You promise to write every day," she said.

"I promise."

"I'll keep you up to date on everything that's happening here."

"And you'll check on Scooter and my parents?"

"Yes."

"And all the news from Lake Forest?"

"Every detail."

The moment Katie was dreading arrived much too soon. The doorman in charge of the gate came to the top of the stairs. He was dressed in a black suit and wore a station master's cap. In a loud, deep voice he called out the train that would be taking Joe away. Joe put his arms around her and held her tight. "I love you, Katie."

I'm not going to cry," she said.

"I know. Tomboys never cry."

"I love you with all my heart, Joe Wilson." They separated as Shorty walked over with Corky. He gave her a hug. "I'm going to miss you, Squirt."

She held tightly to him for a moment. Images of their childhood raced through her head. She turned to Corky. "You see that he behaves himself."

Corky hugged her. "You take care of yourself Katie." He stepped back. "If you have time, will you check on the house? You can use it whenever you want."

"I'll go by once a week without fail."

Scooter walked up to Shorty. "See ya, Shorty. Don't forget my Jap souvenir."

Shorty rubbed the top of Scooter's Cardinal baseball cap. "Keep after those ground balls, Scooter." And then Emma was in his arms. "This town is going to be awfully dull without you, Callahan."

"Is that your way of saying you're going to miss me?"

He gave her a long, lingering kiss. "Don't you dare get married while I'm gone," he said.

"I'm the no-commitment girl, remember?"

The boys were having a hard time separating themselves from their loved ones. Shorty had to get them going or they would miss the train. "All right, you guys! Let's get going!" he ordered. "They ain't going to win this war without us!"

Katie spotted Father Dugan making his way through the crush of people. She rushed over to greet him and then led him to the gate where the boys had gathered.

"Hello, Father," Shorty greeted him with a handshake. He had gone by the church last month and thanked Father Dugan for writing the letter to the court.

"Hello, Shorty." Father Dugan motioned with his hands for all the boys to gather round. "If I can be of any help to you on this end, just write me. He paused for a moment, searching the faces of the young men. "You're embarking on a long and dangerous journey. Always remember that God and your loved ones are with you in spirit."

Katie knew she had better speak up before Shorty bolted for the stairs. "Will you give them your blessing, Father?"

Father Dugan nodded. He waited until everyone had bowed their heads. "May God be your protector — be at your side in times of trial." He held up his right hand over the heads of the young men. "May almighty God bless you — the Father — the Son — and the Holy Spirit."

"Thank you, Father," Katie said. She turned to Joe for one last embrace. They held each other tightly. Katie clung to him and would not let go. He firmly separated her arms from around his neck and kissed her gently on the lips. She reached for him, but he moved away through the crowd. He stood with Shorty at the top of the stairs, gave one last wave, and then he was gone.

Katie just stood there, numbly looking at the empty gate. She looked so sad and forlorn that Emma came over to comfort her. "I'm sure they will get some leave time, soon," she said.

Katie nodded.

"Tell you what," Emma continued. "My father still owes me many acts of contrition for interfering in my personal life. He can pay the phone bill when we make our weekly call to Cheyenne, Wyoming."

Katie looked at her hopefully. "I'll be able to talk to Joe?"

"Every Sunday without fail," Emma promised.

"Oh, Emma," Katie hugged her gratefully.

Rita and the other girls from the Chesterfield Club were stuck behind a VFW parade that had blocked the south-bound streets to Union Station.

"I told you we should have left earlier," Peggy scolded. "We're going to miss the train."

Rita gunned the engine as the last float went past, and headed down Grand Avenue to the station. She parked the car in a spot reserved for taxis and they all ran inside. In the north waiting room they were informed by a doorman that the train was pulling out.

"Where's the first stop?" Rita asked.

"That's a troop train lady. It ain't stopping for nobody."

"The hell it ain't," Rita said. She and the girls rushed past the astonished doorman and down the steps to the train sheds. When they arrived a porter pointed out the train as it was leaving the station.

"Damn!" Peggy said.

"What was the engine number?" Rita asked frantically.

"Beats me," the porter answered. He read the look of distress on Rita's face. "Hold on a minute," he said. "Leon knows every engine that comes through here. Hey Leon!" he called to another porter. "What was the engine number on that troop train?"

Leon walked over. "Number 299," he said. "It's one of the few 2-8-4 steam locomotives that come through here. The government uses them for troop trains because they're fast and they don't break down."

His explanation was lost on the girls, who were already running back up the stairs.

It took a hair-raising ride in Rita's convertible and a visual search of several trains before Rita finally caught up with engine #299 just west of Topeka, Kansas. They were on a straight, flat stretch of highway that ran adjacent to the railroad tracks. The young recruits on the train were leaning out the window and whistling and yelling at the girls.

"It's time to do your number, Mae!" Rita shouted above the train noise and the wind.

"Number?" Mae questioned.

"Start taking it off! How do you think we're going to stop engine #299!"

"You're kidding!"

"You've always said those tits will stop traffic! Let's see if they'll stop a train!"

The challenge appealed to Mae. She had never worked this big an audience. As the boys on the train continued to shout and whistle, she stood up in the back seat and seductively shook her breasts at the speeding train. Windows went up in all 12 cars and heads started popping out everywhere. Mae started slowly unbuttoning her blouse as the troops shouted their enthusiastic encouragement. She braced her leg against the back of the front seat to keep her balance. She was used to dancing on precarious table tops, so the motion of the car was not a problem.

"For God's sake! Will you hurry up!" Rita shouted. "We're going to be in Denver before you get your knockers out!"

But Mae had her audience and she was not about to be rushed. With the expertise of a pro, her blouse magically disappeared, and the troops went wild. She reached behind her and teasingly acted like she was going to unsnap her bra. The boys on the train were reduced to pleading and begging as Mae seductively pursed her lips and blew them kisses. She teased them for another few minutes and then she let her bra fall free. Her huge upturned breasts jiggled with every bump in the highway and the troops went berserk.

Corky was sitting next to Joe. They were both quietly musing about their departure and what the future might hold. Shorty and the other guys had already organized a poker game in the car ahead. Corky moved over to the other side of the train to see what all the commotion was about. He squeezed into a place by the window, peered out at the speeding car and instantly recognized Mae. He would never forget those bare breasts from the night swim that summer at Lake Forest. He immediately ran to get Shorty.

When Shorty and the gang made it to a window, Mae had her skirt off and was seductively bent over moving her bottom at her appreciative audience. They were begging her with shouts and gestures to pull down her panties. She wagged her finger at them like they were naughty boys, and that made them beg all the more.

"Okay!" It's time to make our move," Rita shouted. "If they want to see it — they have to earn it. Motion for them to pull the emergency cord."

Mae and Peggy started pointing to the spot on Mae's anatomy the troops wanted to see and then making a gesture with their arms to show they wanted the emergency cord pulled. It took several repetitions, but the troops finally got the picture and someone pulled the cord. When Mae heard the train brakes go on she frantically started putting her clothes back on.

Rita knew they only had a few minutes before the porter figured out what had happened and got the train moving again. She quickly pulled the car off the road. The girls got out and ran up to the train.

"Hey baby! Get on board!" one of the troops shouted. "Show it to us, sweetie!" another said. "You promised!" All the troops started shouting for more.

Rita motioned for them to be quiet. "Okay, you naughty boys!" she shouted. "We'll give you what you want, but first you have to find Shorty Callahan for us."

The troops started frantically shouting Shorty's name up and down the train.

A few moments later Shorty and the gang jumped off the train and ran up to the girls. There were hugs and kisses all around. The girls paid special attention to Duff and Corky because they knew the boys had no family to see them off.

Rita wrapped her arms around Shorty. "We've had some fun times, Callahan."

Shorty kissed her. "Promise me you'll be faithful until I come home."

Rita laughed. "About as faithful as you're going to be."

She became serious for a moment. "You take care of yourself. I don't want anything happening to you, even if you did dump me for that college girl."

"We'll always be friends, Rita."

"I know. That's why I'm here. Will you write to me?"

"Every day," Shorty said with a mischievous grin on his face.

Rita laughed again. "I love it when you lie to me, Callahan."

The train whistle sounded.

"Time to go," Shorty said. "This was a great send-off, Rita. I'm going to miss you."

"You get back on the train and I'll show you what you're going to miss," Rita replied. There were shouts of envy from the troops as Shorty and the gang were smothered in good-bye kisses from the girls. They reluctantly separated themselves and jumped back on the train.

The girls ran back to the car. Rita climbed into the backseat and Mae took over the wheel.

"Let's give these boys a send off they won't forget," Rita said. The train whistle sounded and the train lurched ahead.

Mae started the car and moved it slowly ahead. Rita turned away from the troops and started moving her bottom in rhythm with each chug of the steam engine. As the engine picked up speed so did her bottom and the troops went crazy. With the expertise of an experienced stripper she made an exaggerated move and her skirt fell off, exposing a tiny pair of red panties. The troops let out a collected groan of appreciation. Rita bent over and started slowly and seductively to roll down her panties. She could tell from the silence on the train that she had them collectively holding their breaths, so she tantalized them unmercifully.

The silver dollar girl knew how to work an audience, so she would halt the progression of the red panties until they pleaded for more. To the delight of the troops she had finally worked her panties down until just a sliver of red covered the object of their interest. Rita started nodding her head; asking the troops if they wanted more. The troops starting chanting: "yes — yes — yes." Rita shook her head in the negative and rolled up her panties. She was greeted with a collective chorus of boos.

"Speed up the car," she said. "We'll meet the train up ahead."

Mae hit the gas and the car sped about a mile ahead of the train. The troops had their heads craned out the window, searching for the girls.

"Stop the car up ahead in the bend of the road," Rita ordered. She had picked a spot close to the tracks.

Shorty and the gang were taking some heat from the other troops about the abbreviated strip show when the train whistle went on and continued unabated. A huge roar went up from the west side of the train and everyone scrambled to a window.

The convertible was parked next to the railroad tracks. In their best Vargas Girl poses. Rita, Mae, and Peggy were standing with their naked backsides exposed to the train. Each of the girls had a high-heeled foot propped up on the running board of the convertible and they were bent over in a fashion that left nothing to the imagination of the troops. As each car of the train rolled past, some of the young men yelled and moaned with delight, and others just stared with their mouths open in wide-eyed appreciation. As the last car rumbled past, Rita and the girls waved and blew kisses to the young men going off to war.

The incident with the girls made heroes of Shorty and the gang. By the time they reached Fort Warren they had made a lot of new friends. It didn't take long for news of the incident to spread around training camp, and within a week everyone knew that Shorty was a man to be reckoned with. He became fast friends with several of the training sergeants and he was never given the menial tasks like KP or guard duty that were required of most recruits. After the first two weeks he was promoted to squad leader, and then to platoon leader. He had a natural ability when it came to soldiering; everything seemed to come easily for him. He became an expert marksman with the Springfield rifle, although Duff scored higher on the rifle range, and he was always the last one left standing on the field of calisthenics or after a forced march. He just never seemed to wear out. He was good at military tactics and strategy, and he welcomed all challenges. It was obvious to his superiors that he loved soldiering, and within a month he was made an acting sergeant. Franky and the other guys relied on Shorty. He had been their leader in civilian life, so it seemed perfectly natural for his role to continue in the service. He also kept a watchful eye on Joe. The first couple of weeks Joe was down because he missed Katie so much. Shorty found the solution was to give him just enough time to write letters and then keep him busy. Joe was assigned more extra duty than anyone because Shorty didn't want him lying around feeling sorry for himself. With his R.O.T.C. background, and under Shorty's tutelage,

Joe was becoming a very good soldier.

Corky was the exact opposite; everything about soldiering was a struggle. He would probably be drummed out of the service if not for Shorty. The straps on his backpack were a never-ending puzzle, and during close order drills, he was forever trying to keep in step with the rest of the company. The first time he fired the Springfield rifle from the squatting position the weapon kicked him backwards and he ended up flat on his back looking at the sky. The rifle was heavy and cumbersome and he was constantly bruising his thumb trying to close the bolt. He could break the weapon down to clean it, but putting it back together was a challenge. And he hated getting out of bed before the sun came up. He referred to reveille as the bugle from hell. Shorty would pull the covers off him every morning and help him get ready to face the day. And Corky had his nemesis: a soldier from New York City named Bo Brainar who was constantly giving him a hard time about his shortcomings as a soldier. He had to line up every morning next to Bo in the back of the formation. Bo was a cocky, former light heavyweight in the Golden Gloves, and he loved to intimidate people. In the back row of the formation he could torment Corky away from the watchful eye of Shorty and the other guys. In a match of wits, Bo was no contest for Corky, and to the delight of the troops, Bo was losing the verbal battles taking place in the back row of the platoon. Bo's pet name for Corky was Curlylocks. Corky retaliated by calling Bo, No Brainar. By the fifth week of training camp Bo's inability to intimidate Corky and the daily losses in the battle of wits were wearing on him.

It was on a Monday, the fourth week of training camp, that everything came to a head. The troops had returned from their first one-day pass in Cheyenne. Most of them had stayed out all night and had to drag themselves to the company formation with a hangover. Shorty was no exception. He stood in front of the formation with his platoon sergeant, quietly nursing a swollen head and waiting for the first sergeant to arrive. Behind him the troops were mumbling and grumbling in the half light of the new day. Bo stood next to Corky in the back row. "Did you get laid last night, Curlylocks?" he challenged.

Corky had a bit of a hangover himself, and was in no mood to put up with Bo. "What business is that of yours, No Brainar."

"That means you struck out, Curlylocks. Me, I had all the pussy I could handle."

"Where did you happen upon the flock of sheep?" Corky asked.

Bo noticed the shoulders on the troops in front of him start to shake.

"Don't push your luck, Curlylocks. You're makin' my head hurt."

"How's that possible? Your head is empty."

Bo heard the laughter from the other troops and in a flash of anger he hit Corky in the side of the head with a straight right hand. Corky's helmet liner went flying and he fell to the ground in a heap. He shook his head, trying to clear away the stars.

Shorty and the platoon sergeant were in the back row in an instant.

"What happened here?" the sergeant asked.

Corky shook his head and rose to his feet. "Sorry, Sergeant. I stumbled. I had too much to drink last night."

Bo smiled wryly. He was afraid he was going to be in big trouble, but Curlylocks knew better than to rat on him.

"Bo punched him in the head," one of the troops said.

"He what?" Shorty looked at Bo and then back at the soldier.

"He sucker-punched him," another soldier said.

Shorty was in Bo's face. "You hit him?" he asked in disbelief.

Bo remained silent. Shorty shoved him backwards out of the formation. "How would you like to hit me, Bo?"

"I'd like that, Callahan. If you weren't hiding behind those phony sergeant's stripes."

Shorty pulled the band of stripes from around his upper arm and handed them to the platoon sergeant.

The first sergeant walked up. He was a grizzled, no-nonsense, World War 1 veteran named Balino. "What's going on here, Sergeant?"

"These two are looking for a fight."

"We'll settle this later," Balino said gruffly.

"Let's settle it right now," Shorty said hotly.

Balino paused thoughtfully. The troops needed some excitement to counter the Monday morning doldrums.

"Not a bad idea, Callahan. We can settle it the Army way and save me and the company commander some paperwork. Get back in formation." The first sergeant went to the head of the company. He called them to attention, gave them a right-face command, and marched them away from the company area. He called them to a halt near some abandoned barracks.

"Callahan and Brainar! Fall out!"

Shorty and Bo went to the front of the company.

"These two idiots can't wait for the Japs and Germans, so they decided to fight each other," Balino said. "The loser of this fight has KP every day for a week, and the winner has a week of guard duty. There will be no fighting in this company unless I say so!" Balino turned back to the combatants. He was an old China hand and had seen his share of brawling. "No kicking, biting, or gouging," he ordered.

Shorty squared off with Bo. He had sized up his opponent and planned his strategy. Bo was six inches taller and twenty pounds heavier. Shorty knew he would have to attack quickly and work from the inside, or Bo would cut him to pieces with hooks and jabs. Bo shuffled his feet, and to confirm Shorty's assessment he flicked a left jab that caught Shorty above the eye. Shorty circled him menacingly as Bo continued to back away and hit him with flicking left jabs. The punches hurt, and the areas above Shorty's eyes were starting to swell. Bo was gaining more confidence with each jab and a smirk creased his face as he lashed out at Shorty's head. Shorty took a few more jabs until he had Bo backed into an area where the barracks formed a V. Bo realized he had his back against the barracks and tried to shuffle away, but Shorty had staked out his territory, and when Bo violated the space Shorty attacked him in a fury. He hit Bo with a vicious right hand and knocked him back against the barracks. Shorty stayed low to the ground and punished Bo with lefts and rights to the body. When Bo tried to cover up with his elbows, Shorty hit him with a left hook to the side of the head. Bo hit the barracks with a thud. He would have gone down, but Shorty was once again inside, holding him up and punishing him with lefts and rights to the body. Bo was grunting with each blow to his ribs. He went into a crouch to protect himself. Shorty hit him with an upper-cut that broke his nose. Bo covered his face with his left arm and Shorty gave him another wicked shot to the ribs and Bo hit the barracks again. Shorty moved in relentlessly. He reached back to throw another punch, but he was jumped from behind by Balino and another sergeant.

"That's enough, Callahan!" Balino shouted. Shorty tried to throw another punch, but Balino had him firmly by the arm. They both watched as Bo slid down the wall of the barracks and collapsed to the ground.

"Save the rest for the Japs, Callahan," Balino ordered.

14

Katie was miserable the first week Joe was gone. She could hardly wait for Sunday to come so they could talk on the telephone. Their first conversation had helped a lot. Joe had told her the only way either of them would survive the separation was to pitch in and help win the war as quickly as possible. She knew he was right, so she quit her job at the Post Office and started working part time at the North American Aircraft Factory in the Fairfax District. North American was building the B 25 airplane.

She also kept a full load at school, and by the time she finished studying and crawled into bed it was usually close to midnight. The only way she could alleviate the loneliness was to work herself to exhaustion. And it was the first time in her life that she hadn't been able to rely on Shorty. His absence made her realize how much she had depended on him. Her only recreation was an occasional movie with Marie and Judy, but these outings always made her wish she was with Joe. She had lunch with Emma every Sunday, and also made it a point to see Joe's parents and Scooter as often as possible. She volunteered her remaining time to several collection committees and she coordinated the waste paper drive by Scooter's Boy Scout troop. The city had geared up for war production, and nothing seemed too inconsequential to save: old tires for use in gas masks, stockings to make powder bags for naval guns, papers for packing cartons, baking grease for ammunition, even old tin cans and tooth paste tubes were being used in the war effort. It was a national sin to discard anything that might be used by the armed forces. Katie was determined to do her part to help bring the boys home as soon as possible.

On the last day of training camp, Shorty was in the barracks with the rest of the gang waiting for word of their destination. He feared they might be split up and sent to separate duty stations. The gang had learned a lot about soldiering these past eight weeks, and they were ready to fight. Duff was an expert marksman and he took to soldiering from day one. Franky bitched a lot about Army life, and bemoaned the fact that he wasn't home chasing skirts and having fun, but when he wanted to, Franky could soldier with anyone. McClusky made the smoothest transition from civilian life. He had an easy-going Irish temperament and his training as a police officer was a natural lead into the military lifestyle. Joe was a picture of quiet determination as he went about the daily business of soldiering. He was a quick learner and he took on every task as if its completion would help end the war. And then there was Corky. Shorty wondered if he would ever get the hang of military life. Everyone in the gang pitched in and helped him out.

Sergeant Morrales entered the barracks. "Callahan! The first sergeant wants to see you in the orderly room!"

Shorty grabbed his cap and headed out the door, eager to learn his fate. Balino had his head down, going over a stack of papers. He was of medium height with broad shoulders and a massive chest. His nose was large and flat and he had bushy black eyebrows set above light blue eyes that seemed to take in everything.

"Sit down, Callahan." Balino put his pen down and scrutinized Shorty. "How do you like this man's army?"

"I didn't know I had a choice."

Balino smiled wryly. "If you had a choice between infantry, artillery, or armor, what would you choose?"

"Infantry," Shorty said.

"Why the infantry?"

"I want to see combat."

Balino grunted. "That's because you've never seen combat." He leaned back and put his hands behind his massive head. "One of the benefits of being in the old army is having my choice of duty stations, Callahan. Before Pearl Harbor I was just an old noncom ready for retirement. Now look at this." He picked up a stack of papers. "I've got every colonel I've ever served with looking for a top sergeant." Balino chose one of the papers and studied it carefully.

"This one's from Colonel McClaren," he said. "I served with him back in 1916 when he was a fresh-faced lieutenant in the 35th Infantry. We were on border patrol in Nogales, Mexico. Mexican irregulars attacked the customs house in Nogales. It was the first time I was ever under fire." Balino paused reflectively. "If life is a circle, Callahan, it's time I completed mine. I'm going back to the 35th Infantry. How would you like to come along?"

"I would like it fine."

"Good. I get to cherry pick the best men from this battalion. The 24th and 25th Infantry are being broken up and Colonel McClaren is assigned to reform the 25th Infantry into a new fighting force."

Shorty felt pride that he was picked, and then he remembered the gang. "What about the other guys I joined up with?"

"Sergeant Morrales can pick the men he wants. We're shipping out at 0900."

Shorty was elated, and then he remembered Katie.

"No leave time, sergeant?"

"In case you've forgotten, Callahan, there's a war on."

"Where are we headed?"

"Schofield Barracks."

Shorty looked at him questioningly.

"Wahoo, Callahan. 'The rock.' Better known to civilian types as the island of Oahu in Hawaii."

Shorty went over the list with Morrales. Corky was the only one they couldn't agree on.

"The kid can't soldier," Morrales said.

"He's getting better at it all the time," Shorty argued.

"The 35th is a tough outfit, Callahan. Balino wants only the best."

"Corky's good for morale. He keeps everybody loose."

"Sorry, Callahan."

"Look, Morrales. We all joined up together. It would be like breaking up a family." Shorty knew Morrales came from a close-knit Hispanic family.

"An infantry platoon on the line is only as good as its weakest man, Callahan."

"I'll take that responsibility."

Morrales paused for a moment. "Okay. But if the kid doesn't shape up in Hawaii, we make him a company clerk."

"Fair enough," Shorty agreed.

Shorty formed up the platoon. Morrales started calling off the names of the men going to the 35th, and they stepped forward.

"We need one more, Callahan," Morrales said. "Who do you want?"

"Brainar," Shorty said. "He can soldier with anyone."

Shorty saw the look of surprise and pride on Bo's face as he stepped forward.

Katie waited in eager anticipation for Joe's voice on the other end of the line.

"Joe?"

"Hi sweetheart. It's so good to hear your voice."

"Oh, I've missed you so much."

"I've missed you, too. Are you okay? How's the new job coming along?"

"I'm fine. The job is taking some getting used to, but I'll figure it out."

"I don't doubt that for a minute. You're the most resourceful person I know."

"Did you find out where they're shipping you? Will you get some leave time?"

There was a pause on the other end of the line. "I'm sorry, Katie. We ship out in the morning. There won't be any leave time."

Her heart sank in disappointment and then she remembered Father Dugan's words about being supportive.

"I'm sorry too, but there is nothing we can do but make the best of it. Where is the Army sending you?"

"Hawaii."

"Hawaii?" She had been praying for a state-side assignment. "Any chance I could follow you?"

"That was the first thing I checked into. Hawaii has been declared a war zone. The military has sent all dependents home."

"Oh."

"It seems that we can't catch a break, sweetheart."

"I know." The telephone was pure torture: listening to his voice and not being able to see him or touch him.

"How will you get to Hawaii?"

"Military Air Transport."

"You'll write me every detail about Hawaii?"

"Of course."

"How's Shorty?"

"Same as always: giving orders and keeping everybody loose. He's here waiting to talk to Emma."

"Put him on so I can say hello."

There was a pause as he called Shorty to the phone.

"Hello, Squirt."

"Hello, brother. Are you behaving yourself?"

"Have to. The military keeps a close eye on me. How's Mom and Grandpa?"

"They're doing fine. I miss you, Shorty. Somehow life was always more exciting with you around."

"That's because I was always giving you something to worry about. Are you doing okay?"

"I'm fine. Just hurry up and get the war over with so we can all be together again."

"You can count on it," he said confidently. "You take care of yourself, Squirt."

"I will. And you do the same. Here's Emma."

"Hello, Callahan."

"Is this the most beautiful girl in Kansas City?"

"Flattery only works on girls that don't know you."

"I miss you, Emma."

"Then how come I've only received two letters since you've been gone?"

"Letter writing isn't something I do best. Are you dating that Mission Hills lawyer yet?"

"Wouldn't you like to know?"

"Do you miss me?"

"I'll never tell."

He laughed. "Haven't you heard that you're supposed to be true to your man in uniform? Builds morale and all that kind of thing."

"I have a feeling that in your case devotion is a one-way street, and I've never known you to have a problem with morale."

"You are one hard woman."

"And don't you forget it."

There was a pause as they both searched for something to say.

"I want us to be married after the war, Emma."

"You're just saying that because you're lonely and far from home."

"All I'm asking for is a chance to compete."

"You will always have that. Now stop getting mushy on me and go win the war."

"Yes Ma'am. I really look forward to your letters."

"I'll keep writing. You are one terrific guy, Callahan. Take care of yourself and tell Corky and the gang I said hello." She handed the phone back to Katie.

"Joe."

"I'm here."

"I love you and I'll pray for you every day."

"I love you too. Keep your spirits up, be brave, and we'll make it through this crazy war."

"I will. Please don't say good-bye, just tell me you love me."

"I love you, Katie."

She hung up the phone. Maybe it was better this way. She didn't think she could bear to see him again and then have to tear herself away.

The engines on the C-130 Military Air Transport churned above the calm waters of the Pacific. The plane's arrival time in Hawaii was an hour away.

Everyone in the gang was elated about the assignment, although Joe was really down about not getting to see Katie before he shipped out.

"I can hardly wait," Franky said. "I"m going to stick my dong in the backside of one of those dark-skinned Hawaiian girls and beg her to do the hula."

"Why am I not surprised?" Corky said. "The most romantic place on earth and all you can think about is your dong."

"Tell me about it, twerp. I don't remember you reading poetry to Shirley Polansky."

Corky blushed as the other guys laughed.

An hour later the plane banked to the left and they could see Diamond Head and Waikiki. The barbed wire and other fortifications strung along the beach looked out of place in the pristine setting of the Royal Hawaiian and Moana hotels, but nothing could detract from the blue ocean, palm trees, and golden sand. The place looked like paradise.

"It's beautiful," Corky said, looking out the window. "Do you think we'll be allowed to go to Waikiki?"

"You'll probably be guarding it," Shorty said. "There's still the chance of an invasion by the Japs."

As the plane banked away from Waikiki Beach they could see the traffic on Kalakaua Avenue and the water in the Ali Wai Canal. Beyond the canal the landscape gradually rose until it vanished into the low clouds that hung with a promise of rain over Saint Louis Heights.

A moment later they came face to face with the sobering reality of the war. The troops grew quiet as the plane passed low over Pearl Harbor and they viewed the damage of the devastating raid by the Japanese. They could see the outline of the battleship *Arizona* nestled in its watery grave — the *Oklahoma*, righted but beyond repair — the *California* and the *West Virginia* massively damaged, and four other battleships that were under repair. The Navy had also lost three light cruisers and three destroyers. The final casualty figures of the raid had totaled 2,403 dead and 1,178 missing.

"We'll pay back those dirty bastards," Shorty said, giving voice to every man's thoughts.

A few minutes later the plane touched down at Hickam Field and tax-
ied to a halt. Shorty stepped from the plane into the bright sunshine and
the contrasts that were wartime Hawaii: the anti-aircraft guns protecting
the field were set against a pale blue sky and sheltered by palm trees blowing in a tropical breeze. As he walked past the bullet-riddled barracks and
buildings of Hickam Field, he could smell the aroma of tropical flowers
that were blooming everywhere. War seemed so out of place in this beautiful setting.

The troops were met by a sergeant and loaded on a truck for the trip
out to Schofield Barracks. The island was alive with activity as all the
branches of the military geared up for an all-out war with Japan. There
seemed to be a never-ending stream of military vehicles passing by, and
construction and repair crews were working at a frantic pace.

Schofield Barracks sat on the central Leilehau Plateau — the post's
15,000 acres stretching from the Waianae Mountain Range to the city of
Wahiawa. As the truck was waved through the Post gates, Shorty took in
the sights and sounds of Schofield: the various battalions were housed in
three-story concrete structures that formed a quadrangle around grass-
covered squares. Noncoms shouting cadence and boots in synchronized
march echoed out of the quads as the truck passed by. In the fields of
green surrounding the barracks, other troops were engaged in various
forms of combat training. And off in the distance was the slit in the
Waianae Mountain Range that was Kolekole Pass, where the first
Japanese planes had flown through to attack Schofield Barracks and Pearl
Harbor.

The truck drove into one of the quads and stopped in front of B
Company of the 35th Infantry Battalion. The troops piled out and headed for the barracks.

Shorty was glad to see Balino's massive frame behind the desk in the
orderly room.

"Welcome to Wahoo and the Hawaiian Division, Callahan."

"Thanks. It was a long trip."

"Morrales arrived yesterday. He's going to be your platoon sergeant.
Your squad will bunk on the second floor, so get your bedding and some
sack time. You can draw the rest of your supplies in the morning."

"When do we start training?"

"Tomorrow, 5:00 a.m."

Shorty's eyes flickered open and then closed as the sound of a bugle
interrupted his sleep. A warm breeze blew through the barracks, rustling

the palm trees out in the quad. A chorus of tropical birds was in full voice, anticipating the dawn. Around him he could hear the other troops starting to stir.

"Would someone shut that bugler up!" Corky moaned sleepily. "He keeps following me around, playing the same stupid song over and over again."

This got a laugh out of the troops and helped them struggle out of their cots as the call to reveille gave birth to another day at Schofield Barracks.

After breakfast they went to the supply room and were issued new gear, including the Gerand M-I rifle that had recently replaced the Springfield, and the much heavier chamber pot helmet instead of the old tin hat.

Later that morning, after a welcoming speech by Colonel McClaren, Balino called Bravo Company to attention and introduced Captain Reynolds, the CO, and his two lieutenants, Kern and Dolan. The Captain was regular army, but Kern was fresh out of West Point and Dolan had recently graduated from Officer Candidate School. Captain Reynolds had been with the Hawaiian Division for the past four years.

"Thank you, Sergeant Balino," Captain Reynolds began. "Let me join Colonel McClaren in welcoming all of you to the Hawaiian Division. The first step in defeating the Japanese will be taken here in the Pacific, and it will include this division. Our training will be tough and intense. My estimate is that we have about 90 days to get ready for combat. Components of the 25th Division have been training here at Schofield Barracks since 1920, and as a Pacific Division we know the Japanese very well. They are a tough and formidable enemy, but they made a big mistake when they attacked us here in their own backyard. They brought the war to Hawaii, and it's our job to take it back to Japan. Good luck, train hard, and remember Pearl Harbor!"

Sergeant Balino took command of the company and started reading off personnel changes. "Callahan and Wilson are promoted to corporal. Callahan will be second in command of the Third Platoon, and Wilson will be a second in command of the Fourth Platoon."

Shorty was expecting the promotions, but had no idea Joe would be moved to the fourth platoon. Joe's departure made Shorty uncomfortable because he didn't like the gang being split up. Joe was too good a soldier to be kept down in the ranks, so there was nothing Shorty could do but accept it and offer his congratulations. One good thing about Joe's promotion was that his new responsibilities would give him less time to pine over Katie.

As Captain Reynolds promised, the training was intense. When B Company wasn't guarding some area of the coastline in anticipation of a Japanese invasion, they were marching through miles of pineapple fields or taking part in jungle training in the mountain ranges around Schofield Barracks.

The troops trained hard through June, July and August, and as September approached they were ready to stop training and start fighting. The American Naval victory in June at Midway had halted further Japanese expansion in the Pacific and given a much-needed victory to the allies. The troops were ready to get off the defensive and start taking the war to the Japanese.

It was the last day of August. They were on another forced march in the highlands around Schofield Barracks. Morrales put up his arm and halted the platoon in the middle of a dirt road that led through a pineapple field.

"Fall out and take a break!" he ordered. "And remember, the penalty for stealing pineapples is five years in prison and a $50,000 fine!"

Shorty immediately went into a field and started harvesting pineapples. "Dole's contribution to the war effort!" he yelled as he tossed pineapples to the troops.

Morrales stabbed a pineapple with his bayonet and started carving the fruit. "Thank you Senor Dole," he said.

"I wonder when we're going to start carving Japs instead of pineapples?" Shorty said as he bit into a juicy piece of fruit.

"Before this war is over you'll have all of the Japs you want," Morrales answered.

"Well, it won't be too soon for me," Shorty said. "I'm ready to get off 'the rock' and get on with the war."

"You don't like it here in beautiful Hawaii?" McClusky asked. "Tourists spend hundreds of dollars to come to Wahoo and you get to enjoy it for free, courtesy of your Uncle Sam."

"The difference between tourist Hawaii and our Hawaii is the difference between paradise and perdition," Corky said.

"You mean you would rather be sunbathing on the beach than enjoying the pleasures of a pineapple field?" Joe asked as he walked up from the Fourth Platoon. "Where's your sense of perspective?"

"Careful," Corky cautioned. "I wouldn't use that big a word around Franky."

"Screw you, college boy," Franky shot back. "Hey, Duff. Are we going down to Hotel Street tonight? My dick is telling me it must be the weekend."

"I'm ready when you are," Duff said.

"You mean that Okie has a voice?" Morrales asked. "That's the first time I've heard him speak."

"He only talks when you mention the finer things in life," Franky said. "Pussy, beer, and a hell-raising good time."

"Known in intellectual circles as wine, women and song," Corky said.

"Why don't you kiss my achin' ass, mister arteest," Franky said good naturedly. "A few beers and you'll be begging me to find you a piece of ass."

"Only if I'm up-to-date on my shots," Corky said to general laughter.

"How about going to Honolulu with us tonight, Joe?" Shorty asked.

"He's too busy recording stuff in his journal and writing to Katie," McClusky said. "After the war we'll all be reading about ourselves in his novel."

"That's right," Joe said."So you had better improve your behavior."

"Come on, Joe," Franky said. "A few beers and we'll put you back on the bus to Schofield. You can have some fun and still be loyal to Katie."

"What do you know about loyalty?" Corky scoffed.

"I'd be loyal until my balls started to ache," Franky replied. "Shorty has the right idea. He cares about Emma, but he also has a nice shack job down at Fort Shafter. A man has to take care of his needs."

Shorty had met a nurse at a quiet bar near Tripler Hospital. Her name was Ronni, and she was married to a sailor who had gone to sea. Ronni was no Emma, but she was convenient, had her own place, and she was good in bed. And she didn't mind if he stayed out late with the gang. He had his own key, and Ronni never asked questions. When he finally shipped out there would be no recriminations and he never had to write. A man couldn't ask for more.

"You guys are very generous and I appreciate you looking out for my welfare," Joe said. "But I have to catch up on my reading, and write my letters."

"Those Army manuals you keep studying are really exciting," McClusky said. "I don't know how you put them down."

"He's bucking for the officer corps," Morrales said.

"We'll be saluting this guy in a few months."

"One thing I've learned from the manuals is when to retreat," Joe said. "I'm going back to my platoon where I'm out of range of these verbal assaults."

"Go ahead," Corky said with a hint of self pity. "Leave me alone with Cro-Magnon man."

"Cro what?" Franky said. "You better talk in language I understand."

"I don't know that many two-letter words."

"Screw you, twerp."

"You two have been insulting each other since you were kids," Shorty said irritably. "Don't you ever get tired of it?"

Franky and Corky looked at each other and then back at Shorty.

"No," they answered in unison.

15

J oe said good-bye to the guys and watched from the second-floor porch of the barracks as they made their merry way across the grassy square and headed for the bus that would take them to Honolulu. Around the quad, screen doors slammed and footsteps beat heavily on the tiers of porches as the troops hurried to distance themselves from Schofield Barracks. He was amazed at how quickly everyone could clear out on a Friday night. Across the way, a finger of sunlight at the top of the barracks was all that remained of the day. As the tropical sun faded, a cool breeze caressed his face and created ripples through the palm trees lining the square. High in the Waianae Mountain Range he could see a buildup of dark clouds promising rain above the lush pineapple fields. Dusk began to shade the mysterious V in the mountains that was Kolekole Pass.

He turned away from the scene and went back into the barracks to pen a long letter to Katie and to work on his novel. He knew that once the division went to war he would have little time for writing. He missed her even more than he had imagined, and working on the novel helped bridge the long expanse of ocean that separated them. He could immerse himself in the past, back in the Dutch Hill and Union Hill neighborhoods, and set scenes using all of the haunts he and Katie had shared.

Although he desperately missed Katie and his family, he had a strong sense of duty and he believed passionately in the cause he was fighting for. He took his duty as a soldier very seriously and tried to instill in his men a sense of camaraderie and attention to detail that would pay off later in combat. He went quietly about the work of building the platoon into a fighting force and he was a friend to everyone in B Company.

He gazed out the window of the tiny room he shared with the platoon leader and watched as stars began to blanket the evening sky. If the world were in its proper axis, he would be walking hand in hand with Katie on this warm starry night. He took pen and paper out of his foot locker and began sharing all of his thoughts with her.

Shorty led his gang out of a bar on Hotel Street. He weaved his way through the payday crowd of soldiers and sailors packed along Hawaii's version of 12th Street. They walked past liquor stores, restaurants, and photo shops. Oriental prostitutes lingered seductively on every street corner, working the crowd. When a deal was made, a simple nod of the head led a serviceman up one of the staircases that rose mysteriously out of the streets and alleys of the Red Light district.

"Do you want to get a massage, Shorty?" Franky yelled above the noise pouring from the bars and arcades. "I know this Philippino girl who is great with her hands."

"Concert pianist?" Corky teased.

"Yeah," Franky answered. "Only she plays 'Rhapsody in Blue' on your dick."

"Another exercise in your never-ending pursuit of the fine arts," Corky replied.

"Why don't you go to the library and get your rocks off, twerp."

"I say we pool our money and get us some China girls for an all-nighter," McClusky said, breaking up the good-natured kidding.

"China girls are all ass and no tits," Franky replied. "I need something to hold on to."

"You guys do whatever you want," Shorty said. "Me and Corky are headed for Fort Shafter."

Corky stopped walking. "Fort Shafter. Me?"

"Yeah, you."

Corky looked at him, puzzled. "I don't want to be in the way," he said as the crowd nudged him along the street.

"What's he going to do?" Franky asked. "Draw pictures while you get laid? You better stay here with us, twerp."

"He's going with me," Shorty said matter of factly.

"You'll be sorry," Franky teased as he molded an imaginary female figure with his hands. "We'll tell you about it when we meet back at the barracks."

"A lesson in anatomy," Corky guessed.

"Yeah. One that will cure your boner."

"Hey. Look at this." Duff said as he stopped outside a shooting gallery. "Let's go in and take some target practice."

"Come on, Okie," Franky ordered. "The shooting we're going to be doing won't be in no gallery." He led Duff and McClusky down the street and they were swept away by the mob of soldiers.

Shorty and Corky stepped off the Fort Shafter bus and started climbing the hill that led to Ronni's house. The evening breeze rustled palm trees along the street. The blackout was still in force, so the stars seemed to glitter with added luster and a full moon lit the way. They had spent their time on the bus reminiscing about home.

"I really miss Katie and Emma more than I had imagined," Corky said.

"Yeah. Me too."

"Do you ever . . . you know . . . feel guilty about fooling around on Emma?"

"What's there to feel guilty about? We're not married."

"No. But you and Emma are a team. You'll probably get married after the war."

"So I'll worry about it then. Do you think Emma is sitting home every night waiting for me?"

"I don't know."

"Well, I guarantee you she ain't. Women have their needs just like a man. Ask any of those sob sisters back at the barracks who are crying over their Dear John letters."

"Sounds like you don't trust women."

"Women are mysterious and unpredictable. They only show a man what they want him to see. Take Ronni, for instance; she's the loving wife in letters to her husband, but she's shacking up with me. She realizes that it's going to be a long war, so she has her fun and then goes back to playing the role of the loyal, faithful wife."

"Rather shallow, don't you think?"

Shorty laughed and smacked him on the back. "So what? That's how some of us lead our lives. We skim the good stuff off the top and leave the loyalty and commitment to you deep thinkers."

He stopped at a small white house. Corky followed him up the steps and stood nervously behind him as he knocked on the door. The door opened and a shaft of light pierced the darkness. "Get in here, soldier boys," a feminine voice ordered. They moved quickly inside the house. Ronni had done a masterful job of maintaining security. The house was well lit, but nothing had penetrated her blackout curtains.

"Hello, you gorgeous girl," Shorty said as he took her in his arms. "I want you to meet my friend, Corky."

Ronni disengaged herself and gave Corky a hug. "I've heard a lot about you."

"Don't believe anything he told you," Corky replied.

"Actually, it was all good." Ronni said, grinning. She had an accent that was definitely Southern, and strawberry blond hair that fell to her shoulders. She had on white shorts and a pink halter top. Her legs were short and a bit on the plump side, and she had full breasts that jiggled seductively above her halter top.

"Don't you think she's the best-looking girl in Hawaii, Corky?"

"Ha!" Ronni said. "Look at these legs." She held one out for them to survey. "They're white as a sheet. I feel guilty trying to get a tan with you boys off fighting the war."

Corky stared at her soft skin and manicured pink toenails. "You look awfully good to me," he said respectfully.

"Well aren't you nice," Ronni said.

She was so bubbly and kind that Corky liked her instantly. "Atlanta, Georgia," he made a stab at her accent.

"Nice try, but it's Rocky Mount, North Carolina. How would you soldier boys like a cold beer?"

"She's not only gorgeous, but a mind reader," Shorty said.

"Allison!" Ronni called. "You can't hide in there forever. Please bring out the refreshments."

Corky looked at Shorty questioningly, and then Allison entered the room carrying a tray. She was a tiny, thin brunette. Her hair was tied in a pony tail, and she had on a white summer dress and sandals. The glasses she wore gave her a studious, professional look.

Ronni made the introductions, and everyone but Allison took a beer. She had an iced tea.

"Allison helps run the library at the hospital," Ronni said.

"What I do is file books," Allison corrected. "Ronni mentioned that you're an artist."

"Art student."

"He's the best artist in Kansas City," Shorty said. "Thomas Hart Benson is an amateur compared to this guy."

"He's my agent, so don't take him seriously," Corky said. He glanced at Allison's left hand and it was ringless. "I thought you local girls took classes on how to avoid servicemen," he said.

Allison smiled wryly. "That was before Pearl Harbor. We now realize that you guys just might be useful."

It was Corky's turn to smile. "I appreciate your support of the war effort. How did you end up in Hawaii?"

"It's my place of origin. My father is a plant manager for Dole."

"Uh oh," Corky said, looking at Shorty. "I knew they would eventually catch up with you."

Allison looked at him questioningly.

"When we're out on maneuvers, Shorty feeds the troops with your father's pineapples."

"Don't they taste wonderful fresh from the field?" Allison said. "When I was a little girl my father would take me with him on inspection trips and all the workers would feed me samples."

"Yes. But you ate them legally."

"I promise to keep your secret," Allison whispered conspiratorially.

Shorty listened patiently to another half hour of conversation. He was glad Corky and Allison were hitting it off, but he wanted to be alone with Ronni. He managed to catch Corky's eye, and with a nod of his head gave him the signal to get lost.

Corky took the hint. "How about a breath of fresh air, Allison?"

"Let me refill our drinks and I'll meet you on the front porch."

When the front door closed, Shorty walked up behind Ronni and cupped her breasts in his hands. "Talk about pineapples," he said. She smacked his hand playfully and he immediately tried to slide it into the front of her shorts.

"Would you quit. We have company."

He picked her up and carried her into the bedroom.

"You stop it, right this minute," she protested half-heartedly.

"You're such a naughty girl. I bet you don't even have on your panties."

"That's none of your business."

"Sure it is," he said playfully. "If you're wearing panties I'll know that you weren't planning to seduce me." He reached for the zipper on her shorts and she turned away. "Come on. Let me see. Good girls have nothing to hide." He started slowly unzipping her shorts as she eyed him seductively. "Just as I thought," he said admiringly.

"You are such an animal," she said as she kissed him passionately and then pulled him onto the bed.

Katie poured a cup of tea for one of her guests and sat down. She was the hostess for "letter-writing night," a Friday night gathering of all the war wives in the neighborhood. She found it comforting to be with other women in her circumstances. After a few meetings they all became good friends and could talk about anything. The first hour was reserved for discussing the latest war news, and also what was happening in the work place. Almost everyone had a job outside the home, so "letter-writing night" had also turned into a support group for working women. Tonight their discussion had covered everything from gas rationing to the love lives of movie stars. The conversation had seriously cut into letter-writing time.

Katie had to stand up to make herself heard. She put her fingers on her lower lip and gave one of her tomboy whistles. It got a laugh and everyone's attention. She held up her pen. "There are a bunch of lonely guys out there waiting to hear from us, so we had better get started." The chatter ended with a rustle of purses and paper and everyone settled into a comfortable writing position..

October 17, 1942
Dear Joe,

As always, I'm missing you more than words can say.

It's "Letter-Writing Night" and we were just discussing the latest war news from the Pacific. There seems to be a lot of action taking place in the Solomon Islands. The newspapers say the Marines are putting up a good fight on an island called Guadalcanal. I'm glad you're safe in Hawaii.

The days are warm, but the nights are starting to cool.

I know you're missing the change of seasons. The trees have turned and the parks and boulevards are a wonder of color. I was out visiting Aunt Martha and Uncle Ray over the weekend, and the lake was a mirror reflecting the reds and golds of the surrounding hills. Your descriptions of Hawaii make me wish we could see it together. Maybe we can take a second honeymoon after the war.

Scooter and your parents are doing fine (except for missing you). This coming week I'm helping host a Halloween party for Scooter's Boy Scout troop. I'm sure Scooter will tell everyone how he, Shorty, and Orson Wells managed to make us look foolish on the night of "War Of The Worlds." Scooter promised me he would come over to the house on Halloween and help give out treats. I'm going to miss your ghostly impersonations that always failed to frighten the neighborhood kids.

I was almost tempted to raid our piggy bank last week. The Jones Store had a three-piece solid maple bedroom set on sale for $49.95. I thought it would be perfect for our first home, but decided to delay all major purchases until we can make them together. I did splurge and buy myself two cardigan sweaters that were on sale for $1.00 each, then scolded myself when I got home for being so extravagant.

My new part-time job is coming along fine. The work is classified so I can't tell you any details; it would never get by the censor. (Hello, if you're reading this). Suffice it to say they wanted to make me a secretary, but I would have none of it, so they put me on an assembly line where I can really contribute to the war effort.

On the homefront, some of the city's matrons are lamenting the loss of their cooks; they're taking jobs as riveters, and sugar and gasoline are being rationed. (All of this was in the newspaper, Mr. Censor.) I get a few extra gallons of gas because I'm doing war work, so I give rides to our neighbors who are not as fortunate.

Abbott and Costello are starring in "Pardon My Sarong" at the Linwood Theatre (I know how hysterical they make you), and your favorite actress Rita Hayworth is starring in "You Were Never Lovelier" at the Lowe's Midland.

There are so many good-paying jobs in the newspaper that I'm surprised anyone stays in school. The college grounds look like a girls academy with all you young men gone to war.

I can see some of my guests dropping their pens, so I had better close for now. Please tell that brother of mine to try and behave himself and the rest of the gang that I said hello.

You are in my thoughts every minute of every day. I can hardly wait for the sun to set because it means another day is over that we've lived apart, and it brings us closer to the end of this horrible war. I love you with all my heart, and exist only for your return.

Hugs and kisses,
Katie

Katie said good-night to her last guest and closed the door. Her mother walked into the room. "It sounded like everyone had a good time."

"Yes. The meetings seem to get more rowdy with each passing week."

"A wonderful support group, though."

Katie nodded and began helping her mother clean up the plates and saucers scattered around the room.

"You look awfully tired, Katie."

"I'm okay. It was just a very long day."

"You can't do everything, you know. With the cold weather coming on I'm afraid you're going to be so worn out you'll catch a chill."

"I like to stay busy. It helps the time pass."

Ann Callahan reached out and brushed Katie's hair with her finger tips. Katie gave her a hug. In the months after her marriage she had grown closer to her mother, and she could appreciate some of the things her mother had experienced. "How did you ever manage the loneliness after Pop died?"

Ann was taken aback for a moment. "It was different with me. Your father had been sick for a very long time."

"It still had to be devastating."

"Yes," Ann sighed. "One of life's experiences that no one can help you with. I just had to let time pass and hope it would get better."

"And did it get better?"

"Yes."

"Do you still miss Pop?"

"Every day. I think he would be so proud of the way you're managing your life."

Katie was so tired and lonely that for a moment she let her defenses down. "I miss Joe so much, Mother."

"I know you do, sweetheart." Ann held her tightly in her arms. "Go upstairs and climb into bed," she commanded. "I'm going to fix you some warm milk, and then come up and tuck you in."

"You haven't tucked me in for years."

"I know. You had better humor me or I just might read you a story."

"You're really regressing now," Katie said, managing a smile.

After her mother had closed the door and said good-night, Katie lay awake listening to the sounds of the night. She was in a state of nervous exhaustion that refused to let her sleep. Off to the west she could hear the rumblings of an approaching thunderstorm and the wind starting to tug at the giant oak tree outside her window. The trains rumbling in and out of Union Station had become such a part of her existence that she could easily distinguish the heavy freighters from the sleek passenger carriers by the way the cars clicked along the tracks. The first fingers of rain tapped against the window pane and a train gave an answering whistle to a clap of thunder. She reached out and touched the sheets on Joe's side of the bed. They had loved to snuggle up close when it stormed. As the rain started beating on the rooftop, she felt an overwhelming sense of loneliness, so she climbed out of bed and went to the window. A flash of lightning lit up the city and for an instant she could see everything from Quality Hill to City Hall. It was the same view she had always had from her oak tree, and it comforted her. She watched the colorful lights on the spire of the Power and Light building, standing like a sentinel against the darkness. I have to keep it together or I won't be any good to Joe, myself, or my family, she whispered to herself. Just work hard, hold on, and everything will be okay. As the lightning flashed and the thunder rolled, she closed her eyes and said a silent prayer for Joe, Shorty, and the rest of the gang.

LATE NOVEMBER 1942

Shorty stood next to Corky in the latrine. They had just returned from a week of field maneuvers and they were getting ready to head for Fort Shafter. Shorty ran his razor through a week's worth of beard while Corky surveyed the mirror for the first hint of facial hair.

"Don't you ever shave?"

"Once every two weeks whether I need it or not," Corky replied. "It's a requirement of this man's Army," he said, making his voice sound gruff.

Shorty laughed. "You've never told me how it's going with Allison."

"You surely wouldn't be referring to the physical aspects of our relationship."

Shorty looked at him in the mirror. "Are you getting laid or not?"

"Or not," Corky replied.

"How come? I thought you guys were hitting it off."

"We are. Did it ever dawn on your hormones that a relationship doesn't have to be physical to be exciting?"

"Not in a million years."

"Well, you're wrong. Allison and I have a lot in common and we love to talk."

"All women love to talk. If you're good at telling them what they want to hear, you almost always get to bury the sausage."

Corky narrowed his eyes at him in the mirror. "At times you can be really disgusting."

"I believe I've heard that somewhere before. You're not falling for this girl, are you?"

"No. We're just friends."

Sergeant Morrales came into the latrine. "Could I see you for a minute, Callahan?"

Shorty looked questioningly at Morrales. He put down his razor and followed him outside the latrine.

Morrales took out a cigarette and offered one to Shorty.

"No thanks. What's up?"

"I just wanted to tell you to enjoy your 'last' weekend in town."

"You mean. . ."

"That's right, Callahan. Keep a lid on it. This is confidential information." Morrales struck a match and lit his cigarette. "We won't know the destination until we're aboard ship, but it's sure to be somewhere here in the South Pacific."

Shorty pondered for a moment. "I think we're ready."

Morrales took a long drag on his cigarette. "We sure as hell better be." He turned and started to walk away. "Oh, by the way. What about Corky? I can recommend having him assigned to the skeleton force we're leaving here at Schofield."

"What are you trying to do, jinx us? It's bad luck to break up a platoon before going into combat. And besides, Corky's good for morale."

"He does keep everybody loose," Morrales agreed.

"And he's done a hell of a job of soldiering here in Hawaii," Shorty argued.

"He's shown improvement all right, but is he ready for combat?"

"You can ask that of any man in the battalion. The answer won't come until we're under fire. I guarantee you he won't fold up like some of these sob sisters."

"Okay, Callahan. You've made your point. You had better go try and squeeze a lifetime into one weekend."

Ronni had fixed an elegant candle lit dinner. After the meal they sat back contentedly with their glasses of wine.

"Ronni, that was an excellent meal," Corky said.

"Delicious," Allison agreed.

"Thanks," Ronni said, pleased.

Shorty was enjoying every last moment of the weekend. He was on his third glass of wine and feeling very melancholy. He thought it very unfair that because of security considerations he was allowed to savor these last few days with his friends while they had no idea what was going on. "I would like to make a toast," he said, holding up his glass. "To friendship, and to you lovely ladies who have taken the time to make our stay in Hawaii so enjoyable." They clinked glasses and drank. He could tell they hadn't picked up on the hint, so he raised his glass again. "And may special friendships always be remembered, no matter what."

Ronni looked at him knowingly. "You're shipping out," she said.

Shorty stared at her but remained silent.

Ronni got up and started nervously clearing away the plates. "I knew this had to happen sooner or later, I was just hoping it would be later."

Shorty followed her into the kitchen.

"I think that's our cue to go outside," Allison said.

Corky grabbed his wine glass and followed her out the door. They sat together on the stoop, silently watching the stars.

"Where do you think you'll be going?" she finally asked.

"I have no idea."

"This confirms our decision not to get involved."

"Yes. The world is too uncertain to make plans or build relationships."

"You're so different," Allison said. "I've dated other servicemen and they always treat me like a female and never like a person."

"One thing on their minds?" Corky guessed.

"Some great lines, though," Allison laughed. "Want to hear some?" she moved over close to him.

"Sure."

"You may be the last girl I ever see," she said solemnly, as she pretended to be a soldier going off to war. "How could you live with yourself if you refused me and I never came back?"

"Not bad," Corky said respectfully.

"And here's my all-time favorite: 'I'm going off to war a virgin and I might die having never been with a woman.'"

Corky reached into his pocket. "I guess I had better scratch those two lines off my list."

Allison laughed. "I love your sense of humor," she said. She stayed close and cuddled up to him. "How come you've never made a pass at me?"

"I don't know. I guess I didn't want to take a chance on upsetting you."

"Inspiring, but not very flattering," she replied.

He squeezed her hand. "Am I hallucinating, or was that an invitation?"

She kissed him gently on the lips. "Come on. Let's go out and get in

Ronni's car," she said.

His heart pounding, Corky followed her down the steps. She was wearing one of those long flowing Hawaiian mumu's that hid her figure, but would be easily accessible if things led where he thought they were leading. They opened the car door and climbed into the back seat.

He kissed her, and fondled her under the mumu. She felt so soft and warm and it had been such a long time since he had been with a woman. "I don't think I'm going to be able to stop."

"Who said anything about stopping," she said, tugging at his trousers.

He freed her from her underpants and got in position.

"What about protection?" she panted.

"Protection?" The thought hadn't crossed his mind.

"Yes. Protection."

What to do? he wondered in a panic. "Hold on. I'll be right back."

He tucked his swollen member under his shirt and ran bare assed up the steps and into the house. He could hear the mattress squeaking in the bedroom. He had to hurry or Allison might change her mind. He opened the bedroom door. "Shorty," he whispered loudly. The mattress stopped squeaking.

"What?"

"Do you have any. . .ah. . .protection?"

"Protection from what?"

He could hear Shorty and Ronni giggling from the bed.

"Come on, Shorty. Help me out here."

"Do you mean rubbers?"

"You know darn well what I mean."

"Since when did good conversation require a rubber?"

"Don't do this to me," Corky pleaded. He could hear more laughter from the bed.

"We have some rubbers," Shorty said. "But I don't think they're big enough to cover your brain." He and Ronni were laughing hysterically now.

"Come on, you guys. I'm in agony here."

"So what. A relationship doesn't have to be physical to be exciting."

"You bastard," Corky said mournfully. He heard feet hit the floor and a drawer opening. Ronni walked up to him in the darkness. In the moonlight he could see that she was naked and her breasts loomed large and inviting. He became even more excited, and as he reached for the rubber she was holding out, he popped from beneath his shirt, and left nothing to her imagination.

"Well, Allison is in for a real surprise," Ronni said admiringly as he burned with embarrassment. He tucked himself back under his shirt and ran quickly out the door.

16

At sunrise the troop ship Ernest Hine lay heavy in the water as it eased away from the pier and slowly headed out to sea. For security reasons there had been no fanfare at the dock.

The battalion had driven the thirty miles from Schofield Barracks in total darkness and loaded everything aboard ship before dawn. Shorty stood at the rail of the ship with the rest of the troops watching the departure. Honolulu looked peaceful and inviting as it nestled against the shining sea. The *Ernest Hine* slipped through the channel and away from the slumbering city. His thoughts were of Emma and also of Ronni fast asleep in the hills above Pearl Harbor. He was in love with Emma, but Ronni had been a very good friend and it had been hard to say goodbye. She had promised him she wouldn't cry, but the promise had ended in a flood of tears as she realized she would probably never see him again. The ship sailed slowly past Moana Park, then Fort De Russey, and finally Diamond Head. He continued to watch until the lush green island was a speck on the sea.

"What a wonderful place," Corky said. "I hope we get to come back some day." His thoughts were of Allison and Ronni and the cozy nest at Fort Shafter.

"I'm going to bring Katie back after the war," Joe said.

"She will love Hawaii."

They continued to stare silently out to sea, savoring the romance of the moment and watching the horizon until the island of Oahu was lost from view. A seagull made one last run at the wake of the ship and then turned and headed back to Hawaii.

"Do you think there will be any broads where we're going?" Franky wondered.

Corky turned and looked at him in disgust. "I've had it with you, Franky. Hold his arms, Shorty." Shorty grabbed Franky from behind and held him tightly as Corky and the rest of the gang started playfully punching him until they all fell laughing into a heap on the deck of the ship.

The next day they learned their destination was New Guinea. The division would be joining General MacArthur's Southwest Pacific theatre of operations.

"Where's New Guinea?" Franky wondered from his bunk in the bowels of the ship. "Anybody got a map?"

"If we had one you couldn't read it," Corky shot back.

"Mr. wise ass strikes again," Franky sneered. "I know more about the world than you think I do."

"Only if Captain Marvel has been there," Corky said, referring to the comic book character.

"Very funny, twerp."

"Where's Shorty?" Duff asked.

"Topside with Joe," McClusky answered. "They're meeting with the brass about a change of orders."

"Just when I had my heart set on New. . . whatever," Franky said. "Send me anywhere but get me off this tug. How does the Navy expect me to sleep jammed up against this ceiling."

"You wanted the top bunk," Corky said. "Now you're mad because you don't have room enough to flog your dong."

"Ain't that the truth. I got a rise last night and lost it somewhere in the hot water pipes," Franky replied to general laughter.

Shorty returned with Joe and everyone gathered around.

"What's up? McClusky asked.

"The transport ship *President Coolidge* has been sunk off Espiritu Santo," Joe replied. "She was carrying all the ammunition and artillery for the 172nd Regimental Combat Team. We've been designated by Admiral Nimitz to take the place of the 172nd."

The gang looked at him questioningly.

"We are going to relieve the 1st Marine Division on Guadalcanal."

For a moment there was quiet as everyone digested the words.

"Holy shit!" Franky finally said. "Maybe being on this tug ain't so bad after all."

December 16, 1942

First Sergeant Balino gathered the company topside on the forward deck. It was their last evening on board. The sun had disappeared over the bridge of the *Ernest Hine* and was slowly sinking into the sea. Balino had a series of maps and charts spread out on the deck. He paced back and forth and waited patiently for everyone to settle down.

"All right, everyone. Listen up. Our assignment tomorrow will be to relieve the First Marine Division on the perimeter of Henderson Field.

The Marines have carved out a strong foothold around the airfield, but Navy intelligence estimates there are still over 25,000 Japs on Guadalcanal. I want you to spend the daylight hours learning the lay of the land. The Japs love to attack at night, so it's going to get real tense after dark. Keep your wits about you, and do not underestimate your enemy. The Japs are raised on the bushido code of the samurai: honor above life. They will never give up and it's a privilege for them to die for their emperor. We want them to do just that, so let's kick some ass and get out of here as quickly as we can. I want one last weapons check tonight, and I want you to be prepared to disembark on Guadalcanal at 0500. That is all."

Balino picked up his charts, folded them carefully, and put them away. He could feel a gentle roll under his feet as the ship glided smoothly through the Solomon Sea. Somewhere out there on the pink and purple horizon lay the island of Guadalcanal, or as it was now known in all the services, "The Island of Death." The casualty figures were confidential, but anyone with a source knew that over 5,000 Americans had already died on that awful island, with thousands more wounded. Malaria, dysentery, and jungle rot ran rampant through the troops, and the fighting conditions were some of the worst in the world with dense jungle, heat, and incessant rainfall.

The Japanese had fared even worse, with five times as many battle casualties. In one Banzai charge against the marines guarding the perimeter of Henderson Field, the Japs had lost over a thousand combat troops.

The waters off Guadalcanal had become a graveyard for both navys and had earned the name Ironbottom Bay because of all the ships sent to the bottom. And in the battle for control of the air, the Japanese had lost over 800 planes and 2,300 crewmen. And still the battle for Guadalcanal raged on as both sides committed the men and material to make the island the decisive battle of the Pacific war. The troops knew none of this, of course. They were young and green and ready for combat. Balino just wished they had been given an easier assignment their first time under fire. He stayed at the ship's railing until the pink and purple horizon faded into the darkening sea. With an ever-increasing sense of foreboding, First Sergeant Balino left the deck of the ship and went below to check on his men.

Katie was having lunch with Emma at Blender's Barbecue. Boogie woogie music blared from the juke box in the corner. Joe used to love to come here. He had his favorite table, where he would lean his chair back against the wall and feel the beat of the music. Outside the window a light mist was falling with an occasional flurry of snow.

"Have you heard anything from Joe?" Emma asked.

"No. It's been two weeks and I'm worried sick."

"Maybe they've shipped out."

"That's what worries me. Have you heard from Shorty?"

"No. But that's not unusual. He hardly ever writes."

"I haven't heard a word from him, either."

"Corky writes to me every week and lets me know how everyone is getting along," Emma said.

"I hear from him too. He can make light of the most serious situation and somehow make it all bearable."

Emma studied her for a moment. "You seem apprehensive and on edge, Katie. Why don't you try to relax and have some fun. It's not a crime to be happy."

"I don't imagine that Joe is having any fun."

"Maybe not. But he certainly wouldn't want you to mope through the holidays. Look at all the smiling faces of the people passing by. Most of them have loved ones in the service."

"I'm just not in the holiday spirit."

"I hope that attitude isn't spilling over into your letters."

"No. I won't let that happen. I'm just amazed that everything can go on as usual. Sometimes the newspapers have the war news mixed in with the Christmas ads. It just seems so unfair that our young men are off fighting the war and all of these people are out having a good time."

"Life goes on, Katie. We're all so far removed from the war that it's hard to appreciate the sacrifices that are being made."

"I know, but it really bothers me when people complain about food and gas rationing when young men are being killed and wounded trying to protect our way of life."

"You have to quit being so judgmental. What happened to the Katie Callahan who always made allowances for everyone?"

Katie took a sip of wine. "You're right. I promise to do better."

"That's the spirit. Have you seen the Christmas window at Woolf Brothers? They're displaying gifts that are compact and easy to ship overseas. I'm going to send Shorty a set of playing cards in a leather-bound case. He loves to play poker."

"That's a wonderful idea."

"What are you sending to Joe?"

"I haven't decided. I only know that it has to be the perfect gift."

"Well, come on. I'll help you pick it out."

"Okay."

It was the first time Emma had seen her smile. "I'll pay the bill," Emma said.

"You certainly will not. I'm a working woman and you're a struggling art student."

"We'll split it then. I've started doing some design work for some of the department stores and advertising agencies in the city."

"Your own business? How exciting! Congratulations, Emma!"

"Thank you. It helps pay the bills and the tuition."

"Are you still mad at your father?"

"No. But our relationship is shaky. I don't know if I will ever forgive him for interfering in my personal life."

"Talk about judgmental."

Emma smiled. "Touche."

A handsome young man stopped at the table. "Hello, Emma. I missed you at school today."

"Hi, Perry. This is Katie Callahan."

"Hello, Katie."

"Hello."

"Are we still on for tonight, Emma?"

Emma paused for a moment, looking at Katie. "Sure," she said.

"Good. I'll pick you up at seven. Nice meeting you, Katie." Perry walked away.

Emma sipped her tea and looked at Katie. "You're disappointed in me," she finally said.

"Why would I be disappointed? You're not engaged or married."

"Because you have a strong sense of loyalty."

"To tell you the truth, I've always admired you for your free spirit. You're honest and forthright and you didn't make any promises to Shorty that you weren't prepared to keep. Is Perry a classmate?"

"A lawyer. Painting is his hobby so he's taking a few classes at the Art Institute. I've known him for a long time."

"Someone your parents would approve of?"

"I'm afraid so. Sometimes I wonder if we're not all destined to end up on a prearranged social register."

"You are too independent to believe that. Although if you're thinking along those lines, it must be serious."

"Perry arrived on the scene at a vulnerable time in my life. However, you happen to be right; no one is going to tread on my independence. I told your brother he would have his shot, and that's a commitment I'll honor — although it may be difficult to keep Perry dangling for the duration of the war."

"You can do it if anyone can," Katie smiled.

"You know, I think you're right. Now let's go pick out that gift for Joe, and we'll get presents for everyone in the gang as well."

Daybreak found the *Ernest Hine* anchored off Lunga Point on the island of Guadalcanal. The troops were still apprehensive about the landing, but it was comforting to see American troops on the beaches helping unload cargo from the various ships. Balino gave the signal and they climbed over the side of the ship and down the cargo nets to the waiting Higgins boats. The boats circled out to sea and then headed to Beach Red at the mouth of the Tenaru River.

"This place smells like the West Bottoms on a bad day," McClusky said, as the odor of diesel fuel filled the air.

"Or Franky's room on any day," Corky chimed in.

"How would you like my rifle up your ass, twerp."

"Only if you promise to take the bayonet off, darling," Corky replied.

Shorty kept his eyes locked on the landing area as he listened to Franky and Corky throw barbs at each other. He would normally tell them to knock it off, but everyone was nervous and they were just trying to keep them loose. He was thankful for the unopposed landing and for the job the Marines had done in securing this portion of the island. The Japs were out there, however, and it would be up to the infantry to dig them out and secure the rest of the island.

The Higgins boat made it to shore. Everyone followed Sergeant Morrales onto the beach, and they gathered in a coconut grove.

"Hey, Cousin! Is it me or is this island moving?" McClusky yelled at Duff.

"It's moving all right," Duff said. "That tugboat will be with us until we get our land legs."

"Are we in Oklahoma yet?" Corky asked as he surveyed the island.

"No. But I sure as hell wish we were," Duff replied.

Sergeant Morrales walked up. "The Navy is making a mess of the beach. Our supplies are scattered everywhere. Let's go help clean it up."

The men of the battalion spent the rest of the day in waist-deep water passing boxes of ammunition and other supplies to the beach, where they were sorted and put in supply dumps. After the sun went down Morrales moved them back to the coconut grove, where Joe was waiting with the rest of his platoon.

"What have you goldbricks been doing all day?" he chided them good-naturedly.

"Waiting for you guys to clear the island of Japs," Shorty answered. "If you're finished I'll pass the word and we'll head back to the ship."

"You had better give us at least a day or two," Joe kidded him back.

"When will the mail catch up with us?" McClusky wondered.

"It will take about a week," Joe said. "I should have a stack of letters from Katie built up by now."

"Hey, Morrales!" Franky yelled. "Where's the barracks? I'm ready for a good night's sleep."

"You'll be digging your bed tonight," Morrales said. "You better hope the marines have done it for you because you ain't too good with a shovel."

"I'll only dig deep enough to cover my nuts," Franky said.

"Since you have your head up your ass that should also protect your brain," Corky said as everyone laughed.

"That was a good one, twerp. How would you like to sit outside my foxhole while I sing 'Hirohito is an asshole' to the Japs?"

"Sorry, that song's not on my Hit Parade."

"Okay, you comedians, let's saddle up," Morrales said. "It's time to relieve the Marines at Henderson Field."

Darkness was closing in as they made their way to the perimeter around the airfield. A Marine gunnery sergeant accompanied Sergeant Balino and pointed out the various locations of foxholes and machine gun emplacements. The bearded, haggard-looking Marines were more than glad to give them up. Shorty separated his squad into two-man teams and helped get them into position. Franky and Corky had the first foxhole. Shorty offered cigarettes to the two Marines crawling out of the hole.

"Thanks, Mac. Where you from?"

"Kansas City. How about you?"

"Birmingham, Alabama."

"I wish I was in the land of cotton," Corky said.

"Ain't that the truth," the Marine sighed.

"What's it like out here at night?" Franky asked.

The Marine paused for a moment. "Hard to explain. I guess it's something you have to experience to appreciate."

"Any advice?"

"Keep your eyes open and a tight asshole. The Japs like to work up their courage before an attack, so they will let you know when they're coming. Watch for the flash of swords. The Jap officers like to flash them around in the night before a Banzai charge."

"Maybe I'll just take a rain check," Corky said.

"That's gratitude for you," the Marine said. "Uncle Sam gives you a box seat at the war and you're complaining."

"It's just that I had theatre tickets for tonight," Corky replied.

"Try that humor on the Japs. A lot of them speak broken English, so we keep throwing insults back and forth. Just don't say anything nasty about the emperor; it really pisses them off, and believe me, you don't want them pissed off."

"Anything else?" Shorty asked.

"I see that you guys have the new M1 rifle. The Japs are used to hearing the crack of our Springfields. They listen for five shots and then they move in. You have a six-shot clip, so I would pause after five shots and save the sixth. It will give you an extra edge and the Japs won't know what hit them."

"Maybe you guys have given them all they want and they won't come back again," Franky said.

"They'll come all right. We're protecting the air strip that holds the fighter planes and dive bombers. The more of our planes they put out of commission, the better their chances of winning the war."

"Thanks for the advice," Shorty said.

"Anytime, Mac. Good luck, and look me up if you're ever in Birmingham." The Marine hurried off to the staging area near the beach.

It was pitch black by the time Shorty got everyone in the platoon into a foxhole. He and Morrales took the machine gun emplacement a few yards away from Corky and Franky. The night had turned deathly quiet; the only sound was the rustle of palm trees and the far-off call of a jungle bird. Wide-eyed with fear and anticipation, they waited.

Katie secured the last section of the instrument panel in the cockpit of a B25. She gave the "thumbs up" sign to a co-worker on the floor of the factory. Around her everyone was working at a furious pace on row after row of partially completed airplanes. She and her co-workers felt a great sense of satisfaction in doing a job that contributed to the war effort. President Roosevelt had said the war would be won by the workers of America and everyone was determined to do their part. She gave the signal signifying the completion of the airplane to her crew chief. He blew a whistle and everyone gathered round. Katie climbed down the ladder and joined her fellow workers. She was the crew captain on this particular plane, so it was customary to give a short speech and be the first one to ceremoniously sign her name on the body of the airplane.

"Congratulations, everyone, for a job well done," she began."I'm not much of a speech maker, but I hope this airplane is a safe haven for those who fly her, and may she be used to bring peace to the world."

"Well said, Katie!" a man shouted.

"Way to go, Katie," another worker said.

With cheers ringing in her ears and feeling a great sense of pride, she stepped up to the plane and signed her name in wide sprawling letters. Her co-workers swarmed over the plane like bees on a beehive and covered every square foot with signatures.

"We're going over to the Tap Room after work and celebrate, Katie," a co-worker said. "Why don't you come along?"

"Thanks, but I have a lot of studying to do and some letters to write."

"Come on, Katie, you need some fun in your life."

"You're all very kind and I appreciate your concern, but I'm saving all my fun for the return of my husband." She reached in her purse for one of her precious five dollar bills. "But that doesn't mean that I can't buy a round of drinks for everyone." she handed over the money.

"You're quite a gal, Katie," a man said. "We really admire you for your loyalty and dedication."

Katie blushed. "Thank you very much. It's a pleasure to work with all of you."

After her shift was over she walked outside and was delighted to see large flakes of snow drifting down. She turned the ignition on Shorty's Cord Phaeton and headed across the viaduct for home. The snow was falling heavier as she passed in front of Union Station and turned up the Main Street hill. The hill was slick and she had to maneuver the car back and forth to keep from getting stuck. She was almost home when the tires started spinning and refused to move ahead. She tried everything, but the car was stuck. She put on the emergency brake and got out of the car.

"Does Shorty know you're treating his car that way?"

Katie turned around. Scooter was standing across the street with his gang of friends. He walked over to her with a smile on his face.

"No, and you had better not tell him," Katie said, grateful to see a friendly face on a stormy night.

"Then we had better get you home," Scooter said.

"Who's she?" one of the boys asked.

"His sister-in-law, you dope," another answered.

"Get in the car and we'll push you up the hill," Scooter said.

"No. You might get hurt," Katie said. Her protest made the boys hoot and tease each other about being careful. "We've been doing it ever since the snow started," a snow-covered lad said. "It's an easy way to make money."

"Okay," Katie said. "If you're sure." She got in and restarted the car. The boys began pushing and in no time she crested the hill and pulled to a stop in front of the house. Out of breath, the boys gathered around the car.

"Thank you so much," Katie said as she opened her purse.

"Oh, no you don't," Scooter said. "You're not getting off that easy."

"What do you mean?"

"I told these guys you were the best sledder ever to ride the Main Street Hill."

"I don't know about that."

"Shorty told me you were the only one in your gang to make it all the way around the driveway in front of Union Station."

"The conditions were just right and I got lucky."

"Then show us how it's done," a boy said.

"Yeah, come on!" they all shouted.

Katie was trapped. She had to pay them back for helping her up the hill. She was dressed in coveralls and an old denim long-sleeve shirt, so she couldn't use her clothes as an excuse. "Okay guys. Let me get my boots and some wax paper and I'll be right with you."

The boys were gathered at the top of the hill when she arrived with her sled.

"What kind of sled is that?" a boy asked as he eyed her narrow, flat-bottomed board. It was made of thin oak with the runners curved up and back.

"It's my grandfather's toboggan," Katie replied. She took out the wax paper and began expertly rubbing down the runners.

"Why are you doing that?" a boy wondered.

"Speed," Katie replied. "It makes the runners slick. I have some for everyone. Give it a try."

The boys rubbed the wax paper on their runners.

"Okay, let's go," a boy shouted. "We can beat a girl any old time."

"Let them go first," Katie whispered to Scooter. "We'll follow in their tracks."

With shouts of joy the boys got a running start and took off down the hill.

"Okay, Scooter. I'll show you how Shorty and I always won every race on the hill. You get us moving and then jump on my back. I need the weight to make it all the way to Union Station."

Scooter got them moving down the hill.

"Faster," Katie said.

Scooter was running full tilt. "Okay. Jump on!" Katie commanded. Scooter almost fell off, but he wrapped his arms around her shoulders and held on.

She maneuvered onto the tracks of another sled for more traction and they picked up speed. Wisps of snow swirled into her face and the wind stung her cheeks. It was exhilarating. For the first time in months she forgot the war and all of her responsibilities and she was a kid again. There was no traffic on the hill, but she would have to watch for cabs around Union Station. The sled was half way down the hill and really moving.

"Go Katie! Go!" Scooter yelled above the swirling wind.

"When we get close to the bottom we have to guide right and lean left!" Katie shouted. "If we don't get it just right we won't have enough speed to get around the corner and still make Union Station. I'll tell you when."

"Wow! This is fun!" Scooter said as he held on tightly.

"This is a real racing sled!"

They were rapidly approaching the bottom of the hill.

"Get ready!" Katie shouted. Down below she could see the boys sprawled in the snow. They had failed to make the corner. She deftly guided the sled to the right side of the street. "Now!" she shouted. They leaned left and executed a perfect turn. The sled shot across the street over the snow-covered streetcar tracks, just missed the pedestrian island, and headed for Union Station. "Lean forward with your legs up," Katie said. She made a right turn and they coasted into the driveway of the station.

"We're going to make it," Scooter said, as the runners glided swiftly through the snow.

"We may have enough speed," she said hopefully. Halfway around the horseshoe-shaped driveway, a man and woman stepped out into their path.

"Uh oh," Katie said. She swerved the sled around them and kept going. Scooter's gang had run to the finish line and they were urging them on. Katie turned into the final leg of the horseshoe. She and Scooter coaxed the sled the final few yards and, to the cheers of the boys, made it to the finish line. They fell laughing into the snow and Scooter clasped her hand in his and raised it triumphantly into the air.

"The winner and still champion of the Main Street Hill!" he said. "I guess you guys can't beat a girl any old time after all!" he shouted.

Katie lay flat on her back letting the snowflakes fall gently on her face. It felt so good to laugh and be young at heart again. She jumped up out of the snow. "Come on, you guys. Let's go inside Union Station. I'm buying everyone a hot chocolate."

The boys followed her happily into the station.

17

It was two days before Christmas. The troops had spent an uneventful week in the foxholes surrounding Henderson Field. The heat, rain and mosquitoes made living conditions miserable. Shorty was thankful that everyone in the squad had remained healthy. Darkness was closing in as he left his machine gun nest and went to check on his men. The jungle was alive with birds trumpeting the end of the day. Along the perimeter the troops were checking their weapons and preparing for another tense, sleepless night. Shorty's last stop was at Corky and Franky's foxhole.

"Hey, Shorty," Corky called. "We need a corpsman up here. These mosquitoes keep biting Franky and passing out."

"I've got something you can bite, twerp."

"How are you guys doing?"

"Never better. I would invite you in but the Missus hasn't had time to tidy up. You can leave our Christmas presents on the door step."

"You see what I have to put up with," Franky complained. "A week of living with this guy is about all. . ."

Corky put his finger to his lips and motioned for quiet.

"What?" Shorty whispered.

"Something's not right. Do you hear the bird that sounds like a barking dog? He's really raising hell."

"So what?"

"I've been listening to him all week and he's never been this agitated."

"Maybe he's getting laid," Franky said.

"No. They're coming, I can feel it."

"Cut it out," Franky said. "You don't know what you're talking about."

"Listen," Corky insisted.

"It was then that they heard it. A rustle and the clink of metal from somewhere out in the jungle. Shorty scampered down the line and passed the word to the rest of the squad. He made it back to the machine gun nest. "Did you hear it?" he asked Morrales.

"Yeah. I heard."

Shorty fingered the safety on his Thompson submachine gun. He had traded his MI rifle and all of his remaining cigarettes to a Marine for the weapon. His throat felt dry and he could hear the beating of his heart. The noises were becoming louder and more frequent as though a large force was gathering somewhere out in front of them.

Suddenly a flash of rifle fire cracked from out of the jungle and instantly the hiss of bullets filled the air. The entire perimeter erupted as everyone returned the fire. The shooting ended as quickly as it had begun and quiet once again settled over the sector.

"That was a probe to find our positions," Morrales said.

The unmistakable sound of swords being unsheathed and weapons made ready filtered out of the jungle.

"Hey, GI! We come for you now!" A Jap called out from the jungle. A chill went up Shorty's spine.

"Hey, GI! You ready to die?!" another voice called out in the darkness.

Shorty could hear the Japs milling around in the jungle and the sound of their excited chatter. As the minutes passed the tension became unbearable. The Japs seemed to be working themselves into a frenzy. Then in one terrorizing chorus they screamed "Banzai! Banzai! Banzai!" The ground shook and the jungle erupted as they charged. Flares fired all along the perimeter, exposing the Japs in an eerie white light. The first wave was caught in the barbed wire fortifications constructed by the Marines. Shorty, Morrales, and the rest of the squad laid a withering fire into the onrushing enemy. The thump thump of mortar fire from the American lines was continuous, and artillery shells raked the jungle where the Japs had gathered. The first wave was sacrificed in the barbed wire and land mines. The second wave rushed forward and used their fallen comrades as stepping stones over the fortifications. The flares went out and for a moment all was chaos as everyone kept firing blindly into the darkness.

A clip flew out of Corky's MI and he quickly loaded another and kept firing. Another flare went off and the second wave of Japs was butchered under the intense fire. They seemed to melt into the fortifications. The firing stopped all along the line. Quiet settled over the battlefield as the Japs retreated back to the jungle to regroup.

"Hey Shorty! Are you okay?" Corky called out.

"Yeah," Shorty answered. "Check on McClusky and Duff."

Corky called down the line and reported back to Shorty that everyone was okay.

"How's your ammo?" Shorty asked.

"It's getting low. How about yours?"

"The same."

"Here they come!" Morrales called out. He started raking the area in front of him with machine gun fire. A flare lit the sector and Shorty could see a large force of Japs attacking his right flank. If they broke through, the entire battalion would be overrun. Morrales swung the machine gun to the right and they both began firing. The Japs were falling everywhere but they kept coming.

"Shit!" Morrales yelled frantically. "The gun jammed!" Shorty kept firing the submachine gun until he ran out of ammo.

Corky heard the firing on his right cease and he knew Shorty was in trouble. Another flare went off and he could see Japanese soldiers closing in on the right flank of the line. He climbed out of the foxhole. "Come on, you guys!" he yelled. He charged forward and prayed that the rest of the squad was behind him. Shorty and Morrales were frantically working on the machine gun. Corky led the squad in front of the line and they began firing into the onrushing enemy.

Several of the Japs almost made it to the machine gun nest, but they were cut down and the main force faltered and fell back.

Shorty and Morrales finally got the machine gun working again.

"Fall back!" Shorty called to the squad. They moved back behind the protective covering fire of the machine gun. The Japs were retreating back into the jungle, so the firing stopped all along the line. Everyone in the squad was breathing hard and wide-eyed with terror.

Shorty caught his breath. "Nice going, Corky," he said.

"Yeah," Morrales joined in. "You put your ass on the line and saved ours for sure."

"Everybody pitched in," Corky replied.

"Yeah, but you led the way," Morrales said. "We owe you one." Another flare exploded and the battlefield was bathed in light. The moans and screams of the wounded and dying pierced the night as smoke drifted over the battlefield.

"I knew it was going to be bad, but I never dreamed it would be like this," Corky said as he looked out at the carnage.

"You'd better get used to it," Morrales said. "It's going to be a long war."

Sergeant Balino appeared from out of the night. "You and your men did a fine job holding the line, Sergeant Morrales. That flanking movement by the Japs surprised everyone."

"It was close," Morrales said. "Did the line hold?"

"The Japs broke through a sector controlled by the Fourth Platoon, but they were beaten back in hand-to-hand combat,"

Shorty was worried about Joe. "Any casualties?" he asked.

"We lost Lieutenant Dolan and six other men. Corporal Wilson is okay if that's what you're asking. He helped rally the men and closed the gap in the line." Balino looked out at the hundreds of dead Japanese littering the battlefield. "The arrogant bastards continue to make the same fatal mistake," he said scornfully. "They think they're fighting the Chinese." He walked away into the night.

"We were lucky, Callahan," Morrales said thoughtfully. "If Corky hadn't rallied the squad, the Japs would have broken through. It's a good thing I made the decision to bring him along."

"You're a real genius," Shorty said derisively.

Morrales laughed, then went to check on the rest of the platoon.

The day dawned hot and sticky. The troops gathered outside their foxholes and surveyed the battle scene. The smell of decomposing bodies permeated the air, and some of the troops were getting sick. The engineers on the bulldozers worked frantically to dig a trench to dispose of the bodies rotting in the heat. Battalion headquarters had reported that the remaining Jap force was in full retreat and there was no longer any danger to Henderson Field.

Corky popped the top on a can of Spam and started eating the contents with the tip of his bayonet.

Franky looked at him in dismay. "What are you doing?"

"What's it look like I'm doing?"

Franky stared at Corky and then at the can of Spam. He put his hand over his mouth and ran to a trench and started throwing up.

"Come on, Franky," Corky called after him. "You're ruining my breakfast."

Joe walked up with Sergeant Morrales. "Is this the squad that saved the battalion?" he asked.

"Hey, you guys! It's Joe!" Corky called out to everyone and they gathered round.

"It's no longer 'Joe'," Morrales said. "From now on its 'Sir'."

The gang looked at him questioningly.

"You are now addressing Lieutenant Wilson. He was given a battlefield commission this morning."

"An officer?" Shorty questioned.

"I told you that one day we would be saluting this guy," Morrales said.

"It was tough losing Lieutenant Dolan," Joe replied. "I just hope I'm up to the job."

"You'll make a fine officer," McClusky assured him.

"I heard it was rough over here last night."

"We were all scared shitless," Corky said. "Any more Banzai charges and we're going to forfeit and go home."

"You can go home a hero. Sergeant Morrales put you in for a bronze star for action above and beyond the call of duty. It has been approved by Captain Reynolds."

"Me? I didn't do.—"

"Knock it off," Shorty said. "You're also being promoted to corporal."

"Way to go, Corky" Franky and the rest of the gang congratulated him.

"Speaking of home, I've got a surprise for you," Joe said as Morrales walked away. He reached in his pocket and pulled out an envelope. "The mail finally caught up with us. I have a letter from Katie that I'm supposed to read to you. Let's take a break over there in the shade." He led them over to a grove of palm trees. Everyone waited eagerly as Joe took out the letter and carefully unfolded the pages. To a man they were suffering the effects of combat shock, and they were hot, tired, and covered with grime. The letter was from a world they longed for and wondered if they would ever see again.

Joe began to read:

> Hello to that gang of mine. I want to wish everyone a Merry Christmas and say that I miss you very much. The old town isn't the same without you, so get the war over with and hurry home.
>
> We had the first snowfall of the season yesterday, and it was a doozy. The streetcars were the only thing moving, and the view from our second floor window was spectacular. Union Station was veiled in snow and looked like a picture postcard. Scooter and his gang were sledding down the hill most of the day and it was a joy to once again hear shouts of laughter in the neighborhood.
>
> I had lunch with Emma yesterday. She is well and looking as beautiful as ever. We did some Christmas shopping for our favorite soldiers and your presents should be arriving soon. The Plaza lights will be dark this year and remain off for the duration of the war. I look forward to the day when we can all be together again and count down the seconds to the Christmas season.
>
> Scooter and I went out into the country and cut a seven-foot Scotch pine that was even larger than our imaginations and then realized there was no one to help

get it in the stand. It was a real struggle, but the tree is decorated and now stands majestically in the front window. It is a lovely beacon on a stormy night and even though you're far from home, it shines brightly for all of you. I wish you the best of the holiday season and hope that everyone is well and in good spirits. I light candles every night and pray for your safety. We're all proud of you and grateful for the sacrifices you're making. I love you all very much and miss my gang more than words can say.

>Your sister,
>Katie

They sat quietly digesting the words. Katie's descriptions of snow and the joys of the holiday season were such a contrast to the heat, the jungle, and the killing, that it was hard to comprehend.

"Katie is quite a girl," McClusky said respectfully. "All those years we treated her like one of the guys and took her for granted."

"Remember how we always made her carry her sled back up the Main Street Hill?" Corky said. "She never complained, not even once."

"And no matter how badly we treated her, she always stood up for us," Franky said.

Shorty listened as they continued to reminisce about Katie and their childhood. His separation from her had made him realize how much they had always depended on her. Even now, she continued to encourage them through her letters. He rose to his feet.

"All right, you sob sisters, this ain't home and it sure as hell don't feel like Christmas. You have weapons to clean and this area to police, so get off your asses and get back in the war." He walked away with their curses ringing in his ears.

January 9, 1943

The day broke windy and cold. Outside the kitchen window Katie watched a redbird peck at the ice in the birdbath.

The Christmas snow had melted and left the landscape barren and bleak. For her, the weeks following the holidays were a time of reflection. The excitement of the new year had given way to the realization that spring was still two months away. The warmth and goodwill of Christmas always carried her through January, but February loomed, and in this part of the country it could last forever. She turned on the faucet and ran some warm water into a pan. Her boots felt warm and cozy as she slipped them on, opened the door, and made a quick dash for the birdbath. The winter wind whipped at her bathrobe and seemed to penetrate every pore of her body. She quickly poured the water in the birdbath and dashed back to the warmth of the kitchen.

"Are you trying to catch your death of cold, young lady?"

"Good morning, Grandpa. Would you like some breakfast?"

Her grandfather sat down at the kitchen table. "Just some coffee, if you don't mind." He opened the newspaper and started scanning the pages. "I don't see much of you anymore, Katie."

"I'm busy, Grandpa."

"You can't win the war all by yourself, you know."

"I can't if I don't try."

"You youngsters. I envy your energy."

Katie poured his coffee and placed it on the table.

"There's an article here on Guadalcanal," he said. "The army is starting a push to clear the island of Japs."

Katie continued to move busily about the kitchen. She never read the war news, afraid that it might make her more anxious and afraid.

"I don't imagine the Japs will have much of a chance against that brother of yours."

"Probably not," she smiled.

"Did your mother leave early?"

"Yes. She had to catch up on some work."

"The newspapers say that Pendergast isn't allowed to dabble in politics anymore," he mused. In March of 1940 Boss Tom had been released from prison. He was forbidden by the courts to use his political office at 1908 Main. Ann Callahan had followed him to his business office at the Ready Mix Concrete Company.

"He's been good to Mother."

"They say he takes care of his friends, but buries his enemies in Ready Mix concrete."

"That sounds like something that was hatched at Republican headquarters."

Her grandfather snorted into his coffee cup.

"How's the Civil Defense job coming along, Grandpa?"

"One idiot scheme after another," he said scornfully. "Last week they had me watching for saboteurs at Union Station. I wouldn't know a saboteur from a hockey player. I'm sure they hatch these assignments to keep us busy."

"Civil defense is important to the security of the country. I'm proud of you for donating your time to help the war effort."

He snorted again, but Katie could tell that he was pleased.

"I wouldn't be the least surprised to hear that you're secretly advising President Roosevelt, Katie. You seem to be doing everything else. What's on your agenda for today?"

"I'm picking up Emma. It's Scooter's birthday so we're going to a party at the Wilson's."

"Thank God the snow has melted. I won't have to be terrorized by Scooter and the rest of his gang of sledders. The ice is bad enough without having to worry about my feet being cut from beneath me."

"You know you're exaggerating, Grandpa. You would love to race the old toboggan down the hill again."

"There's some truth to that, all right. I could show these youngsters a thing or two."

"Want some more coffee?"

"No thanks. I'm off to another meeting. Probably an assignment to watch for enemy subs in the Mighty Mo." Katie raised her eyebrows at him.

"Okay, Katie. I'll do my best for the war effort."

She kissed him on the cheek. "That's the spirit, Grandpa."

Katie gave a polite tap on Emma's apartment door before entering. "Emma! Are you ready?"

Emma came out of the bathroom toweling her face. "Hi, Katie. I'm running a bit late."

Katie looked around at the charts and drawings covering the walls. "So this is advertising," she mused.

"Quite a change, huh? At first I was disgusted with myself for taking time away from my sculpting to pursue a business career, but I now realize that I can do both."

"You know what they say about serving two masters."

"Aren't you one to talk."

"My guess is that you will settle into advertising and one day become very rich and very successful."

"Well, thank you. But I have no intention of becoming my father's daughter."

"Maybe you already are. I'm sure he's very proud of you."

"I doubt it. He won't be proud until I'm properly married and spewing out little bankers to carry on the family dynasty."

"You're so hard on your parents."

"It comes from years of association."

"Speaking of marriage, how's Perry?"

"Now we're getting personal."

"I just wondered," Katie said as she traced her finger around a piece of sculpting.

"You're protecting the interests of your big brother and we both know it."

"Me? Ulterior motives?" Katie said, pretending shock. "Heaven forbid."

"Perry wants a commitment and you know how I feel about that."

"Indeed I do. The epitome of the independent woman."

"Now you're patronizing me."

"Certainly not. I'm a great admirer of yours."

"I'd better go put my makeup on before I get too suspicious of your motives."

Katie grinned. "Hurry up. We don't want to miss any of the party."

"Happy birthday to you! Happy birthday to you! Happy birthday, dear Scooter — happy birthday to you," sang everyone assembled at the party. Scooter made a wish and then blew out the candles.

"A teenager," Katie said. "It's impossible to believe."

"Impossible but true," Mrs. Wilson laughed. "It seems like yesterday that I was burping him on my shoulder."

"Oh, Mom," Scooter said in embarrassment.

"You promised not to get sentimental on us," Mr. Wilson reminded her.

"You can start opening your presents," Katie said. She felt at home with the Wilsons, and had become a member of the family in spirit as well as by marriage. The Wilsons treated her like the daughter they had always hoped for. They fawned over her shamelessly and were always inquiring about her welfare. They had wanted her to come live with them while Joe was gone, but understood her desire to stay home. They insisted that she come to dinner at least twice a week, and informed her immediately when they heard from Joe.

"Open this one," Katie said. "It's from Emma."

Scooter tore at the wrapping paper and uncovered two brand-new baseballs.

"A reminder that spring isn't very far away," Emma said.

"Thank you, Emma," Scooter gave her a hug.

"Now mine," Katie handed him her present.

"A football almanac! Just what I wanted, Katie."

"I'm glad you like it."

After Scooter finished his presents everyone gathered in the kitchen for ice cream and cake. "Now I have something for all of you," Scooter said. He reached in the back pocket of his jeans and pulled out an envelope. "A letter from Joe." He carefully unfolded the letter and began to read:

> Dear Scooter,
>
> I can hardly believe that you're a teenager. It seems like only yesterday that you were eight years old and making the big catch that saved the day against our rivals from the west side. And by the way, Shorty still talks about that catch. He has enclosed the belated five dollars that he owes you for the Cardinals winning the 1942 World Series. The entire gang sends their best wishes for a happy birthday. We all promise many future outings to your favorite sporting events, and Franky and Corky are hoarding war souvenirs for you.
>
> The weather is hot and humid here on Guadalcanal. I envy you the winter weather. After this experience, I will never again complain about snow. Katie mentioned that you and your gang have taken over sledding rights to the Main Street Hill. Our gang will challenge you when we get home.
>
> The Guadalcanal campaign is moving along on schedule, so we hope to be leaving here very soon. I'm sure we will be sent somewhere else in the South Pacific. Everyone feels that the tide has turned in our favor and that it's only a matter of time before we win the war. However, there is still a lot to be done and we have learned not to be over-confident.
>
> Well, that's it from here. My very best wishes to you on your birthday and on becoming a teenager. Tell Mom and Dad I said hello and that I miss them very much. My thanks to all of you for taking care of Katie. Until we're throwing the old pigskin around again.
>
> Your brother,
> Joe

Scooter folded the letter neatly and put it back in his back pocket.

"And now I have a surprise for you," Katie said. "Joe wanted me to save it for Scooter's birthday party. When you write to him, you will have to address the envelopes to Lieutenant Joe Wilson."

They all looked at her, puzzled.

"Joe has been promoted to second lieutenant. He's an officer!"

"Wow!" Scooter exclaimed. "That's really something!"

"We're all proud of him, Katie," Mr. Wilson said.

"I'm proud of him too," Katie replied. "Although I can't picture Shorty and the rest of the gang saluting him and calling him "Sir.""

"I'm sure they will find a way around it," Emma said. "Congratulations Katie. How does it feel to be an officer's wife?"

"Not anywhere near as good as being the wife of a civilian."

"Let's go into the dining room and celebrate with some wine," Mr. Wilson said.

After the party Katie drove Emma back to the Art Institute.

"You seem more relaxed and able to enjoy yourself, Katie."

"I feel better. They say with repetition you can get used to anything. I'll never be completely comfortable until I'm with Joe, but I've settled into a routine. With work and school and war committees, the days are passing more quickly than I could have imagined."

"And you're more optimistic?"

"Perhaps. Sometimes I get down and feel like I'm barely holding on, and then I get a letter from Joe that picks me up again." Katie glanced over at Emma. "Do you miss Shorty? You never say."

"Of course I do. I've found that pretending I don't care sometimes makes things easier to bear."

"You don't mean to tell me there's a soft spot under that tough, independent exterior."

"Please keep my secret. You're the only one who knows."

"Having you for a friend has really helped, Emma. Sometimes when I start to break down I conjure up this image of you, so reserved and regal and full of confidence."

"That sounds more like a description of you. I have my moments of weakness that you would never succumb to. You're the person everyone admires."

"I don't think that's true, but thank you for saying so." Katie stopped the car in front of Emma's apartment. She leaned over and kissed her on the cheek. "Even if you don't marry my brother, I want us to be friends for life."

"So do I, Katie. I'll call you later in the week."

18

The sun was sinking slowly into the Solomon Sea as Captain Reynolds gathered B Company in a staging area near the airfield. Joe and Lieutenant Kern were at his side, and Sergeant Balino stood a few yards away watching the troops gather round. After a few minutes Balino stepped forward. "At ease, everyone. You can light up if you want, but keep quiet and listen carefully to what Captain Reynolds has to say."

The Captain moved to the front of the company. "Thank you, Sergeant Balino. I want to offer all of you my congratulations on a job well done. Henderson Field is now secure, so we can go on the offensive." He pointed to a spot on the map Joe was holding that showed an area of ocean between the Solomon Islands. "In the past the Japs have been able to bring troops and supplies down these sea lanes known as 'the slot' with little resistance. I'm happy to say that is no longer the case. We have put the Tokyo Express out of business and our Navy has control of the waters around Guadalcanal." He pointed to another map held up by Lieutenant Kern. "Our new assignment is to push the Japs off the island. To accomplish our objective we have to take this mass of hills shaped like a sea horse and relieve the 132nd Infantry on the heights of Mount Austen. The 132nd has seized the mountain top, but they are surrounded by Japs. You can expect stiff resistance. The Japs control the high country and they are heavily fortified. They also realize this will be their last chance to save face and to die a glorious death for their emperor. We know they won't surrender, so be prepared for anything. Good luck and be ready to jump off at 0600 in the morning."

Shorty led the squad back to their positions around Henderson Field.

"Does this mean that I have to leave my foxhole?" Corky joked.

"I was hoping he would congratulate us on a job well done and announce that we were going back to Hawaii," MeClusky said.

"Fat chance," Franky said. "I liked it a lot better when the Japs were coming to us. The jungle scares the hell out of me."

"What's there to fear?" Corky said. "Just snakes, crocodiles, and some little yellow people running around trying to cut off your nuts."

"Thanks, twerp. That's just what I wanted to hear."

"Quit worrying," Shorty said confidently. "We're going to be okay.

When we're in the jungle be alert and watch each other's backs. Corky and Franky will alternate on the point and Duff will hang back and watch for snipers. You'll need to carry several canteens, but don't carry any more equipment than you have to. We're going to be hacking our way through some dense jungle. Check your weapons before turning in and try to get a good night's sleep."

At daybreak, Shorty looked down the line and saw Joe leading the Fourth Platoon into the jungle. Joe waved to him and disappeared into the foliage. Shorty led his squad under the canopy of trees and they were swallowed by the jungle. Above them, the huge hardwood trees rose 150 feet into the sky, blocking out the sun. The jungle was like a sauna bath. The troops were already starting to pop the snaps on their canteen belts. "Conserve your water," Shorty ordered. The denseness of the underbrush and the fear of the enemy kept them at a slow pace through the first half of the day. After noon, they became more familiar with their surroundings and picked up the pace. Hours later they came to a branch of the Matanikau River. Shorty posted Andy, Duff, and Bo with a machine gun to cover their right flank as the platoon crossed the river. Shorty watched as the troops waded waist deep into the muddy waters. The platoon was almost across the river when he waved for the machine gun crew to follow. Suddenly, a burst of rifle fire raked the jungle. Shorty hit the ground and crawled back to his men.

"They're coming right at us," Andy said, pointing to an area in front of their position.

Shorty peeked above the ground and saw a large force of Japs moving steadily through the jungle. "Come on," he said. "There's too many of them. We have to get out of here!"

When Bo and Andy raised up to follow, Shorty heard the slap of bullets against flesh and saw them both go down. He crawled back to Andy and rolled him over. A bullet had badly shattered his upper arm. Duff took over the machine gun, and his heavy, accurate firing slowed the Jap advance. Shorty crawled over to Bo and saw that half his head was missing. There was no need to check for a pulse. He paused for a moment trying to figure out what to do.

"Come on, Shorty! Move it!" Corky shouted. He and the rest of the squad had doubled back when they heard firing break out. The Jap riflemen continued to zing bullets overhead with machine gun and rifle fire. Corky and Franky helped Andy to his feet and got him moving toward the river with Shorty and Duff protecting their retreat. Shorty watched as they moved out into the river. "Okay, Oklahoma. Give me some steady fire with the machine gun. Rake the entire area in front of us and I'll throw all of our grenades. We only have until the smoke clears, so when I give the signal, let's haul ass out of here."

Duff started laying a withering fire in front of their position. Shorty pulled the pin on a hand grenade and threw it out in front of him. He tossed four more grenades as fast as he could pull the pins. "Run!" he shouted. He and Duff hit the water at full speed and started lunging across the river. Half way across, Shorty's lungs started to ache and his legs felt like they were on fire. The Thompson submachine gun he held above his head seemed to weigh a hundred pounds. They were almost across the river when bullets from Jap .25 rifles started whizzing by their heads and slapping at the water. They made it to the far bank and dove headlong into the jungle. The platoon had set up machine gun positions and were returning a protective fire back across the river.

"Way to go, Callahan," Morrales said as he crawled up next to Shorty. "It's a good thing you posted that machine gun. The bastards were lying there waiting to ambush us when we crossed the river."

"We lost Bo," Shorty said.

"Sorry, Callahan."

"How's Andy?"

"The corpsmen are working on him. It looks like he's going to lose that arm." Morrales slithered away down the line.

Shorty dropped his forehead onto the ground. He lay there for several minutes trying to catch his breath. After he recovered he got up and walked over to where Corky and the guys were watching the corpsmen work on Andy.

"How's he doing?"

"We've stopped the bleeding and given him a shot of morphine," one of the corpsmen said. "We have to evacuate him if we're going to save his arm."

Shorty knelt down beside Andy. "It looks like you're going to be heading home, you goldbrick."

"Yeah. A million-dollar wound," Franky said.

Andy opened his eyes. The morphine had drugged him against the pain. "Hey, Corky," he whispered. "Draw me a picture of Betty Grable."

"You'll soon be dating all the Betty Grables you can handle," Corky replied.

"I don't imagine too many girls will be standing in line waiting to date a one-armed cop."

"Don't talk like that, Cousin," Duff encouraged him. "You're going to be okay."

"Let's get going," the corpsman ordered. "We have to evacuate you back down the Matanikau."

Shorty and Duff helped Andy to his feet. "You guys take care of yourselves," Andy said. "Sorry to be running out on you."

"You'll be back with us before you know it," Shorty tried to encourage him. Andy put his good arm around the corpsman's shoulders and began walking away unsteadily. The gang watched until he disappeared into the jungle.

"Let's move out!" Morrales commanded. "We have to make the foothills of the Sea Horse before dark."

Shorty helped Morrales get the platoon moving and an hour later they had left the jungle behind and were climbing upward into the foothills of the Sea Horse. The open terrain was a welcome sight. The rolling hills were arid and covered with brown cogan grass. They made it to their destination just before nightfall and began digging in. Morrales took the first watch as Shorty collapsed into his foxhole. He was exhausted from the battle on the Mantanikau and he was depressed about losing Bo and Andy. He fell asleep sitting up with his head leaning back against the wall of the foxhole.

At daybreak, he discovered that the Fourth Platoon had moved into position on his left flank. He found Joe at a command post going over some maps.

"How you doing, Joe?"

"Shorty!" Joe jumped up and shook his hand. "I'm glad you made it okay. How is everyone in the gang?"

Shorty told him about the battle on the river and losing Bo and Andy.

"I'm sorry. When the next messenger goes out I'll find out how Andy is getting along."

Shorty nodded his thanks. "What's our assignment for today?"

Joe looked up the slope of the Sea Horse. "Battalion headquarters has identified at least six heavily fortified pillboxes that will have to be cleared. We begin the attack in a few minutes."

"I'd better get back to the squad."

"Good luck, Shorty. My platoon will be on your left flank, so let me know if you need anything."

"Okay, Joe. I heard you guys had it rough yesterday."

"Ten men killed and five wounded. The Japs are putting up a stiff resistance."

Shorty headed back to his men. A few minutes later the signal was given and both platoons headed up the south slope of the Sea Horse. The going was rugged for most of the day. They soon discovered that battalion headquarters had vastly underestimated the number of pillboxes. By the end of the day the battalion had cleared out 40 Jap positions and had captured the heights of the Sea Horse. As the sun began to sink behind Mount Austen, the Third and Fourth platoons started digging in before the Japs counterattacked. Joe stopped by Shorty's foxhole. "I've got news about Andy."

Everyone put down their shovels and gathered around.

"How is he?"

"They've evacuated him by air to Hawaii." Joe paused for a moment. "He lost his arm. As soon as he goes through rehabilitation the army will be sending him home."

Shorty remembered Andy's comment about being a one-armed cop. He knew how much the police force meant to Andy and he wondered if he would be able to continue working.

"Can you find out what hospital they're sending him to so we can drop him a note?" Corky asked.

"Sure."

"At least he's going home," Franky said, trying to make the most of the bad news.

"I bet his first stop is the Chesterfield Club," Duff said enviously.

"He was a good soldier. Now get busy and finish digging those foxholes," Shorty ordered. He took Joe by the arm and they walked a few yards away. "Do you think the Japs will hit us tonight?"

"Yes. They have to regain control of the high ground or they're finished on Guadalcanal. They also realize we can use Henderson Field as a staging area on our march to Japan, so they will probably hit us with everything they have."

"I think we have them beaten."

"So do I. Now all we have to do is convince them."

Joe took off his helmet and ran his hand through his hair. "The Second Platoon lost both of their NCOs today, so I'm going to take command. We'll be behind you covering the north slope of the Sea Horse."

"Who's taking your place in the Fourth Platoon?"

"Sergeant Morrales will be in command. You've been promoted to staff sergeant and you're now in command of the Third Platoon. Captain Reynolds also put you and your machine gun crew in for Silver Stars."

"We were just protecting our asses," Shorty said.

"Your actions saved the platoon from being massacred in the river."

"Maybe it will mean something to Bo's parents," Shorty said reflectively.

"And show Andy that his sacrifice is greatly appreciated by his country."

Shorty nodded. "I guess I had better go check on my men."

"Good luck, Shorty."

"You too, Joe."

It was almost dawn when the rains came. Corky was awakened by rain drops beating down on his steel pot. "Terrific," he said. "I bet it hasn't rained in these Godforsaken hills in six months. Did you bring a poncho, Franky?"

"Sure. I also brought umbrellas and some galoshes. Eleanor Roosevelt will be here in a few minutes to slip them on our footies."

"No need to be sarcastic," Corky said as he moved up next to Franky and peered out at the darkness.

"Man, this fog is thick."

"Tell me about it. You can't hear anything with the rain slapping down on the dry ground."

"Do you remember when we were kids?" Corky said. "How we used to sneak down to the sheds at Union Station and watch the trains slip in and out of the fog."

"And make up stories about all those mysterious places we wanted to see."

"Istanbul, Calcutta, and Casablanca," Corky remembered.

"Yeah. And Andy would always fall asleep when the rain started beating down on the roof of the sheds."

They paused for a moment, thinking about Andy.

"I hope he's okay," Corky said.

"Me too."

"You guys keep it down!" Shorty called softly from the foxhole to the right of them.

"Hey, Shorty," Corky called back. "We need a lid for this foxhole."

"You need a lid for your mouth," Shorty called back.

"You're not exactly my idea of a good neighbor," Corky responded.

"If you don't shut. . ."

"Banzai!" The terrifying scream pierced the night as hundreds of Japs charged up the slope, having used the rain as cover to sneak up on the American lines.

"Fix bayonets!" Shorty shouted. The Japs were too close for mortars or artillery so it was every man for himself. Along the perimeter of defense there was a deafening roar as weapons fired simultaneously into the wave of Jap soldiers. The wave bent for a moment, but there were too many and the Japs drove into the American lines. Shorty sprayed fire from the submachine gun until the Japs were on top of him. "Out of your fox-holes!" he yelled frantically. A flare went off and he could see Japs all around him. He hit one with the barrel of the submachine gun and he shot another. A blow knocked his helmet off and he fell to his knees. He could feel warm blood gushing down his face.

In the light of the flare, Corky saw Shorty go down. A Jap officer was poised over him with a sword. Corky fought his way past two Jap soldiers. He plunged his bayonet into the ribs of the Jap officer. The man screamed and fell to his knees. Shorty hit him in the jaw with the butt of his sub-machine gun and the officer tumbled down the hill.

The hand-to-hand combat continued with the platoon fighting fierce-ly until the Japs were driven out of the American lines. The surviving Jap soldiers retreated back down the slope. An occasional crack of rifle fire sounded as stragglers were cut down. "Franky! Are you okay?" Corky hurried over to the foxhole. There were two Jap soldiers lying where Franky was supposed to be. Franky clawed his way from beneath them. He took several deep breaths to calm himself. "I shot them and they fell in on top of me," he said.

The Japs had simultaneously attacked both sides of the Sea Horse. Joe's carbine felt hot in his hands as he fired the weapon into the Japs storming up the north slope. They were putting heavy pressure on both flanks of his line of defense — the same tactic they had used at Henderson Field. Joe knew they would put tremendous pressure on the flanks and then storm the center and try for a break-through at the first possible moment. He was out of his foxhole, running up and down the line, encouraging his men and helping out where he could. He was on the left flank of the line when the Japs made an all out assault on the center. He hurried over to help hold the line. The battlefield was lit with flares. Bright red tracers fed down the slope, probing for the enemy. Joe could see that the Japs were making headway up the slope. If they broke through the line, they would hit Shorty's platoon from the rear and drive them off the Sea Horse. Joe moved out in front of the line and laid a dev-astating fire down the slope as he rallied his men to hold.

He ran out of ammo and was reaching for a clip when he felt a a ter-rific blow to his chest. He fell to his knees and tried to catch his breath, but the air wouldn't come. He tried to stand, but his body would not obey the command. All of the feeling left his body in a rush and he collapsed on his side. Out on the horizon the clouds had cleared and he could see the North Star shining brightly down as the chaos of the battlefield swirled around him. He felt strangely detached from it all. As he continued to watch the star, it started to dim. He wondered about that. He tried to hold on, but was too weak. Everything started to slip away.

His last thought was of Katie staring at him from across the dance floor at the Pla-Mor.

As the dawn began to break, Shorty could see soldiers from both armies sprawled over the battlefield. Duff walked wearily up to them. Shorty started to ask about Andy and then he remembered that Andy was gone. It was such a relief to know that everyone in the gang was okay. He checked on the rest of the platoon and discovered that eight of his men had been wounded, and three were dead. It was tough to lose men he was responsible for.

"Hey, Callahan!" Morrales called. "Sergeant Balino wants to see you at the command post!"

"Take over, Corky. I'll go find out what Balino has planned for us. The Japs are finished in this sector so start preparing the men to move out."

"You'd better see a corpsman and get that head wound bandaged," Corky said.

"Yeah. I'll take care of it." As Shorty walked along the crest of the hill he looked at the terrain leading up to Mount Austen and realized there would still be some difficult fighting ahead to clear the remaining Japs from the island. Balino was down on one knee in a grove of palm trees going over some maps. He stood up when he saw Shorty approach. Shorty could tell from Balino's expression that something serious was brewing. His platoon was probably going to be given another dangerous assignment.

"What's up, Sergeant?"

Balino took out a handkerchief and put it gently against Shorty's head. "What happened to you?"

"A Jap officer thought my head was a coconut."

"You'd better see a corpsman."

"What did you want to see me about?"

Balino paused for a moment. "There's no easy way to say this, Callahan, so I'll give it to you straight. Lieutenant Wilson was hit last night on the north slope of the Sea Horse."

Shorty felt his knees grow weak and his mouth go dry. He tried to speak, but nothing would come out.

"They've evacuated him to a hospital ship off Lunga Point."

"How bad was he hit?" he finally managed to say.

"I don't know. He was evacuated during the assault."

"How can I find out?"

"We're being relieved, so you can check on him when we get back to the beach. Get your men ready to move out."

Shorty walked numbly back to the squad. He kept telling himself to keep calm and everything would be okay.

Corky read his expression. "What's up?"

"Joe was hit last night," Shorty said.

For a moment they stared at him in stunned silence.

"How bad?" Franky finally asked.

Shorty shook his head. "We'll find out when we get back to Henderson field."

"Another million-dollar wound," Franky said hopefully.

"Some guys have all the luck," Corky said. "He's sure to get some leave time." He took Shorty by the arm. "Come on. Let's get the platoon formed up so we can get back and check on Joe."

The ship-to-shore landing craft cut through the blue waters around Lunga Point and headed for the hospital ship anchored offshore. No one felt like talking so they sat in silence, watching the bright red cross on the side of the hospital ship. Shorty turned and looked back through the boat's wake at the island of Guadalcanal. It looked so green and peaceful, with gentle waves rolling onto palm-covered beaches. As the cross on the ship grew larger, he became more apprehensive. He took a deep breath and tried to calm himself. The engine on the landing craft was cut and they drifted up to the side of the ship. He and the other guys helped the corpsmen on board lift the wounded into bay doors and then jumped on board. Shorty stopped a doctor who was hurrying past. "We're looking for Lieutenant Joe Wilson," he said.

"When did they bring him on board?"

"This morning."

"Check up on the main deck. They've set up a processing center for the wounded."

Shorty led the guys up three decks of stairs and onto the main deck. On the forward deck a nurse and several doctors were going over various forms spread out on a make-shift desk. Shorty walked over to the nurse. She looked up at him and saw the wound on the side of his head. "The aid station is one deck down."

"I'm not looking for aid. I'm trying to find my brother-in-law. His name is Lieutenant Joe Wilson. He was brought in this morning."

"Oh," the nurse said. "Let me look at the list." Shorty watched as her finger traced down the names on each page of the clipboard. Her finger stopped abruptly and she looked up at him. "If you will wait here for just a moment, I have to confirm something and I'll be right back."

Shorty paced back and forth, nervously looking out to sea and wondering why it was taking so long. When he turned around the nurse was popping through the door of the hold. She was followed by an army chaplain.

"This is Father Ryan," she explained.

"What's going on, Father? What's happened?"

The chaplain took Shorty gently by the arm and led him over to the rail of the ship. He paused for a moment, looking out to sea and trying to form the words. "I'm sorry, Sergeant. Lieutenant Wilson didn't make it. He died a few hours ago."

Shorty heard the words, but they refused to register.

"No. That can't be," he said. "There must be a mistake."

"I'm sorry," the priest repeated. Shorty felt like he was going to come apart. He wanted to scream, but he just stood there staring at the chaplain.

"Where is he?" Corky asked.

"Over here," the priest said as he led them across the deck. "The dead have been prepared for burial at sea."

In a state of shock Shorty and the guys followed him across the deck of the ship. He pointed to an area of the fantail where nine canvas-covered bodies lay.

Shorty walked numbly over and knelt down. "Which one is Lieutenant Wilson?" he asked the sailor on duty.

The sailor checked his clipboard.

"Third from the left."

Shorty took out his knife and started cutting away the bindings on the canvas.

"You can't do. . ."

Father Ryan put his hand up and silenced the sailor.

Shorty slowly unwrapped the canvas covering and the bandages, hoping and praying with all his being that it was going to be someone else.

He pulled back the last wrapping and stared at Joe's face. He looked so peaceful in death.

"You can be assured that he is with God," Father Ryan said, trying to comfort him.

Shorty turned and looked at the guys. They were staring at Joe in shock. Corky had tears running down his cheeks.

"How was he killed?" Shorty asked as he reached out and touched Joe's face.

"He was hit twice in the chest with bullets from a machine gun," Father Ryan said as he helped Shorty to his feet. "The doctors and nurses did everything they could."

Father Ryan conferred with the sailors and they began preparing the bodies for burial at sea. "It's time to begin," he said, as the sailors secured the dead on canvas stretchers.

"But Father," Shorty said frantically. "Can't we take Joe back to the unit?" This was all happening so fast and he had to do something.

"I'm sorry son, but we have to follow regulations. The heat requires that we move swiftly."

Shorty felt a strange detachment set in. This couldn't be real. It was one of those dreams that you would wake up from and. . .

"I am the resurrection and the life, saith the Lord: he that believeth in me, though he were dead, yet shall he —"

Father Ryan's words seemed to be coming from far, far away. Shorty's thoughts were of Joe and Katie and home. It was springtime and they were kids again running through the parks and hanging out at Union Station.

"Our Father, who art in heaven, Hallowed be Thy Name. Thy Kingdom come. Thy will be. . ."

He had talked to Joe last night. They were going to wrap up the campaign and maybe even get some leave time. Joe had to eventually go home. He had never considered that. . .

"Unto Almighty God we commend the soul of our brothers departed, and we commit their bodies to the deep; in sure and certain hope of the Resurrection unto eternal life; through our Lord Jesus Christ. . ."

He kept telling himself to step forward and do something, but he just stood there feeling helpless and empty.

There was a rustle of canvas; a gentle splash in the sea, and all was quiet. From somewhere on Lunga Point came the sound of a solitary bugle playing taps. The notes carried crisply away from the land and out to sea.

Day is done. . .
Gone the sun. . .
From-the-lake. . .
From-the-hill. . .
From-the-sky. . .

Shorty thought back to that summer night at Lake Forest that seemed an eternity ago. He was almost asleep when Katie had called to him:

"Shorty?"

"Yeah."

"Do you think there will be a war?"

"I don't know."

"If there is a war, you have to watch out for Corky and Joe."

"Yeah. I'll do that."

Rest in peace. . .
Sol Jer brave. . .
God is nigh.

As the last note was carried away on the wind, Shorty looked out at the setting sun and knew with certainty that Katie would never forgive him. She held him responsible for Joe's safety, and when he lost Joe he had lost them both.

19

Ann Callahan sat dejectedly at Aunt Martha's kitchen table. Tears streamed down her face.

"I don't know what to do, Aunt Martha," she sobbed. "It's been two weeks since Joe's death and I've tried everything, but Katie's not coming out of it."

"There, there, my dear." Aunt Martha put her arm around Ann and tried to comfort her. "You must hold on and hope for the best. Are the doctors still diagnosing amnesia?"

"Yes. The news of Joe's death was so traumatic that she couldn't handle it. They say it's the type of amnesia that occurs with a lot of war veterans."

"What is the long-term diagnosis?"

"The psychiatrists don't know. The amnesia could last for weeks or even months, but at some point she will come out of it. If and when that happens she could go into a severe depression or even become suicidal."

"I was hoping the memorial service would bring her back to reality."

"She has never acknowledged the memorial service. It's so heartbreaking to listen to her talk about Joe and still keep planning for the future." Ann dabbed at the tears on her face. "She walks around in a trance and she has no appetite. You can tell that she knows something, but her mind just won't accept it. If she could just come to terms with what has happened, then she could go through the grieving process and begin to heal. You can imagine what it's like for Joe's parents to lose a son and then have to deal with this on a daily basis."

"I'm sure they are very understanding."

"Yes. But until Katie's condition is resolved they have to keep up this pretense."

Aunt Martha took her hand. "It may take a while, but I promise you that we are going to get her back." She paused for a moment contemplating the problem. "Perhaps a change of scenery would help. Do you think we could get her to come out to the lake for the weekend?"

"It's worth a try. She has always been able to confide in you."

"Have you heard anything from Egan?"

"No. We've received letters from Corky and Franky, but nothing from

Egan. I'm sure Joe's death must be devastating for him. He had such confidence that he could bring everyone in his gang home safely."

"At the moment our main concern has to be Katie's welfare, and then we can worry about Egan."

Ann nodded. "You're right of course. It's going to take all of our efforts if we're going to save her."

Katie glanced over at Emma. It was "letter-writing night" and they were at the home of one of the war wives in the neighborhood. "I'm glad you came with me," Katie said. "Last week it was Marie and Judy. Letter-writing night is becoming very popular."

Emma nodded. Katie looked ashen and very tired. If something didn't break soon she would probably have to be hospitalized. Emma was aware of the nervous glances from the other women, who were clearly uncomfortable having them there as a visual reminder that with the simple delivery of a telegram they could go from wife to widow.

"Does Shorty ever answer your letters?" Katie inquired.

"Hardly ever. He tells Corky what he wants me to hear, and Corky always includes it in his letters."

"He does the same thing with Joe. I think he has an aversion to pen and paper."

"How's your letter coming along?"

"Okay. It's hard to not be repetitive. I'm sure I bore Joe with all the details of life on the homefront."

Emma searched for something to say, but nothing seemed right and she remained silent.

Katie broke the silence. "How's your business doing?" She could be perfectly lucid for a moment and then she would fall back into a trance.

"I've moved the business out of my studio and into an office on the Plaza."

"I knew you would be a success."

"Thanks for the confidence you've shown in me."

"As if that meant anything. You're like Shorty. You have enough confidence for ten people."

"I hope that's a compliment." Emma glanced over at the page Katie was working on and saw that it was blank. Katie seemed very agitated. She kept nervously rubbing her hands together and biting at her lower lip.

"Why don't we wrap it up and try again later," Emma suggested.

Katie nodded.

Emma gave regrets to their hostess, and noticed the look of relief on the woman's face.

They bundled up against the February wind and hurried to Katie's car.

"I was wondering if you would like to work with me in the advertising business," Emma said as Katie started the car.

"I appreciate that, but I'm too busy with the war effort."

"I mean later, after the war. The business is growing so fast that I need a partner."

"I don't think so, Emma. I have my heart set on teaching school and raising a family."

"I'll leave the offer open in case you change your mind. What are you doing this weekend?"

"Aunt Martha has invited me out to the lake. I haven't been back since Joe and I were married."

"I know your Aunt Martha would love to see you."

"Why don't you come along, Emma?"

"I can't. I have to get caught up on my work."

"We can have Uncle Ray's cabin all to ourselves."

"You need some time to yourself, Katie. I'll call you on Monday and see how you're getting along."

Katie stood at Aunt Martha's picture window watching snow flurries blow across the lake. The landscape looked barren and cold and she shivered.

Aunt Martha watched her. She seemed as rigid as a statue. "If the temperature drops tonight I bet the lake freezes over," she said as she walked up and put her arms around Katie.

"The weather was like this when Joe and I were married."

"Yes. I remember. You're so cold, Katie. Would you like a sweater?"

"No, thank you."

"You hardly ate a bite of your dinner. Why don't you let me fix you a piece of apple cobbler."

"Thanks, Aunt Martha, but I'm not hungry."

"I understand, dear. Why don't I go turn down your bed so you can get under the covers and read."

"I would rather stay at the cabin."

"The cabin is closed for the winter."

"If you let me stay there, I won't be any trouble. I can build my own fire and clean up when I leave."

"It isn't the trouble. I just don't think it's a good idea for you to be alone."

"Why, Aunt Martha?"

"Well I. . ."

"Maybe I should go home. I don't want to be a bother to you and Uncle Ray."

"Since when have you ever been a bother? Uncle Ray will be happy to open the cabin and build a fire for you."

Uncle Ray put down his paper. "Of course I will. I need to check on the place and be sure the raccoons haven't carried away my winter supplies." He put on his coat and hat and hurried out the door.

Aunt Martha coaxed Katie away from the window. "Come into the kitchen and I'll fix you a cup of warm milk. You can sip it while I brush your hair."

"I don't want my hair brushed," Katie said matter-of-factly."

"But why? You've always loved it so."

"I don't know. . . I don't want to be pretty anymore."

"Why, Katie? Why don't you want to be pretty?"

Katie looked like she was going to cry.

Aunt Martha stroked her hair. "It's all right, sweetheart. Don't tire yourself anymore. Uncle Ray will be back soon."

"The fire is roaring and the cabin is nice and warm," Uncle Ray said as he entered the house. "If you're ready I'll walk you to the cabin."

"Thank you, Uncle Ray, but I would rather go by myself."

Her aunt and uncle exchanged glances.

"I just want to be alone," Katie assured them.

"All right, dear. Uncle Ray will check on you in the morning." They watched as she started down the path leading off the hill.

"I'll go check on her before it gets dark," Uncle Ray said reassuringly.

"We have to watch her closely," Aunt Martha said. "She's showing signs of breaking and I don't want her to be alone when it happens."

The snow was starting to fall in large gentle flakes as Katie walked onto the porch of the cabin. Images of the past kept penetrating her consciousness. It was her wedding night and Joe had her in his arms, carrying her across the threshold. Inside she took off her coat and looked around. Everything felt cozy and familiar. Firelight danced off the cabin walls. She walked into the bedroom, remembering the excitement and romance of her wedding night. She sat rigidly on the bed trying to recall every detail. Through the window of the cabin she could see the snow tumbling down and the ground covered in white.

Suddenly, all of her fond memories faded and she became very agitated. She felt like she couldn't breathe, and the cabin walls seemed to be closing in on her. The firelight that was warm and friendly turned sinister and threatening. She had to get out of the cabin. She hurried out of the bedroom and ran out the front door. Her shoes left prints in the snow as she followed the path down to the lake. Her coat was back at the cabin, but she felt insulated from the cold. Her thoughts were of a summer night that seemed an eternity ago. She and Joe were together in Uncle Ray's canoe. She walked over to the shed and opened the door. The canoe was where it was supposed to be. It was light and slid easily through the snow and into the lake. She climbed in and grabbed an oar. In the distance the clubhouse was veiled in snow, and a cold wind blew swales across the lake. But for her it was a warm summer night and she was once again in Joe's arms listening to music flowing from the clubhouse.

"Do you love me, Joe?"

"You know I do."

"You couldn't love me as much as I love you."

"How much is that?"

"More than I can say."

"Do you swear by the ghost of Chief Spotted Tail that you will always love me?"

She steered the canoe toward the island, remembering their last 4th of July together. The stars were shining down in all their luster and she was in his arms, dancing around and around the island. The night was warm, romantic, and wonderful. She kissed him gently on the lips and pulled him to the ground away from the glare of Shorty's spotlight.

"Lovers caught in a passionate embrace," he said.

"The Scandal of Lover's Island," she whispered. "I love you, Joe."

"I love you too, Katie."

She felt so safe in his arms. "Will our lives always be so perfect?" she sighed contentedly.

"Probably not. But we'll manage as long as we have each other."

And just as quickly Joe and the warm summer night were gone and she was alone on the lake. The landscape looked barren and cold and the night was closing in. The wind picked up and blew the snow squall away to the east. The heavens opened and the stars shone down in all their wonder. She sat in the canoe studying the sky, her eyes scanning the Big and Little Dippers and then becoming transfixed on one of the planets. She tried to remember which one it was. Suddenly, a star entered her field of vision and came tumbling across the evening sky. It seemed so out of

place in the natural order of the universe. Her Grandmother always said that if you saw one it meant that someone you knew was going to. . . Katie turned her eyes away. She was standing in a doorway. There was a soldier in uniform standing on a porch and he was holding a telegram. She tried to turn away, but the telegram was in her hands and she was slowly opening the envelope and reading the words. 'We regret to inform you. . .' and in that one awful instant she knew that Joe was gone and that she would never ever see him again. The realization was too much to bear, so she curled herself into a ball and slipped head first into the freezing water.

The phone rang and Uncle Ray picked it up.
"Hello."
"Ray, this is Tom Watts. What has gotten into that niece of yours?"
Uncle Ray was instantly alert. "Why? What are you talking about?"
"She's out in the lake in a canoe."
"She's what?" Panic gripped him.
"She's out in the lake and she doesn't even have a coat on."
Uncle Ray dropped the phone and started running upstairs to his telescope.
Aunt Martha was on his heels. "What's happened?" she asked fearfully.
Uncle Ray put his eye to the telescope. He scanned the lake and found the canoe. "Oh my God, No!" he yelled. He was already running down the stairs. "Call for an ambulance, Martha!" He ran outside and started frantically ringing the fire bell.

Katie kept going down and down until she could feel the silt and mud at the bottom of the lake. She thought back to those hot summer days when she was a little girl. The lake would be warm as a bath and she would seek out one of the cold springs here in the deep. Joe was standing a few yards away. She could see him so clearly. He was reaching out to her. . .
Uncle Ray stumbled and slipped his way off the snowy hill. The fire bell had rousted all the neighbors. "Get the boats!" he shouted frantically. "My niece is in the water!"
"Where?"
"Out by the point on the island."
Some of the men quickly shoved boats in the lake. They headed for the empty canoe bobbing in the water.

"Keep your eyes peeled on the surface," one of them said. "She has to come up."

"Thank God for the moonlight," another said. Some of the men had spotlights they were scanning back and forth across the water.

With each beat of his heart, Uncle Ray could feel the seconds ticking away. They would have to find her soon or. . .

"There she is!" a man shouted. The spotlight revealed a form, face down in the water. There was no hesitation as two of the younger men dove in and pulled her limp body to a boat. They lifted her out of the lake and someone immediately began trying to resuscitate her.

Aunt Martha was waiting when they hurried her to a waiting ambulance. She clutched Uncle Ray, her expression grave.

"We have a pulse, but I'm afraid she's in bad shape," Uncle Ray said somberly.

Aunt Martha climbed into the ambulance. Katie's face was blue and ashen. "My poor, poor baby," she said, wiping the matted, auburn hair from Katie's forehead.

In the jungle, night was closing in fast. The platoon was dug in on a ridge on the south slope of Mount Austen. Their objective was a fortified area known as the Gifu.

Corky left his foxhole to check on Shorty. He crawled over to the machine gun nest. Morrales was staring off into the jungle.

"Where's Shorty?"

"He's out there again," Morrales said, nodding his head toward the jungle.

"He's gone?"

"Yeah."

"Damn!" Corky slammed his fist into the ground. "Why did you let him go?"

"What am I supposed to do?"

"Give him a direct order to stay at his post."

"I tried that three nights ago and he told me to fuck off."

"He's trying to get himself killed. You could tell Balino that he's not well and get him out of here on a section eight."

"No chance. He's killing too many Japs, and he's the best source of information on enemy troop movements. Balino thinks he's the best soldier in the Division."

"He's out there killing for revenge."

"So?"

"What are you trying to say — that we just let him go on risking his life until one morning he doesn't come back?"

"Listen, Corky, if he's hell bent on getting himself killed, there's not much we can do about it."

Corky peered out into the darkness, wondering where Shorty was and worrying that this might be the night when he failed to return.

"Tell you what," Morrales said. "If you go see the chaplain, I'll back up your story. I hate to lose Callahan, but he has definitely gone off his nut. Maybe we can get him some leave time back in Hawaii."

Shorty lay on his back beside one of the supply trails used by the Japanese. He lay quietly listening to the sounds in the night. When he had lost his fear of death, war had also ceased to be frightening. The jungle that was once hostile now seemed almost friendly. Out here he didn't have to worry about anyone but himself and he was free of all the responsibilities of command. There was no one to report to and no one to protect. The only things he feared were the jungle rats. They were as big as beavers and sometimes sniffed him out. He kept a machete handy to dispatch them when they came too close. He had been raising hell with the Japs the past week. They had always owned the nights on Guadalcanal, secure in the knowledge that the Americans would dig in before dark. With his night forays into the jungle, all that had changed and the Jap foot traffic had slowed to a trickle. He hadn't had any luck the last two nights, so he had switched to a different trail. He had avoided several ambushes, so he knew the Japs were trying to get him. If the bastards didn't like to chatter so much, they would have had him by now. He knew they would get him eventually. If not here, then on one of the other islands leading to Japan. His thoughts were interrupted by footsteps on the trail. He could hear the clink of metal and whispering. The Japs would never learn to keep their mouths shut. In one motion he rolled out onto the trail into the path of the Japanese and squeezed the trigger on the Thompson sub-machine gun. The roar of the weapon was deafening against the quiet of the jungle. It was over in an instant. He could hear the moans of the dying and then all was quiet. He rolled back into the jungle and waited. At daybreak he would get a head count of the dead.

"Nice job, Callahan," Balino said as he studied the Japanese maps Shorty had brought out of the jungle. "Where did you get these?"

"I ran into a Jap patrol last night. The officer in charge was carrying them."

"How many Japs were there?"

"I don't know. There were ten bodies on the trail this morning. I think I got them all, but in the dark you never know."

Balino studied him for a moment. "Morrales is worried about you. He and Corky had a visit with the chaplain. They think you've gone off your rocker."

Shorty looked at Balino in surprise. "Why would they think that?"

"You have to admit that it's a bit unusual to go off into the jungle alone and fight a one-man war."

"I'm taking the war to the Japs. Seems to me that's what we're here for."

"Corky seems to think that you're trying to get yourself killed."

"Maybe he's turning into a sob sister."

"I wouldn't call the most decorated soldier in the battalion a sob sister."

Shorty shrugged.

"How would you like a couple of weeks back in Hawaii?"

"No way. My platoon is leading the attack on Mount Austen tomorrow."

"Okay, Callahan. I can't afford to be without you until we finish the campaign on Guadalcanal. When it's finally over I'm relieving you of duty."

Shorty nodded. The chances of him surviving the assault on Mount Austen weren't too good anyway, so what did he care.

Balino grabbed another map. "The Japs are heavily dug in at the Gifu. They have artillery and mortars, so it's going to be a tough fight. I want you to take a squad out this afternoon and scout the jungle. I don't want the Japs to hit us from the rear when we begin the assault."

"Okay. We'll get it done."

The mid-day jungle was hot and humid. Shorty was already soaked in sweat. The gooney birds were in full chorus as the squad advanced through the jungle. Duff and Franky were up ahead on the point. Corky was in the rear, keeping his eye on the trail they had just traveled. They had been scouring the jungle for over two hours, making sure there were no Japs around to interfere with the planned assault on Mount Austen. Shorty returned to the rear to be with Corky.

"It's really hot," Corky said. "Do you remember those hot summer days at the lake when we used to spend the entire day lying out on the raft? When we couldn't stand the heat anymore we just rolled over into the water."

"Yeah. I remember."

"That's what I'd like to do right now — just roll over into the water."

"You'd better quit daydreaming and keep your mind on the Japs."

"I think about them, but they're not an obsession."

"Are you going to preach?"

"If I thought it would do any good."

Shorty saw Duff's hand go up, halting the squad. He waved his men back into the cover of the jungle.

"They're coming this way," Duff whispered as Shorty moved up next to him.

"Okay, this is it," Shorty whispered to the others. "Don't fire until I give the signal."

The Japanese appeared from out of the jungle, trudging resolutely along under the weight of their packs. They carried rifles at the ready. Shorty counted 15 of the enemy. He gave the signal and the squad opened up. The enemy soldiers were slaughtered in the withering fire.

"Cease fire!" Shorty yelled, as he released the trigger on his submachine gun. The squad moved carefully out onto the trail to check the dead.

"Put a bullet in their heads before you get too close," Shorty warned. "The bastards can pull the pin on a grenade with their last breath."

"Shorty! Over here!" Corky called to him. Shorty walked over. One of the Japs was on his knees with his hands behind his head. He was bleeding from a superficial leg wound.

"He must have been shielded from the heavy fire by one of the other Japs," Corky said.

Shorty walked up and put his gun to the Japanese soldier's head. The man cringed and waited. Corky angrily knocked the gun away. "What are you doing?"

"We're not here to take prisoners."

"What's the matter with you? We're soldiers, not murderers."

"You'd better watch your mouth and realize who's in command here."

"Who is in command? Not anyone that I know."

Shorty pushed him. "Get out of my way, Corky."

"You think killing him will bring Joe back, Shorty? Is that it? You kill enough Japs and Joe will appear magically from out of the jungle."

"Shut up, Corky. I'm warning you." Shorty put the gun back to the Japanese soldier's head. Corky doubled up his fist and hit Shorty with everything he had. Shorty stumbled backwards, losing his steel pot, but holding onto the sub-machine gun. A trickle of blood ran down from a cut below his eye.

"Look at what you've become, Shorty," Corky said. "Katie and Joe would be real proud of you."

Shorty came back at him menacingly.

"Callahan is going to take him apart," one of the men said.

"He won't lay a hand on him," Franky replied knowingly.

It was then that they heard it. The sound of an artillery piece firing from somewhere up on Mount Austen, the whine of the shell growing in intensity as it bore down on their position. Shorty and Corky just stood there staring at each other as the rest of the squad dove for cover, and the Japanese soldier bolted for the jungle.

"Take cover!" Franky shouted. But it was too late and his warning was drowned by the exploding shell.

Shorty was in the air, tumbling head over heel. Funny, but he didn't feel any pain. He could see Corky in the air tumbling around and around. He hoped that Corky would be okay. Everything was moving ever so slowly as the ground rose up to greet him. His last thoughts were of Emma, and then darkness mercifully enveloped him.

20

Katie lay in her room with the blinds drawn. The doctors had told her that she was lucky to be alive. The cold waters of the lake had slowed her metabolism and saved her life. She had spent a week in the hospital, and then six weeks in a psychiatric center. She wished with all her heart that she had never awakened. What was the point of going on? There was no joy in life and nothing to look forward to.

There was a knock at the door, and then her mother entered.

"Emma is here."

Katie looked away.

"It might make you feel better to see her."

Katie remained silent.

"Hello, Katie," Emma walked into the room.

"I'll leave you two alone." Katie's mother quietly slipped out the door.

"How are you feeling?" Emma asked.

Katie looked blankly at the wall.

"I received a letter from Corky today. He and Shorty have finally been released from the hospital."

Katie laid her head back on the pillow and stared at the ceiling.

"He said they both have enough shrapnel in them to be poster boys for a scrap metal drive. The army has declared them unfit for military duty, but they have no idea when they will be discharged."

Katie showed no emotion. There was no joy in Emma's news. It was as if she were droning on about complete strangers. All she wanted was for Emma to go away and leave her alone.

"Why don't you come outside on the porch with me? The tulips are in bloom and it's a beautiful Easter Sunday."

Katie pictured Father Dugan at the altar of her church giving the sacraments and then she had a momentary flashback to Union Station. Father Dugan's right hand hung suspended in the air. Heads were bowed. "May God be your protector — be at your side in times of trial. . ." But there had been no protection and she had lost faith in anything to do with religion. Father Dugan had stopped by to see her on several occasions to offer words of encouragement, and to urge her to keep the faith. But to have faith she had to have hope, and there was no longer anything to hope for.

"I'll come back to see you when you're feeling better," Emma said. She walked out of the room and quietly closed the door. Katie's mother was waiting at the foot of the stairs.

"Any response?"

"No," Emma said. "I'm sorry."

Shorty looked out the window of the train at the vastness of the Kansas prairie. It seemed endless compared with the jungles of Guadalcanal. He reached down and massaged the muscles above his knees. His legs were still a bit sore and he would need crutches for a few more weeks, but he had been lucky: shrapnel from the artillery shell had hit him in both legs but left no permanent damage. Corky had been hit in the back and in the right arm. The arm would always be a little stiff, but would not interfere with his painting.

"How about giving me a shot of my bourbon?"

Corky took the pint from the sling on his arm and passed it to Shorty. "Why didn't you want to tell anyone we were coming home?"

Shorty shrugged. "I thought it would be better if we just slipped back into town and had some time to get adjusted."

"There goes my parade," Corky kidded. "Will you at least call Emma when we get to the station?"

"No. I think I'll wait awhile."

"How come?"

"I don't want to go barging back into her life. She has a new business and she's probably made new friends."

They sat for awhile listening to the steady clack of the train along the tracks.

Corky studied Shorty. "Don't throw away your relationship with Emma because of Katie. In a perfect world we would all be having joyful reunions."

Shorty stared out the window at the landscape clipping past. "We left the perfect world at Union Station and I guarantee you it ain't going to be there when we get back."

"Maybe not. But at least we have a chance to make something out of what we find."

"A better chance than Joe, you mean."

Corky leaned his head back on the seat. "That wasn't fair and you know it."

"Maybe not. But that's how I feel." He took a swig from the bottle. "I want to thank you for all you did for me on the Canal and in the hospital. I wouldn't be going home if it weren't for you."

"You don't need to thank me for anything. You have been taking care of me since I was six years old."

Shorty offered Corky a drink from the bottle.

Corky shook his head. "Will you go see Katie and your mother when we get in?"

"Maybe later," Shorty hedged, as he took another swig from the bottle. He was not ready to see anyone. It was going to take some time before he could make sense out of anything to do with family or relationships. As the western edges of the city came into view he thought about Franky and Duff back on the Canal. They would soon be joining the invasion of New Georgia. A part of him wished that he was still fighting in the jungles of the South Pacific.

"What about Joe's manuscript? Will you give it to Katie?"

"Not for awhile."

"I never thought we would make it," Corky said, as he looked out the window at the familiar surroundings. The train followed the flow of the Kansas River as it meandered peacefully toward a rendezvous with the Missouri River at Kansas City. A few minutes later the train braked and slowed as it left the river behind and headed for Union Station. To the north they could see the tall buildings that made up the core of the city and to the south the familiar spire of the Liberty Memorial. Shorty thought about the irony of war. A few inches in the trajectory of a bullet and instead of returning home to loved ones, they carved your name in granite in some cold lonely place visited by school children and old veterans on Armistice Day. As the train pulled into Union Station he felt no sense of satisfaction or joy in finally returning home.

Corky pushed open the door of the house and Shorty followed him inside.

"I can't believe it," Corky said as he looked around. "Everything's the same. It's like we put on our coats and went to get a beer."

"A lot cleaner than I remember," Shorty said, as he threw his duffle bag down on the couch.

"Katie and Emma must have kept it up." Corky went from room to room checking out his boyhood home. "Funny, but I keep thinking that at any moment Granny is going to come shuffling out of a room."

"Yeah. I feel it too. Let's go down to 12th Street and get that beer you were talking about. We can call Andy and have him join us."

"I thought you might want to go to the Chesterfield Club."

"I'm not up to celebrating. I just want a few beers and a good meal."

In spite of their protests, they received a grand reception at a 12th Street tavern. Everyone wanted to buy them drinks and their war wounds drew the sympathy of every female in the place. They were into another round when a familiar voice rang out in the tavern. "Has anybody seen a couple of goldbricks in here trying to impersonate soldiers?"

"Andy!" Corky yelled with delight. Andy appeared from out of the crowd. He stopped short and looked them over. "What happened to you guys? Are you okay?"

"Never better," Shorty said as he shook Andy's hand. It was the first time in months that Corky had seen Shorty smile.

"Man, I thought I was hearing a ghost when Shorty's voice came over the phone," Andy said. "How did you get hit?"

"We tried to do the Missouri Waltz with a Jap artillery shell," Shorty explained. He noticed the empty sleeve of Andy's police uniform. The sleeve was pinned up at the shoulder.

"Wow! Look at all that salad," Andy said respectfully as he checked the decorations on their dress uniforms. "How are we going to win the war without you?"

"I see you're back on the police force," Shorty said.

"I'm a dispatcher."

Shorty didn't press him for more.

"Have you seen Katie?" Corky asked. "How's she doing?"

"I've been to the house a couple of times," Andy said. "She's not up to seeing anyone just yet."

"Then she's out of the hospital?"

"Yes. I'm sure it will do wonders for her to see the two of you."

"You've put on weight since the Canal," Shorty said, changing the subject.

"That's because I don't have you ordering me around anymore."

"You look good."

"Thanks." Andy took his beer from the bartender. "I heard from Duff yesterday. He and Franky really miss you guys."

"I miss them, too," Shorty said.

"I know the feeling. I felt guilty about running out on you."

"You did your part," Shorty said.

Andy took another swig of his beer and became somber for a moment. "I was real sorry to hear about Joe."

Shorty nodded. "What's the chance of getting a decent meal in this town? Do you know how long I've been dreaming about a Kansas City steak?"

"Well, let's get going," Andy said. "I know just the place. Your old friend Solly Weinstein has opened up a supper club over on Walnut Street. It's the 'In' place for high rollers and the upper crust."

At Solly's Place they waited for a table at the bar as a steady procession of finely dressed men and women were whisked past them and into the restaurant.

"Do you get the impression that we're being ignored?" Shorty said.

"It might take a while since we didn't have reservations," Andy explained.

"I don't think so." Shorty narrowed his eyes at the head waiter. "I believe we have a man here who doesn't like soldier boys."

"There he goes being paranoid again," Corky said to Andy. "He still has a touch of malaria from the Canal and he has a tendency to be belligerent."

"What's the Canal have to do with it? He's always been belligerent."

That created a laugh and broke the tension. Shorty bought everyone another drink. They waited for another thirty minutes and then Shorty had had enough. He moved up to the head waiter. "How long does a man have to wait to get a table around here?"

"We're exceptionally busy."

"That's bullshit. You've seated people ahead of us who didn't have reservations."

"I assure you. . ."

"Is Solly here?"

"I'm sure I wouldn't. . ."

"Well go find out. And when you do, tell him to get his ass out here pronto."

The head waiter smiled at Shorty like he was kidding and then realized that he wasn't. "I'll be right back."

Shorty was at the bar when he saw Solly come out into the lobby and look around. "A numbers man is still a numbers man even in a million-dollar joint!" he yelled at him.

Solly walked into the bar. "Well I'll be damned! It's Shorty Callahan home from the war." He walked over and shook Shorty's hand.

"Hello, Solly."

"It's good to see you, kid. This town has been awfully quiet without you."

"You mean Tony Bonatto hasn't been keeping you entertained?"

"Tony went down with Pendergast. This town has gone legitimate, Callahan. All the interesting people are either off to war or doing time."

"It looks like you're doing okay," Shorty said as he eyed the expensive furnishings of the supper club.

"It's a living," Solly said. "Have you guys had anything to eat?"

"We can't get a table. Do you know anyone with pull?"

"I'll see what I can do." He motioned for the head waiter. "Give these gentlemen my personal table, and bring the bill to me."

"You don't have to do that, Solly."

"The hell I don't. You guys have been out busting your ass for guys like me and I want to show my appreciation.

"How are those legs, Callahan? Any permanent damage?"

"No. A few weeks of rest and I'll be taking on Jesse Owens."

"That's great. You guys enjoy your dinner. I'll stop by your table and have a drink."

Solly's table was on a second tier and commanded a view of the entire restaurant.

"Now this is more like it," Shorty said as he stretched out his legs and surveyed the crowd on the main floor of the restaurant. "Fine wine, good food, and we can sit back and watch Mr. and Mrs. America at war."

"Did I detect a note of sarcasm?" Corky asked.

"Maybe a touch. Somewhere in the world there's a soldier getting his ass shot off so these people can have a good time."

"It's best not to think about such things."

"You're right." Shorty held up his glass. "Waiter! Another round of drinks for the table!"

They spent the next hour reminiscing about the past and enjoying the best meal they had had in years. The waiter was pouring some brandy when Shorty heard Corky suck in his breath. He turned and followed his gaze. Three couples had walked jauntily into the restaurant. They were laughing and having a good time. One of the young men was extremely handsome and debonair, and the woman he was pulling along by the hand was Emma. She had on a black cocktail dress and black heels. A single strand of ivory pearls decorated her neck and matched ivory earrings that accentuated her dark black hair.

"She's even more beautiful than I remembered," Corky said.

Shorty stared at her as he went through the gamut of emotions. He wanted to rush over and put his arms around her, but at the same time he was jealous that she was with someone else.

"She came to see me several times when I was in the hospital," Andy said.

Corky stood up. "Let's go say hello."

"No. I need another drink first," Shorty said.

Corky didn't like the look he was reading on Shorty's face. "You're going to be nice, aren't you?"

"You tell me."

"Come on, Shorty. Don't do this," Corky pleaded.

"Don't do what?"

"You know what. Don't take your frustrations out on Emma."

"How about on her boyfriend?"

"I think you've had too much to drink."

"Come on, you guys," Andy said. "I'll drive you home and you can go see Emma when you're sober."

"You're a good man, McClusky. A damned good man," Shorty said. He took another drink and then rose to his feet. "I believe it's time to go say hello to Miss Emma and her boyfriend."

"Don't forget your crutches," Corky said.

"Screw the crutches," Shorty replied as he squared his shoulders and walked confidently away.

She was huddled close to her date and didn't see him stop at the table. For a moment he just stood there staring at her.

"Can we help you, Sergeant?" one of Emma's companions asked.

Emma looked up and saw him, and her hand went to her mouth in shock.

"Hello, Emma."

"Shorty. What in the world. —" She got up from the table and put her arms around him. She was aware that he didn't hug her back. "Are you okay?"

"Yeah. I'm okay."

"When did you get in?"

"This afternoon."

"Where's Corky?"

"He will be along in a minute."

Emma introduced Perry and the rest of her friends.

"So, you knew Emma before the war," Perry said.

Shorty ignored his outstretched hand. "Yeah. That's right. I'm surprised that she hasn't mentioned me."

"She has, actually."

"I hope it wasn't in the middle of a passionate embrace."

"There's no need to be rude."

"Rude? Am I being rude?"

"Hello, Emma," Corky said as he walked up to the table.

"Corky!"

Corky hugged her and kissed her on the cheek. "Let me me look at you," he held her at arm's length. "You're lovelier than ever."

"Thank you. How's the arm?"

"Almost as good as new."

"Would you like to join us?" Perry asked.

"No," Shorty replied. He put his gaze on Perry. "Are you a doctor or a lawyer?"

"Lawyer. Why do you ask?"

"I just wanted to see if my prediction was coming true."

"What's that supposed to mean?" Emma challenged.

"You figure it out."

Emma narrowed her eyes at him. She knew he was trying to provoke her, but she couldn't figure out why. "This isn't the way I envisioned your homecoming."

"Maybe I should have given you some warning. You could have worked me in between dates."

"Are you looking for trouble, Sergeant?" one of Perry's friends said.

"If I were, you couldn't give it to me," Shorty replied. The people at the surrounding tables were staring and the restaurant had grown quiet.

"Nothing ever changes does it, Callahan," Emma said. "Are you determined to make a scene?"

"I haven't decided."

Solly walked up to the table with two of his bouncers.

Shorty looked around at him. "Have I worn out my welcome, Solly?"

"Not a chance, kid."

Andy walked up with Shorty's crutches. "You're the only guy I know who would pick a fight on two bad legs. Take these and let's get out of here."

Shorty put the crutches under his arms. "I'm sorry about the disturbance, Solly."

"I know you are. When you get well, come back and see me. I've got a proposition that might interest you."

Shorty turned to Emma. He looked into her eyes for a moment and then turned on his crutches and left with Andy.

Corky took Emma by the hand and sat with her for a moment. "I want you to know this had nothing to do with you."

"Why the hostility?"

"He's trying to alienate you, because he feels guilty about Joe."

"I don't understand."

"Katie doesn't have anyone coming home."

"Oh. I see."

"A lot happened to him during the war, Emma. He appears to be the same brash, confident, Shorty Callahan that you said good-bye to at Union Station, but he's not. I hope you will give him some time and not take any of this personally. When he's ready, he will come to you and apologize."

She nodded. "I want you to know how happy and grateful I am that you both made it home safely."

Shorty and Corky walked slowly around the grounds of the Art Institute. A gentle breeze ruffled the trees, carrying the smell of spring flowers to every nook and cranny of the campus. Corky took a deep breath of air. "Remember when we used to lie here in the grass and watch the girls?"

"That seems like a lifetime ago."

"I know. Everything's the same, yet somehow different. Do you know what I mean?"

"Yeah. I noticed."

They continued walking through the grounds, listening to the birds and enjoying the day.

"Your legs are still weak, so we can't keep circling the campus," Corky said. "Why don't you quit pretending that you wanted to see the Art Institute and go across the street to Emma's apartment?"

"She might not want to see me."

"Really? You were such a nice guy when we last saw her at Solly's place."

"Don't be a wise ass."

"You've been home two weeks and you haven't so much as given her a call."

"What do you want me to say?"

"You had better think of something, because she just walked out of the building."

Shorty watched as she crossed the street to the campus. "She's coming this way. What are we going to do?"

"What do you mean, we? I'll be in the library when you're ready to leave." Corky walked away.

Emma was heading toward him, so he stepped behind a hedge until she walked past. He followed her for a ways and then moved up beside her. She glanced over at him.

"Excuse me, Miss, but I used to know a girl who looks just like you."

Emma smiled wryly. "I had no idea you knew Betty Grable."

They walked along silently for awhile.

"I want to apologize for what happened the other night, Emma."

"I'm not sure that's acceptable. I spent two years thinking about our romantic reunion at Union Station."

"I know. It's the one thing that kept me going."

"Another chapter in a relationship of contradictions."

"Yeah. I guess so. Is there a chance we could take up where we left off?"

Emma stopped walking and studied him for a moment. "What makes you think that I could make you happy? We haven't exactly been faithful to each other."

"I'm not worried about that. I know that once you make a commitment you'll stick with it."

"And what about you?"

"You're the only girl I'll ever want. I just wonder if I can make you happy. We come from such different backgrounds."

"That's never been an issue. We have a lot more to clean up here than our past. Have you seen Katie?"

"No. I stopped by the house and talked to my mother and my grandfather. Katie stayed in her room."

"Did you make an effort to see her?"

"No."

"Then you have too much unresolved in your life to start thinking about us."

"Maybe that's just an excuse and you're tied to Perry."

"I'm not going to dignify that with an answer, and my relationship with Perry is none of your business." Her features softened for a moment. "How are your legs? I see you're off the crutches."

"I'm getting stronger every day." He moved closer to her. She had on an old sweat shirt, shorts, and tennis shoes, and yet she was as alluring as ever. "Where are you going?"

She eyed him warily, but she didn't back away. "I'm picking up some things at the book store."

He pulled her to him and kissed her. "I"ve been thinking about that for a long time."

She tried to pull away but he held her tightly to him.

"Are you going to hold a grudge about the other night?"

"No. I'm only interested in why it happened," she pulled away from him. "Are you going to tell me about Joe?"

He backed away. "There's nothing to tell."

"Then we have nothing left to discuss." She turned to leave.

"What are you trying to prove?"

"That you have to resolve this with Katie. If you can't talk to me, then what chance will you ever have of talking to her?"

"I need more time."

"Time has nothing to do with it. If you don't come to terms with Joe's death, you'll be running from it for the rest of your life."

He suddenly felt very tired. "Can we go over there and sit down?" He led her over to a bench. After they were seated, he took her hand in his and sat quietly for awhile. "I can't begin to tell you how great it is to be with you again," he finally said. She squeezed his hand and he began telling her everything that had happened on Guadalcanal.

"Hello Katie," Emma said as she entered Katie's bedroom. She walked over and threw open the blinds. "Were you aware that Shorty and Corky have been home for two weeks?"

Katie glared at her, surprised that she had barged into the room unannounced.

"I thought not. Taking an interest in someone other than yourself would be too much out of character."

Katie picked up a pillow and squeezed it against her chest. She turned her face to the wall.

"I'm not going to go away so you may as well look at me."

"I want you to leave," Katie said quietly.

"I'll leave but not before I speak my mind. Have you given one thought to how your behavior is affecting everyone around you?"

"No. Because I don't care."

"I'm not surprised. Sometimes I think we all might have been better off if you had succeeded in your mission at the lake."

"Maybe next time," Katie threatened.

"Then you should do it and let us get on with our lives," Emma said. "You're slowly but surely taking everyone down with you and we could at least make a new start."

"I'm not doing anything to anyone," Katie said spitefully as she narrowed her eyes at Emma.

"Oh, certainly not," Emma mocked her. "What about your mother? She has to spend every waking moment wondering if you're going to be alive when she walks into the room. And Joe's parents: they lose a son and you compound their grief by trying to take your own life. Scooter is the saddest example of all. He should be out playing ball with his gang, but instead he goes down to Union Station and hangs around. He sits there on the oak benches just staring off into space. Did it ever dawn on you, Katie, that it's your duty as Joe's wife to take care of his family? Joe Wilson deserves more than you're giving him and he would be ashamed of you for the way you're behaving."

"Shut up!" Katie shouted angrily. "Who are you to tell me anything! You wouldn't know the first thing about love or dedication or faithfulness!"

"Perhaps not. But I do know about simple human decency, and that's something you've forgotten. I planned to have a life with Shorty, but that's all been put on hold. He has this strange notion that you are holding him responsible for Joe's death and until that is resolved he can't get on with his life."

"He is responsible," Katie said hatefully.

"Oh, I see," Emma said. "There was not one thing he could possibly have done, but you're still holding him responsible."

"Yes! He was the one who couldn't wait to join the stupid war! He promised me that he would watch out for Joe!"

Emma paced back and forth, never losing eye contact with Katie. "That's how it's always been for you, Katie. Shorty was your own private protector who could always make things right. Anything that threatend you would be taken care of by your big brother. And then he failed you, and the one time in his life that he needs you, you are too self-centered and selfish to respond."

"Stop it!" Katie shouted. "I want you out of here!"

"I'll get out when I'm finished!" Emma shouted back. "Shorty was so devastated over Joe's death that he did everything he could to get himself killed. He knew you would hold him responsible and he couldn't live with that. And what about the rest of the gang? You're the one they all look up to and respect. They went out of their way to always try to please you. I remember how they were so careful not to swear in your presence, or bring their girlfriends around because you might not approve. And you repay those years of devotion by turning Andy and Corky away when they pay you a simple courtesy call. For God's sake, Katie, Andy lost an arm in the war and Corky went through hell. You could have at least offered some sympathy and support."

"I don't have any sympathy and support to give!"

"No. You're too busy wallowing in your own misery."

"You have no idea how I feel. Don't you understand?" Katie cried as she wiped tears from her face. "I thought everything would be okay if I worked hard and put my faith in God. I prayed for Joe's safe return and was confident that if I did the right things he would be protected. Now he's gone and I have nothing to live for."

"You have everything to live for. There are people who love you and need you. If things were reversed do you think Joe would be acting this way? Of course not. He would be doing something worthwhile with his life."

"I'm not Joe. And I don't want to go through life without him."

"Then make that decision and get on with it."

"Get out of here right now!" Katie shouted. "Get out!"

Emma had to leave before she lost her composure. She turned away and ran down the stairs and out of the house. Why had this happened to Katie? She was the sweetest, kindest person in the whole world and she deserved better. Emma knew she had taken a big risk in trying to shame her into wanting to live. She sat down in the grass at the side of the house and covered her face with her hands. She hated everything about the war. It was slowly but surely destroying the lives of everyone around her. The tears streaming down her face surprised her. It had been such a long time since she had cried, but God! how she needed to. She started sobbing and cursing the war for everything it had done to Katie, to her friends, and to her generation.

21

nother week had gone by and Katie felt exhausted from depression and the long months of grief. Emma was right in saying that she was drowning in her own misery, and hadn't considered what losing Joe had done to anyone else. His passing had taken the meaning from her life, but there was still an obligation to those who had loved him, especially Scooter. She had failed Joe in that respect. Emma's lecture had also made her realize how much of a burden she had put on her brother. After Pop died she had depended on Shorty to handle all of her insecurities, and that wasn't fair. She didn't know if she wanted to go on living, but Joe would want her to try.

There was a knock at the door and her mother entered.

"Good morning, dear."

"Good morning, Mother. What day is it?"

Ann Callahan looked at her in surprise. "Why, it's Sunday."

Katie pushed the covers away and slowly climbed out of bed. "I'm going to get dressed and go to church," she said.

Ann Callahan stifled an impulse to cry. "You get in the tub and I'll have your breakfast ready when you come downstairs."

Katie took the wafer that symbolized the body of Christ, and then she felt Father Dugan place his hand gently on her head. She moved reverently back to her pew. Any hope of recovery would have to begin here with Father Dugan and the church. She said a silent prayer and then listened to the resonating voices of the choir singing the 23rd Psalm.

"My Shep-herd is the Lord, nothing in-deed shall I want." For the first time in months she felt a moment of peace.

When she arrived home her grandfather was working in his victory garden and her mother was nervously cleaning the house. She went upstairs and changed into her jeans and an old shirt.

"I'm going outside and help Grandpa in the garden," she announced to her mother.

"All right, dear."

The noon-day sun was shining brightly and a warm breeze tugged at her hair.

"Hello, Grandpa."

"Hello, Katie." He was surprised to see her, but tried not to show it. "Would you hold the end of this string? I can never seem to get these rows lined up straight."

"And when you do, you lose the seed packets and can't remember what you planted."

"Now I remember why you women were never invited to work in the garden," he said with a grin.

Katie helped him get his rows lined up and evenly spaced. "I'll do the digging and you do the planting," she suggested. He started to protest.

"I need the exercise," she assured him. She began digging with the shovel. It felt good to block everything out and do physical labor again. They worked together the entire afternoon, and when the garden was finally planted she was exhausted. She sat down in the dirt and wiped sweat from her face.

"Thank you, Katie. I had almost forgotten how industrious you are. This planting would have taken me a week."

"Thank you, Grandpa. I'm still a bit weak, but it feels so good to work again." She followed him into the house.

"You two have put in a hard day," her mother said.

"Who was on the phone?" Katie asked. "I heard it ring."

"It was Aunt Martha. She was checking on your welfare and she wanted your grandfather to come out to the lake for dinner."

"Why don't you both go?"

"We couldn't possibly. It's your first day. . ."

"I'm fine, Mother. You've worked so hard these past few months that you need some rest. I insist that you accept her invitation, and I want you to spend the night at the lake."

"Katie, I. . ."

"I'll be okay. I want to invite Shorty home so we can talk."

"It just doesn't seem right. . ."

"I give you my word that everything will be okay."

"All right, dear. If you're sure."

Katie stood in the lobby of Union Station. It was late Sunday evening and the station was packed with people. She looked around the grand old building that held so many memories, then closed her eyes and took a deep breath. She had to set aside all of her emotions if this was going to work. She walked slowly ahead and passed under the giant clock guarding the entryway to the north waiting room.

It took a few minutes of scanning the cavernous room before she spotted him. He sat on one of the long, straight-backed, solid oak benches. He was wearing his Cardinal baseball cap, and he was watching people go down the number 10 stairway where they had said their last good-byes to Joe. She turned away and fought tears that were starting to form, then took a deep breath and composed herself before walking up to him.

"Hi, Scooter."

Scooter looked around. He was surprised to see her. "Hi, Katie. What are you doing here?"

Katie sat down beside him. "I saw Whitey waiting patiently out on the street, so I thought you might be here."

"Yeah. He won't stay home, and they won't let him in the station. Are you feeling better, Katie?"

"Yes. Your mom tells me you come here a lot," Katie said.

Scooter shrugged his shoulders. "I guess so."

"How come?"

Scooter turned his gaze back to the people hurrying down the stairs. "I don't know," he said.

Katie reached over and put her arm around his shoulder. She summoned all of her courage, and for Scooter's sake, said the words she thought she could never say. "Joe's not coming back, Scooter."

Scooter turned and looked at her. "I know he's not," he said defensively.

"Then why do you keep coming here?"

Scooter took off his baseball cap and worked the bill back and forth in his hands. "Because I can see Joe a lot clearer when I'm here," he said.

Katie bit down on her lower lip. "You have his picture."

"I know, but it's not the same. I miss Joe more than anything, Katie."

Katie didn't think she could possibly have any tears left, but they began to fall.

Scooter reached over and took her hand. They sat for awhile, listening to the call to trains echo through the station and watching people hurry to the numbered stairways.

Katie composed herself. She squeezed Scooter's hand.

"When you feel like you have to come down here, I want you to come and see me instead. We'll talk about Joe."

"It won't be the same, Katie."

"I know. All I'm asking is that you give me a chance."

Scooter thought for a moment and then nodded his head. He took one last look at the stairway. "Let's go, Katie."

Outside the station, Whitey followed them to the car.

Katie walked numbly ahead. She wondered how the world could function with so much loss and so many broken hearts. She looked up at the night sky. The stars were shining brightly above the Main Street Hill and above the old oak tree where she had first met Joe. She pictured herself dancing across the yard in his arms with the coolness of the dew on her feet. And she remembered her mother's words from a childhood that seemed an eternity ago: "You don't want to get involved with that boy, Katie, he's a ghost dancer." But she had always loved him so much, and loved him without reservation. Perhaps he was up there somewhere in the vastness of the universe, a ghost dancer, wandering among the stars in the warmth of the mid-April evening. She had to believe that, or she couldn't go on.

"What are we doing here?" Scooter asked as she stopped the car in front of Corky's house.

"I want to say hello to Shorty and Corky."

"I wanted to come and see them, but Mom said they were recovering from their wounds."

"They're okay now," she assured him.

Shorty, Emma, and Corky were having a drink in the kitchen.

"What did Solly Weinstein mean when he said he had a proposition for you?" Emma asked.

"He needs a partner so he can branch out into other things. When the war is over he thinks real estate will boom."

"I can't picture you selling houses."

"He wants me to take over his restaurant and several of the bars that he owns. I told him he would have to make Franky a partner as well and he agreed."

"Sounds like a good opportunity."

"Then it's okay with you?"

"You want my approval?"

"For the rest of my life."

"That sounds very much like a proposal."

"And?"

"And we are going to lean in that direction, but give ourselves at least a year to sort everything out."

"You mean about Katie and the war."

"Exactly. You guys have been through more than you realize and you need some time to make certain adjustments."

"But we are engaged?"

"Engaged sounds so definite."

"Okay. Not engaged, but way ahead of Perry."

"Perry is not even in the race."

"Well, what do you know," Corky said. "You two have managed to stumble around and almost make a commitment." He held up his beer. "I propose a toast to almost being engaged."

Emma laughed. "Well, what do you expect? I. . ." she was interrupted by a white dog that came yapping into the kitchen. "What in the world. . ."

"That dog looks like Whitey," Corky said. Shorty carefully lowered himself to one knee and started rubbing Whitey's ears. "I think you're right. It does look like Whitey. What are you doing here, boy?"

"He came to bet on the Cardinals," Scooter said as he entered the kitchen.

Shorty stood up. He fought hard to control his emotions. It was uncanny how much Scooter looked like Joe. Shorty walked over and pulled Scooter into his arms and gave him a hug. He stepped back and looked him over. "What happened to you? You're all grown up."

"I'm glad you're home," Scooter said.

"Hello, Scooter," Corky shook his hand.

"How's the arm, Corky?"

"Almost as good as new."

Emma wrapped her arms around Scooter. "Are you still my boyfriend?"

"You bet. It looks like Whitey remembers you guys."

"How could he ever forget us?" Corky said.

They were so caught up in greeting Scooter they didn't realize Katie was standing in the doorway. Corky was the first to notice. "Katie," he whispered.

They all turned and stared at her, too stunned too speak. Shorty thought she looked very thin and fragile. Her eyes were hollow, and a trace of sunburn failed to hide the paleness of her skin.

"Does anyone remember how to say hello?" Katie asked, breaking the awkward silence.

Emma went to her and kissed her on the cheek.

"Thank you for everything, Emma," Katie whispered as she gave her a hug. And then Corky embraced her.

"Hello, Katie. It's been a long time."

"Yes. Yes it has."

There was a moment of hesitation as she looked at her brother, and then she was moving across the room and into his arms. "Hello, Shorty."

"Hello, Katie." It almost broke her heart that he hadn't called her Squirt.

"I'm glad you're home."

"Yeah. Me too." He held her tightly for a moment before letting go. "How are you doing?"

"I'm all right. It's you guys that I'm worried about."

"We're okay. Although Corky's cooking has set us back a few weeks."

"I beg your pardon," Corky protested.

"How long have you been up and around?" Emma asked.

"This is the first day. I helped Grandpa in the garden, so I'm a bit worn out."

"Let's go into the living room and sit down," Shorty suggested.

"I'd better get back home," Katie said. "Scooter and I stopped by to see if you and Corky would like to spend the night with us at the old homestead. Mother and Grandpa are staying at the lake."

"Are you sure you're up to having company?"

"Yes. I would like it very much."

"Just like old ti —" Corky started to say, before remembering that it wouldn't be, without Joe. Embarrassed, he turned away.

"It's okay, Corky," Katie said. "I know what you meant." She turned to Emma. "Will you come too?"

"For a little while. I have an early meeting with a client so I can't spend the night."

"If your offer of a summer job is still open I might like to apply."

"The job is still open, and it's yours for the asking."

"Well then, let's get going," Katie said. "We have a lot to talk about."

Later that night she lay in bed listening to the trains pulling in and out of Union Station. Shorty was in his bedroom across the hall and Corky and Scooter were sleeping downstairs. She had spent the evening enjoying their company and discussing everything but the war. It would be a while before she was ready to talk about the war. The day had been tiring and so much had happened that she couldn't sleep. She had been isolated by depression and had forgotten what a wonderful feeling it was to have the support of family and friends. Corky had taken her aside and said that he would always be there for her no matter what, and his words seemed to have something special in them. The war seemed to have given Corky the strength and confidence that it had taken from Shorty.

Off to the west she could hear the approach of another thunderstorm. They seemed to rumble in every evening in the spring. The lonesome sound of a train whistle broke the still of night and she thought of Joe. That old familiar feeling of loneliness and loss returned. She shook off the depression that was starting to build and tried to think of something else. It was disappointing that she hadn't found a way to tell Shorty that she loved him and that he wasn't to blame for what had happened to Joe. Her thoughts drifted back to their childhood, when life had seemed so bright and full of wonder. And as she remembered those days, she discovered what she had been searching for. Instinctively she knew that her brother was still awake. "Shorty," she called out to him. Time passed and she thought he hadn't heard.

"Yeah," he finally answered.

"Would you turn on the carousel?"

There was a few moments of silence and then from across the hall came the old familiar melody that was so much a part of their childhood. She listened as each comforting note sounded so clear in the night. The music ended and quiet once again settled over the house.

"Good night, Shorty," she called. And then she waited for the sound of his voice that had always made her feel so safe and secure in the dark.

"Good night, Squirt."

And she knew then that she was going to make it.